The Heart Tattoo

The Heart Tattoo

Joseph A. Liebreich

Chapter 1

$\mathcal{S}$he leaned forward, her face almost touching the mirror on her dressing table, and whispered to the image, "Enough being subtle. It hasn't worked before, and I won't do it any more. Today I'll be direct. I'll get him alone at the reception and flat-out say, 'How about going to bed with me?'" With a pinky she smoothed a wayward eyebrow hair into place. "Well, maybe not those exact words, but I'll make it clear what I want."

Humming softly to herself, she put the finishing touches on her makeup. She carefully dipped a brush into the blush powder and stroked it gently on each cheek then spread flaming red lipstick, which closely matched her hair coloring, across her lips. She pursed her lips together to even it out then dabbed on a final touch of gloss.

With great concentration she inspected the reflection in the mirror. The red hair topped what she judged to be a still desirable, almost hourglass figure. But still she had doubts. She twisted her head first to one side and then the other and wondered, do I still have it? Can I pull it off or is he only interested in the young bimbos? The joke of wanting to trade in the forty-year-old wife for two twenty-year-olds flashed through her mind. After staring intently for a full minute she concluded, I'll be all right. Even at forty-plus, even having delivered two children, I still *look* twenty. She smiled wryly. Okay, twenty-something.

"Kate Mallory, aren't you ready yet?" her husband shouted up from downstairs. "What's taking you so long? You don't have to look perfect."

Oh, yes I do, she thought. Only perfect is going to get him into bed.

"You're not the bride today," his voice sailed up to her.

She didn't bother answering him—it was the third time he'd yelled at her in the last fifteen minutes, and he'd have to wait. No I'm not the bride, she thought. I'm not Nancy. I'm only one of her friends from high school. And so is that bitch, Judy Fanelli, the one I'm going to get even with. She felt tension pain mounting in her back and began to talk out loud to make it go away.

"Whenever I think of what she did to me, and me not paying her back yet, it really pisses me off. Whoever said 'revenge was a dish better tasted cold' was full of shit," she muttered through clenched teeth while she twisted her body to ease the pain. She continued to cock her head from side to side studying her reflection in the mirror. "This has been eating at me for years. Every time I've tried to get even with her I've struck out. Time is running out, and today's going to be the day things start going my way."

She closed her eyes and pictured that night long ago when Judy Fanelli had hurt her so deeply. Twilight was drizzling down, when she had stood by the window and watched with horror the scene unfolding beneath her. Dominic Micaletto, the love of her life, (she would do anything for him—and had), held a young woman's hand, led her jauntily to his car and, with a flourish and an over-the-top bow, opened the door and ushered her in. He had made no secret of the fact that he dated other women—his feelings for her were nowhere near as intense as her feelings for him. But her initial dismay had turned to revulsion and then shock when she realized the girl he had in tow was Judy Fanelli, her best friend. Riveted to the spot, she could not move, could not run downstairs and confront them. She could not will her mouth open to speak. She could not bring herself to shout out, "Where are you two going?" She knew where they were going and what they were going to do and could not stop them.

Two hours later when they came back she was still standing at the window, staring out into the night. Under the glaring light of the porch lamp she saw a disheveled Judy frantically stuffing her half-tucked-in blouse into her jeans, then quickly jerking her fingers through her splayed-in-all-directions hair. Etched forever in Kate's memory was "the look." Halfway up the front steps, Judy stopped, turned, and looked at him. It was the look of a girl who had just become a woman. "The look"—eyes sparkling like diamonds, a look not of gratitude, but of adoration.

"I'll never forget that look," Kate said to her face in the mirror. "And I'll never forget that that whore tried to steal my boyfriend. She caused me a lot of heartache and screwed up my life but good. If not for her, I could have married him. But now I'll get even; I'm going to break up her marriage. I'll sleep with her husband, and if that doesn't do it I'll try something else and keep on trying until I have my revenge. She's going to be as miserable as I was, and nothing's going to stop me. Nothing."

Why has it taken so long? she wondered. It's because I haven't had many chances to get her husband alone, she thought. And when I do get him alone he pats me on the head like a friendly dog. I haven't been aggressive enough. But today will be different. No more pussyfooting around; today it's the direct approach.

"C'mon. Hurry up." Greg was screaming from downstairs. "You've been at it an hour and a half already. You'll never look better than you do now. We're gonna be late. It's after five."

Shut up, buster, she thought to herself. I've got to look stunning. I can't have the bastard ignoring me any more. I'm not going to have him say 'no' when I ask him to bed.

Very carefully, so as not to muss her hair, she slid the glittering emerald green dress on over her head, shimmied her hips to settle it on her shoulders, then flattened the long sleeves down her arms. She grabbed the lapels, which bordered the low-cut "V" in front and gently tugged them down, then smoothed the dress over her hips and cinched the bow around her waist. She stepped back from the mirror for one last look and let out a low whistle. Wow, she thought, if he doesn't pay attention to this gorgeous woman, he's probably dead.

"Finally," her husband said as she sauntered down the stairway with heel-in-front-of-toe model steps. "I was ready to go by myself," he groused.

"Don't give me a lot of shit," she teased as she caressed his cheek with her fingertips; then she stepped back and studied him. While she was tall at five-nine, he was even taller. He was barrel-chested

("Like a stevedore," she would say.) and sported the beginnings of a potbelly that she did not like. "It's from sitting at a desk all day long," he would explain as she frowned. Even so, she thought, he was a knockout today in his black tuxedo and stark white, pleated shirt dotted with mother-of-pearl buttons.

"My god you look handsome," she said smiling at him suggestively. "Let's forget about the wedding, go upstairs, and rip each other's clothes off." She reached out for his hand.

He looked at the vision in front of him and his heart beat fast. He knew she was not teasing but thoroughly, seriously in lust with him. There seemed to be something about him all dressed up that drove her wild—wilder than usual. Six months ago they had been preparing to go to an uncle's fiftieth wedding anniversary party at a fancy French restaurant. After he had zipped up the back of her dress, she shivered then slowly turned around and stared at him, drop-dead handsome in his formal dress, for the longest time. Without a word she had unbuttoned his jacket, peeled it back over his shoulders, then started on his shirt. That time he had given in. Clawing at each other with animal desire, they collapsed on the bed.

Two hours later, hopelessly trying to smooth their rumpled clothes and mouthing a lame excuse ("We were held up in traffic. There was a detour because of a fire.") they arrived at the party. His sister snickered to her husband, "Yeah. I'll bet. More likely it was a detour to the bedroom. And I know the kind of fire she means."

Now he flushed as he briefly considered leading her to their bed, stripping her naked, and burying himself in her body. But instead he took her by the shoulders and held her at arm's length. Reluctantly. For even after twenty years of marriage, he wanted her as much as he had on their first date. He picked up her coat and held it out for her. "We'd better go to the wedding now and save the sex for later," he said quietly.

She savored the thought. There would be sex later, she hoped. With Tony Fanelli.

Chapter 2

"*W*hat kind of dummies plan to get married in February, for chrissakes?" Tony Fanelli complained to his wife. He pulled the living room curtains aside and looked out the window hoping to see a blizzard so he could have some ammunition for not going, but it was only gray and cloudy. "What kind of sense does that make? It could snow and really mess things up, and half their friends are away on some Caribbean island anyway. Who's even gonna be there?"

As usual Judy Fanelli paid little attention to Tony's grumblings. She stepped in front of the full length mirror in the hall for a last minute inspection on their way out. A five-foot four stylish brunette with shoulder length hair draped in a black off-the-shoulders Anne Klein II dress looked back at her. She poked an out-of-place hair back into its nest as she thought: I look great.

Years ago she wouldn't have thought that. No one ever told her to not to compliment herself, but as a young girl she watched her mother, her role model, ignore herself and defer to her father's every whim. From this she assumed that women were second-class citizens who were put on earth to tell men how great *they* looked and not to praise themselves. When did she change? It had been a slow process, but one important event was when she enrolled in college (over her mother's whining—"You weren't a good student in high school, and now you're going to college?") and graduated.

She turned away from the mirror and faced her husband expectantly. When he did not say the "You look nice" she would have liked, she rattled off in staccato fashion, "It isn't snowing, so stop crabbing. And it's not our wedding so why should we care who's there and who isn't? They chose February because this is the six-month anniversary of when they met, and they didn't want to wait any longer to get married. I think it's romantic. Look on the bright side. How often do we get to go Philadelphia's fancy Four Seasons Hotel?"

Feeling he was right but further argument was useless, Tony stifled a response but said, "I can't keep all your friends straight. Tell me about Nancy again. You said this was her second marriage."

"Right. She married late in life the first time. She was thirty-three. He was a sharpie, her first husband, with a lot of charm. But I thought he overdid it—I thought he was oily, maybe even slimy. But he must have charmed Nancy. She's no dope."

Tony was sorry he had asked. This promised to be a never-ending, pointless story. He wanted to jam his fingers in his ears but did nothing.

Judy continued, "The story goes that he supposedly went on a business trip to Iowa (I think he sold computers for IBM), so Nancy went to visit her mother who still lives in the house she grew up in—it's in our old neighborhood. Two of Nancy's nephews were also visiting; she caught a cold from one them and decided to go back to her own home rather than infect everyone else. When she walked into her living room, she saw a bare bottom bouncing up and down over the back of the couch." Judy glanced at Tony for his reaction. Instead of the glazed over look she had expected, he was paying attention. "Fascinated she watched for a few seconds and then recognized the bottom was her husband's. She walked around to investigate and noticed there was a body underneath him—which was obviously not her body. With a shriek that rocked the house she kicked the two of them out."

"Did she let him put his pants on?" Tony snickered.

Judy ignored him. "Out of the house and into divorce court. See what can happen."

Tony knew what was coming next. She always managed to steer one or two conversations every day around to the subject of fidelity.

It wasn't hard to figure out why, he thought. When she was seven years old, her mother's brother left his wife and two children and ran off to California with a sexy young manicurist who wanted to be a movie star more than anything else in the world. She had latched on to him as her ticket west. Judy's aunt was so upset that she had to "go away to the country" for a month, and while she was gone her children were parceled out to relatives—one of them stayed with Judy and her family. She cried all the time and cursed her father for leaving them alone. This taught Judy a lesson—infidelity brings pain and suffering.

Now she said to Tony, "And let that be a lesson to you. Some of us women are strong about fidelity. It's very important to us. Remember before we were married you promised . . . ," she began.

Here she goes again, he thought. "How can I forget?" he interrupted. "You remind me at least three times a day." This is a scene from *All in the Family*, he thought. Here I am being strangled to death by Edith telling me the same old dingbat story. He felt like yelling, "STIFLE!" but he didn't.

It had been different when they were first married. Then he had thought her stories were novel and cute. But after almost twenty years of marriage, he had heard all of them more than once, and the repetition grated on him like fingernails on a blackboard.

He opened the front door in the middle of one of her sentences and waved her outside. The sharp cold of the late February afternoon stung their cheeks as they hurried to the car. Tony slid behind the wheel and became very quiet as he drove. Troublesome thoughts throbbed in his head. He had tried to be faithful; he had tried very hard. And he had succeeded . . . for a while. But for Tony seven-year itch had come early; after five years. What was it that pushed me over the edge? he wondered.

He remembered when they were newlyweds. Life was so fresh and exciting. He couldn't wait to get home after work and share the day's events with his wife. "My bride," he would call her and sweep her into his arms as he stepped into the house. But as time passed "fresh and exciting" turned to same-old-same-old. The hello-I'm-home kisses changed from marathons of mutual mouth-exploration to light pecks on the cheek, and then to air-kisses blown gently in the direction of the other. And in the bedroom, Tony thought, screwing her had changed from sensational adventure to boring routine. A rut, he thought. We fell into a sex rut. The same thing over and over again with the same woman. It was like having a duty and doing it. Like taking the trash out. I needed someone different for the thrill of it, he thought. The thrill of the chase, the thrill of the conquest. It's not my fault; he rationalized not fully quenching the guilt. I wasn't meant to be happy with one woman, and life's too short not to be happy. Besides, what's wrong with an occasional piece of ass on the side? I keep it quiet; nobody knows; nobody gets hurt, and the women are just as hot for me as I am for them.

Women seemed to fall into his lap. As a salesman, he called on purchasing managers in a variety of businesses. Receptionists and secretaries would come on to him by dropping hints about being free that evening. "Maybe we could have a drink?" was an invitation he had received a thousand times. Once in a while a waitress would be friendlier than she needed to be just to get a bigger tip. Opportunity knocked repeatedly with little effort on his part, and finally after five years of marriage, he answered the knock. If he met a woman who was something special, he would take her phone number and call her next time he was in town. His "little black book," which he hid in his glove box (Judy never drove his company car), bulged with numbers of his past conquests.

What's the harm in what I do as long as Judy doesn't find out? he asked himself. Of course she would be hurt if she found out, but who's going to tell her?

"You're so quiet. What are you thinking about?" Judy asked.

"Er . . . I was wondering. Did you have any . . . feelings about Nancy's marriage?" he asked.

While she didn't make a big deal out of it, Judy professed to be a witch. A good witch, she would hurriedly add when questioned, but a witch nonetheless. Sometimes she had forebodings about the future—visions and spells. And occasionally she could see auras and halos around people. An hour before her father died, she visited him in the hospital. While she watched in alarm, she saw the halo around his head fizzle from a bright, glittering, sunshiny ring to a cloud of gray dust which crumbled onto his shoulders. She had burst into a torrent of tears.

"What did you see?" he had asked in a hoarse whisper.

She didn't answer, but he knew what she saw from the tears which grew in the corners of her eyes. He shuddered, then sighed.

And now she closed her eyes and waited. She felt nothing definite only a vague feeling that something horrible was about to happen to her. She shivered and shook it away.

"No," she said to Tony. "No premonitions."

Chapter 3

Judy was the first to be surprised at the wedding.

The ceremony was over by seven and after the Fanellis shook hands down the receiving line and kissed the bride, they went into the reception. The immense Ben Franklin Room on the hotel's main floor had a dozen stations scattered around its perimeter. Each offered food from a different culture: Chinese, Indian, Italian, Thai, French. "The United Nations must be meeting here today," Tony joked as he lifted two glasses of champagne from the tray of a passing waiter, handed one to Judy, clinked it with his own, and downed it in two gulps.

Tony spotted one of his cousins in the crowd and drifted away to join him. As Judy flitted from station to station sampling here and there, she noticed a handsome, fortyish man following her and looking at her quizzically. Finally he approached her and said, "I can tell you don't remember me. I've watched you look right through me a dozen times." He paused. "But I remember you."

She studied him carefully: Warm smile. Thin face, thin body, a fraction this side of emaciated, like a ballet dancer. His thinning dark black hair showed a few traces of gray sprouting at the sideburns. She had noticed that he had some effeminate traits, not quite the exaggerated limp wrist, and he didn't lisp, but the tone of his voice was slightly higher than that of a macho male and his speech pattern was a little whiny. On the spot she decided she liked him.

"You don't look familiar," she said.

"How quickly they forget." He smiled broadly. "You are Judy, aren't you?" He glanced down at her left hand and spotted her wedding ring. "I don't know your married name, but you were Judy Orsini, weren't you?" She nodded. "I'm Carlo Fiore," he went on. "I was your senior prom date. When was it? Twenty-something years ago."

She closed her eyes and gradually matched the face of the shy, young, boy who had been her prom date with the face of the man standing in front of her.

"I remember you now," she said.

She didn't add that if she didn't remember him it could hardly be her fault. The prom was their one and only date. He was polite and well-mannered at the prom, but after two dances with her, his cousin, Dominic Micaletto, had invited him outside for a few quick ones, which turned out to be more than a few. Unaccustomed to heavy drinking, Carlo had gotten trashed beyond drunk. He had spent the rest of the night and the next morning at the after-prom party, zombie-like, in a world of his own.

Judy finished munching on a miniature egg roll, swallowed it, and said, "I'm Judy Fanelli now. And that's my husband, Tony, over there."

She indicated a corner of the room where Tony was surrounded by a group of four good-looking, young women. Two of them hung on his arms, held spellbound by his sparkling smile, dazzled by a story or joke Judy could not hear. Suddenly they all burst into hearty laughter.

"He seems to be quite a charmer," Carlo said. "I'll bet he's a salesman."

"Good guess. He sells office supplies. And does very well at it," she added defensively. "They've given him a lot of raises and responsibility."

She had become used to sticking up for Tony and his profession from the beginning of their relationship. The first time she brought Tony home to meet her parents, her mother had said, "A salesman?" with a touch of disdain in her voice.

Judy glared at her mother and didn't wait for Tony to defend himself but quickly countered, "Yes a salesman. Anything wrong with that?"

"What does he sell?" her mother had asked, backing off a little; but then she bored in with: "Does he make a living at it?"

As she felt her man being attacked, Judy exploded. She read her mother the riot act and was prepared to do the same to Carlo if he turned snotty, but he changed the subject.

"How long have you been married?" Carlo asked.

"Our twentieth anniversary is coming up this June. I can't believe the time has passed so quickly."

"Do you have any children?" Carlo asked.

"You're getting *too* personal," she balked. She felt her eyes misting. "And that's a sore point."

Talk about children always upset her. She and Tony had wanted children and had tried to get pregnant when they were first married. After two years with no success, they visited a fertility doctor. Tony grinned like a little boy when the results of his sperm count came back show he was at the high end of the normal range, but when the doctor turned to Judy and said, "Let's talk in my office," and motioned the two of them in a chill went down Judy's spine.

"This is a bit technical. Why don't you sit down?" he said as he gestured them to chairs. The doctor explained there was an obstruction in Judy's fallopian tubes which prevented fertilized eggs from getting to the uterus, implanting in the wall, and growing. Tony looked confused. Judy gasped.

"I found scarring, probably from a previous pelvic infection," the doctor went on. "The scarring blocks the tubes. We can't operate, and there are no known drugs to correct this. There's nothing anyone can do. I'm sorry, you simply can't have children."

Devastated Judy dragged Tony to two more doctors who agreed: "What you have is impossible to correct. Maybe in twenty years we'll know how to deal with this."

"Look on the bright side," Tony said when they were alone again, "We don't have to worry about birth control."

His inconsiderate and uncaring words cut her like a knife, and after he went to work she cried for an hour without stopping. She certainly didn't want to tell this to Carlo, who was virtually a stranger, so she said sadly, "No. We have no children."

Suddenly she felt very uncomfortable. She didn't want to be rude, but she had to get away from Carlo; the discussion about children had upset her, and she didn't want to cry in front of him. She looked around the room and pretended to catch Tony's eye. "I've got to go; Tony's signaling me," she said.

"Can we have a dance later?" Carlo said to her back as she walked away.

"Sure," she said over her shoulder.

She hurried over to where Tony was standing and pulled him aside. As she started to invent an excuse for dragging him away from the group around him, a waiter zigzagged through the crowd politely announcing that the meal would be served in an adjacent room. Tony crooked his arm in Judy's direction. She hooked into it and let him lead her to their table.

*　　*　　*

An hour later it was Tony's turn to be surprised.

The conversation at the table made him uncomfortable since it centered on who was more important, the accountant, the doctor, or the lawyer. When they started discussing their "toys," Tony squirmed noticeably in his seat.

"I've ordered the big Mercedes," the accountant said.

The doctor butted in. "Why don't you get the 740i? It's a better car and . . ."

The accountant ignored him. "They can't build them fast enough. The waiting list is so long that I can't get delivery for six months."

When the lawyer started in on the benefits of a Jaguar, Tony tuned them all out.

Judy had tried to help by chiming in with her "selling is a profession like medicine or law" speech, and even though she defended him for not having gone to college—"you don't have to go to college to be successful or to be a good person"—he still felt stereotyped as inferior. So he was happy when Judy gave him an excuse to leave the table.

"Wanna get me a refill, hon?" Judy said to him. "Another Merlot, please. And, here. Ditch the empty." She handed him the empty glass.

As he crossed the hardwood dance floor, Kate Mallory fell in step behind him and caught up with him at the bar. She leaned her arms casually on the counter and turned in his direction.

"Oh, Tony. How're things?" she purred, pretending to have just noticed him.

At the sound of her voice, he turned to face her and blinked at the shimmering emerald green dress which sparkled seductively even in the dim light. Even though she was Judy's closest friend, and he placed all of Judy's friends off limits, he couldn't help himself. He eyed her up and down and mentally undressed her. Nice, he thought, very nice.

"Oh, hi Kate, haven't seen you in a while," he said nonchalantly.

She slid down the bar closer to him making sure to bump his elbow with hers. Tony felt a tingling go up his arms to his shoulders. He loved women, all women; and he would be happy to flirt with Kate, but he didn't believe in innocent flirting. If flirting didn't lead to the bedroom, he reasoned, then it's a waste of time. And why should I waste time?

He remembered that he had brushed her off at a picnic she threw last summer. Kate had sidled up to him, and after some small talk had said, "Let's have lunch sometime, Tony. We could find a lot to talk about."

Tony parried that with, "Okay, I'll see when Judy and I are free."

"No, not with Judy. Just you and me." she said angrily.

He had turned his back on her and hurried away without responding.

And that wasn't the only incident. Some of Judy's other friends had made suggestive remarks, but he went out of his way to avoid becoming too friendly with any of them. That's all I need, he thought, is to start up with one of her friends and have her find out. There'd be hell or alimony to pay.

On the other hand, he had always found Kate attractive, the most attractive of Judy's friends. And if I did start up with any of them, he thought, Kate would be the one. He peeked at her out of the corner of his eye; he scanned her hourglass figure one more time and in spite of her being "off limits," wondered how she'd be in bed.

"Anything new and exciting in your life?" she said in a husky, sexy voice.

He twisted his head to look away from her, searched for the bartender, and answered her with a disinterested but forced, "Ummm."

"This may be harder than I thought," Kate muttered to herself.

Tony spotted the bartender at the far end of the long bar busily filling orders for a noisy crowd of ushers. As he began to signal to him, Kate slipped behind the bar and draped a napkin over her arm, tilted her head upward in a haughty manner and said: "Can I get you anything, Sir?" She phrased this with a strong accent on the "anything." Tony smiled, but didn't answer, and continued to wiggle his index finger at the bartender.

"C'mon. I'll tend bar for you. Try me," she slid the words slowly out as she took a small sip from a glass of champagne and made a point of sensually trying to lick some imagined drop from the corner of her mouth. Tony mumbled a few words, turned away again, and tried again to catch the harried bartender's eye.

Damn, she thought, the sonofabitch isn't even giving me a chance to get to the punch line. She waited until he turned toward her again and leaned over the bar, tilting her shoulders forward to make sure her dress fell away from her upper body. To emphasize that she wanted his attention she took hold of his sleeve and pulled him toward her. She had to smile as she watched his eyes slowly zero in on her cleavage then dart guiltily away, like a child caught with his hand in the cookie jar. Men are so easy, she thought. What I've got down there isn't much different from anything he's already seen on Judy or any of the other women he's gone to bed with, and yet he's dying to get a look.

"I've got something important to talk to you about, Tony," she confided to him. "But I don't want the whole world to hear." She pulled him even closer to her; she almost had her mouth in his ear. She touched his ear lobe ever so gently with her tongue, so gently he wasn't sure if she had done it or not.

"Y'know," she whispered, "I've been keeping a secret for a long time."

"Mmmm," he replied glancing around. Secret or no secret, now that the show of flesh was over he had lost interest.

"Wanna know what it is?"

"What what is?"

She clenched her fist and summoned all her strength to keep from socking him on the jaw.

"I said," she squeezed his arm, "that I've been keeping a secret for a long time, and I'm ready tell you what it is." Without waiting for a response she blew lightly in his ear and said in a staccato burst in her best slinky, silky, siren voice, "I've always wanted to go to bed with you. You've always been the handsomest stud around. Looking at you I get this sexy feeling, and I know we'd be dynamite together." Inwardly she could hardly keep from laughing. It sounded so trite and insincere, like something a no-talent, porn star would say in an X-rated movie.

So she was surprised when she saw the effect of her words on Tony. He had swiveled his head to face her. His eyes were wide open and lit up like the White House Christmas tree. He stared at her as if she was a Martian.

"Yeah. Me too," he stuttered without quite knowing what he was saying.

In spite of all the times he had been propositioned he wasn't expecting this one. The sheer surprise of it jumbled his powers of reasoning, and his long submerged lust for this redheaded bombshell overpowered him. He quickly convinced himself that if he went to bed with just one of Judy's friends—this one—somehow that would be all right.

"Sure. We'd be great in bed together," he said confidently. He had regained some of his composure and was now on auto-pilot. His eyes darted around the room. "We can't talk about it here. I'll call you in a couple of days and we'll set something up."

No, I need something more definite, Kate thought. He'll only be interested in me until there's another dress to look down.

"When's the next time you'll be out of town?" she cooed.

"I've got to be in Baltimore sometime next month. It doesn't matter exactly when. But that's the first time I'll be out of town."

"Okay let's make it Thursday, March 20th." That was one of the five days she had carefully set aside in her busy schedule a week earlier. "I'll set things up for us. You be sure and call me in a couple of days and I'll lay out" (she grinned wickedly at him) "the details." She walked around to the front of the bar and when she was next to him, slipped a card from her purse and tucked it into the side pocket of his pants. She playfully tickled him while slowly sliding her hand out. "My business card with my private cell phone number on it," she whispered conspiratorially. She wriggled her fingers "bye-bye" at him and slunk away not looking back but careful to swivel her hips sensually. Numbly Tony returned to the table empty handed.

Judy looked at him quizzically and asked, "Where's my wine?"

He had forgotten all about it. "Uh. They were too busy at the bar. I'll go back in a few minutes for it."

Judy went back to talking to the woman next to her not noticing the dazed expression on his face.

A few minutes later Tony left the table again on a wine run, and within seconds Carlo tapped Judy on the arm.

"C'mon," he said and holding out his hand, "We can dance while we talk. That way nobody will interrupt us, and I can make up for all those dances we didn't dance at the prom."

As she stood up, Carlo studied her carefully, comparing her with the teenager he had known so long ago. The years had dealt kindly with her; she was as appealing to him now as she had been years ago. Smooth skin. And while she's not slim and svelte like a fashion model (Who was, beside a fashion model? he asked himself.), nevertheless she's managed to hold onto her figure, Carlo thought as he led her to the far side of the dance floor and opened his arms. She smiled and stepped inside primly, keeping a proper distance.

"Do you work?" Carlo asked trying to break the ice with small talk. "I remember at the prom you said you were in the high school secretarial program."

You got so smashed that night, Judy thought, how could you remember anything? But she said, "That's right. And when I graduated I took a receptionist's job at Neuberger Roe & Price."

"The law firm?" he asked.

"Yes. The law firm," she answered. "And I still work for them, but I'm not a receptionist any more. They thought I had potential and twisted my arm to go on with my schooling. I went to college at night—they even paid for it—and earned a Bachelor's Degree in pre-law. I'm real proud of that. After I graduated, I was promoted to paralegal, and that's what I do now."

"A lawyer," Carlo said.

"Not quite a lawyer. I help the lawyers."

Nervously he swiveled her around and peeked over her shoulder to see if her husband had come back yet. Then he thought, so what if he has? I'm not doing anything wrong. I'm only dancing with another man's wife. Calmly he continued to dance with her.

"Do you have any hobbies?" he asked.

"I'm into flowers. I read books about flowers; I look at flower catalogs. This is the time of year I plan my flower garden. What do you do?"

"I'm a writer. For the paper. The Philadelphia Inquirer. Look for my byline on local stories." He looked into her eyes and when she looked back he changed the subject. "Some day you'll have to fill me in on what happened at the prom. I don't remember too much about it." He did remember up to where he began drinking heavily, but after that he drew a complete blank on the rest of the evening. "We could talk over lunch or a cup of coffee."

"Lunch would be nice," Judy said without hesitation. "Call me."

"Okay. But it'll have to be soon. I'm starting on a new job April fifteenth and it's out of town. Way out of town."

"Out of town where?"

The music stopped, and the dance was over. He curled his hand lightly around her waist as he accompanied her back to her seat.

"I'm going to Rome. Italy," he buzzed with excitement and flushed as he sat down next to her.

Tony returned with the wine, and Judy introduced the two men to each other. Carlo rose from his chair and motioned for Tony to sit as he mumbled a "glad to meet you." Then with a hasty goodbye he left. Tony set the glass on the table in front of Judy and asked, "Who was that?"

"My senior prom date, Carlo Fiore," she answered. "He asked me to have lunch with him some day. Are you jealous?"

Tony eyed him carefully. "No," he said confidently, "You can have lunch with him."

I wasn't asking your permission, she thought to herself; but out loud she said, "You don't have to worry about him. He's leaving town soon."

The male conversation at the table centered on the chances of the Philadelphia Eagles being in next year's Super Bowl, something Tony could talk about comfortably. As he turned to add his comments about the team needing a new coach, Judy thought back to her senior prom. It was an important night in my life, she thought. A night I'll never forget. The first time I let a man touch me. More than touch me. It was the first time I let a man go all the way.

And the man wasn't Carlo.

Chapter 4

As he drove away from his sister's house after a disturbing lunch, Dominic Micaletto tried not to let it bother him. After all, it wasn't his daughter. His short marriage had been childless, and as far as he knew, in spite of the many women he had bedded, he had never fathered children with any of them. Maybe, he thought, that was why he had such strong feelings for his niece.

"How ya doin' in school?" he had asked his 12-year old niece, Tina, that afternoon.

His sister, Denise Demarest, had asked him to come to lunch so they could discuss "something important," and they had just finished eating.

"Why're you asking?" an angry Tina snipped at him. "It was Mom put you up to it, wasn't it? Now you're gonna snoop into my life like she did." She stomped from the table and upstairs to her room without waiting for his answer.

Dominic's mouth dropped open. This was not the Tina he knew who had always been such a loving child. When she was little, she would push her older sister out of the way to climb up on Uncle Dominic's lap. Once settled there, she would put her arms around his neck and squeeze him as hard as she could and tell him how much she loved him. Until today, he could always count on her for a serious hug whenever he came to visit. But today something was wrong. She gave him a weak "hi" when he came in and busied herself setting the table for lunch and paid him no further attention.

"What was that all about, Maria?" he asked her older sister, who was sitting next to him spooning the last bit of ice cream from her plate to her mouth.

"Don't get me mixed up in this," she bristled. The spoon clanged on her dish as she dropped it and ran from the table.

Dominic stood up so fast his chair thunked into the wall behind him, and he thundered to the empty room, "Somebody tell me what the ffff . . . ," (he caught himself in time) "is going on here."

Denise, startled by her brother's bellowing, came flying out of the kitchen just as Maria slammed her way out the front door.

Dominic planted his knuckles on the table, hunched over, and glared at her. He liked his life to be on an even keel and had no tolerance for anybody who or anything that threatened to upset it.

"Why the fuck did you ask me here today?" he muttered to his sister through clenched teeth.

Denise had never gotten used to hearing him use his favorite adjective and winced at the obscenity, but decided not to comment. "This is hard for me, Dominic," she started. "I've never come to you with family troubles before, even after Harry died so young." Her husband, Harry, had died a year after Tina had been born. Denise had managed as a single mother with substantial financial support from Dominic. "You've taken care of the bills, and I appreciate that, but now . . . this . . . I can't handle this on my own." She started to cry.

Softened by her tears, he mellowed a little. "What is it? What's the 'something important' we've got to talk about?"

She screwed up her courage. "It's Tina. I found some stuff in her room. I wasn't snooping. I swear I wasn't snooping. You know me Dominic. I don't snoop into their things."

"What 'stuff' did you find?" he said.

"In her waste basket, like she wasn't even trying to hide it . . . a plastic baggy with some white dust in it. Oh, Dominic . . ." In between the huge sobs that racked her body she managed to push out, "She's . . . doing . . . drugs."

He made no effort to console her but said, "Yeah. Well, lotsa people do drugs, and it doesn't seem to hurt them."

"Can't you see? This is the start of something bad. If she gets hooked, her life won't be worth nothing. Help me, Dominic. Help her. Talk to her."

"I can't talk to her. She ran out on me just now, and I only asked her how things were in school. She's trying something new to act grownup. Wait a few weeks, she'll get over it."

"She's not gonna get over it. It's only gonna get worse," Denise wailed. "I'm scared. You gotta do something."

Her request for action grated on him. Action was not his problem-solving and decision-making style. He much preferred to do nothing and hope the problem went away or things got better. He reached over and patted her on the head, like he would a friendly dog, waited until her crying subsided, then let himself out.

Hunched over the wheel he bulled his way through traffic and tried to slough off the whole incident. Though he strained as hard as he could to put it out of his mind, it wouldn't go away. His associates knew him as the consummate macho-male tough guy; more than once he had used his fists to persuade others to agree with him. The one chink in his armor, his Achilles heel, was his love for his nieces. Tina on drugs—in his gut he knew it wasn't going to get better.

Chapter 5

$\mathcal{M}$onday morning after the wedding, Tony and Judy were having one of their silent breakfasts together. Judy was usually bright and cheerful in the morning. She would bounce up as soon as the alarm went off, sit on the edge of the bed, stretch first one way and then the other, then jump up full of early morning energy. Tony was the exact opposite. He would smack the snooze button at least three times before he grudgingly got out of bed. He remained quiet and sullen until he reached his first appointment of the day, at which point he installed his salesman's personality and perked up.

The Fanellis had the paper delivered daily but most days ended up throwing it away unopened in the plastic bag it came in without reading it; they preferred to get their news from the parade of TV programs from five to seven. So this morning Tony was caught off-guard when Judy said, "Did you see this article in the Inquirer?"

"When do I ever read the paper?" Tony grumbled, barely awake.

"Maybe we ought to start. There's a story here by Carlo Fiore," she said, pointing to the bottom of page one.

"Who?" Tony asked. He took another sip of coffee and tried to concentrate on how he would approach his first sales call. He had developed the habit of planning his sales calls in his mind before he actually made them, and he wished Judy would stop talking and let him think.

"Carlo Fiore. You met him at Nancy's wedding. He was my senior prom date."

"Umm. So who cares if he wrote a story?"

"I care. And you ought to care, too."

"Why should I care?"

"Boy, is this a stupid argument."

"You're the one that brought it up."

Judy snapped the paper wide open, clutched it tightly, and hid her face behind it so Tony couldn't see the tears welling in her eyes. He's dumping on me more and more every day, she thought. I feel like I'm his punching bag, and I don't deserve it. I haven't done anything to him. Why can't he be like he used to be when we were first married?

And Tony thought: There she goes again with her pointless blubbering. Right now I need quiet to think and plan. Can't she see that? It's her fault I have to find other women; she doesn't understand me any more. How in hell am I supposed to be faithful to her when she annoys me all the time?

He turned his thoughts to Kate. She sure looked sexy at the wedding, he remembered. He began to fantasize about being in bed with her.

*   *   *

While the Fanellis brooded, Kate was already at work, congratulating herself on finally landing Tony. Hot damn, she thought, it's finally gonna happen. She left the office at eleven saying she was taking an early lunch, but skipped eating and went to the public library. Now for phase two, she said to herself. She read down the spines of a stack of thick phone books, pulled out the one marked "Baltimore," and thumbed through the yellow pages until she came to detective agencies. The large ad for Omega Investigations had the come-on "THE MATRIMONIAL SPECIALISTS" in big letters. Just what I'm looking for, she thought as she copied down the phone number. Before she shut the book she wrote down the phone numbers of two other agencies. For backup, in case Omega doesn't work out, she reasoned.

When she got back to her desk she noticed the boss was out, so she went into his private office and shut the door. She settled into his high-back, amply stuffed swivel chair, pulled out the private phone he kept in his top desk drawer, and dialed Omega's number.

"I need some . . . matrimonial work done," she told the receptionist who answered.

"I'll put John on the phone. He's the only partner with free time right now," the operator said.

A moment later a sugary voice spoke into the phone, "This is John Christopher, how can I help you?"

"It's like this, John. I won't bore you with the details but cut right to the chase. I'll be going to bed with a married man at a motel in your area, and I want someone to take pictures of us and send them to his wife."

"I'm afraid I'll need more than that," he said fidgeting in his chair. He was uncomfortable with what she had outlined, since it was not exactly in line with his regular business.

"There isn't any more than that. Well, actually there are a few little details."

"And what would they be?"

"First of all my face isn't to show in any of the photos. I don't want his wife to know who he's in bed with." Yet, she said to herself. "Second, I want you to call his wife afterwards and tell her she will be getting pictures of her husband screwing another woman. And third, don't come breaking the door down and barging in on us. These pictures have to be taken on the sly, through a window or whatever. He's not to suspect anything. Can you handle all that?"

Christopher sighed. "Frankly, this is not quite what we ordinarily do. I have to consider if there is anything illegal about this. I can't afford to be sued by an angry husband or wife or lose my license. Give me a second to get my thoughts together."

"I'm not asking you to do anything illegal. I'll pay for this in advance with a cashier's check. That will protect both of us. You won't know who I am, and I can't prove you did anything. When you call her on the phone, you don't have to identify yourself. And when you mail the pictures, use a plain envelope. Damn, why am I doing all the thinking for you?"

He thought about the shrinking balance in the business' bank account and the bills on his desk which were overdue. Recently Omega had been stiffed by a large account that had gone bankrupt. John and his two partners had been forced to layoff all of their investigators since they couldn't pay them, and had been carrying the business with their personal money. And now that was running out. We sure need her money, he thought. Let's see if she'll pay twice our usual fee.

"Okay we'll do it. I'll do it personally. The fee is $2,000," he said in a professional tone.

"Agreed," she said. "The check will be in the mail today. And here's a phone number where you can reach me." She gave him her cell phone number. "Set things up for March 20th."

"Good. That gives me about three weeks. Now here's what we do to catch a cheating husband." He proceeded to outline a plan. "Can you manage that?" he asked.

She broke into a broad grin. "Nooooo problem. I can manage that just fine," she said.

* * *

Late that afternoon John Christopher limped into the office of a nondescript Maryland motel. Seven years ago when he was a star detective on the Baltimore police force, he had burst into a suspect's room in the middle of the night. He had hoped the man would be in bed sleeping. He wasn't. He was hiding in the bedroom closet. Fortunately he was so high on drugs that when he pulled a gun and fired wildly at the police no one was killed, but John was shot in the leg before his partner could subdue the gunman. John managed to live with his handicap, grudgingly, until he overheard one of his supposed friends at the station say behind his back, "John, you know, the cripple." It was more than his ego could bear. He took early retirement, joined with two other ex-policeman, and established Omega Investigations.

Now he studied the man behind the motel counter. A new face, he noticed. He stood off to one side and waited until the clerk, sporting a unkempt Vandyke beard badly in need of trimming, finished checking in an older man/younger woman couple with no luggage. As they walked away, he strode up to the check-in desk.

He held up his private investigator's badge in the palm of his hand. "I'm John Christopher, private investigator," he said. "I've never seen you here before."

"Yeah, so?" the clerk said, glancing disinterestedly at the badge as if it were junk mail. He turned away and started to walk into the office.

Christopher leaned forward, bellied onto the counter, grabbed the back of the clerk's shirt, and dragged him back. With his free hand he twisted him around and yanked hard on the clerk's beard. He screamed in pain.

"Have I got your attention now?" the detective asked.

The clerk shoved John's hands away, rubbed his sore chin, and nodded.

"Are you new here?" John demanded. Sullenly the clerk nodded.

"Are you the night clerk? Four to midnight?" Another nod.

Not exactly a world-class conversationalist, John thought.

"Do you work Thursday nights?"

"I have Sundays and Mondays off," he said unenthusiastically.

"On Thursday, March 20th save the 'special' room for my clients. Understand?" The clerk picked up a pencil.

"No," John warned him. "Don't write anything down. I'll be back before then to remind you, and besides I have to identify the man and woman for you."

"There's one problem," the clerk said. "I don't know anything about any 'special' room."

"You *are* new here, aren't you?" Christopher sighed. "Ask your boss about the room with the mirrors. And then you make sure give that room to my people. If you screw up, I'll . . ." He left the sentence unfinished. "Here's my card." He slapped his business card on the counter. "If there are any problems, anything at all. You call me. Remember. I've got that room reserved for March 20th. Don't give it to anyone else."

"Yeah. Yeah. I understand." The clerk nodded as the detective limped away.

When he got back to the office John called his client to confirm what he had set up. "It would be helpful if you could send me a picture either of you or of him for the room clerk."

"I don't have a picture of him," she said. "And remember I said not to photograph my face. I don't want you to know who I am."

"Lady," John said. "If I'm going to take pictures of you in bed with a man, there's not going to be any part of you I'm not going to see."

"Even so, I'm not sending you a picture of me. Tell them to hold the room for . . . Murphy."

"Okay, Mrs. Murphy. It'll be waiting for you."

Chapter 6

Two days later Charles Price, Jr., Charlie to his friends, left his law firm, Neuberger Roe & Price, early. Mr. Stratham H. Neuberger, the firm's doddering, eighty-seven year old founder, had summoned him to the Philadelphia Country Club. "You c'mon over here. There's a man looking for a lawyer," he had harrumphed over the phone, "but I can't understand what he's saying."

You haven't understood much of what anyone's been saying for the past five years, Price thought to himself as he buzzed for his secretary and told her where he could be reached.

Charlie drove up the club's circular driveway and parked under the canopied front entrance. The valet greeted him with a "Hello, Mr. Price," as Charlie tossed him the car keys. He knew where the old man would be waiting and went directly to the dark-mahogany-walled bar. In the dim light he did not see Mr. Neuberger right away, but he could hear him shouting, "Slow down. I can't understand you."

"Millions. We're dealing with millions," the other man was saying as he gestured enthusiastically.

Neuberger rose creakily from his seat as he noticed Price approaching and slapped him on the back. "Glad to see you, Charlie," he said. "This fellow here needs a lawyer." He nodded to the man behind him. "I didn't get his name," he muttered in a stage whisper loud enough to be heard a mile away.

"It's Leon. Short for Leonardo," the man said. He rushed on with his story without waiting for Price to be introduced. "It's like this. I have relatives in Italy who are starting a toy business. They plan to manufacture toys, but they also want to get licenses to sell toys in Italy that are made here in the States, so they need a lawyer who can understand these kind of contracts. I've decided to back them financially, but before I send them a check, I need someone to go over there and make sure everything is . . . you know, okay. They *are* my relatives, but we're talking about a lot of money here."

Price fiddled nervously with the knot on his tie, settled into a chair, and said, "Our firm can certainly be of service. I, myself, have a lot of experience with contracts. And as for looking out for your financial interests, I'm a CPA in addition to being a lawyer."

Leon raised his eyebrows in admiration. "You'll also need someone who understands Italian," he said. "They don't speak English very well."

Neuberger suddenly experiencing a wave of understanding butted in, "That's not a problem. We have quite a few employees of Italian ancestry. I'm sure one of them can handle the language problem." He looked expectantly at Price, who had no idea who in the office could translate Italian.

"Okay," Leon said to Price. "Your partner has convinced me that you're a reputable law firm. Let me contact the people in Italy and before I send them a check, I'll arrange for you to go over there and meet with them."

Price was elated as he drove home. This was going to be a bonanza if the firm could enter the international market. And he would find a way to personally take credit for the flood of new business that would surely result. Mentally he began spending his bonus.

Chapter 7

$\mathcal{L}$ate that same afternoon Tony Fanelli was north of Trenton finishing up his last sales call for the day. On the way out he stopped to get another look at the leggy, miniskirted, bombshell receptionist and to find out if she was bedable. While her face, Tony judged, was okay—nothing to get excited about, her body was movie star quality. Bulging Dolly Parton breasts over a wasp waist anchored by Betty Grable legs would start any man's blood running hot, and Tony was no exception. She knew exactly the effect she had on men and smiled warmly at Tony, stood up, then bent over to pick up her purse from under her desk. Tony, watching her short skirt ride up her legs, felt sexual desire twitching in his groin.

"Done for the day?" Tony asked alternating his gaze between her overflowing blouse and her gorgeous legs.

She returned his admiration with a beaming smile. "I hope I'm not done for the day," she snickered. "The good part of the day starts now." Tony gawked at her. "The good part of the day is," she said emphatically, "when I go home to my boyfriend."

The fact that she had a boyfriend didn't faze him. He'd learned that a woman was just as likely to cheat on a boyfriend as a wife on a husband. Tony's mind swirled with images of a handsome man undressing this goddess of a woman.

She went on, "We've only been living together for three weeks, and you know how it is at the beginning. We can't get enough of each other. Sometimes we even skip supper and go right to bed."

Jauntily, she waved goodbye and bounced out the door. Tony admired her swaying hips until she was out of sight, then whispered, "Whew, that's one lucky boyfriend," and headed for his car.

He pulled onto I-95 south and headed toward Philadelphia but immediately got caught in the middle of a traffic jam. Impatiently he drummed his fingers on the steering wheel, and lecherous thoughts of non-stop love-making ran through his head. He tried to remember: Was it ever that way with Judy and me?

His thoughts raced back to their early days together.

A week after he proposed, Judy began to tell him of her plans saying, "And let's go here for our honeymoon." She handed him a brochure for a Pocono Mountain resort and jabbed her finger at a couple with their arms around each other in a bright red, heart-shaped tub with water bubbling and foaming around them.

"Wherever you'll be happy," Tony had said barely looking at the pamphlet. He didn't care where they went. He was crazy in love with her and wanted to be with her. The location didn't matter.

After their wedding, they drove to the Paradise Lodge, and as soon as the bellboy left the room, he began to claw at her clothes. She twisted away from him.

"Mrs. Fanelli wants some romance first," she said keeping him at arms length. "Some flowers, some wine, some dancing. Then you won't have to rip my clothes off. I'll do it for you."

"What the hell is this?" he said angrily. "Before we got married you were happy to jump into bed with me without any of this fooling around."

"Well, now we *are* married, and this is our honeymoon, and I want to be treated as a wife. I need some romance."

Tony grumbled something under his breath, but took her down to the ballroom. After they had danced for an hour, he led her to the gift shop and bought a dozen red roses, then took her up to the room, called room service, and ordered champagne.

That night they made love four times. The last time was five in the morning. At seven he felt her hands running over his chest.

"I love you so much Tony," she said as she wrapped her arms around him and rubbed her naked body against him. "I want to make you happy."

He blinked and the memory disappeared. He stared at the not-moving cars in front of him, and sighed. Those exciting days are gone, he thought. He and Judy had become an old, married couple each with a job and a career. They were locked in a dull, boring routine, and the good times they used to have together were getting fewer. He escaped from this torture the only way he knew—in the arms of other women. Which reminded him about Kate. At Nancy's wedding she had put her business card in his pocket and said, " . . . call me in a couple of days." He had been meaning to call her, and now since he would have a lot of time until traffic started moving again, he decided to do it. He rummaged through his attaché case until he found the office furniture catalog where he had hidden her card, then dialed her number on his cell phone.

After five rings she picked it up. "Hello," he said. Traffic inched forward a few yards.

"Hello," she said. "Hold for a second whoever you are. I'm finishing up on another line."

Three minutes later she was back.

"It's Tony," he said. "Can you talk?"

"Oh, Tony," she twittered. "If I had known it was you, I would have . . . Am I glad to hear from you. I'm kinda busy—I've got two clients coming in shortly, so we'll have to make it a quickie." She giggled at her own joke. "What's up?"

When he didn't laugh, she nervously combed her fingers through her hair wondering if her "quickie" joke had turned him off.

"In general things are okay. But right now I'm stuck in traffic, so I thought I'd give you a call to see if everything is . . . set up," he said.

I haven't done it quite this way before, she thought. (Though I've done it almost every other way.) It's always been spontaneous, not set up in advance like this; and the man always set up where we'd go. I don't want to let him wriggle off the hook, and I've got my little surprise for him, so I've got to take charge here. But I'm not sure how to play it. Should I come on like a Madonna or a whore? Given Tony's reputation (she had heard stories about his major sexual appetite), she decided on the latter approach.

"Everything is taken care of," she cooed. "I've planned a big surprise for you. It'll be something special, something different from anything you've ever had before. Oh, Tony. I can't wait for you to light my fire. I know it's gonna feel soooo good. And I'm gonna give you the thrill of your life. You're gonna remember this night forever." Oh, shit, she thought, I hope I'm not overdoing it.

Her words and tone of her voice sent Tony's mind reeling. What could the surprise be? he wondered. All sorts of possibilities raced through his head as he replayed erotic scenes from his favorite pornographic movies.

He said, "I can't wait, either. You're getting me all worked up and horny just thinking about it."

"You stay that way and we'll have a great time together. Now here's the details," she twittered. "On Thursday the twentieth, at seven o'clock meet me at . . ." She gave him the address of the Calvert Inn in Laurel Maryland, which was the motel outside Baltimore John Christopher had told her to use. "I'm so excited about this. I'm . . . I can't think of the words." She almost said, "I'm gonna wet my pants just thinking about it," but thought that would be a little too much.

"Same here," Tony said. "I'm excited too."

Her secretary motioned that her next appointment had arrived and was waiting impatiently. "Gotta run," she said, tweaking a tiny kiss into the phone, then clicked off.

A horn blared behind Tony shattering his daydreams. Traffic had started crawling again and there was too big a space in front of Tony to suit the driver behind him. He squashed the urge to salute the honker with his middle finger, eased his foot onto the accelerator, and slowly closed the gap.

Chapter 8

$\mathcal{W}$hen the phone on the far corner of her desk rang, Judy Fanelli pushed aside a pile of folders in order to reach it. She had been glued to her computer screen at Neuberger Roe & Price since early that morning. Her fingers had danced over the keyboard as new ideas popped into her head and was so absorbed in her research that the lunch hour came and went She didn't notice and didn't stop to eat. Now as she answered the phone, hunger pangs rumbled in her stomach, but she ignored them.

"Judy Orsini," she said into the phone.

"That's how I remember you, but I thought you were married to Tony Fanelli," the voice on the other end said.

"Carlo?" she asked, recognizing the distinctive sound of his voice.

"Yes, it's Carlo. Did you divorce Tony?" he joked.

"No, we're still married, but I use my maiden name at work so the cranks and creeps won't be able to trace me. How did you know where I work?" She had forgotten their conversation at the wedding.

"At the wedding you told me you were with Neuberger. I looked up the number, called, and asked for Judy Fanelli. They connected me with you."

"I hate to rush you, but I've got a lot of work to do today . . . ."

"Since you're busy I'll make it quick. I want to take you up on the lunch date I promised. You do remember that, don't you?"

"Yes. I remember." She smiled.

"And you remember I'm leaving for Rome in three weeks so we'll have to make it soon."

"No problem." She glanced at her wall calendar. "Today is Thursday, March 20th. How about next Tuesday, the 25th?"

He cradled the phone with his shoulder as he paged through his pocket scheduler. Tuesday's lunchtime block was empty. "I'm clear. I'll pick you up at your office around noon."

"I'm penciling you in as we speak. By the way, you know my parents were both born in Rome, and my mother talks about how great it is to be Roman all the time, so we'll have something to discuss at lunch."

"My family's from Abruzzi, and I still have some cousins over there. I've been writing to them since I was a kid. I had a journalist hiding in me even 'way back then. I'm going to see them when I get to Italy. Hey, look. We'll talk more on Tuesday. I've held you up too long already."

I never expected to hear from him, Judy thought as she hung up the phone. I would have bet big money it was one of those "we must get together" pleasantries that are never followed up on. Carlo, hmm. Carlo. I wonder why he asked me out to lunch, if he's leaving town? Why is he interested in me? Then again why shouldn't he be? Why wouldn't any man be interested in me? She took a compact from her purse, flipped it open, and studied her reflection in the mirror. So far I've managed to keep from looking my age.

Judy more than prided herself; she was obsessed with maintaining a youthful appearance. With great effort she forced herself to eat as little as possible, and she noted with satisfaction that she only weighed five pounds more than the day she was married. Every other week her colorist tinted out the gray from her hair; and every morning and night she used an assortment of creams and lotions to keep her skin soft and wrinkle-free. She smiled when her friends commented that she looked much younger than she was, and she would glow when people often mistook her for thirty-one instead of forty-one.

There was one aspect of her appearance that had disturbed her when she was a child—her aquiline nose. Her mother haughtily referred to it as a "perfect Roman nose," and insisted that it was an asset. "I like mine," her mother had said proudly. "You'll get to like yours." And Judy had; over the years she decided her mother was right. It made her look aristocratic, noble. She was not unhappy that her mother had talked her out of the "nose job" she had begged for in tenth grade.

She shook her head to clear these thoughts away and returned to work. At four fifteen she felt increasing pain and stiffness in her back, and it broke her concentration. She stood up, stepped to the doorway of her cubby, rubbed her eyes gently, and looked down the corridor to the large, floor-to-ceiling window at the end. From forty floors up she gazed absent-mindedly at the skyline outside. The skyscrapers seemed to shimmer and ripple as they reflected the sunlight from their glass, metal, and stone facades, and in the distance Billy Penn seemed to be smiling at her from his perch on top of City Hall a few blocks away. Beautiful day; not a cloud in the sky, she thought. She glanced at her watch: four-thirty.

Suddenly, the unnatural quiet startled her. Where was the low hum of voices she was accustomed to? Where was the clicking of keys on keyboards? She looked around and noticed there were no people scurrying through the hallways. Then she remembered: it was Thursday; the next-to-last Thursday in the month. Most of the employees of the law firm left early to get a head start at the company-sponsored happy hour at TGI Friday's on City Line Avenue. Judy rarely missed these get-togethers and found them fun—a good way to meet everyone from the top brass (who usually gave everyone a quick hello, then sat at an isolated table in a corner shutting themselves off from the rest of the group), down to newly hired secretaries. She liked getting away from the stiffness and formality of the office. At Friday's there was easy banter and camaraderie. Here her co-workers were willing to let their hair down and be real people.

What the hell, Judy thought, even though it's not five o'clock and I'm in no hurry—Tony won't be home until Saturday—I'll call it quits too. Working briskly, she straightened up her workspace—plopping pencils and pens into the Temple University mug on her desk, and stuffing papers into file folders.

As she pushed her chair under the desk and smoothed her tweed jacket and skirt, a fierce tremor snaked through her body. It started with a crawly, tingling sensation (it felt like a nest of spiders had been dumped on her head), which then exploded in the roots of her hair. Quickly it increased in intensity causing her to shiver and shake uncontrollably. A fraction of a second later a wave of prickles flooded down her spine, surged into her feet, and cramped her toes. She shuddered violently and began to lose her balance. Bile rose to her throat—she felt as seasick as she had on last year's vacation with Tony. The cruise ship to Bermuda had run into a hurricane and was tossed violently in its huge waves. And now as a bitter, acid taste seeped into her mouth, she clenched her teeth and dug her nails into her palms to fight the mounting nausea and summoned all her strength to keep from falling. Like a punch-drunk boxer attacked by a relentless opponent, she staggered and reeled as wave after wave of some vague, evil force pounded at her.

Gradually it subsided leaving her physically and emotionally drained. But in its wake she was left with a fear, a fear of some undefined disaster approaching. Cold drops of perspiration formed under her arms and started to trickle down her side; her heart beat faster and faster, and she wobbled unsteadily. To brace herself she clawed her fingers deep into the soft upholstery on the back of her chair.

Slowly she regained her self-control. Hand over hand she worked her way around and collapsed into her chair as a dozen jumbled thoughts raced through her head. Is this a heart attack or another of my witch's spells? she wondered.

As she continued to return to normal, she decided it wasn't a heart attack—no chest pain, no pain anywhere. Instinctively she knew it must be a warning, a warning about some evil, some tragedy waiting in the wings ready to come into her life.

Preoccupied with her thoughts she didn't notice that Sara Parker, the secretary from down the hall, had stuck her head in the doorway. Sara was the resident free spirit at Neuberger. She dressed in unusual clothing—today she wore a long, flouncey, multi-colored peasant skirt and a stark white blouse. She looked ready to burst into a gypsy dance at a moment's notice. Her long, black, hair was tied in a ponytail with a wide bow of material that matched her skirt.

How Sara got any work done was one of the mysteries of the office. She spent most of the day collecting gossip from those willing to talk, and the rest of the day passing it along to those who were willing to listen. Judy called her "the office flit" to which Sara would reply: "Somebody's got to do the dirty work around here."

Sara stood nervously twisting her hair and tapping her foot. When Judy still didn't notice her, she rapped gently on the doorjamb with her long fingernails. Judy swiveled to face her. Sara took one look at her, pale and shivering, and the wind whooshed out of her like a punctured balloon.

"God, you look awful," Sara said, a frown furrowed on her worried and frightened face. "You're white as a ghost. Are you sick? Should I go call a doctor." She turned to leave, but Judy raised her hand to stop her.

"I'll be okay," Judy replied with a quiver in her voice. The color began returning to her face.

"Are you sure? Do you need any help?"

"No. I felt sick for a second, but I'm better now. I think it was one of my spells."

"Are you sure it's nothing serious?" Sara didn't believe in spells or Judy's claim to be a witch. "You've really got me worried."

"I'll skip Friday's and go home. I don't think I'm up to it."

"Okay, but let me take you." Sara held up Judy's coat and one at a time slipped its sleeves onto her arms. "You're in no shape to drive."

"Thanks for the offer. I'm going to take you up on it," Judy said, leaning on the younger woman. Noticing the grave concern on her face Judy repeated, "I'm okay. Really. I'm sure it was one of my witchy things—something weird came over me. It threw me for a loop, but it's gone now."

On the drive home she closed her eyes and fought to shake off the evil premonition. It wouldn't go away.

Chapter 9

*L*ate that same afternoon John Christopher returned to the Calvert Inn. A professional's Canon camera with a protruding lens hung around his neck. In his attaché case he carried an extra roll of film, a peanut butter and jelly sandwich, a flashlight, and the current issue of Playboy magazine.

Had he not been trained as a detective, he would not have recognized the clerk. Someone must've told him to straighten up his act, John thought. The clerk's scraggly beard was gone; he was clean-shaven. He wore a tie, neatly knotted and up close to his neck; the top button of his shirt was buttoned, the shirt was carefully tucked into his pants and smoothed around so there were no wrinkles.

"Remember me?" John asked.

"Yes, Sir," came the crisp reply.

"Tonight's the night," John said as he told the desk clerk about "Murphy."

"I understand," the clerk said. "I'm to look out for a party named Murphy, and he or she gets the 'special' room. Is that correct?"

"You got it. And it'll be a 'she.' We've planned that she will pick up the key so there'll be no mistake in getting the right room." He looked at his watch. "It's five o'clock now. She's supposed to arrive at seven, but she could be here any time from now on, so watch out. Sometimes people come early. By the way, do you get a replacement for supper break?"

"No. I eat right back there," he nodded to a door behind him, "and when the office door opens a buzzer rings, and I come out here. There's no chance anyone else will be here or that I won't be here, or that I won't hear them."

"Sounds good," the detective said. "I need . . ."

"Here it is," the clerk reached under the counter and pulled out a room key chained to a eight-inch paddle.

Christopher walked around to the side of the motel and opened a door marked "LINEN CLOSET-2." He judged the room to be about twelve feet by ten feet. The wall in front of him and the wall to his left each had half a dozen shelves piled high with sheets and towels. On his right there was a three-foot by three-foot glass window in the center of the wall, and in front of the window was a recliner patched with peeling duct tape that partially covered a multitude of rips in the fabric. Through the glass he could see into a darkened motel room—only a small night-light glowed on the switch plate by the door. He could barely make out a gigantic circular bed covered with a garish gold and purple spread.

The detective unzipped his windbreaker, hung it on a hook on the back of the door, then settled down in the chair, and took the camera from its case. He flipped off the lens cover and sighted through the viewfinder. Satisfied he set the camera gently on the floor and leaned back in the chair. Look at me; I'm Allen Funt, he thought. He opened the magazine—this will keep me awake, he had thought when he packed it—aimed the flashlight at it and began to thumb through the pictures. When the endless parade of naked women started to bore him, he began to read the letters to the editor. "Unbelievable," he said out loud as he read about a couple plastering honey all over themselves and then licking it off. "Who writes this shit?"

Half an hour later he got up from the chair, stretched, opened the door a crack, and peeked out. The setting sun painted the sky a dazzling orange-yellow, then winked twice in quick succession and disappeared over the horizon. As he watched the grayness of twilight shroud down, he was startled by his stomach growling, reminding him that it was past his usual suppertime and he had not eaten. He shut the door, sat back down, pulled the sandwich from its wrapper, and began to nibble on it.

Chapter 10

Driving toward the motel, Tony remembered how excited and nervous he had been the first time he went to bed with a woman—a girl really. When he was fourteen years old, he was caught off guard in a lively conversation with his best friend Bob, and blurted out before he could censor it, that he was still a virgin.

"You mean you ain't been laid yet?" Bob had said incredulously. "We're gonna change that. I'll fix you up with Betty. She'll fuck anything. Even you." He laughed raucously.

Betty turned out to be a thirty-year-old mountain of pudgy flesh topped off with dirty blonde hair. However, Tony was wound up so tight by the time he met her, that he wouldn't have cared if she was Godzilla's sister. She played her part well and moaned and twisted under him (but continued to chomp on a wad of pink bubble gum), and after he had finished, she held out her hand.

"What's that for?" he asked.

"The twenty fuckin' dollars I get," she said.

"I don't know anything about any twenty dollars," Tony said, "and besides I ain't got no money on me."

"You'll fuckin' pay me, or Bob's in big trouble," she threatened.

"I'll pay you tomorrow."

He never did.

There had been many since Betty, but each time Tony was on his way to meet a new woman he felt the same blood-throbbing, lump-in-the-throat excitement. His whole body tingled imagining what new experience awaited him. That was the key, wasn't it? he thought to himself. The key to feeling alive. Always having something different, something new to look forward to. Judy's like an old shoe. Comfortable, reliable, broken in. I know exactly what to expect; and that has its place in my life. But screwing a new woman, that's the spice of my life. He hummed softly to himself and tapped his fingers on the steering wheel. He looked up and saw he was heading south on I-95 and approaching the first exit to Wilmington. An hour later, he took his cell phone from his pocket and dialed Kate's car phone number.

"Tony?" said the female voice at the other end.

"Yeah. It's me. I'm south of Wilmington. Where are you?" he asked.

"You sound impatient," Kate teased.

"Sure I'm impatient. Aren't you? And what's the surprise you said you had?"

"You'll have to wait, 'cause if I told you what it was, it wouldn't be a surprise would it? So I'm not telling you anything. Anyway, you're way ahead of me," she said. "So you'll get there first. Wait in your car near the office for me. Don't go get the room. I'll get it when I get there. It's part of the surprise."

"Okay. But check to see if anybody's following you. And look out for any suspicious cars or people around the motel. I'd like to keep this between you and me."

"Who the hell do you think is interested in us? The adultery police?" She laughed.

"Just be careful and look around," he insisted.

"Yeah. Yeah. I hear you. See ya soon."

An hour later Tony drove up to the motel. He parked near the glitzy red and blue sign which announced: The Calvert Inn in Laurel, Maryland. He tilted the seat as far back as he could, turned on the radio, and leaned back against the headrest. He tried to relax but found himself tense with the expectation of a new woman in bed; and what could her surprise be? Ten minutes later, she pulled up next to him. He let out a low whistle when he saw the fire-engine-red, 2-door, sporty Pontiac Sunfire, (she must have got a new car, he thought) then got out of his car. Kate rolled down the driver's window, and he leaned his elbows on the sill. To make it easier to drive she had hiked her tight skirt up almost to her waist, and Tony's eyes bulged as he stared at her exposed legs and the white wisp of underwear peeking from her crotch.

"A-A-Anyone f-f-follow you?" he stammered.

"No," she answered as she leaned over and kissed him lightly on the mouth. "You see anybody behind me?" She jerked her head toward the highway.

He glanced out toward the road and regained some composure. "Nope. Nobody there," he said.

"I'll get the room key. You wait here 'til I come and get you," she said.

She slithered out of her car paying no attention to Tony's gawking, and without a backward glance she walked to the door marked "Office." As she opened the door she heard a muffled buzzer sound. Immediately a man emerged from the doorway behind the counter.

"Can I help you?" he asked.

"Yes. I'm Mrs. Murphy," she said.

"Oh, yes. We've been expecting you," he said. He reached into one of the cubbyholes on the wall behind him and handed her an oversize, shiny, gold room key. "It's number twenty-four, over that way." He pointed to her right. "The key turns to the left. Everything's ready for you. Have a good evening."

She returned to where Tony was waiting and said, "Let's go, stuuuud." She slurred the last word suggestively. After he slid out of his car and stood up, she faced him, stuffed her hands in his back pockets, jiggled her fingers seductively, and pulled him toward her. She rubbed her body up and down against him and raised her face to his.

"It looks like this is going to be a real fun evening with what I feel growing in your pants," she said. "I can't wait to get my hands on that."

Tony put his arms around her and kissed her passionately. As he explored her mouth with his tongue, he eased his right hand under her jacket and massaged her breast. Slowly she broke away.

"Save me some of that for inside the room," she purred. "I don't do public shows." She reached into her car, took out a garment bag, and handed it to him. "Carry this for me, would ya?" she said.

"What's this for?" He slung it over his shoulder. "You staying here for a while?"

"Change of clothes. I have to go to work in the morning."

She took his hand and led him down the row of rooms, unlocked number twenty-four, and playfully pulled him in behind her.

"Leave the lights off," she said, quickly stripping down to bra and panties. "Surprise number one will be more dramatic that way." She dropped her clothes in a pile on the floor then threw off the spread and the blanket, sidled under the top sheet, and took off her underwear. "C'mon Tony, get those clothes off," she said, "and get in here next to me."

Tony hurriedly took off his clothes and crawled in next to her. She plumped up the pillows. "Sit up. Here, next to me."

"That's the surprise? We're going to do it sitting up?"

"Shut up, and pay attention."

She pressed a button in the nightstand by the bed. A six-foot square panel in the wall facing them slid silently sideways uncovering a huge TV screen. She pushed another button. A VCR hummed to life and a movie started to play: a couple sat down in a restaurant to eat. As the waiter took their order and left, the female dropped her napkin. When she stretched under the table to retrieve it, she tickled her hand up her partner's leg. Leering at the camera, she mouthed, "I can't reach it," and crawled under the table. Forgetting about the napkin, she massaged his crotch, then unzipped his fly, extracted a huge penis, licked it twice before burying it deep inside her mouth. Slowly at first, then faster, she bobbed up and down. In her excitement she eventually knocked over the table but never missed a beat. Shocked diners looked on with expressions varying from delight—some of them applauded—to astonishment.

"Looks like fun, doesn't it, Tony?" she said as she threw back the sheet and began licking the inside of his thighs.

The actor and actress on the screen got up from the table and retired to an adjacent room which had mirrors on all four walls and the ceiling. They undressed, dropped onto a conveniently placed bed and began to fornicate in earnest.

Coming up for air she twittered, "Get ready, Tony. Surprise number two; coming up."

He tensed not knowing what to expect. She stretched her hand out and pressed a third button on the nightstand. Gradually other panels started moving: the first retracted exposing a mirrored ceiling flecked with tiny bulbs which flickered like stars in a summer sky.

The other receding panels revealed, except for the area with the TV, mirrored walls.

"Is that bitchin' or what?" she exclaimed. "We can watch ourselves fucking like the couple in the movie."

At a loss for words, Tony, roused to fever pitch and bursting with lust, rolled her onto her side, lifted her face to his, and plunged his tongue into her mouth. She threw her top leg onto his waist, jabbed him inside her, and began to rock back and forth. She buried her head between the pillow and his cheek and called the tempo by digging her heel into his butt. Behind him she formed an "O" with her thumb and forefinger and waggled it twice at the mirrored wall.

Later she asked him, "One more time?" She slithered her naked body on top of his and reached between his legs.

"Lemme rest for a minute. I'm not nineteen any more."

"Okay. We can talk while you rest." She slid off him and pulled the sheet up to her neck.

Tony shut his eyes. He didn't want to talk, he wanted to re-enjoy everything that had happened—the porn film, the mirrors, the twinkling ceiling, and most of all the thrill of a new female body under him. He replayed the evening in his head, decided it was one of the best ever, and started to think about how he could get her in bed again.

"Is this a one night stand or do you do encores?" he asked.

Kate thought: I'm not sure how much this is going to hurt Judy. If everything goes right, this might be all I need to pay her back. But just in case something gets screwed up, I'd better not burn my bridges behind me. I'll play it safe. I can always cancel later on.

"Of course I'd like more," she said. "What I feel for you isn't going to die after one night. Seems to be the opposite. Tonight was like pouring gasoline on the fire. I'm hotter for you now than I was before. How about you? Would you like to see me again?"

"Oh, I'd like to for sure," he said.

"Umm," she purred serenely.

She lay on her back and locked her fingers behind her head, taking care to let the sheet fall to her waist. Tony raised himself on an elbow and looked down on her.

He slid his hand up her side to her breast and felt nineteen again.

*　　*　　*

John Christopher looked at his watch. It read nine o'clock. He gathered up his camera, magazine, and windbreaker, and prepared to leave his hideout. No use sticking around here, he thought. The rest of the night is going to be an instant replay. I've got all the pictures I need. He closed the door carefully behind him making sure it didn't slam and without a word to the watching clerk, dropped the key on the check-in desk.

He drove slowly away from the motel scanning the edges of the highway. Two miles down the road, he spotted a pay phone outside a gas station and braked to a stop. He took a scrap of paper from his pocket on which he had written a phone number and smoothed it out on the counter under the phone. He had already memorized the number, but not one to take chances, he read it out loud to himself from the paper as he lifted the receiver and poked the keypad. While the phone was ringing, he held his watch up to the dim light in the booth. Almost nine thirty. She should be home by now, he thought.

Chapter 11

$\mathcal{A}$fter she had eaten supper, Judy Fanelli kicked her shoes off, settled on the couch, and pulled her legs under her. She fluffed open the newspaper—she had started reading it religiously looking for articles by Carlo—turned to the local news page, and tried to relax and forget the cloud of doom she felt was hanging over her. After a few minutes her eyes started blinking, the paper fell from her hands, and she dozed off.

Her sleep was interrupted at nine thirty by the ringing of the phone. She jerked awake, raced into the kitchen, and grabbed the receiver from the wall.

Out of breath she panted, "Hello."

After a short pause, a gravelly voice on the other end sounding like Marlon Brando's mouth-full-of-marbles "Godfather" said, "Is this Mrs. Fanelli?"

"Yes. Who's this?"

"Your husband's Tony Fanelli?"

"Yes. Why?"

"Wanna make sure I got the right Fanelli."

"Did something happen to him? Was there an accident? What's wrong?" Her voice quaked. She nervously brushed a stray lock of hair from her face with the back of her hand.

"Nothing's happened to him . . . yet. But something's *going* to happen to him. Lady, your husband's screwin' my girlfriend, and if you don't do something about it, then I will. And it ain't gonna be pretty!"

"Say WHAT!!?" She fell back against the kitchen counter and propped herself up with her free hand. Her mouth fell open; she couldn't think of anything else to say.

The voice on the phone demanded, "You still there?"

"Still here," she answered haltingly as she stumbled to one of the dinette chairs, pulled it from under the table, and flopped into it.

"Don't tell me this is the first time he's run around on you. A pretty boy like him."

Another period of stunned silence. The caller became annoyed.

"Hey, you listening to me, or what?" he said.

"I'm listening, but I'm having a lot of trouble believing what you're telling me."

"Believe it. I just got done taking pictures of the two of them in bed at this here motel near Baltimore. They'll get you all excited," he snickered. "They're real dirty pictures. Like what you see in an X-rated movie. Pictures of them nude and all twisted up together."

"Pictures?" Judy repeated sluggishly.

"Yeah. X-rated," he repeated. His voice turned ugly and threatening. "I'll send you a couple of the best ones. But you'd better do something about him, lady, or I'm going to hurt him—bad."

"Why are you doing this to me?"

"Didn't you hear me?" Now the voice become angry. "I told you. I was happy with my girlfriend until your husband showed up. After he started screwing her, she doesn't want anything to do with me. She doesn't even want to sleep in the same bed with me. Your bastard husband is gonna pay for this. I want her back, and I'm giving you one chance to straighten him out before I do. I'm counting on you to do something—I don't care what—to get that asshole away from her. If you don't, then I'm gonna kick the shit out of him for starters. And hey, if you can't straighten the bastard out, then you should divorce him 'cause he's gonna be nothing but a bloody lump of meat when I get done with him."

Judy listened in stunned silence. Beatings, divorce. Tony cheating on her. Her head was spinning.

"Pictures," she said as if in a dreamy trance.

"Yeah, pictures. Gimme your address and I'll mail them to you."

She snapped awake. "I'm not giving you anything until you tell me who you are."

"I told you who I am. I'm the boyfriend that's getting shafted here. Now gimme your address," he demanded angrily.

Dazed, bewildered, and cowed by his tone of voice, Judy gave him her address and hung up the phone without saying "goodbye." Damn, she said to herself as she recovered from the shock, I just gave our address to a total stranger who doesn't have the kindest of feelings toward Tony. Dumb! Dumb! Dumb!

Judy cradled her head in her hands and planted her elbows on the kitchen table. Who was this man on the phone? she wondered. The voice didn't sound familiar and he sounded serious, so it's probably not one of our friends playing a joke. They wouldn't joke around with something as serious as this, would they? Maybe I'm making too much out of nothing. After all Tony knows how important it is for him to be faithful to me. He knows how upset I'd be if he screwed around with another woman. This can't be true; he promised he'd be faithful.

But did he keep his promise? she wondered. He certainly would be attractive to women. Sure, I warn him about the love handles around his waist. Still, taking the pluses with the minuses, he's a real hunk.

Tony's good looks were a major asset in his career. Not long after he began selling, he realized his specialty would be cold calling. Handsome Tony had no trouble getting around the salesman's first obstacle—the receptionist. Patting and smoothing his hair into place, he dazzled them with his smile. Invariably the smile was returned and Tony quickly followed with a line of friendly patter which he had carefully refined. As the receptionists fell under his spell, they forgot the instructions their purchasing agents had given them: "Keep the damn salesmen out of my office so I can get some work done." They managed to find some reason to get Tony admitted.

So, Judy thought, let's add this up. He is charming, handsome, and attractive. He has the opportunity: he's often away overnight. And most likely he has a following of panting women (or women without pants. She allowed herself a bad joke): four states worth of charmed receptionists. But even though he had the opportunity, would he?

Her thoughts returned to the man on the phone. I wonder who he is, she thought. How did he know Tony's name? And was this the coming disaster that I felt at work? "Get hold of yourself," she said out loud. "This is silly. I'm only hearing one side of the story. I'm sure Tony is innocent, and I've got to give him a chance to explain." But the nagging doubts continued as she walked to the living room and settled back on the couch. Could it be true? Would he go to bed with another woman? The thoughts kept plaguing her and refused to go away.

There's no reason for him to need another woman, she thought. If it's sex, he should have no complaints. We make love about twice a week, and he never seems to be disappointed or want more. I've offered to go with him on his trips, but he's never wanted company.

I haven't found any signs, she thought. Of course, I haven't been looking, she added hastily. There's been no lipstick smears on his shirts; no unusual smells on his clothing; no strange phone callers hanging up when I answer; nothing to hint that there's another woman. Tony's sensible and not a gambler. With the all the AIDS out there it doesn't seem likely that he would want to play Russian roulette with his life.

But, she thought, staying alone on those long evenings away from home didn't sound like Tony. He was more likely to look for company—go to a bar and talk to the bartender. If a woman happened to be in the bar looking for a man, Tony would be her first choice. Tony, with his polished small talk; his honeyed voice—like a radio announcer's; Tony, with his movie-star looks; Tony, with his light blue eyes like bottomless pools of the clearest water. The question was: would Tony make it plain from the beginning that all he wanted to do was talk or if she gave the right signals, would they end up in a bedroom?

Though she wrestled with the question for a long time, Judy couldn't decide what Tony would do if the opportunity presented itself. I just don't know, she concluded. I don't know for sure what he would do. Her train of thought shifted to what she would do if it *was* true? She bolted upright and angrily punched her fists into the leather couch cushions; her face turned crimson. I'd really be pissed off, she fumed. More than pissed off. After he promised. And didn't *I* pass up opportunities to start something with other men? Just last week at the grocery store, that young, handsome man followed me out to my car and offered to help me with my bags. And Carlo at the wedding. I wonder if he's trying to hit on me? No, he's nice, and besides he's leaving for Italy soon.

Enough of this self-torture, she thought. I need someone to talk to, a sounding board. Her head pounded. Someone who can help me think clearly. Someone who can offer me some good advice. She glanced at her watch. It's too late now, she thought. Tomorrow I'll call Kate. Kate's my best friend, my confidante, my psychiatric surrogate. Talking to Kate will help.

Too exhausted to go upstairs to bed or even to take her clothes off, she curled up on the couch and closed her eyes. In two minutes she was fast asleep.

Chapter 12

*B*RRRRNG. The phone rang in Room 24 at The Calvert Inn. Kate snapped awake and arched up from the pillow. BRRRRNG, it shrilled again. She reached over the man snoring softly next to her (How can he sleep with this goddamn phone shrieking? she thought.) and grabbed the receiver.

The emotionless, synthetic, computerized voice on the other end said, "Good morning. This is the wakeup call you ordered. It's four o'clock. Have a good day."

She groaned. "Fuck you and your good day," she grumbled into the mouthpiece then dropped the phone on the floor. The "clunk" woke Tony; Kate fell back on her pillow and paid him no attention. She mumbled to herself, "Damn. I hate getting up this early in the morning."

"Who's on the phone?" Tony said brushing the cobwebs from his eyes.

"My wakeup call," she said.

"Wakeup call? What wakeup call?" He rose on one elbow.

"Some of us have to go to work," she answered. "I've got a client coming in at nine, and it's a long drive. You go back to sleep if you want. Or," she hesitated and changed the tone of her voice to sexy, "we've got time for one more quickie if you're up to it." She tickled the pouch between his legs.

He gently pushed her hand away as she knew he would. He turned over on his stomach without answering and fell back to sleep. After four hours of almost non-stop sex and only five hours rest, she was positive he would be exhausted. Not like her first lover; not like Dominic, she remembered wistfully as she locked her hands behind her head and gazed at the ceiling. He was insatiable; he was *always* ready for one more. She was the one who had to beg him to stop.

"I'm so damn sore down there," she would sob. "I can't do it again. It hurts like hell."

He would laugh and reply, "I'll lick it and make it better."

But that was years ago, and she hadn't met anyone with his recuperative powers since.

I wonder what Dominic's doing right now, she daydreamed. In spite of the way he treated me—like a piece of shit—I always loved him. I'll always have a place in my heart for him—he was my first, and he was the best. Then there were the others who thought they could use me and dump me, and one by one I got even with them. I got even with all the people who screwed me over, except one, this asshole's wife. She glanced contemptuously at Tony sleeping alongside her. Judy's gonna pay for what she tried to do to me. She tried to take Dominic from me and screwed up my life. But now I'll pay her back.

She glanced at the alarm clock-radio on the nightstand by the bed. Damn, look at the time, she scolded herself. Enough of the past, I've got to get ready for the present. She showered quickly, and as she blow-dried her pageboy she admired herself in front of the mirror over the sink. I'm not in bad shape for an old broad, she kidded. She tried circling her waist with her hands and laughed when she fell far short. She had come a lot closer when she was a teenager, she remembered ruefully. Nevertheless, she liked what she saw—nice boobs, perky, youthful figure. Minimum damage from child bearing. She twisted first to one side and then the other and judged herself to be plenty sexy. For a woman who looks like me, she wondered, why had it taken so long to get this asshole to bed? From what I've heard the fuckin' bastard's screwed everything that moves and breathes. Oh, well; all's well that ends well.

She finished putting on her makeup, then dressed. She tossed her cosmetics into her Coach bag and dropped it on a chair near the door. For a second she stood hands on hips and looked down scornfully at Tony who was still sleeping. She scooped up her dirty clothes and was about to stuff them into a pocket of her garment bag when she got an idea. She pulled her bikini underpants out of the pile and shoved them into the wad of his underwear which lay in the corner. "A surprise for Judy," she snickered. Thanks, sucker; it's been fun, she said to herself. She slung the garment bag over her shoulder, pulled the door open, and grabbed the Coach bag by its leather strap. Once out the door she noisily kicked it shut behind her.

When she stepped outside and prepared to set her luggage in her car, something twinkling inside Tony's car, which was parked next to hers, caught her eye. She looked closely and her mouth dropped open. The window on the passenger's side had been smashed— all the glass had been poked out—and the door hung wide open. At first she thought there were snowflakes all over the inside, but on closer inspection she saw they were shards of glass which had created the sparkle that had caught her attention. A jagged hole stared at her from the dashboard where the cassette player/radio used to be. For a moment she wondered what had been in a second rectangular hole; then she remembered that lately thieves were breaking into cars and taking air bags. The contents of the glove box had been scattered all over the front seat. She noticed maps, an owner's manual, a box of Kleenex, and his Pennsylvania motor vehicle registration card. Suddenly she noticed a small black address book lying on the floor. Cautiously she reached in, brushed the broken glass away from it, and picked it up. As she opened it she noticed it was Tony's—he had written his name and address inside the front cover. Leafing through the pages she let out a low whistle in amazement—look at this, she thought. There must be over a hundred names and phone numbers here—all women. Some of the names were followed by one, two, or three hand-drawn stars. The bastard must have a rating system, she thought. Wonder if my name's in here yet. She searched but could not find it. I'm keeping this; it may come in handy later, she decided. She stuffed it into her purse and banged on the door to Room 24.

She said in a loud voice, "Get up Tony. You have a problem."

When he opened the door, she almost burst out laughing. He was halfway through shaving. One side of his face was covered with white shaving cream and the other side was clean shaven. He looked like the Phantom of the Opera with two different sides to his face.

"Close the door. It's freezing outside. What's the matter?" he asked.

"It's your car. Come out and look."

He quickly finished shaving, put on his jacket, and followed her outside.

"Holy shit!" he said when he saw the damage. "What the fuck happened here?"

"Probably a druggy looking for something to sell. You'll have to call the police and report this. Sorry, but I'm leaving. I've got appointments to keep, and I don't want to get involved in this."

"This really pisses me off," he exploded. "Some goddamn asshole is causing me a whole bunch of trouble. I don't care about the damage; it's the company's car, but I'm gonna lose a lot of time getting estimates and getting this fucker fixed." He clenched his fists and pounded the hood. "Don't they have any goddamn security at this fucking motel?"

"I wish I could help," she said insincerely.

She blew him a kiss and got into her car.

Tony stood shaking his head and cursing. "What kind of a fucking society do we live in?" he shouted at no one in particular.

As she pulled away, she took a last, brief look at him, smoothed her skirt, and pulled onto the highway. She glanced at her watch and decided it was too late for breakfast; then she began to think about the private investigator she had hired to take the pictures.

I wonder if he was even there, she thought. I didn't see anybody. But of course that's the whole point—if he's doing the job right I shouldn't see anybody. I didn't expect him to batter down the door in the middle of the night and come barging into the room with his camera flashing. He told me there would be a one-way glass and he would be behind it. I suppose . . . Enough, she said to herself, he must know what he's doing; after all this is his business.

But even if the investigator screwed up, she chuckled to herself. I tossed in that little present for superstud to take home to his wife. I'll bet Judy gets a real kick out of finding a strange woman's underwear when she does Tony's laundry.

She flipped down the sun visor and snapped open the vanity mirror. When she stopped for a red light, she stared smugly at the face looking back at her and silently congratulated her image. It's taken a long time, baby, she thought, but if those pictures and that surprise can convince her he's cheating and give her some major heartache . . . or worse, then I'm gonna be happy. Very happy.

The light changed to green. As she clicked the mirror shut and sped away, she thought: It's taken much longer than I thought it would, but I'm finally gonna get even with that bitch.

Suddenly she had a troubling thought. What if, she wondered, what if all this didn't do the trick. Suppose that shithead talked his way out of it. After all he was a salesman with the gift of gab. And, even after his guilt was exposed and proven beyond any doubt, suppose, just suppose Judy decided to forgive him? If I haven't caused enough heartache and pain to pay her back, to make us even, what would I do then?

No plan formed in her mind but she swore if this didn't work, she would do something nasty. Real nasty. But I *will* get even, she promised herself, one way or another I *will* pay her back.

She slammed the accelerator to the floor and yanked the steering wheel hard to the left to swerve around a big semi. The highway in front of her was open. She sped toward her office in Philadelphia.

Chapter 13

On the evening Tony and Kate met at the Calvert Inn, Tina Demarest, Dominic's niece, had pleaded with her sister. "You've got to go with me, Maria. Mom will never let me out of the house alone. Ever since she found the drugs in my wastebasket she doesn't trust me." Tina was lying on her bed nervously jerking her fingers through her short blond hair.

Maria replied angrily, "Can you blame her?" She crossed her arms across her chest and stared down at Tina. "How badly are you hooked?"

Before she could catch herself Tina jumped up and exploded, "I'm not hooked at all. I'm not a junkie! I can take it or leave it." Remembering she needed her sister to chaperon, she quickly lowered her tone of voice and apologized. "I'm sorry, Maria. I didn't mean to blow up at you. You're the only friend I've got in this house."

"It's your own fault Mom's mad at you. Why the hell did you start with drugs? You know how dangerous it is."

"All my friends do it. I wanted to see if I was missing anything." Tina looked down at the floor unable to meet her sister's piercing gaze. "Come with me to this party tonight," she whined. "You'll see how it is. I only take enough to feel good. And it does feel good. Please come with me. Pretty please. You're my ticket out of here tonight. Without you . . ." When Maria didn't respond, Tina continued angrily. "If you won't come with me, I'll get out of here any way I can, even if I have to crawl out a window."

Maria thought to herself: Maybe it's better if I go with her and am around to keep an eye on her, rather than have her on the loose by herself.

"Okay. I'll go with you," Maria said unenthusiastically.

Tina clapped her hands three times. "Good," she said.

With a hasty "Goodby, Mom. We're out of here" the two sisters hurried out of the house before Denise could ask where they were going. She could only plant her hands on her hips, shake her head, stare wistfully at the closed door, and hope they didn't get into trouble.

Tina took deep breaths of the unseasonably warm night air, and spotted two boys lounging on the corner. She greeted them familiarly. "You guys doin' anything tonight?" she asked. They shook their heads no. "Wanna go to a party?"

"Sure," they answered.

"It's in West Philly, Powelton Village," Tina said. "We need your car."

"No problem. Let's go," they said and began walking toward a dark blue Crown Victoria parked halfway down the next block.

Tina pulled the back door opened, pushed her sister inside, and slid in after her.

The boys drove past Drexel University's campus and then through the adjoining University of Pennsylvania campus. Following Tina's directions they drove down a quiet, tree-lined street and pulled up in front of a Victorian house set back from the curb.

Maria noticed that lights were on in every room both upstairs and downstairs, and even though many of the windows were open, there was an eerie quiet around the house. It didn't fit her preconceived notion of a wild, noisy drug orgy with the neighbors ready to call the police.

When they opened the door, Maria was struck by a haze of wispy smoke which hung in the air. She sniffed cautiously and identified cigarettes and marijuana, but there was another component in the smoke, pungent, but unfamiliar. She tried not to breathe too deeply but felt a very relaxed sensation welling up inside her.

Without a word and before Maria could stop her, Tina left the others standing by the door and hurried off toward a slender man with short, kinky hair and a thin black moustache. From his light tan complexion and small, fine features, he could have been Jamaican, African, or a mixture of races.

"Hi, Eddie," she whispered as she squeezed his arm. "I brought you a new customer."

His eyes lit up. "Where?" he said.

"She's over there by the door. Standing with those two guys." She nodded toward her sister.

"And what's her name?" Eddie asked.

"Maria. She's my sister."

"Sister," Eddie repeated matter-of-factly. She's so fuckin' hooked she gives me her own sister, he thought to himself. "Let's go over and say hello to your sister," he said to Tina. He put his hand in the center of her back and nudged her toward the trio.

"First give me my free package," Tina said, bracing against his push.

"You'll get it after you introduce me. In this business I don't trust anyone. You deliver, then I'll deliver." He smiled showing a set of even, beautiful, shiny white teeth.

"I need it now. I need it bad," she whined. In spite of the warm evening, Tina had started to shiver.

"You'll have it the second after you introduce me. Now let's go."

Tina allowed herself to be guided through the crowd.

As she approached her sister she said nervously, "Maria, this is Eddie. Eddie, Maria."

Eddie looked the buxom sixteen-year-old up and down while she eyed him suspiciously. Tina stared expectantly at him, and when he ignored her she tugged at his elbow. She glared at him and silently mouthed, "Now."

He fumbled in his back pocket, surreptitiously pulled out a plastic baggy, and tried to slip it to Tina without anyone else seeing. Tina yanked it from his hand, edged away, and rushed into the dining room out of her sister's view. The two boys followed closely behind her. Maria heard one say, "We're the ones who brought you here. We should get a cut."

"So you're Tina's sister," Eddie oozed at Maria. He put his arm around her shoulder. "Want to feel warm and fuzzy?"

"I already do," she said, twisting around to get loose from his grasp. "I'm high from breathing the smoke in here."

"That's nothing but a buzz. Come with me. I'll give you a sample of the real stuff. Then you'll really be flying."

"No, thanks." She stiffened.

"You haven't done it before?" he asked with phony incredulity.

"No. And I'm not starting tonight. I'm not going to be a zombie dope addict." But in spite of her words she wondered what it would be like to be high on drugs. After all, she thought, I'm only going through this life once, and I don't want to miss out on anything. If I try it once, just once, what harm would there be? And besides, if Tina's getting some happiness out of it, why shouldn't I?

"Look around," he said gesturing with a broad sweep of his hand. "Everybody here's doin' it. Does anybody look like a zombie? Don't they all look like they're having a good time? Let's find your sister." He took Maria by the hand and led her into the dining room. They stood behind Tina who gazed peacefully at the ceiling. "How's it going?" Eddie asked her.

"I think I'm in heaven," Tina said. "Not a care in the world. I feel wonderful." She tilted her head down, turned, and noticed her sister. "Oh, hi Maria."

"Go easy on that stuff," Maria said.

Her words lacked emotion as she felt herself getting more and more curious about how she would feel under the spell of the forbidden drugs. After all, she thought, I'm the older sister. It's not fair that she's the one who's floating on air, and I'm on the outside looking in.

"What have you got to lose?" Eddie said to Maria. He stretched out his hands palms up. "Try it once. I guarantee you'll feel better than you ever felt before." He paused a few seconds for effect. "And if you don't like it, you never have to do it again." Sensing her resistance was ebbing he pushed a little harder. "You can't get hooked after only one . . . Here, I'll show you how."

He led her to a couch in the corner of the room, sat down, and patted the seat next to him. As Maria sat down next to him, he slid another packet from his back pocket.

*   *   *

Over the years Carlo Fiore had taped or bought more than a dozen Humphrey Bogart movies. His favorites were *The Maltese Falcon*, *Casablanca*, and *The Treasure of Sierra Madre*. Tonight he had shoved *Casablanca* into the VCR and was empathizing with the loner, Rick, being too noble to pursue Ilsa because she was married. Just as Bogart delivered, "Of all the gin joints . . . ," his phone rang. He recognized his old friend, Steven Nestor, Narcotics Division, Philadelphia Police Force.

"You sleeping?" Nestor asked.

"No. I was watching TV," Fiore answered.

"A Bogart movie, I'll bet."

Carlo smiled. "*Casablanca.*"

"You want in on a raid right now?"

Carlo had established a friendship with Nestor that dated back many years. From their early contacts, Carlo had been impressed with how the policeman tempered his professionalism with a genuine concern for addicts as human beings in trouble. He had written flattering stories about him, and once did a three-part feature story about the hazardous life of a drug-enforcement officer with Nestor pictured as the outstanding example of how a policeman could cope with the excruciating pressures of this difficult job. Nestor attributed his rapid promotions to the story and reciprocated by periodically allowing Carlo come along on drug raids.

"Can you pick me up?" Carlo asked.

"I'm in my car and on my way right now. You be out front in five minutes."

Carlo recognized the black, unmarked Buick Park Avenue a block away, slid into the back seat next to the policeman, and greeted him with a quick "hello."

"We're after a major dealer named Eddie," Nestor said, after which the two men sat silently.

They drove to West Philadelphia following the same route Tina and Maria had taken a few hours earlier. Powelton Village was a neighborhood of stately old homes, but in recent years it had fallen prey to the urban problems of graffiti, drugs, and violence. As they drove down the quiet street, only the Victorian house had any lights on, and these blinked three times in quick succession as the police approached.

"Shit," Nestor exclaimed, "A lookout must've spotted us and alerted them. Maybe we can still catch Eddie coming out the back if the guys in the alley get in place fast enough."

* * *

When the lights blinked in the house, Eddie immediately headed for his escape route. As he yanked the door open which led to the cellar, Maria caught him around the waist.

"Where are you going?" she said in a bleary haze.

"I'm getting the hell out of here," he said in hushed tones. "Did you see the lights blink? That means the cops are coming."

He tried to brush her away, but she managed to grab onto his belt and held tight.

"You'll have to take me and my sister with you, 'cause I'm not lettin' go of you," she said.

"Let go my fuckin' belt," he snarled.

Suddenly Tina appeared next to her sister and threw her arms around Eddie's chest pinning his arms to his sides.

"I ain't got no fuckin' time to waste," he said, and slamming the door behind them, dragged them both down the stairs, battering them against the walls and steps. At the bottom he stopped and listened. For a second he heard nothing and saw no one following him. Suddenly the sounds of the front door splintering came from above. Angry voices shouted, "Everybody down on the floor and don't make any trouble." He heard a muffled voice ask, "Where's Eddie?"

The two girls were barely conscious from the beating they had taken going down the stairs, and Eddie brushed them away easily; they fell to the floor in a heap. At the back of the cellar was a massive metal door which he pushed open. Without a backward glance he scurried to the other side and shouldered it shut. As he threw the three half-inch metal bolts into place, he silently thanked the bootleggers who had built this escape route eighty years ago. In front of him was a tunnel that led to another house he owned across the alley, and waiting there were the lookouts who had alerted him. Smiling broadly, they traded high-fives.

* * *

In spite of the police badgering, no one would tell where the elusive Eddie might be. The addicts knew they were in no danger of being arrested—it was obvious the police were only interested in arresting the dealer—and would not even admit to having seen him. They also knew it was not a good idea to mess around Eddie. At best they would have their supply of "happy dust" cut off, but at worst they would be corpses.

Carlo followed Nestor as he started searching the house from top to bottom.

"Look here," Nestor said, as he pulled open the door to the cellar and pointed. "Think he's down there?"

He clicked on his flashlight and played the beam down the steps. At the bottom of the steps he saw two motionless bodies.

Are they dead? he wondered.

He drew his gun and quietly, cautiously, started tiptoeing down the steps motioning Carlo to stay a few steps behind him. The massive steel door caught the flashlight's beam and reflected it back in their eyes, but Nestor turned his attention to the two bodies at his feet. He quickly felt for a pulse in the neck of each and when he was satisfied they were both still alive, he leaned against the steel door and twisted the handle but could not open it.

"Bolted shut," he said to Carlo. "I wonder where it leads?"

He turned back to the two girls lying at his feet and gently turned them over. In the glow of the flashlight Carlo recognized them and gasped.

"You know them?" Nestor said as he tried to determine if they needed medical treatment.

"They're my cousin Denise's daughters." He felt as if a cold arctic wind had blown on him and shivered.

"I'm sorry."

I can maybe understand Tina being here, Carlo thought to himself. He was not close to the family, but his mother was, and she constantly talked about "Tina. You know; the one with the wild streak."

"When she was twelve," his mother went on, "she took her mother's keys and drove off in her car."

But Maria, Carlo thought, Maria was always the goody-two-shoes. How did she get mixed up in this? As he stood paralyzed, not knowing what to do, the girls gradually struggled to a sitting position and then on unsteady feet stood up and rubbed their bruises. In the dim light they did not recognize Carlo but reached for the railing and pulled themselves slowly up the stairs. The two men trailed after them.

Oblivious to the chaos Tina spotted the two boys who had brought them and waved them over.

One said to the Steve Nestor, "We brought them; we'll take them home."

Carlo cocked his fist and drew it back, but Steve grabbed his wrist and held it firmly.

"Don't fuckin' blame us," said one, cowering behind the other. He pointed to Tina, "It was her idea. She's the one who knew where the party was. She asked us to bring her here."

Though they looked right at him the girls still did not recognize Carlo who now began to shake violently as if he had been thrown naked into a meat freezer. He dropped his hands weakly to his sides and looked pleadingly at Nestor for guidance.

"We can let these four go," he said to Carlo. "We'll catch Eddie another time." He turned to the two boys. "You punks get these girls home okay, 'cause if you don't, your life won't be worth shit. Understand?"

They nodded.

He put his arm around Carlo's shoulder and led him out to the Park Avenue.

*   *   *

Maria had passed out on the ride home, but was awakened by a heavy weight bouncing up and down on her lap.

"Where am I?" she slurred.

No one answered. As she forced her eyes open, she saw an unconscious Tina draped across her, and a moment later she realized she was in the back seat of the Crown Victoria.

When the car glided to a stop, the two boys dragged the semiconscious girls from the car and carefully laid them at the foot of the steps to their house. One of the boys leaned on the doorbell and when he heard footsteps coming, he ran back to the car and slammed the door behind him. With their squealing tires leaving black streaks in the street, they sped away.

Denise still sleep-groggy opened the front door and peered into the blackness of the night. She saw nothing.

"Who the hell's ringing my doorbell at one o'clock in the morning?" she muttered to no one in particular.

When Tina moaned, she looked down and noticed her two lifeless daughters sprawled on top of each other. Her heart skipped a beat, and she slapped her hands over her mouth to muffle a shriek that never materialized.

Maria raised her head. "Hi, Mom," she said weakly barely able to get the words out.

Denise fought first to keep from fainting, then to keep from throwing up. She bent over, grabbed Tina under her arms, and tried to drag her into the house, but Tina was more weight than she could manage. Sobbing with futility, she raced into the house, grabbed the phone, and dialed her brother's number.

The phone rang five times before a barely awake Dominic answered with a snarled, "Who the fuck is this?"

"You've got to get over here," Denise shrieked, ignoring the obscenity. "I can't get the girls into the house."

"Hunh?" Dominic said holding the receiver away from his ear.

"They're lying on the front stoop. Stoned out of their minds, and I can't move them," she wailed into the phone.

Dominic snapped fully awake. "I'll be right over," he said. He smacked his palm to his forehead.

Chapter 14

Judy Fanelli slept without moving on the living room couch until the morning sun streamed in. The warm, bright light played over her face tingling her skin and she blinked awake. For a moment she lay perfectly still, feeling warm and cozy. Only her eyes darted around the room trying to piece together where she was. When it registered that she was not in her own bed, she wondered why she had spent the night fully dressed sleeping downstairs on the couch. At first she couldn't remember any of yesterday's events, but gradually she recalled the traumatic, near-epileptic attack and the harrowing phone call. Even though she fought to squelch it, the thought of Tony in bed with another woman nagged at her as she shook herself awake.

Still groggy, she swung her legs off the couch and stiffly stood up and stretched. After starting the coffee, she picked up the phone and started to dial Kate's number as she had planned last night, but when she glanced at the clock on the wall she realized she had slept too long—she was going to be late for work. She hung up the phone before it could ring and mentally made a note to call Kate from the office.

She reveled in the soothing prickle of the water needles as she showered and wished she could stay in it forever. It was so peaceful—like a tranquilizer; all her problems seemed to be washed away. But she cut it short, toweled off, and dressed quickly. She grimaced as she glanced into the mirror and noticed how pale and haggard she looked. Thank God it's Friday, she thought. If I get through today, I'll have two days to rest up. But right now there's no time for major damage control. I'll have to put on my makeup later.

The receptionist at Neuberger Roe & Price snickered as Judy rushed in, "Hung over and almost an hour late, and I didn't even see you at Friday's last night. Where were you, and what were you doing?"

Judy mumbled a pleasantry though she was thinking: Up yours, sister, and hurried down the corridor to her office. She quickly shuffled through the stack of paperwork on her desk and made a to-do list of her day's work. Satisfied she had things under control, she took a deep breath and dialed the real estate agency where Kate worked.

"Hi. It's Judy," she said as Kate picked up the phone. "Got a minute?"

"Judy. I'm busier than a paperhanger with the itch," Kate replied. She had a penchant for corny, old, one-liners. "But for a friend, I'll squeeze you in. I've got a few minutes between appointments. So, what's up?"

Judy told her about the frightening episode in the office.

"Do you think it was some kind of seizure or fit? Maybe you should see a doctor." Kate said.

"No. No doctor. I'm sure it was one of my witchy spells. But let's drop that. What's more important is the phone call I got last night. From a strange man."

"All men are strange, Judy. I've found that out over the years. There was one . . ."

Annoyed, Judy interrupted her. "Another time with the stories."

"So what about the man?"

"He said Tony had been to a motel with his girl friend, and he would send me pictures of them in bed together. He sounded really pissed. And, he said that if I didn't do something to get Tony away from her, then he would do something. He sounded vicious."

"What do *you* think?" Kate asked almost gaily. "Is Tony playing around or not? He is a very handsome, Sicilian stud, you know. I love that hunky Mediterranean look."

"You don't sound like you're taking this seriously, Kate. You know how I feel about sex outside of marriage. I'm not as laid back about it as you are."

"You're right about that. You know Greg and I have an open marriage. We agreed to let each other to have affairs as long as they don't threaten our marriage. And we don't have to tell each other about them."

"You need a lot of smarts to know when the 'threatening of the marriage' begins.'"

"It's worked for us so far," said Kate coolly.

"So far? You mean after you got married you slept with other guys besides Greg? You never told me about that."

Somewhere deep inside Judy a warning bell went off. Kate was a congenital blabbermouth. Even the most important and personal secrets were secrets she couldn't keep. She had casually given away the surprise 40th birthday party Judy had carefully planned for Tony and never apologized. "You should have known better than to ask me to keep a secret," she had said. "I can't help myself. I'm a talker." And now she was saying she had kept secrets.

"All these years I thought we told each other everything. I thought we were best friends," Judy said.

"We are best friends. Since high school. Say, do you remember the day we met?" She went on without waiting for an answer. "We were standing next to each other by our hall lockers watching Dominic walk by and swooning."

"He was poetry in motion. Like John Travolta in *Saturday Night Fever*," Judy said. "Watching him move was like watching ocean waves roll onto a beach."

"I think he gave me a serious look because of my Irish red hair. That got me hooked. I thought I'd die if I couldn't have him. He was sooo good looking. Then I started gushing to you about how crazy I was about him."

"I remember. That was the start of our friendship. After that you told me everything you and Dominic did down to the last detail. And you told me everything else that went on in your life."

"For a long time he *was* my life." Kate sighed. "Of course I'm over him now. But those, Judy dear, were the days, my friend. He was one helluva man in the sack, too. I'll never forget those times I had with him."

"And you told me about every single one of them. You ought to write it up. It would make a great novel."

Kate said, "You and I were best friends then, and I did tell you everything." Her tone of voice changed to somber, "But as time went by things changed. Now there are some things I keep to myself. But, hey, this isn't helping you with your problem. You're almost a lawyer, so you should know it's going to be hard for Tony to prove that he *didn't* do something."

"So what do you suggest I do about the phone call?"

"I'd tell him about the call, but I wouldn't make a big deal out of it. Why don't you wait for the pictures to come and see what they show? I'd make damn sure the evidence tied a tight noose around his neck before convicting him. 'Innocent until proven guilty' isn't such a bad idea."

Judy thought over her advice. "I guess you're right. I *should* give him the benefit of a reasonable doubt."

"We sound like a bunch of lawyers." Kate laughed. "But then you're in the business. Whoops. My next appointment's here. I gotta go. Bye, Jude."

Judy hung up the phone and spread out the contents of two folders onto her desk. As she started to dig in to the pile of work, there was a knock on her cubicle door. Sara cracked it open and peeked in. Judy motioned her in. Sara wore a wig of shoulder length blonde hair, and a brown, leather miniskirt which was the shortest and tightest Judy had ever seen.

"How do you move in that thing?" Judy asked.

"I take small steps," she answered.

"Don't you have problems sitting down?"

"The way I figure it, I put my ass on the chair and the skirt can do what it wants. Whoever wants to look can look. With all the porn that's around everybody's seen everything anyway."

Judy sighed, and for a fleeting instant a snippet of Carlo surged through her mind. I suppose like any other male, he stares at the girls in short skirts, she thought. And then she wondered, Why do I care if he does? A picture of her in a short skirt preening for an adoring Carlo flashed through her mind. She tried to shake it off, but it persisted.

"I envy you," Judy said.

"Why is that?" Sara asked.

"I'd like to wear those short skirts again," Judy said.

Sara smiled a conspirator's smile, came closer, and whispered, "Didn't you used to go out with Charlie Price?"

"I went out with him once," Judy replied, "and that was twenty-five years ago. Maybe more. Right after I started working here."

"Why only one date? He would have been a prize catch."

"He didn't impress me as anything special. I thought he was nerdy. He tried to get me into the sack on the first date but gave up fairly easily. Look, I've got work to do. We'll save that story for another time."

"He must have changed quite a bit. Today's Charlie Price sounds like he doesn't give up that easily."

"Sara." Judy was exasperated. "I don't have time for this. I'm fighting the clock. Where's all this going?"

Sara twisted her face into a pout and went on, "The rumor in the office is that Charlie is running around with a tanned, busty, gorgeous forty-year-old-who-looks-twenty-five." She paused to build suspense. Judy began tapping her pencil on the desk impatiently. Sara bent down close to Judy. "It's Rita," she whispered.

Rita was Mr. Roe's knockout secretary who wore low cut blouses and who was constantly bending over to encourage anyone who was interested to try and look at her mammoth breasts. Since her religion required her to meet at the church-of-the-tanning-salon at least twice a week, she sported a summer tan all year 'round.

Judy motioned her to leave. "Interesting but I've got to get to work," she said.

"There'll be hell to pay when his wife finds out. She's supposed to be a real spitfire."

"That's his problem," Judy said turning her attention back to the work on her desk. "I've sure got enough of my own."

*   *   *

Charles Price, Jr. walked down the hall past the office where Sara and Judy were gossiping. He was on his way to attend a senior partners' meeting with Stratham Neuberger and Harris Roe. Charlie's father, Charles Price, Sr., had been invited to join the original firm, Neuberger & Roe, fifty-five years ago. Five years ago he had agreed to retire to Florida provided his son would be voted in as a senior partner. Price, Sr.'s stuffy pride and immortality were at stake. He wanted to be sure the name "Price" would remain on the firm's marquee. Neuberger and Roe, anxious to be rid of the irascible Price, Sr., whom they considered a real pain in the ass, acquiesced. Junior, they figured had to be more manageable.

Neuberger had been the CEO since the beginning, but recently, as his senility progressed, his ability to manage had gone dramatically downhill. Although he still came to work (He even showed up one Sunday, confused and angry that everyone had taken the day off. After a forty minute discussion, the security guard convinced him that it was indeed Sunday, and his office was closed.), Roe had gradually assumed the role of chief executive. Neuberger was invited to partners' meetings as a courtesy—Roe and Price often met without him to talk about important decisions—but today Neuberger's input might be helpful.

In Roe's corner office the three men greeted each other perfunctorily, then settled into heavily padded, leather chairs which surrounded a glass-topped coffee table. The room with its overstuffed furniture and dark molded paneling reminded Charlie of the Union League's main sitting room.

After a few minutes of preliminary discussion, Roe said gently to Neuberger, "Stratham, you're telling us that you promised Leon we would have a lawyer fluent in Italian to handle his affairs with his relatives in Italy. Is that correct?"

"Yes. Of course I promised him. How else would you expect us to get his business? And a good deal of business it's going to be. I may be older than any of you," he nodded to Price and Roe, "but it doesn't mean I can't be as good a rainmaker as you or any other lawyer in this firm, or in this city. And furthermore . . ."

Roe interrupted him, "And whom did you have in mind when you promised him this Italian lawyer?"

"Why, no one in particular. I'm sure I've heard some of the employees muttering in Italian from time to time. It shouldn't be hard to find one who's . . ."

"So you had no one in mind." Roe tented his fingertips together, poked them under his chin, and rested his elbows on the arms of his chair. "And this morning Leon called you. He wants to set up a meeting in Rome in about six weeks at which time we've got to provide someone fluent in Italian." Smirking, Roe turned to Price. "Charlie, do you think you can learn Italian in six weeks?"

Price shook his head "no." "Not a chance."

"That's what I thought," Roe mumbled under his breath. "So here we are," he said out loud, "on the verge of expanding the firm's business dramatically by establishing a foothold in Europe, and we're held up by one minor detail." Roe thought for a moment and then decided to pass the buck. "Charlie, this is your baby. You're the one with the CPA. You're the one who's going to Rome to look at the books and make nice with the Italians. You solve the language problem."

"Consider it done," Price said without the vaguest idea where his interpreter would come from. Suddenly he recalled his minister's sermon from last Sunday. It was based on the story of Abraham's attempt to sacrifice Isaac. Price remembered Isaac had questioned his father, "Where is the animal to be sacrificed?"

"God will provide," Abraham had replied.

That's good enough for me, Price thought. God provided for Abraham, he can provide for me.

Harris Roe stood up indicating the meeting was over. He curled his arm around Neuberger's waist and gently nudged him out the door. Charlie Price fell in step behind him.

Chapter 15

Saturday afternoon while she waited for Tony to come home, Judy snuggled on the couch in the living room. She tried to put the thoughts of the phone call out of her mind by studying the dozen flower catalogs she received every spring. Her father had owned a flower shop and when she was a teenager, she was expected to work in the shop after school and on weekends along with her mother and two brothers. Gradually she grew to love the flowers she worked with.

When she and Tony came back from their honeymoon, they discussed moving from their center-city apartment and buying a house of their own.

"I don't want to live a South Philly row house with concrete all around like we grew up in," she said. "I want a big backyard with grass and trees and some room for me to have a flower garden."

"Okay," Tony agreed grudgingly.

As each day with Judy passed, Tony felt another ounce of his freedom and individuality being sucked from him. It had started with the wedding plans. Judy had made all the decisions—where it would be held, how many would be invited, what food would be served, what the theme colors would be. In the end Tony felt like a guest at his own wedding. Now it looked like she had made the decision about where they would live with no input from him. He had given in without argument time after time to marry this girl he supposed he loved, but as she asserted herself more and more he wondered if the sacrifice of his pride, his ego, and his maleness, was worth it.

In order to regain some control he countered with, "We're not moving to the suburbs. I want to stay close to my family."

A month later the real estate agent had shown them a single home in the wooded, suburban-like East Falls section of Philadelphia. The neighborhood's major claim to fame was its illustrious residents, the Kelly clan. Some of Princess Grace's family still lived there, and they attracted others of the city's movers and shakers to the area's large, tree-shaded houses. In spite of the urban decay swirling around it, East Falls remained an oasis of gentility.

"I love it," Judy had said after being guided through the two-story, colonial house. "Look at that back yard. It's huge." Ideal for my garden, she thought.

"It's nice, but it's too close to the street," Tony grumbled. But he agreed to buy it when she argued that the big oak trees out front would provide enough protection from the traffic noise, and since the driveway to the street was so short, he wouldn't have so much snow to shovel in the winter.

Every year in March she eagerly poured over catalogs deciding which flowers to get rid of and which ones to add. The garden was her therapy, her hobby, her obsession. Each spring she felt a burst of joy as she watched the tulips and crocuses poke up from the soil, leaf out, and blossom. Perhaps, she thought, planting the flowers gives me some of the mothering feelings which I missed out on by not having children.

Now it was almost noon, and she had thumbed through the first few pages of the third catalog when she heard a key scratching in the front door. Tony pushed the door open and dropped his suitcase and a plastic garbage bag stuffed with his dirty clothes in the foyer.

"I'm home," he announced, fatigue showing in his voice.

"Hi, Tony," Judy said nonchalantly as she went to meet him. She threw her arms around him and squeezed him tight, but he only returned a halfhearted hug and a feeble kiss. "Did you have a good trip? Sell a million?"

"I'm in a bad mood and really pissed off right now. Thursday night someone smashed the window and broke into my car."

"That's a real bummer. Did they take anything important?"

"The radio's gone. The air bag's gone. The insurance will cover it, but the real pain in the ass is getting the car fixed. I drove it to the body shop this morning on the way home. They need three days, so for the next three days I'm stuck with a loaner. It's a real clunker." He sagged into the recliner in the living room and continued, "Not only that, but it's getting tougher and tougher out there. I don't know how some of our competition can offer the prices I've seen. I'll have to talk to my boss about it this week. And I'm not looking forward to the shit he's going to give me about working harder and smarter." He rubbed his eyes and yawned broadly. "And what's new around here?"

She had agonized over how to tell him about the phone call. I can't dump it on him out of the blue, she thought. I've got to find a way to lead up to it. She decided to start by telling the latest office gossip ending with Sara's news about Charlie Price's escapade. "What an idiot," she said. "If you're going to screw around, you don't do it with somebody in your office so it's bound to leak out. You'd think a smartass college graduate—he even went to two colleges—would have more brains than that."

Tony mumbled a reply and stifled a yawn with the back of his hand. He pushed back in the recliner; his eyes drooped shut.

"Looks like you're out of it," Judy observed. "Why don't you go upstairs and lie down for a while. When you get up, I've got some serious stuff to talk to you about."

Tony bolted awake and snapped the chair upright. "No. Let's talk now and get it over with. I feel so exhausted I may sleep right through tomorrow *and* take Monday off too."

Suspiciously: "What happened to make you so tired?"

Testy: "What else? Business. I work long hours, and it's caught up with me. What's the problem we have to discuss?"

Judy told him first about her seizure at the office. "It left me with a feeling I can't explain," she said. "A feeling that something very bad is going to happen to us."

"You ought to see a doctor if you're not feeling well," he said, and then without waiting for a response, "Maybe it's your own special form of PMS."

She stared at him open-mouthed and bristled when she realized he wasn't joking. Unwilling to start an argument she melted him with an angry look, and began, "You know I'm a witch . . ."

Before she could continue, Tony attacked. "You're an adult. It's time you cut out this 'I'm a witch crap.' Adults don't believe in witches, curses, and premonitions. It's our parents who believe in those things along with the 'evil eye'."

She tried to hold her temper, but didn't succeed. Seething she said, "Maybe *your* parents believe in that 'evil eye' shit. But in my house when I was growing up, the only thing they said about those curses was: '*Cosi Siciliani,*' like the Sicilians. And it wasn't a compliment."

He retreated into furious silence.

She took a couple of deep breaths to calm down, then said quietly, "There's one more thing." When he didn't respond but only stared at her, she told him about the phone call and tried to gauge his reaction. From his response (calm) and his body language (listless), she couldn't decide if he was tired, acting "cool under fire," or really innocent.

He said, "What do *you* think? Do you think I would do something stupid like that and screw up our marriage?" Annoyance crept into his voice. "I know how hung up you are on this being faithful. You remind me often enough . . ."

"Don't get mad," Judy interrupted. "I'm trying to be open and honest with you. I couldn't not tell you about this, could I? Remember he said he had pictures. What am I supposed to think when somebody says that?"

"I'd 've thought you'd have had more faith in me after all these years. I know if it was you who was accused, I'd know for damn sure it was a lie. I wouldn't even have to think twice about it." Mounting fury now. "Anyway, even pictures can be phonied up these days. Air brushing, heads stuck on someone else's body. The tabloids show the President meeting with aliens all the time."

"Who'd want to go to all the trouble to frame you, Tony? Do you have any enemies? This guy sounded nasty. He said he was going to beat you up if you didn't leave his girl alone."

Tiny beads of sweat formed on Tony's upper lip. What the hell is going on? he thought. Who would pull a stunt like this?

"I don't have any enemies. And there's no one for me to leave alone." He enunciated each word with a sharp pause between. He glared at Judy. "It sounds like you believe what he told you."

She said wearily. "That's enough for now, Tony. Let's not beat each other up any more. Why don't you go rest up before we both say things we'll regret. We'll wait and see if any pictures come before we talk about this again."

Tony stalked out of the room and up to their bedroom. Pictures, he thought. That's the damndest thing I ever heard. Who could have taken pictures of me in bed with Kate? I didn't see anyone taking pictures. There can't be any pictures. This must be someone's idea of a joke. It must be one of the wise-asses at work jerking my chain (but how would someone know?). Well, he's had his fun now. I don't think we'll hear anything more about this.

*　　*　　*

Tony napped off and on all afternoon and at supper did his best to avoid any conversation with Judy. That night he slept fitfully—on purpose. He wanted to make sure he would get up and out before she woke so he wouldn't have to face her. As dawn broke, even though he felt like turning over and going back to sleep, he forced himself out of bed. He constantly glanced over his shoulder at Judy to make sure he wasn't waking her. He grabbed his clothes and dressed quietly in the bathroom. He dragged out his gym bag (which he always had packed and ready to go) from behind the shoe rack in the closet and quickly left the house, closing the door silently behind him.

As he drove away, he thought about his relationship with Judy. From past experience he knew the longer he held out, the more likely she was to forget about his blowing up. He thought: I don't need a confrontation with her, especially about fidelity. I've managed to keep my affairs a secret for a long time. How long has it been? More than ten years. Do I feel guilty about them? Hell, no. They've probably helped keep Judy and me together. It's good to have her to come home to, but I like having the others too. I need variety to make life interesting and exciting. And besides, he admitted to himself, it makes me feel real good to know that all those women are attracted to me.

Tony drove to the parking lot behind the gym. Two days a week he sandwiched in a workout between his sales calls, and either on Saturday or Sunday he went for a third time. During the week he rationalized that he was using his lunch hour to exercise; even though he took a lunch hour anyway and often spent more than an hour at the gym. He noticed the desk-bound purchasing agents he called on tended to have midriffs draped over their belts, and this gave him the motivation he needed to keep fit. He swore to himself, I'm never going to look like that. I'm going to stay in shape. And, he thought, I've done a damn fine job of it.

He changed into his shorts and tank top and went up to the running track which was suspended above the Nautilus room. After a few stretching exercises, he began to trot around the track. As he started the third lap, Fred Matthews fell in step next to him and slapped him on the back.

He and Fred went back a long way. They had become best friends when they were bar-hopping bachelors. After Tony graduated from high school, he hung out at the latest "in" singles bars to meet women. As if by some strange ESP, he kept bumping into Fred, and they started calling each other by name. One night in a boozy stupor, they started bragging to each other about their conquests and found there were a dozen women they had both bedded. Rather than feeling they were competitors, this became a bond that pulled them together. When they exhausted stories about their sex lives, they found they had another common interest—the Philadelphia sports teams, especially the Eagles.

Fred sucked in a deep breath and asked, "How are they hanging, Tony?" He began breathing in rhythm—in on two steps, out on the next two—as he jogged.

Tony avoided the expected answer—"Two in a bunch," and puffed, "Not bad." They ran two laps together without talking any more then Tony said, "I have a problem."

"About . . . ?" Fred asked.

"I've got a man/women kind of problem."

"Don't we all?"

"Did you ever go to bed with a girl and then get a lot of shit from an angry boyfriend?" Tony blurted.

"Never did," Fred huffed.

They passed a stunning twenty-year-old with a figure to die for and two-foot long, blonde ponytail. Walking briskly, she held a weight in each hand and swung her arms as if she was slamming a punching bag. She wore a tight pair of gray workout pants with a pink thong accent. They twisted around and smiled at her; she ignored them.

"What do you think those thongs are for?" Fred asked.

"To attract our attention, dummy," Tony responded.

"It did. But you were saying something about an angry boyfriend."

"Did one ever call and warn you about staying away from his girlfriend?"

"Nope," Fred said.

"My wife got a call from a guy who said he took some pictures of me and his girlfriend in bed, and said he would send them to her."

"Pictures?" Fred strained to get another look at the blonde. "If your wife finds out you're cheating on her, you're really gonna be in deep shit."

"The pictures didn't come yet. He only called and promised to send them."

"Then what's the problem?"

"Suppose with me for a minute. Suppose someone sent your wife pictures that showed you in bed screwing another woman. There was no doubt about it; it was you. What would you do?"

Without hesitating Fred answered, "Even if I was guilty as hell but there was some way I could worm out of it, I would deny everything. But if the pictures showed close-ups, and there was no way it wasn't me, then I'd lie my way out of it. I'd beg for mercy. I'd want to keep my marriage. For me marriage has a lot of going for it. Do you remember being single? Remember us trolling for women at the singles bars? It was fun at the time, but how'd you like to do that now? Not me. I get worn out from a day's work. And I like my sex regular, ready and waiting for me when I get home. I don't have the energy to spend a couple of hours every night looking for some woman to fuck. Besides the competition is much younger these days. You think it would be easy for us to get girls? I don't think so."

Two more laps.

Fred added, "And I get my food made and my laundry done."

"Oh, yeah," Tony said, "I almost forgot. This guy also threatened me. Judy said he sounded like he wanted to beat the shit out of me."

"Now that's more serious," Fred said. They stopped running and leaned against a wall. "You'd better be careful. There are a lot of crazies out there today. Serial killers, regular killers, guys who'll kill you if you take their parking place. There's road rage and a whole bunch of other weird stuff going on. I'd watch my ass if I was you, and I'd sure stop seeing her. Screwing around with a woman who has an angry asshole looking out for her doesn't sound like my idea of a good lay. However much she lights you up in bed, it isn't worth dying for."

"Okay. Thanks for the advice," Tony said. "I'm going downstairs to work on my body."

"See you next time," Fred said. "I'm going to take a shower and call it quits for today."

During his ten reps on the abdominal crunch machine Tony wondered what to do now. Should he see her again? She *was* a tiger in bed; and the porn movie, and the mirrors; what surprises might she think up next. No, he decided. Fred was right. It's too dangerous. No kind of sex, no matter how good, no matter what surprises, was worth a bullet in the head from a jealous boyfriend. Come to think of it, he thought, what the hell is she doing with a boyfriend anyway? She's married. Was it her husband, Greg, who called Judy on the phone, or does she have a boyfriend in addition to her husband? Something stinks about this whole thing. If no pictures come, I'm gonna forget about it, but if somebody does send pictures, then I'm gonna ask Kate what the fuck's going on.

He slid onto the red plastic seat under the pull-down bar and adjusted the weights. Then he rubbed his hands together and readied them on the grip. Silently he counted "One" as he pulled the bar down across his chest.

* * *

After his workout, Tony took a long shower then sat on the bench in front of his locker and stared at it for long time thinking. In spite of the strains in his relationship with Judy, he decided he wanted to stay married to her. After all, he thought, Fred's points made a lot of sense. On the other hand, he would continue pursuing other women, concluding that would help his marriage by filling in what he was missing with Judy. Marriage could give him the same-old-same-old and he needed that, but the other women could give him variety, spice, adventure, and thrills, and he needed that too.

He spent the rest of the day in front of the TV at the gym. Late in the afternoon he decided to go home. By the time he got there dinner was already on the table. The tension in the air hung as a backdrop over a silent meal during which neither one spoke to the other. Tony, wanting to smooth things over, was not quite sure how to go about it. And Judy swore to herself she wouldn't be the first to give in and start talking since he was the one who caused this standoff. After dinner, he and Judy tiptoed around, taking great pains to avoid each other and any possible discussion of what had happened the night before.

Later that night, when Judy heard the shower stop running—he went to the gym and must have taken a shower, she thought, and now he's taking another one just to avoid me—she carefully arranged the flower catalogs on the coffee table, and started upstairs, not sure what kind of mood Tony would be in. Ever since he had left that morning she had buried herself in planning the garden and had managed to put him out of her mind, and now she didn't want to face him again. I've had enough punishment for a while, she thought, and I haven't even done anything wrong. All I did was tell him that someone called on the phone. Is that a reason for him to get mad at me? What's the problem with him? I got a bunch of crap dumped on me for something that's not my fault. Well, to hell with who started it, I'm going upstairs right now before he can go to sleep on me and have it out with him. I don't have to live this way any longer.

Walking confidently, she went up the stairs, and stood in the open doorway to the bedroom. Tony had a towel wrapped around his waist and was lying on the bed, hands folded across his chest, staring at the ceiling. He was obsessing about the phone call. Could there really be any pictures? he thought. If there were, who would have taken them? Even if someone followed me to the motel, there's nothing to worry about. They couldn't have taken pictures of us in bed because I didn't see any flashbulbs go off. There can't be any pictures, he concluded. It's what I keep coming back to—this is all someone's idea of a joke. It's the only logical explanation, so I've got nothing to worry about.

It took him a few seconds to notice an angry Judy glaring down at him.

"Look . . . ," she began.

The one word galvanized him into action. He bolted upright and held up a hand to stop her from talking, "Don't say anything. I was going to come downstairs in a minute to talk to you." The lie came easily to him, and others followed without hesitation. "I was way off base. I shouldn't have blown up at you like that. But you have to understand. I'd had a hard week. I was dog-tired. I know that's no excuse."

"I had to tell you about that call." Her voice softened. "If I didn't tell you, I'd feel dishonest. We ought to feel we can discuss anything with each other without getting a whole lot of shit about it."

He jumped up from the bed. The knot in the towel around his waist loosened then slipped apart. Naked he cuddled her in his arms and pulled her close to him. When he felt her softness against him, a rush of real affection, which he hadn't felt for her in a long time, came over him, quickly followed by an avalanche of burning, animal lust.

Unaware of his desire she continued, "It was only a phone call. There may not even be any pictures. Someone's trying to cause trouble between us. Well, we won't let them. Say you're sorry, and we'll forget about it."

"You know I'm sorry, honey." He pulled her even tighter to him, nuzzled into the hollow of her neck, and rubbed her back. He sat her down on the bed, sat down next to her, and put his arms around her shoulders. "Everything's back to normal now. Everything's gonna be all right."

Until the pictures come, Judy thought glumly.

Chapter 16

*M*onday evening, after fighting the evening rush hour traffic, Judy pulled into the driveway, gripped the steering wheel tightly, and rested her head on her hands. After a few minutes, she sighed, then, mustering all her strength, she dragged herself through the front door and dropped her purse on the hall table. Shoes get off my feet, she thought, as she kicked off her high heels and stretched out on the couch in the living room. She grabbed the remote and clicked on to the news, but found herself unable to relax as Jim Gardner on Channel 6 enthusiastically described the latest fires and murders. She forced herself up from the couch and began the one housekeeping activity that she enjoyed most—doing the laundry. It gave her a feeling of accomplishment to take dirty clothes and make them sparkling clean, and when Judy ironed, she was in seventh heaven. She dumped out Tony's bag full of dirty clothes and began sorting the colored from the white.

Forty minutes later Tony unlocked the front door and stared in astonishment at the sight in front of him. Judy was standing with one arm stretched out toward him. Between her thumb and forefinger she dangled a pair of bikini underpants. They were dotted with little pictures of jet-black bulls with devilish faces whose curly tails ended in arrows that pierced tiny blood-red hearts. Slowly she swung them back and forth in front of her flabbergasted husband.

"This is a hell-of-a turn on," Tony said. "Does this mean you aren't wearing any panties?" Did I get lucky, or what, he thought to himself. He didn't care to notice that this was totally out of character for her, and the look on her face was anything but playful/sexy.

"These aren't mine. Are they yours?" she said through clenched teeth.

"Now you're losing me. Of course, they're not mine. They're for a woman. What's all this about?"

"This is about laundry. I'm not going to wash your whore's fuckin' underwear!" she screamed.

"What?" He recoiled.

"You heard me. Now listen carefully," she shouted. "I'll make it real simple for you. I usually do the laundry on Sunday. But yesterday I was still pissed about the phone call, so I didn't do it. I decided to do the laundry today—just now. And guess what I found? Rolled up in your dirty clothes, the ones from your last trip south, were these." She jiggled them closer to his face. He backed away.

Fred's words tumbled through his head. Deny, lie, talk your way out of it. Brain don't fail me now, he prayed. Judy stood waiting and said nothing.

"It's not what you think." He stalled for time. "I can explain this." Suddenly an idea came to him. "It must be the new guy at work. We hired a new salesman, Darin, a few weeks ago, and he's a real practical joker. He even gave the boss one of those exploding cigars. He must've put those in with my laundry to get a laugh." Tony forced a laugh. "Wait 'til I tell him how angry you got."

"Let me get this straight. He went with you on a sales trip, which you forgot to mention to me when you came home, and somehow snuck these . . ." She dropped the pants on the floor as if she couldn't bear to hold them any longer and turned her head away, "into your bag."

"No. He didn't come with me. On the way home, Saturday morning, remember I had to stop at the body shop and drop the car off to get the window fixed. It was close to my office so I stopped there after. I had some paperwork to do. Darin was there. We traded some small talk, and I told him I was coming back from a trip. Now that I remember, he did act sort of stupid. Then he said he was going home, and he left. But I stayed on a while longer because I hadn't finished yet. That must've been when he did it."

"He just happened to have a woman's underpants with him waiting to drop them in your laundry."

"You should see the guy's desk drawers, Jude. They're loaded with all kinds of shit. He's a major packrat. He might even have Jimmie Hoffa buried in there for all I know." He was amazed at how easily the story came to him.

She ignored his attempt at humor and said, "So he took these from his desk without you seeing and went out to your car—the one you always lock . . ."

"This was the loaner . . . from the body shop. Maybe I didn't lock it right. And many times in the company parking lot I don't bother to lock the car. There's a chain link fence around it and a full-time security guard, even on weekends. But that gives me an idea. Next time I park in that lot and I see that guard, I'll ask him if he saw someone fooling around with the car."

Exasperated: "That's the lamest story I ever heard," she said. "You left your car at the shop and were driving a loaner, how would what's-his-name even know what your car looks like?"

"I told him about the broken window, and I showed him out the window—I pointed to the wreck I had to drive. He laughed at it. We both did."

Judy's simmer turned into a violent boil. There's no way I'm buying this, she thought. This is too coincidental—first the phone call saying he was with a woman and now a woman's underwear. But I can't come right out and call him a liar, there is some chance his story might be true. She strained to interpret the expression on his face, but Tony, the super salesman, had mastered a poker face to hide his true emotions and feelings, and in all the years she had known him, she still didn't know for sure when he was telling the truth and when he was lying.

"Maybe we can move on from here." He stepped gingerly around the underwear lying on the floor. "What's for dinner?" he asked in a friendly manner. And when she didn't answer he asked, "Where's the mail?"

"That's it?" she shrieked. "What's for dinner? Where's the mail? Forget about that shit. We never did get to talk about Saturday night. What were you so mad at? I didn't accuse you of anything. Why were you so angry if the man on the phone has no pictures? And now today with the laundry. I want to know what the hell is going on here."

"Hey. Calm down. This isn't getting us anywhere. Let's have dinner, and then we can talk about it." He headed for the kitchen.

"Stop running away from me," she said trailing after him. "Last night you used sex to avoid talking to me, and tonight . . ."

He interrupted. "Seriously, honey. We will talk about it after we eat. I promise."

She took two deep breaths and decided to pull back. "Okay," she said forcing a calmness into her voice she really didn't feel. "I'll nuke something from the freezer." She pulled open the freezer door and started reading the labels on a stack of Weight Watchers dinners.

"Wait a minute. Wait a minute," Tony said, his temper rising. "I'm tired of warmed-up cardboard. On the nights when I'm home, why can't we have home-cooked meals?"

"In case you haven't noticed, I work eight hours a day." Her voice cracked. "A hard eight hours a day. I don't go to three-hour business lunches, then do the bar scene for a couple of hours before dropping into a freshly made motel bed." She began screaming again. "I don't have time to make home-cooked meals."

"You had time before that phone call," he said angrily, matching her voice level.

"Would you rather I hadn't told you? I don't know what you want from me any more." She fought back the rising urge to break into tears thinking: No way this bastard's gonna make me cry.

"What do I want from you?" he snapped. "I want a little more confidence in me than assuming I'm guilty. You think I'm guilty because of pictures that don't exist, and guilty because someone's playing a joke on me. Look lawyer, I want you off my case. And right now I want a home-cooked meal and if I can't have one, then I'm going out to a restaurant and get some decent food." He grabbed his car keys and stormed out.

"But I'm not on your case," Judy wailed mournfully to the back of the slamming door.

The dam broke and tears streamed down her face. Sobbing and crying she slammed a ginger chicken dinner into the microwave, punched the keys, and turned on the kitchen TV. The endless parade of misery upset her even more.

"I'm not watching the goddamn news any more. It's too depressing, and I'm depressed enough," she sobbed.

She forced herself to eat.

Her intuition refused to let it go so easily. A nagging feeling cautioned her that this was the smoke, and there was a fire somewhere. She remembered the premonition at the office that had frightened her so, and her stomach twisted into a knot.

"Tony's cheating and lying," a small voice inside her whispered.

*   *   *

Tony drove away from the house grumbling to himself, "Bitch. She's not the only one who works hard. The money I earn buys her everything she wants, and this is the thanks I get. Well, shit on that." He slammed his palm on the steering wheel, then pulled out his cell phone and dialed quickly. A female voice answered.

"It's Tony. Is he home? Can you talk?" Tony asked.

"No, and yes. He's not home yet but don't come over. He's due any minute." The voice turned velvety and inviting. "I'm glad you called. How've you been, sweetheart?"

"I've got two little problems," he said.

"I know about the car window. I was there," Kate cooed. "What's the other? Anything I can help with?"

"The car window is the least of my worries right now. Starting with the most recent, how did your panties get into my laundry?" he asked. "You knew Judy would find them if you put them there."

"Oh. You mean the ones with the cute little bulls all over them?"

"Yeah, those."

"I wondered what happened to them. I looked through all my clothes when I got home and couldn't find them. I thought with all the . . . excitement I had accidentally thrown them out. Now I know where they got to. You know I bought them special for you. There's this great sex shop . . ."

Tony was not to be put off but interrupted her. "Did you put them in my laundry on purpose?"

"Of course I didn't put them in your laundry. I have no idea how they ended up with your stuff instead of mine. It was early in the morning when I packed up, and frankly I wasn't functioning too well at that point, honey. I was somewhat worn out. I wouldn't put them there on purpose. I have no reason for having Judy find out about us. I had too good a time with you to want to upset things. Didn't you have a good time?"

"Yeah," he answered dejectedly, "I had a good time."

"What did Judy say when she found them?"

"She started yelling and screaming, but I managed to calm her down."

Dejected: "How'd you do that?"

"I made up a story about a guy at work playing a practical joke on me, and she bought it."

If she did she's pretty dumb, Kate thought, but said, "I can't help you with the panties problem. I'm sorry it upset Judy. Now what was your other problem?"

"Do you have a boyfriend in addition to your husband?"

Her voice changed to steely. "That's a real personal question, Tony. Do I ask you about your sex life?"

"Some one called Judy that night and said he had pictures of me in bed with his girlfriend, and he's mailing those pictures to Judy."

"I don't know anything about that either. But since you asked, I don't have a boyfriend, only my husband. And he wouldn't bother to call her, he would talk to me about it first. It wouldn't upset him anyway. After all, he . . . I don't think we're getting anywhere talking about this, Tony. I don't know anything about any pictures or any boyfriend, and that's that. Now, anything else you want to talk about?"

"Nothing else," Tony grumbled. "Bye, now."

Tony slammed the phone shut and stuffed it in his pocket.

Chapter 17

Three minutes before noon the next day, Carlo Fiore got off the elevator on the fifteenth floor of The Packard Tower, a downtown skyscraper, pushed open the glass door marked Neuberger Roe & Price, and smiled at the receptionist.

"Would you tell Judy Orsini I'm here," he said.

"And whom shall I say is calling?" she asked in her snootiest voice.

"Carlo Fiore. She's expecting me. I'm her lunch date," he replied.

When Judy got the buzz that Carlo had arrived she quickly grabbed the mirror from her purse and studied her face carefully. Not too bad, she thought. She was especially worried about her eyes. Would they still look red and swollen from her blow-up with Tony last night? On careful inspection she saw that her eyes were rimmed by perfectly lovely skin, and there was no hint of the previous day's upset. She clicked the mirror shut and put on her jacket. Just then her heart fluttered—a flutter like she felt when she was younger and going on a first date with a new man. She hadn't felt that flutter in a long time and thought, What's going on here? Am I nervous, expecting something to happen between us, wondering if he will he like me? "Enough," she said out loud. "This is only two friends getting together for lunch; nothing more." But, as she walked down the corridor to meet him, her inside voice answered back, you'd like it to be something more, wouldn't you?

Carlo watched her push open the door marked "Private" to the left of the reception area. Although she smiled when she saw him, he studied her carefully and sensed that in spite of her surface attempt to look cheerful, something was wrong, very wrong. In some way he could not explain, he knew that deep down she was miserable and hurting. He felt his heart go out to her.

"Hi. How are you?" he said. And before she could answer, "I've made reservations around the corner, at The Garden."

She took a good look at him and brightened. He really is handsome, she thought. If I were single, he would be on my "A" list. She scolded herself: Now why am I thinking about other men? I suppose because Tony's being such a shit. She felt a warm feeling toward Carlo well up inside her, and it gradually replaced the anger toward Tony she harbored in her heart.

He held the door open for her and with a gracious bow and wave of his hand ushered her through. He ignored the receptionist smirking after them. When they reached street level, they nervously made small talk about the weather ("Warm for March, isn't it?"), and the city ("It's getting cleaner downtown.") as they walked to the restaurant.

The maitre d' led them through a narrow hallway which opened onto a U-shaped dining area. At a corner table for two he pulled out a chair for Judy, opened menus, and placed them in their hands.

"Your waiter, Perry, will be with you in a minute to take your drink order," he said.

Carlo studied his menu for a fraction of a second then laid it down and nervously smoothed a non-existent wrinkle in the white linen tablecloth with a forefinger while he searched for an opening.

"Remember my cousin Dominic?" he began.

"Oh, yes," Judy answered. No chance she would forget him.

He proceeded to tell her about the drug bust. "I hadn't spoken to him in years, but I called him the next day to tell him about his nieces. He already knew, his sister had called him. He was plenty shook up about it."

Judy's eyes had glazed over, she was reliving the prom night. Carlo broke into her thoughts with, "What are you thinking about?"

Before she could censor it, "The prom" came out.

"Let me take a chance here," he said. "What did happen all those years ago back at the prom?"

Before Judy could answer, the waiter came and stood stoically by the table not wanting to interrupt. They looked up at him; Judy awkwardly ordered an iced tea and the first thing on the menu, a turkey club sandwich.

"Bring me the same," Carlo said. He stared at her, unable to shift his eyes away.

"The prom," Judy mused. "Is it okay if I start at the beginning?" He nodded.

"You remember my best friend Kate?" Judy began.

"Sure I remember Kate. She had the serious hots for Dominic, and the four of us double-dated for the senior prom."

Her thoughts momentarily drifted back to Dominic, but Carlo interrupted them.

"You asked Kate to help you find a prom date; she asked Dominic, and he asked me. Well, Dominic never really *asked* anybody; he *told* me to take you to the prom." He stared at her. "I'll never understand why you didn't have a date. You were so pretty." He paused for a second and smiled softly at her. "And still are."

Judy felt a tightening in her chest. Wow! What's happening here? she wondered. I didn't get to know him very well at the prom, but he sure is nice. I think I like him. No, I know I like him. She felt a tinge of red creeping up to her face. This is ridiculous, she told herself, feeling like a teenager falling in love.

"Thank you," she said quietly and hurried to change the subject. "We started out on the right foot. You were so good-looking in your tuxedo; you could have been a magazine fashion model. When you called on the phone to ask me out, you asked me what my favorite flowers were. I said roses. Then you asked what color my dress was. I still remember; it was maroon. You brought me a corsage of beautiful white tea roses. You came with Kate and Dominic to pick me up in his dazzling, white Ford convertible. He was the original testosterone-loaded, Neanderthal, macho male; drove like a maniac. When we got to the gym we danced a few dances before . . ." She didn't want to embarrass him, but his look encouraged her to go on. "About an hour after the prom started, Dominic asked you to go out to the parking lot with him and three other guys. He hung out with a rough crowd; they really looked like trouble. You were gone about a half hour, and then the five of you staggered back reeking from alcohol and roaring drunk. Except for Dominic. He wasn't a roarer. Either he could handle his liquor, or he was a quiet drunk, or he didn't drink as much as the rest of you. He seemed totally unaffected. And you . . ." she smiled at him. "I didn't know how you could even stand."

"This is embarrassing," Carlo said, "but go on." He hung his head and covered his face with his hands. I've come to regret that night, he thought to himself.

"You were like a helpless little boy—like a Raggedy Andy doll. You turned to mush. At least I thought so at the time, but I was wrong."

"Why do you say that?"

"After the prom we were supposed to go with two other couples to a house we rented down the shore. Dominic insisted that you drive. You were so smashed I was sure we'd all be killed, and I started crying and making a scene."

"Why did he want me to drive if I was so drunk?" Carlo interrupted.

"How can I put this delicately? He and Kate wanted the back seat to . . . themselves." Carlo grinned like a schoolboy. "With all the grunts and groans coming from back there you almost broke your neck looking in the rear view mirror trying to see what was going on. I think that's what kept you awake."

"I don't remember any of this," Carlo said ashamedly.

"The way you kept fiddling with the mirror and squirming around to see what was going on back there. I was afraid we'd end up in a ditch."

"We didn't, did we?"

"No. Somehow you managed to get us there in one piece. But shortly after we got there, you excused yourself and went upstairs and took a nap. And that was that. I didn't see you again until the next day when the four of us drove back to Philadelphia. But," she added hastily, "I don't want to talk about the past any more. Let's talk about the here and now." She took a deep breath then blurted out, "Are you married?"

He studied her face for some clue about why she asked this question and thought he saw a glimmer of interest in him.

"No," he said. "I've never found the right woman. I've been a bachelor for so long that my friends tease me about being gay. I suppose that's the fate of any single guy who's over twenty-five today." An impish grin crossed his face. "But I'm not gay. I'll give you some women references if you want to call them."

Judy shook her head "no."

The waiter brought their food and silently set it down in front of them. Then he twisted the plates to the correct orientation for a perfect presentation. At this break in their conversation Judy began to think about Tony's infidelity and a cloud of sadness descended across her face. An alert Carlo noticed her change of mood and said, "Do you know why I was invited to Nancy's wedding?"

"No. She never told me."

"I was a good friend of Nancy's first husband. He invited me over to their house often because we both liked to watch hockey games. So I became friendly with Nancy too. Gradually things changed. I would go over to see him, but he was never home. Then about a year ago she became very introverted and . . ." He searched for the right words. "Acted like a whipped dog." Judy jerked her head up. "That's the only way I can describe it," Carlo continued. "You could see it in her posture. She started looking like a stooped old lady."

"She never told me anything. What was going on?" Judy asked.

"Her husband . . . well, he wasn't very nice to her. Let's just say she suffered a lot of physical abuse. After she told me what he did to her, I hated him. She and I developed a great relationship. We were like brother and sister. She would tell me everything, and I would listen and try to help." He bent over toward her. "So if you ever need a friend, a friend to talk to, I could be that friend. I have experience of being a shoulder to cry on"

Judy remained silent.

Carlo said, "I noticed when I picked you up today that something was bothering you. You looked so . . . down, and now that look is back again. Is there something I can help you with?"

Can I trust him with my deepest thoughts and most personal secrets? Judy wondered. She looked deeply into his eyes and tried to know his soul. Intuitively she judged him to be what he seemed—an honest, open person, eager to help her. Trusting her intuition, she began to tell him everything.

"It started at work last Thursday," she said. "The day you called." Before she could censor it. "That was the only good thing that happened to me that day." slipped out. Hurriedly she went on to cover up. "I had a strange attack. A wave passed through me and left me with a feeling, a premonition that something evil was going to happen to me. And now I'm afraid it's coming true."

"Why? What's happened?" His eyes widened with concern.

"That night a man called and told me he was sending me pictures of . . ." She took a deep breath, and her words came out with a whoosh. "Pictures of Tony in bed with another woman."

"That's terrible if it's true. But you should wait until the pictures come before you condemn him. There are some real nutty people out there these days. Anyone can call anyone on the phone, and pictures can be spliced together to show anything. That phone call doesn't automatically mean Tony's guilty."

I don't think I'm ready to tell him the rest, Judy thought. No, I won't tell him about the panties. "Let's talk about something else, something happy," she said. "Let's talk about you going to Rome."

"You said your parents came from Rome," Carlo said.

"Both my mother and my father were born there and came here in the early days when Mussolini came to power. They hated him, but they loved Rome. While I was growing up my mother kept drumming it into my head how wonderful it was to be a Roman. How Romans were the noblest, most wonderful people in the world. Romans were . . ."

Suddenly she felt ill; no, not ill. She felt pain. It felt as if someone had punched her in the stomach. She pushed the plate of half-eaten food out of her way, folded her arms on the table, rested her head on them. Carlo's eyes widened and he gasped with alarm. Judy fell into a trance.

She could see a white, indistinct form, which gradually took the shape of a woman, wavering ghost-like against a dark blue background. Suddenly the background changed color. Three vertical stripes appeared; lime green on the left, white in the center, and red on the right. Judy recognized the colors of the flag of Italy. A huge hole suddenly burst open in the center and sucked the whole picture into it; Judy now saw only a vast black void. It was all over in a few seconds, and slowly she regained consciousness.

Carlo had jumped up from his chair, hurried to her side, and bent over next to her. "Are you all right?" he whispered into her ear.

She blinked her eyes rapidly and lifted her head. "Yes. I'm okay," she said. "I get these spells from time to time. Like that one in the office I just told you about." She shook her head rapidly from side to side struggling to regain her poise. "But what I didn't tell you is— that I'm a witch."

Carlo snapped upright. I thought I'd seen and heard it all, he snickered to himself. I've interviewed demonic killers, satanic priests, but this was a new one. He smothered a laugh.

"Oh?" he said out loud in a questioning tone of disbelief.

"No. It's true."

He censored a belittling comment and stepped back away from her as if to get a better look at a self-confessed witch.

"Don't worry, and don't be afraid. I'm a good witch." He looked at her like she had just landed from Mars. "Remember Glenda in the *Wizard of Oz*? She was a good witch."

He nodded, now feeling a little uneasy. Could there be witches after all, he thought, let alone good witches? "What was this spell about?" he probed cautiously.

"I'm not sure what it meant," she answered as she glanced at her watch. Excitedly: "Look at the time. It's after two. I enjoyed having lunch with you, but I've got to get back to work. I don't want to get fired."

He signaled the waiter for the bill, and as he signed it, Judy felt a wave of realization sweep over her. I know what that was about, she thought. I'm going to Italy. It was me who was sucked into that Italian flag. As she was about to tell Carlo, he took out a piece of paper and wrote two numbers on it.

"Here's my work phone and my home phone. I'd like it if you would call me before I leave. I do want to keep in touch. And I want to make sure that you're all right." He pulled her chair out. "I apologize for keeping you out so long."

They walked quickly back to the office where he surprised her by kissing her European-style on both cheeks in full sight of the receptionist. In spite of her efforts to stay calm, she felt a warmth for him rising in her, and she blushed like a school girl. Omigod, she thought, I like him. I like him a lot.

"*Ciao*, Judy," he said. "And if you're ever in Rome, promise you'll look me up."

In spite of her recent vision she said, "I don't think there's much chance of me being in Rome."

"But promise anyway. Just in case."

"Okay, I promise," she said smiling.

*   *   *

When she sat down at her desk, Judy dialed Kate's number.

"I had lunch with Carlo today," she said. "You remember? He's Dominic's cousin. From the prom."

"Dominic," she said dreamily. I only think of him every day, she thought to herself.

She tuned out what Judy was saying and allowed herself to daydream. Her thoughts drifted back twenty years to her relationship with Dominic. Initial infatuation had quickly grown into obsession. She was crazy about him, really, actually crazy. She pursued him with every trick she could think of to get him to marry her. Since he had an insatiable appetite for sex, she went out of her way to be there for him so he would have no need of another woman. "You spend so much time with your legs spread, you're gonna end up bowlegged," he would laugh at her. Then he would calmly tell her about the other girls he was dating just to see her become furious. "Your face gets as red as your hair when you get angry," he needled her. None of his crudeness, scorn, or derision managed to turn her off; she remained determined to marry him.

Finally after an exceptionally passionate session of lovemaking during which he had degraded her almost beyond her point of endurance, she decided to get it out into the open. He lay on top of her breathing heavily, totally unconcerned that he was brutally crushing her.

"I love you," she said gasping the words out. "And I want us to get married. Hey, look. If you marry me, you can have this whenever you want." She rolled her hips suggestively and ran her hands down his naked sides and reached between his legs.

He recoiled, braced himself on his elbows, and looked her in the eyes. He said, "Right now I don't want to marry nobody. And besides, you want to get laid so bad, I can have *you* any time I want. And if you don't want to, there are a thousand others girls waiting in line for me. What the fuck should I get married for?"

She bit her lip hard to keep from crying but couldn't quite manage it. As she sobbed softly, she angrily shoved him off her and punched him hard in the ribs.

"What was that for?" he growled massaging the sore spot.

"Serves you right for being . . . cruel," she said.

And in spite of that, she thought, even though he treated me like shit, I loved him like I never loved anybody else. I loved him even more than I love Greg.

She had met her husband, Greg, through her work. After three or four unsatisfying jobs, she had answered an ad for a residential real estate sales agent. The interviewer turned out to be a high school classmate of hers and offered to hire her on the spot. She accepted.

Six months later after she had found she liked the work and had become good at it, the phone rang.

"This one's yours," a co-worker yelled at her. "I got the last one."

The woman on the other end of the line wanted to sell her house. "It's too big for the two of us. There's only me and my son now. He was helping me take care of my poor, sick husband. The dear man had three heart attacks. The last one killed him." She sighed. "Now it's time for my son to move out and be on his own. By the way, you sound like a nice girl. Would you like to meet him? His name is Greg."

Within a year she married him.

Judy's voice brought her back to the present. "Uh, oh. Sorry I can't talk," Kate said. The boss is calling me."

Chapter 18

Two days later the pictures came. When Judy came home from work and walked up the flagstone steps toward the front door, she noticed the nine-by-twelve manila envelope sticking out of the mailbox. "I'm here," she felt it calling to her as it twitched in the spring breeze. She pulled it out and inspected it carefully. There was no return address, but the Baltimore postmark shouted out a warning. She knew even before opening it, that inside were the pictures the anonymous caller had promised to send. And he wouldn't bother sending them, she realized, unless they showed what he promised. She heaved a great sigh and shivered. Her heart started beating erratically.

With a shaking hand she somehow managed to put the key into the front door lock, twist it, and push the door open. Standing in the open doorway, she let the other mail slide through her hands and fall to the floor. She stood stark still afraid to open it as a knot began to form in the pit of her stomach. She forced herself to action: closed the front door, and tossed her purse on the hall table. I suppose, she thought—her heart still fluttering wildly—I have no choice but to open it. It's not going to go away. With quick twists of her wrist she nipped off little pieces down the width of the envelope and let them flutter to the floor.

Her hands trembled as she groped inside the envelope and she felt the slippery, smooth photographer's paper. Maybe there's a letter, she thought, trying to postpone looking at the pictures. I could read that first. She fished around in the envelope but there was no letter. I can't put it off any longer, she decided, I've got to look at them.

Slowly she slid out the first picture straining in the dim early evening twilight to make out the details. No success; it was too dark. She staggered into the living room and dropped down onto the couch.

She snapped on the table lamp and slowly focused her eyes on the photo in her hand. She gasped. The images were as clear and sharp as if the picture had been taken in a photographer's studio. A naked man and woman—in full color—were lying on a bed locked in the missionary position. The woman had her legs crossed at the ankles behind the man's back and appeared to be pulling him into her. The man's body was pressed flat against the woman's, hiding much of her from view. The woman's face was turned to her left, away from the camera, and was nestled behind the man's head which lay on her right shoulder. His hands were buried under the pillow, which he had bent upward around the woman's head making it impossible to identify her. However, from the male's left profile, even without seeing his entire body, Judy knew without a shred of doubt it was Tony. She groaned and let the photo and the envelope slip from her fingers to the floor.

She clenched her fists and winced as her nails dug into her palms. A strange mixture of emotions cascaded through her. She was furious that Tony would cheat on her after all his promises and denials. And yet she was relieved, relieved that the worrying and waiting was finally over. Here were the pictures. They proved his infidelity, and there was no way he could talk his way out of it.

Summoning all her strength she willed herself to look at the other pictures. She bent over and picked up the envelope and yanked the second picture from it. In this one the woman was facing the male who lay on his left side with his back to the camera. Even in this position Judy could again easily identify Tony, but as in the first picture, the woman's head was completely hidden from view. Her torso, from her shoulders down, appeared from under Tony's arms. Her left leg was hiked high up so that her thigh rested on his waist; his right leg was pushed up far between her legs. Like two pairs of scissors trying to cut each other, Judy thought. As she stared in fascination and curiosity at the tangle of legs, a red spot, about the size of a quarter, on the woman's left hip, caught her eye. As tears streamed from her eyes, she strained to make out what it was. She couldn't. I need a magnifying glass, she thought. Then she remembered that Tony kept one in his desk. On wobbly legs she tottered upstairs to his office. Impatiently she jerked open desk drawers, rummaging hurriedly through their contents, tossing Scotch tape, envelopes, and thank-you cards in all directions until she found it.

She laid the picture flat on the desk, turned on the desk lamp, and squinted through the lens of the magnifying glass. "That bitch," she said out loud, "has a heart tattooed there. On her hip. A fuckin' heart tattoo." She felt the blood rushing to her head. It throbbed and pounded; anger like she had never felt before raged through her. She shouted to the empty house: "He's dead meat, that dickhead. And that woman, too. I swear to God I'll find out who she is, and when I do . . ." She couldn't finish the sentence as huge sobs racked her body and left her fighting for air.

She groped her way back downstairs to the living room and stuffed the pictures back in the envelope without even looking at the last one. She threw the envelope as hard as she could in the direction of the front door, then tried pretending the pictures didn't exist, but it was no use. She felt overwhelmed; she felt her world was collapsing and closing in on her. The evil disaster that was predicted was coming true, and there was nothing she could do to prevent it. She threw herself on the couch, wrapped her arms around her knees, and coiled into a fetal ball. If I get all closed up, she thought, maybe I can make this nightmare go away. Slowly she rocked back and forth. It didn't calm her. Huge spasms racked her body. She cried uncontrollably.

*   *   *

Earlier that day three teenagers had been sitting in the wooded area behind their high school drinking beer. Dave Stanley, the ringleader, wore a black, peaked baseball cap with the N-over-Y emblem of the New York Yankees—strangely out of place in suburban Philadelphia—backwards on his head. Shocks of unkempt hair stuck out on all sides.

He had met the other two in the hall after third period class.

"School sucks," he had said. "I'm going wacky cooped up in here. Let's get outta here. Let's *do something*."

"Yeah. Let's go have some fun," they had agreed. "School is so fucking boring."

"We could do some brew," Dave said.

"Good idea," they agreed.

They sneaked down the hallway glancing over their shoulder to make sure they weren't being noticed. The bell was ringing for fourth period class as they walked out a side door. Laughing and joking they walked the five blocks to Dave's house. In the pantry he took the keys to his mother's car from the pegboard where they were hanging.

"Where is she today?" one of them asked.

"Damned if I know. Probably with one of her do-gooder groups. Lucky for us the car is here. Somebody must've picked her up. You guys wait here while I buy the beer. It won't look good if they see a car full of rowdies. They might check my ID."

Dave brazenly entered the beer distributor certain that he would have no trouble buying beer even though he was below the legal age. He credited that to the three-day growth of patchy stubble which he didn't like but tolerated. ("The damned thing itches," he complained, "but I'm keeping it because it makes me look older.") The bored clerk rang up his purchases without questioning him.

Dave returned home, picked up his two friends, and drove back to school. He parked in the last row of the parking lot, tossed each of his companions two six-packs ("I bought 'em, you carry 'em," he said.), and led the way deep into the woods which separated the school from the neighboring properties. Dave hitched up his pants, sat down on a fallen tree trunk, and reached out his hand for a can. As they handed him one, the other two boys snapped open cans and began to drink. The more they drank, the more raucous their voices became and the more they heaped abuse on the teachers they hated. They punctuated their vicious invective by crushing the empties and throwing them violently into the woods.

Two hours later the beer was gone.

"Seeing as how we're out of beer, we gotta find something else to do," Dave said. "No way I'm goin' back to school." His words came out slightly slurred.

"We c'n go to the mall and hang out," one said. The others nodded agreement and they stumbled back to the car.

At the King of Prussia Plaza, Neiman Marcus and Nordstrom were in no mood to have three tipsy, obnoxious teenagers in baggy pants belted loosely around their hips, making rude and vulgar comments to their customers and sales staff. Customers scattered in all directions as the trio meandered down the aisles. When they began to finger the merchandise and derisively shout out the prices, a terrified clerk called store security. As two men fell in step behind them, Dave growled, "We got shadows. Let's get outta here."

They prowled the mall corridors, leered at the few girls they saw, then muttered—but loud enough to be heard—obscenities about them. They soon became tired and bored and started to head back toward the car. As they stood outside the entrance and pulled cigarettes from the pack Dave offered, they noticed a sleek, sporty Jaguar XK8 coupe ten cars down the first row in the parking lot. The sunlight twinkling from its gleaming forest green finish seemed to wink at them, seemed to beckon them.

"Look at that," Dave said in awe. "How'd you like to drive something like that? I wonder how fast it goes? Whatever, it's got to be faster than my mom's Toyota."

They sauntered over to the car. Dave looked in the driver's window and ran his eyes admiringly over the rich, leather interior. He squinted as something silvery glittering near the steering wheel caught his attention.

"Well, I'll be damned. The schmucks left the keys in the car," he shouted. "C'mon. We're going for a ride." He opened the door, bowed from his waist, and motioned them in.

"I'm not helping you steal no fuckin' car," one of his buddies said, shying away.

"We're not stealing it. We're only borrowing it for a little while. We'll test drive it and bring it back when we're done," Dave promised him. "Now get in," he barked, as he shoved them into the car. They meekly obeyed and sank into the plush leather seats. Dave sniffed deeply. "Still has that new car smell," he said. "I like that."

Oblivious of the mall security guards racing toward him, he turned the key and the motor whispered to life. Dave revved the engine and smiled at the low-pitched hum. This is definitely not gonna be like my mother's Toyota, he thought.

As he backed the car out, tires screeching, he narrowly missed crushing a couple putting their infant's stroller in the rear of their minivan. The security guards tried frantically to wave him down, but Dave, nearly running them over, sped toward the nearest mall exit. The guards yelled into their walkie-talkies for the Upper Merion

Township Police to come fast. Dave shot around a line of cars waiting for a traffic light to change, and careened onto the highway, fighting the wobbling steering wheel to maintain control. His horrified friends curled up in the back seat, buried their heads in their hands, and terrified, shivered in silence. Luckily Dave barreled through the intersection without a scratch. He ignored the furious drivers who pointed middle fingers at him and shook their fists.

The sound of sirens in the distance triggered a blast of adrenalin into Dave's nervous system. He floored the accelerator in an attempt to beat the changing traffic light at the Route 202 intersection. This time he was not as lucky. His brain, numbed and dumbed by alcohol, miscalculated badly; the light had been red for a good three seconds when he came hurtling through. With a sickening crunch the Jaguar crumpled into the driver's side of a Chevrolet sedan negotiating a left turn toward the Plaza's parking lot. A cloud of dust fizzled up from the impact followed by the tinkle of falling metal and glass parts; then there was an eerie silence. Shocked motorists, unable to move, stared open-mouthed at the terrible scene of destruction.

A minute later the shrill whine of a siren cut through the stillness, and a police car with its blue and red lights flashing screeched to a stop. The officer took one look at the mangled cars, shook his head, and phoned for an ambulance. I'd be surprised if anyone comes out of this alive, he thought. The Jaguar had accordioned to half its original length. The engine and radiator had smashed into the passenger compartment crushing the life from Dave and his two companions. No hope for them, the policeman sighed feeling for pulses in their necks. He inspected the sedan. The driver showed no signs of life. His left side had been splintered by the impact; broken ribs poked out in all directions. One of them must have punctured his heart, the policeman thought. The passenger, he noticed, was still alive, buckled in her seat belt, but she gasped for air and struggled to breathe. When the rescue squad arrived, he waved at them to hurry and pointed to her.

As he watched the EMTs lift her from the car, the patrolman noticed a wallet sticking out of the driver's back pocket. He gingerly lifted it out, slid out the driver's license, and read the name—Alberto Fanelli.

Chapter 19

$\mathcal{A}$s night fell, Tony returned home. Silently he entered the house hoping to minimize or avoid contact with Judy. Three days had passed since they had fought over the panties she had found in his laundry, and they still had not made up. Judy had purposely refused to pick them up from the foyer, and just this morning Tony had gotten tired of stepping over them and had taken them out to the garage and tossed them in the garbage can. Even with the tension between them, he was not prepared for the blackness that greeted him now; not a light was on in the entire house.

"Judy," he said softly. "Are you home?"

No response.

A little louder: "Anybody home?" he asked with a hint of worry in his voice.

No answer.

What the hell was wrong, he wondered. She should be home by now. He flipped on the lights and walked into the living room. At first he didn't notice her. Then he saw her hunched up like a ball and shaking on the couch. He stood still and looked down at her for a moment startled, not knowing what was wrong or what to do.

He said, "What's the matter, Jude? Are you sick?" Was she in shock? he wondered.

Gently he bent down over her to she if she was breathing. She uncoiled explosively like a wound-too-tight spring being released and barely missed uppercutting his chin with her head. She sat up and began to brush the river of tears from her face with the back of her hand. Startled, Tony jumped back. He was shocked speechless by her appearance—her face was puffy and spotted with red blotches. Judging from her swollen eyes she had been crying for a while. She fixed him with an angry stare; her eyes sizzled and he could have sworn they shot lightning bolts which he actually sensed coursing through him.

He struggled to speak through the tightness in his chest and managed to repeat, "What's the matter?"

"You're what's the matter," she managed to blurt out between sobs. "This is bad, Tony. Very bad. The worst." Slowly she felt her self-control and confidence return, but that was quickly replaced as the sight of her husband, the reason for her pain, caused a volcano of rage to erupt inside her.

"I'm at a loss here as to what's going on," he said. Then he followed her finger as she slowly pointed to a manila envelope that lay on the floor. In the darkness he had walked over it without seeing it.

"Is that the problem?" He nodded toward it.

She shot her words like bullets. "Goddamn right it is." She bolted up from the couch, pushed him back out of her way, and walked over to it. With shout of "Here," she picked it up and fired it at him with a backhand frisbee-fling. It bounced off his stomach and fell to the floor. He looked at her quizzically, bent over, and retrieved it.

He pulled out the first picture, examined it carefully, then deflated and sank into the recliner. How'd they do that? he thought. There was no one else in the room. Where could someone have hidden to get that picture? Suddenly he understood. That was Kate's big surprise—a two-way mirror. Wait 'til I get hold of that bitch, he thought. I'll fuckin' kill her. Jeezus Christ, I should have been more careful. Well, there's no way I can change what's done; let's try to put a positive spin on this. As Fred said, I can't deny, or lie, so I gotta talk my way out of this one.

He studied the picture for a long time desperately searching for words.

"It's me," he said dejectedly, tapping it with his forefinger, "in the picture."

"No shit, Dick Tracy," Judy roared as she balled her fists and repressed the urge to punch him in the face. She stood in front of him, arms akimbo, glaring down at him.

"I made a mistake," he said meekly.

"You sound like a fucking soap opera. Next you'll say, 'Please take me back,'" she screamed showering him with a froth of saliva. He hung his head not able to look her in the eye. "I'm so goddamned mad I can't think straight," she went on. "Those promises you made meant nothing to you. Our marriage means nothing to you. All the trust we had is gone. And you lied when I told you about the phone call. It couldn't be you, you said. I was supposed to have faith in you, you said." She panted for breath then continued. "My mother was right. She tried to warn me about you goddamn Sicilians."

Judy remembered growing up to the sound of her mother's tirades about how proud she should be that she was a Roman. Not an Italian, but a Roman. "Sicilians are nothing but trash," she would say. "They're not even Italians. They're Greeks and Arabs. What can you expect from them?"

Tony, trying for a way out, jarred her back to the present. "Now wait a minute," he said.

"Wait for what? You've been caught fucking another woman. I can't live with that. I can't cope with that."

He headed off in another direction.

"I swear it was the first time." "With her," he added silently to himself. "Judy, we've had twenty good years of marriage. Don't throw it away for one crazy night," he pleaded. "Please gimme a break. I got carried away. I can't give you a good reason for it; it must have been some kind of seven-year itch. Anyway, I won't see her again. It's over between her and me. I know you won't believe this, but I told her weeks ago that that night would be the first and last time." He calmed his voice considerably and spoke in slow, deliberate tones. "I'm not going to see her any more, I promise. It's okay; it's over now." He stood up and reached out a hand to touch her, soothe her, comfort her.

She slapped his hand away, and he slunk back into the chair. "You're damn right it's over. It's over between you and me. I want out. I want the big 'D.' Divorce. We're finished, you shithead, . . . you bastard!" Astonished at the sound of her words, she began shaking.

Tony paled. "Before you say anything else, listen for a second. Think again about all the good years we had together. We had a lot of fun and good times and . . . and there's more to come."

"Stop trying to weasel out of this."

Tony slid to the edge of his chair. "I've done a good job being a husband, and I couldn't have expected more from you as a wife. We've had a too good a partnership to toss it all away now."

"Let's get back to the main subject, Tony. First of all who's the bimbo bitch in bed with you?"

"It doesn't matter. She's not important." He paused for breath as Judy continued to glare at him. "The point here is that I promise to be faithful to you from now on."

"You promised me before to be faithful. We promised each other," Judy said, and despite her effort to hold herself together, began to sob. "And you broke that promise. Now you expect me to believe it when you promise again."

"I sorry; I really am. I'm guilty, and I have no defense. What can we do to work this out?"

Judy flared up, arms windmilling, wild-eyed, boiling over.

"What can WE do? What can WE do? WE can't do anything, because one of WE doesn't give a shit any more. Turn up your hearing aid. I WANT OUT!" Exhausted, she staggered away from him and crumpled back down on the couch.

"I love you too much for this to ruin things between us. You're worth everything to me, and I don't want to lose you. And I don't want to lose us. You want me to be faithful? You got it. For Chrissakes give me a chance—one chance," he pleaded. "Don't toss our future down the drain 'cause I made one mistake. After twenty years don't I deserve a second chance? Just *one* second chance?"

Boy, I must be stupid, Judy thought. He's starting to get to me. I guess I do owe him something. He's been a good husband for all these years—at least as far as I know. Tony saw her face soften and, hoping for an opening, came over to her. He sat down next to her and put his arms around her: this time she didn't resist. He hugged her tight, but she remained limp in his arms and did not hug him back.

"I'm really sorry, Jude. It's you I love. I've always loved only you. I got sidetracked—maybe it was road-loneliness. I swear it won't happen again; ever. And I'll do whatever you want to make it up to you. Don't throw away all the good we've had, and we've got coming, because I screwed up once." (Whoops, he thought, bad choice of words.) "I know we can work this out."

Fury gone, Judy slipped her arms gently around him. "I'll think it over," she said quietly. "We'll talk about it again in a couple of days."

As she turned her face toward him and prepared to rest on his shoulder, the phone rang breaking the mood. She pushed herself free from his grasp. When she picked up the phone, Tony turned his back to her and methodically tore up the pictures into little pieces and stuffed them back into the envelope. "Son-of-a-bitch," he muttered. "I'm gonna kill the son-of-a-bitch that did this."

Tony's sister, Angela, was on the phone. Angela was the family cheerful Pollyanna, always looking on the bright side of every dark cloud, but now her voice was shaking and sobbing; she spoke in an uncharacteristically sorrowful tone.

"I'm glad I got you instead of Tony," she said to Judy.

"What's the matter?" Judy asked. "What's wrong?"

She cried uncontrollably. "It's my parents. Our parents."

"Yes. What happened?" Judy urged her on.

"They were in an accident, an automobile accident."

"What? Are they hurt?" This was turning into the day from hell, Judy thought, as she nervously waited for Angela to pull herself together.

Tony walked over next to her and pulled the receiver away from her ear, trying to hear the other end of the conversation.

"What's happening Judy?" Tony whispered to her.

"Shhh. I'm trying to find out," Judy said. She yanked the receiver from him and placed it tightly against her ear.

"Who is it?" Tony asked.

"Quiet. I'm trying to hear."

"Mama's in the hospital," Angela cried. "She's badly hurt. She'll recover. But Papa . . ." She choked as she searched for the right words. "Papa's not all right. He's not coming home . . . ever again. He's dead."

"Oh my God. That's awful, Angela. When did this happen?"

"This afternoon out at the mall. They called me an hour ago and I rushed right over to the hospital. I'm there now."

Tony noticed tears welling in Judy's eyes and a look of horror pass across her face. "What's wrong? What's my sister saying?" he asked. Judy put her finger to her lips and motioned for him to be quiet.

Angela's voice filled with rage. "Goddamn drunk high school punks. They stole a car and were running from the police when they smashed into . . . The three kids are dead, and I'm glad. Otherwise I would've killed them myself."

"Is there anything I can do to help?" Judy asked. While she waited for Angela's answer, she thought: it's that terrible premonition of evil again. I thought Tony's cheating would be the end of it, but it looks like that was only the beginning. The more she thought about it, the more she had a sinking feeling that this wasn't the worst. Her intuition told her that as bad as things were, this wasn't the end. She sensed that there was even greater misfortune out there waiting for her. She pushed those thoughts from her conscious and looked at Tony standing next to her. Poor Tony, she thought. He adored his father. They were more than father and son, they were best friends, too. Tony will be crushed by his death.

The tearful, trembling voice on the phone, on the verge of breaking down, interrupted her. "I gotta hang up. I don't want to talk about this any more. I can't think straight. You'll have to tell Tony."

Gently Judy hung up, pushed Tony into the recliner, knelt down next to him, and put her arms loosely around his neck. She rested her head on his chest for a second, then looked up into his eyes.

"Tony. Angela had some bad news," she began.

*　　*　　*

"I'm going to the hospital," Tony said, tears streaming down his cheeks, "I've got to go see Mom." He raced out the door with Judy following closely behind.

"I'll drive," she said grabbing the keys from his hand.

He didn't resist but urged her, "Okay, but hurry."

Tony sat, white as a sheet, trembling in the passenger seat. He squeezed his eyes shut and tried to erase the snippets of scenes shuttling in and out of his head. His mother lying in a hospital bed, his father in a coffin. He struggled to cope with the wrenching changes that were happening in his life. My father, my best friend, he thought. I can't believe I'm never going to see him again. And Judy threatening to leave me isn't making this any easier. A terrible wave of depression swept over him. He tried to suppress it by thinking of the good times he had spent with his father.

He used to ask me questions about his business, Tony remembered. I was his marketing consultant. Tony thought of the small tailor shop his father had owned near the house where they lived. As the years went by the customers who had ordered shirts and suits from him began to patronize Wanamaker's and Boyd's. After all those stores had a larger selection, the clothes were cheaper, already made and hanging on the racks, so they could take their purchases home with them the same day. It was Tony who urged Alberto to branch out into dry cleaning. When it proved to be successful, Alberto delighted in telling his friends that it was his brilliant son who had rescued his failing business.

Judy glanced at Tony out of the corner of her eye. He caught her look, and it shocked him back to the present.

"Pop never hurt anyone in his life," he said sobbing and choking on the words. "He was one of the few good guys left in this world. Why did this happen to him?"

Hurting people, Judy thought angrily, the tears began streaming down her face again. He's concerned with people being hurt. Does he know how much he's hurt me? How can he be so insensitive? Well, maybe that's not fair to him; he has his father's death on his mind now, but will he ever realize what he's done to our relationship?

Somewhere in the darkness a clock chimed ten as they ran up the hospital steps. Panting from exertion and emotion, Tony approached the receptionist. He struggled to get the words out: "Fanelli—room number?"

"F-a-n-e-l-l-i," she said as she typed the letters into her computer terminal. She stared at the screen for a moment. "Lucia Fanelli?" she asked. Tony nodded. "She may not be able to talk to you," she said. "She's had a bad time of it."

"If we can't talk to her, we'll sit with her and wait until we can," Tony said. "What's the room number? I'm her son for Godsakes."

"That'll be Room 625. Follow the blue line on the floor. That will take you to the elevator . . ."

Tony cut her short. "Will she be . . . all right?"

"I don't have that information on my screen. You'll have to ask her doctor."

Slowly they pushed open the door to Room 625. A comatose body lay on the bed, eyes shut, propped up on two pillows. Judy's mouth dropped open. She looked like a corpse. Her sallow complexion reminded Judy of phyllo dough, and her chest barely moved, her breathing was so shallow. Intravenous solution trickled down a clear plastic tube that snaked from a hanging vinyl bag into a needle stuck into the back of her hand. What sounded like a chorus of crickets chirped softly in the background—instruments monitoring her vital signs. Tony gulped as he fought the nausea which rose inside him; tears trickled from the corners of his eyes. He clung to Judy's hand like a drowning man to a life preserver.

A nurse stood by the bed gently stroking her patient's face.

"I'm her son, Tony," he said to the nurse. "How is she?"

"Hi. I'm Diane," the nurse said quietly. "Your sister, Angela, just left. You should be able to talk to your mom soon. She wakes up for a minute or two every once in a while and then falls back to sleep. She's had a very rough time, but the doctor said if there are no complications, she should recover. But it'll take a while. She'll be in the hospital a couple of weeks, maybe for a month . . . or two, and then she'll have to recuperate at home for a couple more months before she's a hundred per cent. At her age healing takes a long time."

Lucia Fanelli blinked her eyes slowly, fought to hold them open, and smiled weakly at Tony. She mouthed his name, but no words came out.

"Ma. How are you?" Tony said. He just managed to fight off another wave of nausea that envelped him.

Summoning all her strength, she managed to say: "I'll be all right." Her eyes closed.

"Ma," Tony sobbed.

"It's okay. I'm resting," she said. Her eyes remained closed. "I feel like I'm on a cloud. Floating along."

"She's had a lot of painkiller," Diane whispered.

Suddenly her eyes fluttered open, pink color flooded back to her face. Judy thought, if you could blank out all the medical equipment you'd think she was perfectly normal. She cleared her throat and said to Tony, "I can't talk real good right now, but I've been doing a lot of thinking. And there's something I want to give you." She stopped speaking for a moment and coughed softly. Tony leaned closer to her. "I can't talk no more today. You come back and see me tomorrow. Go home now and let me get some rest."

"You should go now, like she says," Diane said. "Come back in the morning."

As they rode down in the elevator Judy said to Tony: "She seems to be holding her own, and the nurse said she would recover."

Tony: "It's such a shock. I've never seen her sick a day in her life. The only time she's ever been in a hospital was to have children or to visit her friends."

Judy changed the subject: "I wonder what she wants to give you. This'll be a real surprise."

Tony said nothing but thought to himself: I've had enough surprises to last me for a long time. The last one screwed up my life but good. Now Mom's promising another. I hope this one is better than the last one.

Chapter 20

The next morning when Judy and Tony went back to the hospital, they stopped the doctor as he was leaving Lucia's room. He confirmed what the nurse had said the night before—recovery would take a long time—and he added, "I think you'll find her a little better today than she was last night. She's had a good night's rest."

After entering the room, Tony took one look at his mother's pale face and motionless body and couldn't agree. He consoled himself by deciding that she didn't look any worse. He stared at her for a moment; she did not move.

"You awake, Ma?" he whispered.

She didn't answer but blinked her eyes three times in quick succession and strained to sit up. Judy helped her to an upright position and held her there while she plumped up two pillows and stuffed them behind her back. She gently brushed the wisps of hair from her eyes and caressed her cheek. Tony kissed her, pulled up a chair near her bed, and sat down. Lucia reached out a hand, caught Tony's hand, and squeezed it tenderly. Her mouth moved but no words came out.

"How are you today?" Tony said.

With great effort she lifted her upper body and motioned for Judy to put another pillow under her head. After which, she gathered her strength and willed herself to speak. The words came very slowly.

"I'm going to be okay. It's Papa who got the worst of it. They told me this morning that he died," she said in a halting, quivering, high-pitched voice which Tony hardly recognized. Tears crawled from the corners of her eyes down her cheek. Judy pulled a tissue from the box by the bed and gently wiped them away.

"We're all so very sorry," Judy said. "It's a real tragedy about him. But the doctor said you'll be okay in a few weeks."

Lucia took a labored breath. "I didn't even see it happen. We were turning to go into the shopping center . . . It happened so fast. I didn't see anything coming, then I heard a loud crash. And it felt like someone hit me with a hammer. The next thing I know, I'm here in the hospital. I don't remember anything else."

"Goddamn bastards," Tony muttered to himself.

There was an awkward silence with no one knowing quite what to say. Lucia closed her eyes and breathed so slowly that Tony was afraid she was dying.

Finally she spoke in a worried tone. "Tony. There's something around you," she rasped. "It's a cloud. But a bad cloud. Something bad . . . . I saw it last night, but I couldn't talk then." She tried to brush her hands through the air as if to wave it away, but she was weak and her arms fell to her sides after one futile attempt. She crooked a finger at Judy beckoning her closer. "I can't do this. My arms have no strength. You take off my necklace." She pointed to a delicate silver chain with a tiny silver horn dangling from it which hung around her neck. Judy unclasped it gingerly.

"When I was a little girl in Sicily, my mother gave it to me to keep evil away," Lucia said. "I've never taken it off since the day she put it on me. Never. Now I give it to Tony. He needs it. Judy you put it on Tony's neck. It will fight off the evil and bring him good luck. But you," she stared at Tony, "must never take it off. As long as you wear it, you're protected. You take it off and . . ." She left the rest of the sentence hanging.

As Judy started to put it on him, Tony held up his hand for her to stop. "How can you think this is lucky, Ma?" he asked. "Look at you all broken up in a hospital. It brought you bad luck, not good luck."

"You crazy . . . ," she began. Her voice got louder. "Your father died in the accident, and I'm here." She rose from the pillow, sat upright and almost shouted, "ALIVE!" She slumped back exhausted and spoke so quietly that Judy and Tony leaned over close to her mouth to hear what she was saying. "My good luck was that I lived. He didn't. Now you wear it," she commanded.

Judy clipped it around his neck.

The old woman whispered into Tony's ear, "You listen to me, and listen good. You must never take it off. If you do, all your good luck will go with it. Promise me you'll always wear it. Always."

"I promise, Ma," he said.

I know what his promises are worth, Judy thought to herself. I wonder if he'll keep this one.

The door swung open, and a nurse swished in. "Out you two," she said. "Let the patient get some rest." Flicking her wrist, she shooed them into the hall.

In the hall Tony pleaded with Judy, "With Mom laid up like this, let's postpone talking about our . . . problem. Can we? Please?" He automatically flashed his best salesman's smile at her.

How can I be angry with him now, she thought. His father dead; his mother in the hospital. "Okay," she said reluctantly. "But I'm not forgetting about those pictures. We'll have to get that settled *soon*."

I've bought some time, Tony thought. I'll have to think of some way to get around those pictures. He heaved a sigh of relief.

On the way out of the hospital, Judy put her arm around Tony's waist and gave him an "I'm with you" squeeze. He looked at her gratefully and smiled a "thanks."

"Why don't you take the rest of the day off; stay home and relax?" she asked him.

"Sounds like a good idea, but I think I'd feel better if I go to work. It'll help get my mind off it."

"Okay. Drop me off at my office, and I'll see you for supper."

When they reached her building, she opened the car door, gave him a serious kiss on the lips, and rushed from the car. Tony was too dazed to say goodbye, and only an impatient driver honking behind him shook him out of his trance. He congratulated himself on his salesmanship. I talked her into postponing talking about divorce, he thought. Maybe I can get her to postpone it forever. He smiled as he drove away, never realizing that she had only agreed out of pity for him because of his father's death. She had every intention of talking to Bob Dolan, the lawyer in her firm who specialized in divorces, as soon as he had a free minute.

As she opened the door to The Packard Tower, Judy tried to sort out her thoughts. Forgive and forget, she said to herself. I can forgive, but I can't ever forget. I'm going to find out who that woman is with the heart tattoo if it takes me forever. And regardless of what happens to me and Tony, she's going to pay for this.

*   *   *

Judy tapped her foot impatiently as she rode the elevator up to her office. It seemed to stop at every floor and take forever. She raced by the receptionist without stopping, but Sara saw her in the hallway and followed her to her desk.

"I was beginning to worry about you," Sara said. "What happened you're so late?"

"I had to stop at the hospital before work," Judy said.

Sara's mouth dropped open. "Hospital? What's wrong? Who's sick?"

Judy told her about the accident and the death of her father-in-law. Sara expressed her sympathies then launched into a discussion of how to bring up of children properly so they don't steal cars and kill innocent people. Judy flicked her wrist at her to shoo her away; she didn't leave but droned on. Judy grabbed a manila folder from a corner of her desk, flipped it open, and began to type rapidly on her keyboard. Finally Sara took the hint and left without a word.

Fifteen minutes later when she looked up from her work, she noticed the red light had been blinking on her answering machine. She pushed the "play" button and heard her mother's sorrowful voice say, "I just heard about the tragedy. Why didn't you call me right away?" That's right, Mom, she said to herself, lay on the guilt.

She dialed her mother's number and accepted her sympathies about the accident. Then Judy told her about the pictures of Tony.

Her mother lapsed into the high-decibel, agitated Italian she used when she became excited. "See," her mother said animatedly, "that's why we didn't send you to Parochial school."

Judy had heard this story a hundred times and said to herself, Here we go again.

"When you were a kid, you asked why did we send you to public school. You remember?" her mother said in a loud voice.

"Yes, Ma. I remember," Judy shouted in Italian. It was an automatic reflex—when her mother spoke Italian, Judy answered in Italian; when her mother raised her voice, Judy raised her voice. Realizing she could not stop her mother from repeating the story, she closed her eyes. She remembered the first time she had heard this harangue; she was a sophomore in high school.

"You want to know why you go to public school?" her mother had ranted. "I got to open your eyes? You don't see what's going on around here? Look at the Italians who live in our neighborhood. Are they Romans like us? No! They come from Naples, Calabria, or— even worse—Sicily. And who are these people from Sicily? They're farmers, peasants, bandits, scum, *Mafiosi*. You're a smart girl. Where do they send their children to school? Parochial school. So we send you to public school so you won't have nothing to do with them."

And now in a voice so loud Judy was sure they could hear two floors away, her mother added, "After I told you, then what do you do? You marry one of those Sicilians, and he turns out to be a bum. You tell me Tony was with another woman. I tell you I'm not surprised."

Judy said nothing.

In a gentler voice her mother said, "You gotta expect those kind of men to have other women. They all do it. They're pigs," she muttered under her breath but loud enough for Judy to hear.

"Ma . . . ," Judy began.

"Anyway," her mother interrupted, "you married a Sicilian. You do what the Sicilian women do. They look the other way. As long as he is good to you—he don't hit you, does he?" She raced on not waiting for an answer. "You overlook this."

No sense arguing with her, Judy thought. "I'll think about it, Ma," she said. "There's something else," Judy added. "You remember Carlo Fiore, my senior prom date?"

"If he's the one who writes for the newspaper, I know his mother a little. She's always bragging about him, but she's a nice woman. They're from Abruzzi."

"I had lunch with him the other day. He's taking a job in Rome."

"Ah, Rome," Her mother sighed and launched into another favorite harangue. "The rest of Italy isn't worth anything. You never forget, you are a Roman. Your Papa and I were both born in Rome. You understand what that means? Rome is like a magnet for all Italians. Like Mecca for a Moslem. Even the poorest peasant in Italy saves money to travel to Rome at least once before he dies. Newlyweds come from all over Italy to honeymoon in Rome. Rome is the heart of Italy. And to be born Roman is . . ."

"Okay. Okay," Judy interrupted. "Ma I have to go to work now. My desk is loaded with . . ."

"You go, but you remember what I'm telling you." Abruptly she said, "Goodbye," and hung up.

She had heard her mother's speeches so many times over the years that she knew them by heart; but now her words started to sink in. Could my mother be right about Rome and Romans? she wondered. Am I really special? Something stirred inside her, a yearning, a desire, a wish. Someday, Judy thought, in order to be a whole person, in order to be me, I have to go Rome, saturate myself in the culture, and explore my roots. Is this a pipe dream or will I get there someday?

Charlie Price had been on his way to an early lunch and, as he passed by in the hall, had heard Judy Fanelli shouting to her mother on the phone. He had no intention of eavesdropping but slowed down intending to deliver a snide request for order and discipline. Something like: There are people trying to work here, keep it down, he thought. However, when he realized Judy was speaking Italian, he stood rooted to the spot and smiled.

My translator for Leon what's-his-name, he thought. God has provided me with a translator.

*   *   *

That evening as Judy returned home from work and opened the front door she heard the phone ringing.

It was Kate. "It was on the five o'clock news," she said. "I was shocked to hear about the accident and your in-laws. Your poor father-in-law. I'm terribly sorry. What the hell happened?"

Judy plopped onto the couch with the cordless and told her the details.

"How's Tony holding up?" Kate asked.

"It's a real blow for him. He's really shook up." Judy paused for a moment. "On top of that we have another serious problem." She took a deep breath and then let it out. "The pictures came yesterday."

"And what did they show?" Kate asked.

Her body tensed as she remembered the glossy photo of Tony knotted in the embrace of another woman. "T-T-Tony with another w-w-woman . . . ," she managed to stutter.

"Oh?" It came out as a question.

Judy didn't speak for a minute, then said, as she forced herself to stop shaking, "This is hard for me to talk about, Kate; especially with everything else that's going on."

"Take your time. Did they show *everything*? Were they 'admissible as evidence' as you lawyers say?"

She took a deep breath. "There's no doubt it was Tony. And there's no doubt he was in bed with another woman."

"Wow! Tony. Who'd've believed that?" She wondered if she sounded sincere.

"No question about it." Judy felt a wave of sadness come over her, and a tightness in her chest as if someone was sitting on her.

"Any idea who the woman is?" Kate asked.

"No. She's hidden in all the pictures." Judy began to hyperventilate. "Talking to you about this . . ." She gasped for breath. "I can feel myself getting superpissed off at him all over again," she blurted out quickly.

"Judy, you know how I feel about this."

"Yes I do. But think how I feel. It makes me feel like a real loser; as if I'm not giving him everything he needs. What is it he wants that he's not getting from me? Is it sex, or comfort, or a friend to talk to? I've tried my best to give him all those things. But the worst thing is that he broke his promise. He promised to be faithful and broke it. And now he's promising not to do it again. Oh, Kate should I believe him?"

"That's for you to decide. I can't help you there. For me, as long as Greg comes home for dinner most of the time, and he's there when I need him, that's all I expect from a husband. If he screws around on his own time, that's okay with me. Look, Judy, you're too uptight about the whole thing. Nobody's into fidelity any more. Christ, look at our presidents—Roosevelt, Eisenhower, Kennedy, Clinton.

Republicans, Democrats, it doesn't matter. And hey, not only today but in the Bible. King David decided to have another guy's wife, and then sent the husband to die in battle. If that was okay for him, can you blame Tony?"

"Bible stories prove my point," Judy said. "They were written to show us the way to morality, not to encourage us to behave like they did."

"We disagree on this. We always have. End of discussion. So what are you going to do about it?"

"Right now, nothing. He's suffering enough with his mother in the hospital and his father dead. I'm not going to make his life any more miserable by smacking him with a divorce."

"I know you'll think it over carefully before you decide. How's Mrs. Fanelli senior doing?"

"They think eventually she'll be okay. But it'll be a long healing process. We went to see her last night and she looked like death warmed over. Hell, she was almost in a coma. But this morning she seemed better. Which reminds me. Tony made another promise this morning . . . to his mother. We'll see how he keeps this one."

"What was that?" Kate asked.

"His mother gave him a good luck charm, a silver horn, to wear around his neck. She said it would bring him good luck as long as he wore it, so he promised her he would never take it off."

"So what's the big deal?"

"He hates to wear any kind of jewelry, especially around his neck. He won't even wear his wedding ring. It will be interesting to see if he keeps this promise."

"Greg's driving up now," Kate said. "I've got to go make supper. I'll call you soon."

Judy started to hang up the phone when a fleeting thought came to her.

She called,"Kate" into the receiver, but the only answer she got was a dead-line buzz.

In all the excitement, she thought, I forgot to tell her about the tattoo, the heart tattoo. Oh well, I'll tell her next time we talk.

*　　*　　*

Five seconds after she hung up the phone, it rang again. Still feeling shaky, she didn't feel like talking to anybody and let the answering machine pick it up. But her nervousness disappeared when she heard Carlo's voice, and she quickly yanked the receiver off the hook.

"Don't listen to the message, Carlo," she said. "You've got a real, live human being on the phone."

"Are you screening your calls?" he asked.

"I just hung up from Kate and was ready to start dinner," she apologized.

"I'm only kidding. I saw some Fanellis' were in a car crash, and one was killed. Are they any relation?"

"They're my in-laws. Tony is very upset about it. He and his father were really good friends—more than just a father and son."

"I'm very sorry about his father. How's his mother doing?" Carlo asked.

"It looks like she'll recover, but it may take a long time." She paused for a moment. "I've had another bad shock." She took a deep breath. "Remember those pictures?" When Carlo didn't respond, she said, "I told you a man called saying he was sending pictures of Tony."

"I was hoping it would turn out to be nothing."

"No. It was something. They came in the mail yesterday. They showed . . ." She sobbed softly. "Damn. I break up every time I talk about this."

"It's okay. You don't have to tell me the details. What are you going to do about it? Can I help?"

"No one can help what's been done." She choked the words out. "I've got to decide what to do on my own. But with his dad dead and his mom in the hospital, I can't dump a divorce on him too." I don't want Carlo to hear me like this, she thought as she struggled to keep her voice from quivering.

"Excuse me. I've got to go now." And before she could stop herself she said, "I'll call you before you leave for Italy." She hung up quickly, grabbed a Kleenex, and sobbed.

Chapter 21

On Monday morning Tony woke up especially early so he could stop at the hospital to see his mother. He also had a second reason for getting up early. In the four days since the accident, his concern for his mother had lessened. He saw her improving every day, and she was no longer in critical condition. As his fear for her life faded, it was replaced by a burning anger. I'm going to find out who took those goddamn pictures, he thought, and then I'm going to kick the shit out of him.

He cut his morning visit with his mother as short as he could and still be the attentive son, then slid back behind the wheel of his car. He pulled the cell phone from the glove box and dialed Kate at home then pinched the phone between his shoulder and ear while he started the car.

Answer the phone, he thought as it rang for the fourth time. I don't want the goddamn answering machine. He pulled away from the curb, pounding the steering wheel nervously with his palm. The phone rang twice more before she picked it up.

"Can you talk?" he asked trying to conceal his irritation.

"Oh, hi Tony." Kate yawned. "He left for work, and I'm at least three-quarters awake. I'm still lying in bed, but I've got no appointments this morning until eleven. Sure, let's talk. By the way I heard about your parents. I'm really sorry . . . your poor father."

Tony stopped her short. "Thanks for your sympathy, but I don't want to talk about that right now."

"Then why are you calling? You want some more good sex?"

"Did you tell anybody where you were going that night you were with me?"

"Are you kidding? Why would I do that, silly?" She used her squeaky, little girl voice. "I'm a big girl. I don't tell Mummy or Daddy or my husband where I go at night. Or during the day for that matter."

"Did you set me up?" he growled.

She ignored his anger and spoke calmly, "Set you up? What *are* you talking about?" She was wide-awake now. "Set you up for what?"

"Somebody took pictures of us in bed in that motel room and mailed them to Judy. She was really pissed. Do you know who did that?" Tony yanked the wheel to avoid a driver cutting in front of him and the phone squirted from his ear. He shook his fist at the other car and picked up the phone from the floor.

"How could someone take pictures?" Kate was saying. "I don't know of any camera that can see through walls. Maybe Superman with his x-ray vision was spying on us, and he transmitted a picture from his eyes to his brain to a special camera." She chuckled.

"This isn't funny. Judy's ready to divorce me over this."

"Ooooo, that's too bad."

"But I'm lucky. It looks like she's forgiven me." The anger rippled in his voice as he snapped at her. "It doesn't take a rocket scientist to figure this out. You and your surprises. One of those mirrored walls must have been one-way glass, and you . . ."

Provoked by the accusatory tone in his voice, she quickly countered, "Now hold on buster. I don't know anything about any one-way glass. I only asked for a mirrored room with a big screen TV. All the quickie motels have one. No one told me about any hidden cameras. Maybe that's how somebody gets his kicks; taking pictures of the customers. Besides why would I send her pictures of us? If I wanted her to know about us, and I don't, I'd pick up the phone and call her. I wouldn't be sneaky about it."

Calmer: "So you didn't hire a photographer?"

"Are you crazy? What the hell for? No way."

"I don't think we should see each other any more," he said. "The sex was great, but I don't want to risk breaking up my marriage. It does mean something to me."

She nervously combed her fingers through her hair. She wasn't ready to break it off with Tony just yet because it sounded like the pictures weren't causing Judy enough heartache for them to be even. Also, she assumed, their preoccupation with the results of the accident was blunting the impact of Tony's infidelity. No, she thought angrily, my revenge is far from complete. I'd better keep this relationship open in case I have to do a repeat performance.

Before she could stop herself she clenched her teeth and snarled, "Don't make any decisions you might regret."

Tony's eyes widened: Did I hear right? Did she threaten me? he wondered.

Before he could react, she got control of herself and changed her tone of voice. She said sweetly: "Even if you want to call it quits, we'll still be friends, won't we?"

"Sure. Sure," Tony said. "We'll still be friends. Now humor me. One more time around. You don't know anything about the pictures that Judy got?"

She said, "That's right. I don't know anything. Tony, I don't want you to worry about this. Everything will turn out all right. Trust me."

Tony hung up, dropped the phone on the seat beside him, and shoved a tape into the cassette player. As the Eagles sang about a "peaceful, easy feeling," he felt anything but peaceful.

I'll get to the bottom of this, he swore.

*   *   *

When she was sure he had hung up, Kate slammed the phone down. Goddamnthemotherfuckinbastardtohell, she thought to herself. I'm so close to my revenge, but I can't seem to get it nailed down. I dropped the panties and the pictures on her. I went through all that fucking with Tony, not that I minded it, but it all seems to be for nothing. So far. She slammed her fist on the night table next to her bed so hard that the phone jumped up then jangled down.

Trying to calm herself and plan her next move, she flopped back on the bed and concentrated on her breathing. She forced herself to take deep breaths. Slowly in, slowly out. I can't think clearly when I'm angry, she thought. Damn Judy. She humiliated me and caused me a lot of pain, and she hasn't suffered nearly enough for us to be even.

She resolved to keep the heat on and the pressure up, even though she could not think of a specific plan. Something will come to me, she thought.

She dressed and started to go downstairs to eat breakfast. On the landing at the top of the stairs she peeked briefly into her daughter's room. Everything was in order. The twin beds were neatly made. Family pictures were lined up in a perfectly straight row on the desktop. She stared wistfully at the picture of a high stepping, smiling, teenage cheerleader with huge, orange pom-poms on her gleaming white boots. A carnelian and white Cornell University pennant hanging on the pink-and-white candy striped wall was a reminder that a sophomore college student slept here when she came home on break.

She frowned as she looked into her son's room. The clutter shouted the message that this was the home of an eighteen-year old high school senior of male extraction. Dirty underwear and crumpled shirts littered the floor like a picked-over display at a clothing flea market. Papers lay scattered four and five deep over every square inch of his desk. The computer was already turned on; flying windows floated across the screen. Post-it notes were stuck on top of each other down the sides of the monitor. On the corner of the desk, peeking out from under his pocket protector with four different colored pens sticking out, she noticed his latest report card—mostly A's. He's two steps away from being a nerd, she thought. How'd he turn out to be so square with a mother like me?

She stared at his bed and sighed. In spite of her repeated nagging it was unmade; rumpled sheets were twisted around a light blue blanket, and the pillow lay on the floor on top of a pair of dirty jeans. As she stood with her hands on hips looking at the mess, she heard the shower running in the hall bathroom—he's taking one of his fifty-minute showers, she thought. I'll have to ask him if there's a girl in his life now since he's so obsessive about his cleanliness. For years it had been a struggle to get him even to brush his teeth let alone wash his face or, heaven forbid, take a shower. I'll surprise him and make his bed, she decided; but nothing else. If I start to clean up the rest of the room, it'll take forever, and it'll only spoil him. She grinned. And he wouldn't be able to find anything if I did that.

Kate smoothed out the bottom sheet, the top sheet, and the light summer blanket; then started to tuck them in. Her fingers touched something under the mattress which felt like cardboard or paper. Can't be the Penthouse magazines, she thought. He stopped hiding those two years ago. Now he shared them with his father and kept them in the second drawer down in his desk. She lifted the mattress carefully and pulled out a dozen bubble packs of some kind of pills. The words "Rohypnol", "2 mg", and "Roche" caught her eye. What the fuck are these? she asked herself.

The screech of the shower faucets being turned off interrupted her thoughts, and before she could decide what to do next, her son, dripping wet with a towel wrapped around his waist, sauntered into the room. She held out the packets at arm's length and looked at him quizzically.

"Good morning, Mom," he said unconcerned. "What do you have there?"

"You tell me. I'd thought I'd surprise you and make your bed, and I found these under your mattress. Are they yours?" she asked brandishing the drugs.

"Well, yes and no," he answered.

"What kind of an answer is that? Have you been to a doctor? Are you sick? Did he prescribe these?"

"No. I haven't been to a doctor, and I'm not sick."

She said nothing hoping he would explain without her having to Torquemada him, but he didn't. While she watched he undid the towel and, totally unashamed and unconcerned about his nudity, began to dry off. The smooth, taut, young body stirred lustful desire deep inside her. She squelched it quickly. He's your son for Godsakes, you sex maniac, she scolded herself.

"Are you taking these drugs?" she asked.

"Hey. You know me better than that. There's no way I'd start frying my brain with those drugs."

Exasperated: "You're getting me ticked off. What the hell are these? And whose are they?"

"They're 'roofies'," he said cheerfully. "The latest 'in' drug."

"If you're not taking them what are you doing with them?" A terrible thought hit her. "Omigod. You're not selling them are you?"

"No, I'm not selling them. Look, here's the story." He sat down on the bed and began to pull on his socks. "You know my buddy Ramon?"

She didn't remember him speaking specifically about a Ramon, but he was always making new friends so she was not surprised. He had inherited his father's easygoing personality and in spite of his leanings to nerdiness, had attracted a slew of friends from all segments of the high school community. The gays, the dweebs, the beauty queens, the grinds, the athletes were all represented in his group of "buddies."

"What about Ramon?" she asked.

"He moved here from Texas about two months ago." He began to blow dry his hair and stopped talking.

"And?" she shouted over the noise.

He shut off the dryer.

"Roofies are real popular in Texas. All the kids use them down there. They're not prescribed or manufactured in the U. S., but you can get them right across the border in Mexico where they're legal. So Ramon got them from his cousin in Juárez. When his family moved here, Ramon brought a supply with him in order to tide him over until he can find a local supplier. But then he found his younger sister dipping into his stash. So he came to me as a friend and asked me to hold them for a while. He doesn't want his sister to get hooked on them."

"This boggles my mind." She ran her fingers nervously through her hair. "You're talking like these were aspirin. You're holding *illegal* drugs for a friend."

"Yeah. But it's no big deal. I told you I wouldn't take any of these drugs myself, and anyway roofies aren't all that bad. They're made by a reputable drug company," he pointed to the Roche name. "They're the most widely prescribed sedative/sleeping pill in Europe. It's not like it's crack cocaine or some other hard drug."

"How do you know so much about this?" she asked warily.

"From the information highway." He jerked his head toward the computer. "It's all on the Web. The DEA has a write-up on it, and so do other health organizations. The media's giving it a lot of attention right now. They call it the 'date rape drug'."

Kate remembered reading a warning her daughter had brought home.

"Your sister brought home a pamphlet from college about being careful drinking punch at fraternity parties."

"Yeah. Some fraternities use and abuse roofies. If a guy wants to get a girl . . . , you know, this drug has a lot of advantages. First, it's cheap. They only cost a buck or two a pill. Second, it's easy to slip in a drink, and they dissolve fast. Third, they lower her . . . um . . . inhibitions. And fourth, and maybe best of all, most of the time they produce temporary amnesia; so the girl gets raped and later doesn't remember anything. She can't testify against anybody."

Speechless Kate sat down on the bed, her head reeling. She buried her face in her hands trying to sort this all out. Gradually her brain stopped spinning, and suddenly the spark of an idea flickered to life then blazed brightly. When he turned toward the mirror and concentrated on the final primping of his hair, she turned her back to him and furtively stuffed one of the bubble packs down the front of her blouse thinking, I have a use for this. She waited until he turned to her, then ceremoniously tucked the others back under his mattress.

"Whatever the reason you're keeping them, I want them out of here, and fast. Next time I find them, I'll flush them down the toilet."

"Okay, Mom. I hear you. Give me a couple of days. I'll ask Ramon to find someone else to help him out, but I can't talk anymore right now. It's so late I don't even have time for breakfast." He pecked her on the cheek, grabbed his books, stuffed them in his backpack, and raced down the stairs and out of the house.

As she left his room, she took the bubble pack from her blouse and twisted it slowly in her fingers. The corner of her mouth curved up in a malicious grin as she thought of where she had found it—she and her son were on the same wavelength when it came to hiding places. She went into her bedroom, lifted her mattress and slid the drugs under it. At the same time she pulled out the little black book— the one she had taken from Tony's car. "Time for you to go to work," she said out loud as she smoothed the bed covers back into place.

At the desk in the kitchen she found a blank envelope. She made her hand tremble to disguise her writing as she scrawled "Mrs. Fanelli" and the Fanelli address on it. She tucked the book inside, licked the flap, slapped a half-dozen stamps on it, sealed it, then kissed it with a smile, and put it in her handbag.

On her way to work she dropped it in a mailbox.

*　　*　　*

The next morning as Tony opened the front door and prepared to leave for work, he shouted upstairs to Judy, "I'll be home late tonight. Between ten and midnight."

She came to the top of the stairs still in her nightgown and glared down at him, hands on hips.

"I hope you don't mind my being suspicious; but where will you be so late, if you don't mind my asking?"

Testily: "This is for your benefit. I have a five o'clock appointment near Washington, and instead of staying overnight and having you worry, I'm coming home. But I suppose the customer will want me to buy him dinner, and if he does, it'll be midnight before I'm home. Would you rather I stay over night down there and come home tomorrow morning?"

Judy said contritely, "No. Late tonight's okay. I'm sorry, but you can't blame me for being suspicious, can you?"

"I told you it's over, and I'm not going to see her again," he said not bothering to conceal his anger.

"Right. I heard you." Sarcastically: "But you'll excuse me if I'm not too trusting or believing right now. Do you plan on finding another 'her' to replace 'her'?"

As the crimson flush rose in his face, Tony summoned all his self-control and through clenched teeth said, punching each syllable, "Good . . . bye." Damn lawyer, he thought. He felt her eyes boring into his back but continued out the door without looking back.

*   *   *

After his last sales call that afternoon, Tony drove to the Calvert Inn and confronted the room clerk.

"I was here about ten days ago," Tony started, nervously drumming his fingers on the counter.

"About a million people come through here in a week, I hope you don't expect me to remember you," the clerk said superciliously.

"No. You didn't see me. The woman I was with picked up the key. We had the 'special' room."

The clerk eyes wandered around the room. "The one with the mirrors?" the clerk whispered, smirking. Tony nodded. The clerk continued in a monotone. "That room gets rented every night;

sometimes two or three times a night. It's reserved at least a week in advance. It's busier than a revolving door. If you want it again, I'll write you in." He opened a date book and picked up a pen.

The man's attitude irritated Tony who balled his fist and banged it on the counter. "I was set up," he snarled. "One of those mirrors in that room must be a fake—it's got one-way glass in it, and someone took pictures of me in that room and sent them to my wife. You work here so you must know what goes on around here. I want to know who took those pictures. Who set me up?" The clerk continued to sneer as Tony continued, "And if you don't tell me . . ."

"Chill out, friend," the clerk spoke calmly. "I only work here. People come in. I give them the key to the room, and that's all I know. I don't know anything about a fake mirror or someone taking pictures."

Tony used every ounce of his self-control to temper his voice. "You must know what goes on around here. Who was behind that mirror taking pictures?"

"I rent rooms. That's my job and that's what I do. I keep my nose out of other people's business."

"Who owns of this place?" Tony demanded.

The clerk smothered a snicker. "Some big corporation. McIntyre Enterprises or something like that. They own a couple dozen motels and a bunch of restaurants. Don't bother looking for Mr. McIntyre, though; he's been dead for years. The manager told me it's like the DuPonts; there are about a thousand McIntyres that own pieces of the corporation."

Exasperated: "Okay. Okay. Who's the manager?"

The clerk stifled a laugh. "That's even funnier. I haven't seen him since my last payday two weeks ago. He knows less about what goes on here than I do. He's got six motels and three restaurants to look after. All he does is come in here every two weeks, ask if everything's okay, drop off my paycheck, and then he leaves. After that, I don't see him for another two weeks."

Fuming, Tony turned on his heel and stomped out.

Chapter 22

That evening Dominic Micaletto ran into a new problem.

When he was in high school, his father, a penny-ante loan shark, used him as a gofer. But mostly what he went fer was women. Dominic found that women were strongly attracted to him. His friends could never figure out why. "You ugly son-of-a-bitch," they would say, "how the fuck you get any woman you want?" It couldn't have been his smile, he rarely smiled. It couldn't have been his intelligence; he cut school so often he was kicked out of Parochial school, ended up in public school, and barely graduated. For starters he had looks to die for: smooth, swarthy skin; inky black hair which he plastered with the greasiest goo that was sold; his nose, eyes, and lips might have been chiseled by some ancient Greek sculptor trying to get a handle on perfection. As if all this handsomeness wasn't enough, he had the muscular build of a boxer. Combined with a generous dollop of charisma the total package was irresistible to women. But Dominic didn't understand and wasn't concerned about *why* women fell for him so easily. Whatever the reason, he snickered to himself, I'm just going to relax and enjoy it.

His father was the oldest of seven boys, and when the youngest got married, his wife was only a few years older than Dominic. Six months after the wedding, Dominic had gone to his uncle's house on an errand. He wasn't home, but she invited him in. One thing led to another, and they spent the afternoon in bed together. And then another afternoon. The afternoons blossomed into a torrid affair— they would furtively plan their moments alone even if it was only for a half an hour. When Dominic's father found out, he pressured him to break it off. "It don't look right. You and your Aunt," he screamed. "There are plenty of other women you can have; but not family." Dominic said nothing but within three days found a replacement.

A few years later Dominic's father, a three-pack-a-day smoker, died from lung cancer. Dominic took over the family loan sharking business and expanded it into bookmaking and extortion. Soon he became tired of fixing his friends up with women for free, so he started a prostitution/escort service. He had no trouble hiring beautiful and willing women, and it became another profit center in his empire.

He bought his mother a home on three acres of land in New Jersey, and in spite of her urging him to come and live with her—"This house is too big for one person," she nagged. "You come live with me."—he chose to stay in the South Philadelphia house where he grew up in order to be close to his business interests.

Tuesday nights he would assemble five or six of his cronies and take them out to eat at a La Luna, a local Italian restaurant. Afterwards they would gather at his house and play cards. Dominic was obsessed with pinochle and insisted that they play until he had won most of their money or, if he was losing, until the early hours of the morning.

And so when his phone rang at ten o'clock on Tuesday evening, an annoyed Dominic glared at the men at the card table, none of whom made a move to answer the phone.

"Get the fuckin' phone Sal," Dominic said to his chief lieutenant, Salvatore Rozzi, who was lounging in the living room with a half empty beer bottle in his hand. "And see what the fuck they want," he added.

Sal lifted the receiver and listened for only a few seconds before saying, "You better get this one Dominic. This is serious shit."

The worried look on Sal's face failed to register with Dominic, who gave him a disgusted "Why couldn't you handle it?" look.

Dominic grabbed the phone from Sal and gruffly snarled, "Hello."

From the other end of the line, a voice that was all business said, "This is a friend calling from New York."

Dominic recognized the code phrase for the right-hand man of the New York boss of bosses. He had spoken to this man on the phone before and although he had never given his name, Dominic knew who he was. A pall came over Dominic's face since he knew these people were not to be trifled with. A suggestion from them was an order to be carried out without question. Dominic had gazed with horror at the bloody, mutilated corpses of men who didn't understand this. Uncharacteristically Dominic spoke quietly and respectfully.

"What can I do for you?" he asked.

"I'll get right to the point," the voice said. "Our organization has too much merchandise for sale and not enough customers. We're looking to expand into Philadelphia, but the problem is we don't have the salesmen. We need you and your organization."

"But my salesmen don't move your kind of merchandise," Dominic equivocated. "They don't know your business, so I don't see how I can help you."

The caller's tone turned threatening. "A good salesman can sell anything. I don't have time to waste. Are you with us or not?"

"I can't give you an answer right now. Let me think it over, and I'll call you back."

"You've got one week. We can't wait any longer than that because this doesn't involve only us. The manufacturer overseas is pressuring us to get his merchandise wider distribution, since he can produce even more than he does now."

Dominic squeezed his eyes shut and winced. He understood that in addition to arm-twisting from New York, he was being further pressured by even more powerful men—the Sicilian Mafia.

"Yeah. Okay. Gimme a week," Dominic said.

When he was sure the line had gone dead, Dominic slammed the receiver into its cradle. Sal always marveled that he could do this with just enough force to shatter the ear drums of anyone unfortunate enough to be standing close by but not quite forcefully enough to destroy the telephone.

"Goddamn it! God fucking damn it!" Dominic ranted.

"What did they want?" Sal asked.

"What did they want? What did they want?" Dominic repeated. He gripped the card table with both hands and unable to control his fury picked it up—cards flew in all directions—and threw it across the room where it crashed into a brick fireplace. Silently as the men stared at the grotesquely twisted table, Dominic began to kick at it—first with his left foot, then his right, over and over again.

"Drugs. Fuckin' drugs," Dominic ranted. "They want us to push drugs."

"And?" Sal asked, thinking it might not be a bad idea.

All Dominic could think of was the night Denise had called him sobbing for him to hurry over. He found her crying frantically over the two girls lying on the front steps. At first he thought they were dead, but after he checked to see if they were breathing, he had carried them one at a time into the house, up the stairs, and dumped them onto their beds. Unable to cope with this disaster, he had left as soon as he could. From then on Denise was constantly begging him to come over. Each time, he noticed his beloved nieces seemed to be in worse condition than the time before. They were sunken-eyed and sullen; they pulled him aside out of their mother's hearing to beg him for money. He refused and lectured them on the harm the drugs were doing to them.

"They're turning you into zombies," he ranted at them. They ignored him.

Then yesterday Denise had called.

"Dominic," she could barely get the words out from between the tears. "It's the girls."

Not knowing what to say Dominic said nothing.

"They're stealing money from my purse."

"Are you sure?" he asked.

"When I suspected. I started counting it every morning and every night. It's been going on for more than a week now."

"Could it be someone else getting into your purse?"

"There is no one else. I don't know what to do about it." Unable to hold back, she began crying in earnest.

"Get a hold of yourself. Give me a couple of days to come up with something," he had said.

Dominic stopped kicking the table, turned and faced his cronies, and shook his head sadly. "I won't fuckin' sell drugs," he said over and over as if it were his mantra.

"You're a dead man if you don't," one of the pinochle players warned him.

Chapter 23

It's Thursday, Judy thought as she jockeyed her way through the rush hour traffic on her way home from work. Thursday again. Last Thursday was the worst day in my life—the day the pictures came and the day of the accident; but I have a feeling there are more bad times ahead. There's something nagging inside me telling me it's not over yet. She stood outside her house and nervously pulled the mail from the mailbox. Ever since the pictures had come she felt queasy about taking in the mail. Today, as she slid the letters from the box she noticed one envelope had a slight bulge in it. It feels like a small book, she thought as she pinched around it with her fingers. She felt a twinge go through her—this was not good. Something else was about to go very, very wrong, her intuition said.

She held the suspect envelope in her hand, dropped the rest of the mail on the hall table, then carefully inspected it. On the first line of the address was "Mrs. Fanelli" in an unfamiliar handwriting. The letters were scrawled with an unsteady hand, and, in child-like fashion, the address sloped downhill. Curiosity overwhelmed her desire to throw it unopened into the trash. She sank onto the couch in the living room and tore the envelope open. Inside she found a small black book, weathered and well used around the edges. Her stomach knotted, and a sinking feeling welled inside her; instinctively she knew: this was the next part of someone's continuing effort to rub her nose in Tony's infidelity.

She turned back the cover of the book and saw Tony's name and their address written on the first page. It's his handwriting, she noticed. He must have lost this, and now someone's returning it, she thought. The flicker of optimism faded when she remembered that the envelope had been addressed to "Mrs." not "Mr." Fanelli. Slowly she leafed through the pages. Her mouth dropped open as she read page after page of only women's names and phone numbers, all in Tony's handwriting. After most names a single crude, five-pointed star was drawn; a few names had two stars, and every so often a name had three stars. With mixed anger and sadness she wondered, what do I conclude from this? It's obvious the woman in the pictures wasn't Tony's first and only. The lying bastard didn't slip up only once like he said, he has been cheating on me major, big time, for a long time. There have been lots of women, and this is his book of whores. She quickly flipped through the pages again. God, she thought, there must be over a hundred names. And the stars, that must be a rating system. In spite of her attempt to squelch the thought, she wondered how many stars he would give her. Damn, she thought, I was seriously considering forgiving him and giving him another chance, and now this.

She heard Tony's car pull into the driveway and shortly after, heard his key scratch in the door.

"Hi. How was your day?" he asked. He bent over and brushed her cheek lightly with a kiss.

"It was okay until a few minutes ago, and now it's turned to shit," she said through clenched teeth. She struggled to maintain her composure and hold in the anger that was building in her gut.

"What happened?" he said.

She held out the book. "This is yours. Don't deny it. It has your name in it. It came in the mail addressed to me, so I opened it."

He calmly took it from her hand and thumbed through it. "Yeah. It's mine. Thanks. They must've stolen this when they broke into my car. I keep it in the glove box, but I'm surprised they mailed it back to me. Why didn't they throw it away?" He put it in his pocket. "What's for supper? You wanna go out maybe?"

A beet-red flush crept up Judy's neck to her face; she felt her ears burning. She stood up, planted her fists on her waist, and glared at him. "Do you think I'm a goddamned idiot?" she screamed. "This is the 'little black book' you macho guys all joke about in the locker room, isn't it?"

"What the hell are you talking about?" Tony looked surprised.

"This is your bimbo book. Where you keep your babes' names and their scores."

Astonishment swept across his face. "You've got to be kidding," he said calmly.

Her voice rose to a piercing shriek. "There are only women's names in this book, and they're rated with stars. What the fuck am I supposed to think?"

"Take it easy, Judy. Back off. You're way off base on this one. There are only women's names because these are the names of the secretaries of the purchasing agents that I call on. I try to get appointments with their bosses. I have to remember their names and phone numbers don't I? And the stars are the degree of difficulty they give me. If they don't give me a problem they get three stars. They're easy. Understand?" Mentally Tony patted himself on the back. I'm getting good at thinking fast on my feet, he marveled.

Blinding rage surged through her, but try as she could, she couldn't think of a way to punch holes in his story. I know it's a lie, she thought, but I can't prove it. Like lightning in an electrical storm, she sizzled with frustration. She couldn't hold back any longer, broke down, and started to cry. Tony came over and put an arm around her shoulder.

"Tony, Tony," she sobbed. "Can't you see why I have a lot of trouble believing that? It sounds like such a made-up, bullshit, phony story."

"But it's true," he said. "This is the way I've done business for years. I need this book for my job. It's helped me become successful. Is there anything wrong with that?"

Tears of frustration streamed down her face. Over and over "He's lying. He's lying," pounded in her head.

She gritted her teeth. The bastard, she thought. The dirty fucking bastard.

*   *   *

After supper when Tony went upstairs to "do his paperwork", Judy curled up on the couch with the phone and dialed Kate's number. A second before the machine picked it up she remembered Kate wouldn't be home. Kate and Greg had tickets to a play downtown and would have left by now. I really need a consultation tonight, she thought. I've got to talk to someone about this address book. Her thoughts turned to Carlo. He's kind and understanding, she thought, and he did offer to help if I needed it. What the hell; I'll give him a try. She dialed his number. He picked it up on the second ring.

"Carlo, I need someone to talk to," she said. She almost added "and Kate isn't home tonight" but censored it. She carried the phone into the kitchen and closed the louvered doors so Tony wouldn't hear.

"I'm glad you called. What's the problem?" he asked.

She told him about the book.

"It is suspicious. You said there's not one male name in the book?"

"Not one even close to being male. I was hoping there would be a Pat or a Patty so I could think it was Patrick. But there were only two Patricias with Pat in parenthesis."

"And the women's names were in alphabetical order?"

"Yes. What difference does that make?" Judy asked.

"His story would be more believable if they were in order under company names. How would you look up the secretary of the Jones Company? Wouldn't you look under Jones and not her name?"

"You right. Say, you'd make a good detective."

"Remember I'm a reporter trained to investigate thoroughly. But the important question is: Who is behind this? Someone seems determined to give you a bad time about Tony. The pictures, the address book."

"There was something else I didn't tell you because I was too embarrassed."

"Oh? What was it?"

"I did his laundry after he came home from his romp with the bitch at the motel, and someone had put women's underwear in with his clothes from the trip. Tony said someone from work must have done it as a joke."

"I have trouble buying that," Carlo said. He thought for a moment. "This all seems like part of a plot. I suspect the woman, whoever she is, is behind the whole thing, since she's the only one who would be able to put her underwear in with his dirty clothes. She's the one who would have set up a photographer to take pictures of them in bed, because who else would know what motel they were going to. Somehow she got hold of his address book and mailed it to you." He thought for a minute. "Maybe it's one of those women in the book. She might feel that Tony wronged her somehow. Or do you know some woman who has it in for Tony?"

Judy thought for a minute. "No. I can't think of anyone," she said.

"Let's eliminate the obvious. Tony can't be behind this. He'd have no motive for getting you angry at him. If he wanted a divorce, he'd ask you outright and not play these games with you. Did you ask him who the woman was?"

"He brushed me off, and before I could pin him down, his sister called saying that his parents were in the accident. In all the confusion after that I never asked him again. But he looked genuinely surprised when I showed him the underwear and the book. Of course, being a salesman he can put on any emotion on his face he wants. But I'm sure it's not Tony behind this. I can't see any reason why he would do something like this. I can't think of anybody who might want to do something like this."

Neither one spoke for a few moments.

"You're turning out to be a good friend, Carlo," Judy said. "Someone I can talk to and confide in. I feel better just venting. I'll miss you when you go to Rome. When do you leave?"

"A week from tomorrow—Friday, the 11th. I'll have a few days to settle in before the job starts on April 15th."

"Only one week 'til you go," she said glumly.

She felt a warmness toward him stirring inside her. One week. Then he'll be gone, out of my life, she thought. Just when I'm starting to like him . . . a lot. A little drama started in her head—the two of them walking slowly down the aisle in a small chapel toward a minister. He spoke again interrupting her daydream.

"I'd like to see you one more time before I go," he said. "Let's have lunch again."

"I'd love to. But you must have a million things to do before you go. Can you fit me into your schedule?"

She heard Tony coming down the stairs. He's probably hungry and wants to snack on some pretzels, she thought. "Call me at work," she whispered into the phone. "I gotta go."

As Carlo hung up the phone he thought about the women he had gone out with. There was not one that he had dated more than five times. For various reasons he dumped them all. One was too pushy: she nagged him mercilessly to get married after only their second date. Another, extraordinarily beautiful on the outside, bitched at him constantly about every aspect of his life. His clothes were all wrong. "Throw these out," she would say pointing in his closet, "and get some Ralph Lauren Polo in here." And: "Why don't you write a novel?" she whined. "That's where the real money is. You'll never get rich being a reporter." But with Judy, he thought, it's so different. At lunch during our conversation I felt that we were . . . coming together. I felt that she . . . liked me. I wish I had followed up after the prom and dated her again. I know I'll really miss her when I move to Italy. He wondered if he was falling in love with her. Maybe, he thought wistfully, I shouldn't be so helpful with her problems with Tony. If she works them out, there's no "me" in her future.

He turned on the TV and started washing the supper dishes.

*   *   *

Tony got up early Saturday morning and rushed off to the gym. He was determined to work off the tension and frustration which resulted from not being able to find out who was behind the attempt to disrupt his marriage. In addition he was becoming frantic, reasoning that whoever it was, would make more attempts to call Judy's attention to his infidelity. Desperately he had called Fred and made an appointment to meet him this morning.

"Hi, Fred," he greeted him. "Let's go in here." He steered him into one of the empty sales offices and closed the door behind them.

"What's going on?" Fred asked. "You look pretty frazzled."

"I'm gonna level with you," Tony began. "My marriage is in a lot of trouble." He filled Fred in on all the details, telling him the whole truth except for Kate's name.

"I've got to find out who's behind this and put a stop to it before Judy hits me with a divorce. But the only thing I have to go on," Tony confided, "is the damn woman. It was her underwear, and she's the only one who could have put it in my laundry. The only question is did she do it on purpose, or was it an accident like she says. And she must have gotten the address book when they smashed the window on my car. She's the one who told me about the break-in. She could even have broken the window herself to get my address book."

"I don't think so, Tony. How would she even know you had an address book or that you kept it in your car?"

"You're right. But do you think I ought to call her about it? Should I flat-out accuse her of sending it to Judy and see what she says?"

"I don't think that's a good idea. She sounds like a pretty smart bitch. She came up with an excuse for everything else. 'Whoops,' on the panties. 'Who me?' on the pictures. Of course she'll say she didn't take the book; and maybe she didn't." Fred thought for a moment. "Someone must have it in for you, and they're going to a lot of trouble to cause you grief. But you're right. The prime suspect has to be the woman. She's the only one who knew what motel you were going to and when. If someone else is behind this, they must have gotten lucky. They followed you, realized or knew the room had a fake mirror, and then took pictures. Then they would have to be lucky again to stumble onto the address book. Too many coincidences. No. My money would be on the woman."

"I can't believe she's the one behind it. Because like she said if she wanted Judy to know, she'd pick up the phone and call her. She's one aggressive woman and it doesn't fit her style to do something sneaky. Besides, it doesn't make any sense because . . ."

A manager knocked on the door. "We need the room now," he said. "I have a salesman who just finished showing a prospect around. He needs an office to close the sale. You'll have to leave."

"We'll talk some more another time," Tony said.

Chapter 24

*W*hat a week this is going to be, Judy thought. Here it is Monday morning, and I've got to go to Alberto's funeral. Time flies—it seems like the accident happened only yesterday. Friday, Carlo leaves for Rome. That's like another funeral. I'm losing a father-in-law and a friend. A good friend, she hurried to add, not wanting to admit that he was fast becoming more than a friend. He was becoming her fantasy, the one she dreamed about to escape from the present. What would life be like with Carlo? she had begun imagining.

She took one last look in the mirror on the back of her bedroom door: black dress falling just right across the shoulders, black shoes, and black bag. She sighed deeply—what a pity, such a good man—then walked down the hall steps and went into the living room where Tony had been waiting for her. He had been exceptionally nice to her since the address book came, and now, wordlessly, somberly, he gently took her hand and led her out the front door.

She shielded her eyes from the bright April sun as they stepped into the waiting limousine.

"Funerals always make me think of my own mortality," Judy said settling into the plushy seat. "It's a very uncomfortable feeling."

"I feel that way too," Tony said. "But I'm glad it's not my time yet."

"I wonder whose parent or spouse will be next," Judy said. "And then I think about my father. He's been gone ten years, and I still miss him." Her father was the kindest, nicest man she had ever known. Though he never told her he loved her, she could tell by his actions that he did—he was a touchy-feely person. When she was young, he loved to stroke her hair, hold her hand, or cuddle her to him as he told her stories about his life in Italy before he came to the United States. He was a soft-spoken gentleman, a family man; he wouldn't have been involved with a tattooed woman in a sleazy motel, Judy thought. Even so, when she probed her deepest emotions she found that in spite of all that had happened, she felt compassion for Tony. After all, she thought, he did lose his father.

Alberto's funeral was held in the Cathedral Basilica of Saints Peter and Paul in center-city Philadelphia, a huge, stately church. As Judy prepared to sit down in the front row with Tony and his siblings and their families, his sister Angela came over and threw her arms around Tony and began to sob. Tony patted her on the back and struggled to hold back the tears.

"Damn," Angela said. "Damn it all Tony. Papa's dead. And for no good reason." She cried openly.

Judy put her hand around Tony's shoulder as he said, "It's terrible, Angie. But we've got to take care of the living. Ma's too sick to even come here today."

Angela's husband consoled her and led her away to her seat.

Judy turned around every few seconds and gaped with astonishment as a seemingly endless line of mourners continued to stream in. In spite of the size of the church, they filled every available seat. A large crowd for anyone, Judy thought, and Alberto Fanelli was only a dry cleaner/tailor with a small shop, no one special.

She leaned over and whispered in Tony's ear, "Who are all these people?"

"Customers," he answered.

"Your father did a hell of a business. There must be half of Philadelphia here. Do you know all of them?"

"This place holds about twelve hundred. I know most of them. Sshh. They're starting the service."

The choir began to sing, but Judy was unable to control her curiosity and continued, "How come a simple tailor is having a funeral in this enormous cathedral with a *cardinal* officiating? You know a cardinal's only one step down from the Pope."

"Dad was always a sucker for charities. He gave a lot of money to the Catholic Church without making a big deal of it. He made a lot of friends, and this is their way of saying thanks. Now be quiet."

After lengthy prayers and eulogies, the service ended. With a great rustle the congregation rose as the casket was escorted up the main aisle by an honor guard of Alberto's closest friends. Judy and Tony joined in the procession which formed behind it. At the back of the church, Judy noticed Carlo and flushed with excitement.

He nodded to her and mouthed, "I'll see you later."

Tony noticed and asked, "That was Carlo, wasn't it? I recognize him from Nancy's wedding."

Judy nodded. "He's leaving for Rome on Friday. I'm going to have lunch with him before he leaves."

"There's nothing funny going on between you two is there?" Tony asked.

Judy's mouth dropped open. Was he serious? The stern look on his face told her he was.

She yanked on his sleeve and angrily pulled him aside. "Are you out of your goddamn head? Do you really think there's something going on between me and Carlo? And if there was, would I tell you I was going to have lunch with him?" she snarled.

"I thought maybe you'd try to get even with me after what I did. That's not so crazy, is it?"

"Listen here, Tony. That's the furthest thing from my mind. I'm doing the best I can to hang in there and keep our marriage together, and there's no way I'd try to get even. Carlo's only a good friend. Nothing more." Why am I so angry, she thought, if he's only a good friend? Is he more than a good friend? She censored thoughts of Carlo and angrily fell in step alongside Tony.

At the cemetery four men slowly played out the ropes under the casket, and it sank into the grave. Tony's fought to maintain his self-control by methodically clenching and unclenching his fists. The end of his father's life and fury at the senseless accident that killed him were almost more than he could bear. He dug his nails into his palms with rage and frustration. "This is the worst day of my life," he said out loud. His father's death and the realization that he would never see him again gripped Tony, and he winced with the pain of it.

When Tony left Judy and went to Angela to say goodbye, Carlo, seeing Judy alone, came to her side.

"My condolences," he said. "I know this is a bad time, so I'll make this quick. And this is the wrong place for me to ask, but are you free for lunch on Wednesday? It's about the only time I have before I leave. I can pick you up at your office or we can meet at The Garden if you prefer."

"I thought you were going to call me at work?" she said.

"I couldn't wait. Lunch?"

"Wednesday's fine. Pick me up at the office," Judy said quickly noticing that Tony was headed back.

In the limousine as they headed home, Judy said, "Tony."

"Mmmm," he said.

"Promise me that you won't have any other women, ever again."

I was hoping I wouldn't have to do that, Tony thought. But I did it once to get her to marry me, and now if I do it, it's only to keep her from divorcing me.

"I will be a good husband, and as far as I'm concerned that's included. I promise."

And this time don't break it, Judy thought to herself.

Chapter 25

*C*harles Price, Jr. had a tough, touchy situation. He paced back and forth in front of the custom-made, oak desk in his huge office at Neuberger Roe & Price, paying little attention to the expensive, Picasso-like, modern artwork that hung on the walls. Occasionally he glanced out the floor-to-ceiling windows at the late afternoon sun sparkling on the glass and steel buildings of the Philadelphia skyline. I'm stalling, he thought, and that isn't making this any easier. He looked at the date on his wristwatch—Wednesday, April 9th. I can't wait any longer, he thought. We leave in three weeks. I'd better call her in right now and get it over with. He punched the intercom button marked "Secretary."

"Tell Judy Fanelli to come in here right away," he ordered.

While he waited for her, he sat down behind the desk and tried a number of different poses. He came to the conclusion there was no way to hide the fact that his left arm was in a sling. He tucked his right hand behind his head and leaned back in the heavily padded executive's chair taking care to rest his feet on the small footstool under the desk. He detested it when he saw his employees with their feet on their desks and would grumble to himself, "No one has any goddamn manners anymore."

He heard a gentle tapping on the door, stood up and opened it, and tried unsuccessfully to hide his injured arm behind his back. As

Judy Fanelli walked in, he nodded to her and shut the door behind her barely noticing how she looked (quizzical) or what she was wearing (tweed business suit). Wordlessly he ushered her to the chair in front of his desk and gestured for her sit. He had considered having the two of them sit on the couch in front of the coffee table but decided that was too intimate and might scare her off. And he did want her to say "yes."

"Do you want some coffee?" he asked her politely.

She shook her head. "No thanks," she replied. She slid to the back of the chair, straightened her back, crossed her legs primly knee-on-knee, and folded her hands in her lap.

As he walked around the desk to his chair, he kept his eyes on her and scanned her from the bottom up. Nice legs and quite attractive, he noted. But he grimaced as he remembered the one date they had.

It was a week after she had joined the firm, a teenager fresh out of high school. She had appealed to him: all-American fresh, young, and good-looking. Two weeks earlier he had graduated Penn law school in the top ten percent of his class. He was in a mood to let loose and celebrate after his nose-to-the-grindstone life at college. Also he was determined to get the most he could out of bachelorhood as fast as possible. His father had already delivered a blustery, hour-long, lecture demanding that he settle down and get married—and being quick about it. It wouldn't be long, Charlie feared, before the tyrant put his foot down.

He had asked her out, and she said yes. Their evening started off on a high note, and he quickly began to picture Judy in bed with him, wondering what she would look like with her clothes off. Chatting amicably, they had left the office together on a Friday afternoon. During the short cab ride to the restaurant, he was impressed when she held up her end of the conversation whether they talked about current events or the latest hot legal topics. Because she was so young, he had prejudged her to be an airhead; he realized she was far from that. After a lavish dinner at the Monaco in the Olde City section of town, they had leisurely strolled along South Street watching the parade of oddly dressed teenagers passing by. They looked at each other and snickered as a tall girl with pink, spiked hair and loops of gold pierced through her eyebrows stared vacantly at them with drug-crazed eyes.

He asked her back to his apartment. "It's not far from here. And it's got a tremendous view. I'm on the fifteenth floor, and it overlooks Independence Hall," he had told her. Intrigued by what she might see, she agreed to his invitation. He settled her on the couch, opened the glass doors of his enormous bar, and offered her an after dinner drink. She refused and settled for a ginger ale. He poured himself some brandy and drank it quickly for courage. Then off-handedly invited her into the bedroom as if it were a done deal in payment for the dinner he had bought her. The evening went downhill quickly for him after that.

"I really like you a lot, but I don't think it would be a good idea tonight," she sighed. He stared at her not comprehending. "It would be, well . . . messy." He continued to look perplexed. "It's a bad time of month," she blurted out. He harrumphed, suspected she was lying, but remained a gentleman and after some meaningless small talk, took her home in a cab.

He did not handle rejection well. For days after he could feel her lame excuse gnaw at his insides. Am I getting an ulcer? he wondered as his stomach churned. A few weeks later he considered asking her for another date but decided to avoid a possible second unpleasant episode. And soon after, he discovered that he had no trouble finding women more than willing to warm his bed for a shot at marrying one of the richest bachelors in the city. He never asked Judy for another date.

He rubbed his eyes as if to erase those memories from his mind, and stared across the desk separating them wondering if she ever thought about his clumsy effort to bed her. No matter, he thought, that was a long time ago.

"What happened to your arm?" she asked breaking the silence.

Embarrassed, he tried unsuccessfully to twist the arm out of sight. "Oh, nothing serious. A domestic quarrel that got out of hand," he answered. "My wife tends to overreact to . . . certain situations, which leads me nicely to the business I have to discuss with you." He leaned forward, furrowed his brow, and peered at her intently. "How good is your Italian?"

For a second she was taken aback. This was totally unexpected and out of the blue. Where, she wondered, was he going with this strange question? Recovering her composure she answered: "Until I was five and started to play with other kids, it was the only language I heard or spoke. My father refused to speak English until the day he died, unless it was an emergency. So if I wanted to talk to him, I had to speak Italian. My Mom was a little more flexible but not much."

"It's been a while since your father died." Price had reviewed her personnel records thoroughly two days ago. "Have you forgotten how to speak it?" Like a good lawyer he tried not to ask a question without already knowing the answer. He had heard her on the phone talking to her mother and suspected she was fluent.

"No. I have some relatives I speak to in Italian. And my mother. Often when she gets excited, she'll go off ranting in Italian."

"So today if someone was speaking Italian, you wouldn't have any trouble understanding them?"

"Absolutely not. No trouble at all."

"One more thing," he added. "I've studied this language thing carefully. There's a big difference between Italian and Sicilian." Judy was dutifully impressed. "Do you speak Sicilian or Italian?"

Judy smiled as she thought of how her mother would blow her top if someone even intimated that she might be Sicilian. "I have pure, one hundred percent Roman blood flowing in my veins," Judy said. "My father and mother were both born in Rome. But I'm married to a Sicilian, and you're right; I can't understand some of Tony's relatives when they speak. It's almost like a foreign language to me. I really only understand Italian."

"Good," Charlie said. He thought for a second. "How about written Italian? Could you translate written Italian into English?"

"I can't see that being a problem. My father used to read to me and bring me books to read—in Italian. I don't know where he got them. I even saved some of them and have them at home in the attic."

Price planted his good elbow on the desk and looked her squarely in the eye. "Could you understand legal terms in Italian?"

"Probably not right out of my head. But with a dictionary I'm sure I could do it."

As strange as the conversation was, she was totally unprepared for what came next.

"You know I'm having some . . . marital . . . difficulties," he sputtered. She thought it best to remain silent and when she didn't respond, he sailed off on another tack. "As a result of Mr. Neuberger sitting around the country club and chatting with anyone who will listen, the firm now has a new client with an Italian connection. Stratham became friendly with a man who is preparing to invest a substantial sum of money with some relatives in Italy who have started a toy manufacturing/distributing venture. It's a small company just starting out, and they want to sign a royalty agreement with an American toy maker."

Price checked to make sure Judy was paying attention before continuing. Noting her eyes were locked onto his, he took a deep breath and went on. "No sense in dragging this out. Someone has to go to Italy and check this company out. We have to shake hands with the principals and make sure they have their heads screwed on straight. We'll inspect their manufacturing facilities, look at their books, and decide if our client's investment stands a reasonable chance of being successful. After we are certain they can pay our bill," he snickered, "we'll conclude the royalty agreement for them." He leaned back in his chair and relaxed.

"For obvious reasons," Price continued, "Mr. Neuberger will not be going to Italy, and I've been chosen by the partners to handle this work." He paused for a moment to let the importance of that statement sink in. "We've been told the people over there speak little or no English, and I don't plan on learning Italian. There's no time for me to learn it even if I wanted to, which I don't. And I won't hire an interpreter because I don't want any outsiders knowing our business. So I've chosen you to come with me. To Italy. We have a meeting set for May 5th."

Her mouth dropped open with surprise; he misinterpreted her shock and thinking she was going to speak, he held up his hand to shush her. Her mouth closed.

"I don't know about your life outside this office, and I don't care what it's like, but I do know my wife. She'd kill me, or you, or both of us if she found out the two of us went on a trip to Europe alone . . . together. So I have to take a third person along . . . as a fifth wheel." She smiled at his joke. "The next part may sound sexist, but I don't mean it that way. You can pick any male lawyer—my wife would really go bananas if I went to Europe with *two* women—in this firm to go with us. The lucky man gets a free vacation. Of course, I reserve the right to veto your choice, but I don't think I'll have to. You're smart enough to chose properly. Any questions?"

She tried to absorb what was happening, but she had trouble focusing from the cloud nine she was on. Her head reeled; her heart pounded, Car-lo, Car-lo. Things are moving too fast for me, she thought. This is too coincidental. This can't be real; it must be a dream. She briefly considered pinching herself but decided against it. Price would think I'm crazy if he saw me, she thought.

"Judy?" He cocked his head and looked at her quizzically. "Anybody home? Are you there?" She nodded her head but said nothing. "Any questions?" he repeated.

Only one important one, she thought. She said, "Where in Italy will we be going?"

Of all the question she could have asked, this is what she comes up with, he thought. "We'll be headquartered at The Savoia in Rome," he said.

Rome, Rome, Rome. Carlo, Carlo, Carlo. Judy's heart thundered in her chest in rhythm with the words. I'm going to see Carlo in Rome, she thought. I can't wait to tell him at lunch today.

Charlie Price stared at her waiting for her decision. Finally he broke into her trance: "Then you'll go?"

Unable to talk because of the huge lump rising in her throat, she nodded "yes" and stood up.

"One more thing before you leave," he said.

Uh-oh, she thought. The other side of the coin. What's the bad news?

"Next week is our monthly visit to TGI Friday's. I know you come periodically, but you missed the last one. I'd like you to make a special effort to attend this one, and in the future come to them regularly. The partners want to get to know you informally. They're very excited about this Italian client and hope it will be a stepping-stone for us to get profitable business in Europe. This could be a whole new source of revenue for the firm."

He looked at her for some comment but she remained locked in a fantasy about meeting with Carlo in Rome. "You'll be there?" he asked. "At Friday's?"

"Yes," she answered, barely able to get the word out.

Judy floated from his office back to her desk not sure what to do first. She briefly thought about calling her mother, who would surely be anxious to hear this news and would be terribly excited. But she didn't want to hear a lecture right now on how wonderful it would be for anyone to have the opportunity to visit Rome, and how wonderful it would be for her to get in touch with her roots. No, what she really wanted to do—was to talk to Carlo—to tell him the news. She could hardly wait for the time to pass until noon.

She shuffled papers aimless on her desk for the rest of the morning and daydreamed about dating him. What would it be like? she wondered. She visualized a romantic evening in Rome starting at a fine Italian restaurant. Afterwards he would ask her up to his apartment. There'd be some small talk, and then, oh so naturally, they'd end up in bed together. His hands would be soft on her body and she would caress him from head to toe. Passionately but gently they would make love. Why can't it be like that in real life? she thought. In my real marriage I get stuck with an unfaithful shit, but Carlo wouldn't be like that. How do you know? she asked herself. I can tell, she answered. There are some things about people you can just tell. She tingled with the anticipation of meeting Carlo for lunch. I feel like a teenager, she thought. A teenager with a crush. She hugged her arms together across her breasts.

The clock dragged on and on, but finally she was seated across from him at The Garden.

"It's only been two weeks since we were here . . . ," Carlo began.

"Two weeks and one day," she interrupted.

"It looks like you've been keeping track of the time. I like that." He reached across the table and took her hand in his. She didn't pull away.

Sadly Carlo continued, "This was nice—getting to know you all over again. But now I'm going away, and I don't know if I'll ever see you again."

Before she could break in with her good news, Carlo said, "You know this isn't a temporary assignment. I'll be in Italy permanently—for as far into the future as I can see. I love my work, and this is where it's taking me. But maybe you'll come and see me, or I'll come back here to the States." He leaned toward her. "I do want to see you again, Judy."

She put a forefinger across his lips to silence him. "I've got something very exciting to tell you," she said animatedly.

He kissed her finger lightly and she took it from his mouth.

"Oh? What is it?" He arched his eyebrows. "It looks like good news from the look on your face."

"I'm going to Rome," she enthused. "In less than a month." She told him about her conversation with Charlie Price. "Even with the business demands, I should have time to see you. Won't that be exciting?"

"Wow," Carlo said. "Give me a second to absorb that."

The waiter set the food in front of them, but they didn't touch it. Carlo's initial exuberance faded. Judy looked at him quizzically.

"What's wrong?" she asked. "Won't you be happy to see me?"

"You bet I will. But you are a married woman, and that presents some problems. It's not as if we would be free to enjoy . . . everything Rome would have to offer." He grew pensive. "If only you weren't married . . ." He didn't finish the sentence.

She looked at her food then looked up at him. "Okay. If I wasn't married, then what?"

"We'd get to know each other a lot better. I size people up quickly, and I think you're a wonderful person, Judy." He felt his throat tightening and pushed the food away from in front of him.

"Oh, Carlo. I do like you. I like you a lot as a good friend, but I am married, and I don't want you to be expecting any romantic relationship in Rome." Why is my heart thump-thumping so wildly if he's only a good friend? she wondered.

"Okay. I'll respect that," he said. "I'm glad we've gotten close, and I hope the future has some good things in store for both of us. We'll see each other in Rome and see where it leads."

"This is getting too serious. Let's talk about something else," she said.

"Okay. What about all the problems with Tony? What are you going to do about that?"

"For the time being I'll take my mother's advice. I'll overlook all his broken promises and cheating and go on with the marriage. I'm not comfortable with it, but maybe he's learned his lesson, and maybe with time I can learn to live with what he's done. But I'll tell you this. And I mean it from the bottom of my heart. He's promised not to do it any more." What are his promises worth? she thought to herself. "If he ever fools around again . . ." The words "I'll be on the next plane to Rome" popped into her head, but she said, "I'll divorce him. I've talked to Bob Dolan at work. He's the lawyer who handles divorces, and he doesn't see any problems if I decide to go through with it. If Tony cheats on me one more time, I will, Carlo, I swear I'll do it."

Having unburdened herself, her appetite returned, and she nervously stabbed a lettuce leaf and stuck it in her mouth.

Carlo handed her a small piece of paper and said, "Before I forget here's my address and phone number in Rome. Put it away carefully and don't lose it. Call me when you get there."

She took her wallet from her handbag and tucked it away behind a credit card.

Carlo said, "I really blew it at the prom, didn't I? I'm so angry I can't remember most of what happened that night."

"I must have been a hell of a date to leave no impression," she teased.

Carlo began to speak but the waiter came with the bill, and Judy rose to leave. They stared into each other's eyes, each wishing for different circumstances. Carlo, wanting to take her in his arms and kiss her, and Judy, feeling very uncomfortable not knowing where her growing feelings for him would take them.

Flustered by her emotions, she said, "When we meet again, I'll tell you the rest of what happened that night. It's very personal, but it didn't have anything to do with you."

Carlo's ears perked up. She said, "When we meet again," he thought. I'm looking forward to that.

*   *   *

That evening Kate called Judy.

"I haven't spoken to you in a while," she said. "Anything new?"

"I'm going to Rome . . . on business."

Kate congratulated her on her good luck. "I wish I could take a vacation. I'd go anywhere."

"This isn't a vacation, Kate. There'll be a lot of hard work."

"Sure. Sure. If that's what you want me to believe. Oh, by the way," she said offhandedly, "anything new on the marriage front?"

"Tony zapped me with another hand grenade," Judy said.

"Hunh?"

Judy told her about the black book.

"It sure sounds suspicious to me," Kate said. "He said they were secretaries. If it were me, I'd keep the bosses names."

"You're right. His explanation sounds half-assed and not very logical." Judy said.

"I discussed your problems with Greg, and we both think you ought to loosen up a little. We don't mind if the other one has affairs and maybe that arrangement might be healthy for you."

"I know you two have an open marriage, but you agreed to that before you got married. Tony and I promised to be faithful to each other, and it means a lot to me that I'm the only one he sleeps with. You've got your marriage set up in a way that works for you. It won't work for me, and I couldn't stand that arrangement."

"Shoot yourself. I mean suit yourself. If you decide to divorce Tony, I'll be here for you."

Chapter 26

€arly the next morning the phone rang in the offices of Omega Investigations. The caller asked for John Christopher.

"Of course I remember you," Christopher said. "We took the pictures at the motel and mailed them to someone in Philadelphia. Was everything all right?"

"You did fine. The pictures were perfect, but . . . they didn't get the job done," the female voice on the phone said. "I've got to push some more. Harder this time."

Christopher didn't answer. He had skirted close to the edge of the law last time for this client and was afraid of what she might want him to do now.

Kate ignored his silence and went on, "Here's what I have in mind." She described a plan which astonished John Christopher, who thought he'd heard everything. One client had even hinted around asking him to commit murder, and this was nearly as bizarre.

John put his hand over his eyes and slowly shook his head "no." "I can't do something like that," he said. "You want me to break a dozen laws. At best I might lose my license, and at worst I could go to jail."

"How about three thousand dollars to do it?" she asked. "What does that work out to? Five hundred dollars an hour?"

"Now, look. How do I know you're not FBI or some nut out to get me? You could be trying to trap me. The government's always doing stuff like that."

"Five thousand dollars?"

"That's not enough money for the risks I'd be taking."

"So you'll do it? All we have to do is agree on the price?"

The bank account, does it always come down to the bank account? he wondered. Although Omega was gradually pulling back from the brink of bankruptcy, there was still a pile of unpaid bills, and daily, insulting, dunning phone calls that caused him sleepless nights.

"I won't do it myself. I can't take the chance I'll get caught. I'll have to call in some . . . operatives who won't be locals. They can do the job then disappear quickly, and if they're from out of town, they'll be harder to identify." He hesitated for a second. "It'll cost you a lot of money. Let's say twenty thousand dollars. In advance. After I cash your check, I'll see if I can put it together, and if I can't, I'll send you your money back."

"You've got a deal. I'll mail the check tomorrow." Kate smiled anticipating the pain this would cause Judy. "How soon can you do this?"

He thought for a minute. "I can get this set up in a week. No. Make that two weeks. I've got to find the right people, which means a dozen phone calls, wait for callbacks. I don't want to rush this and have all of us end up in jail."

"Okay, okay," she grumbled. "Do it right, just do it."

I've waited this long, she thought as she said goodbye, I can wait a little longer.

John Christopher hung up the phone, put his feet up on his desk, and clasped his hands behind his head. There's no way I'm getting personally involved with this crazy woman's scheme, he thought. It's too dangerous. Wow, she must really hate those Fanellis to want to pull a stunt like this. Now who can I contact for this job?

His thoughts drifted back to his days on the Baltimore police force. Running through the data bank in his mind he decided one criminal he'd run into, Louis Banks, would be perfect. Lou had been arrested for bigamy; he had married three women—rich widows—all at the same time, and then proceeded to squeeze money from them to support a casino habit. He was in his early forties, dressed well, broad-shouldered, handsome, and could talk a woman into doing anything. He's just what I need, John thought. I hope he's not back in jail.

As he thought further he decided that a second person—preferably a woman—might be a good idea. He wondered if Lou was married (he grinned) or living with someone. How can I get in touch with him? John wondered. Contacts, contacts make the world go 'round. I'll start with the parole board, he said to himself, as he picked up the phone. Don Granger owes me a favor.

Lou Banks hadn't learned a trade in jail (and had no desire to), so when he was released, he returned to the only career he knew—being a parasite. It wasn't long before he sweet-talked a waitress he met at a local diner into letting him move in with her. After he had guaranteed his room and board, he tested the waters and found he hadn't lost his touch. He duped a string of women out of substantial sums of money (though he would disappear from their lives when they mentioned marriage). However, his initial success faded, and now he was down on his luck. It had been six months since he sucked every last cent from a recent widow, which he promptly blew at the craps tables in Atlantic City, and he hadn't found a new source of income. He was totally dependent upon the waitress, Frankie (he never asked her what her real name was), for support.

He turned over in bed, looked at the alarm clock, then nuzzled her.

"What time do you go to work today? It's after nine," he said.

She stretched out her not unglamorous body and yawned. "I don't go in 'til eleven, because I switched with Mary. She had to go to the doctor."

"How much money do we have in the bank?"

"Forget it Lou," she said. "You're not going to Atlantic City again for a while. We've got enough to live on for a month and not much more." She stretched like a kitten getting up from a nap. "Y'know what would be nice?" She went on without waiting for an answer. "It would be nice if you got a steady job."

Steady job? Doing what? he wondered. When he was in prison he had worked in the laundry and had hated every minute in that hot, steamy furnace. That, to him, was what a job was—something to be hated, something undesirable. He loved the women in his life—he didn't feel sorry for the ones he had preyed on, because he had to live didn't he? And they got something in return for their money—companionship and affection—didn't they? That's my job, he thought. Giving companionship and affection.

The phone rang. "Get that Lou, will ya?" Frankie said. "I'm going to take a shower."

As she dropped her shorty nightgown on the floor and headed toward the bathroom, he picked up the phone and greeted the caller with a suave "hello."

"This is John Christopher," said the voice on the other end.

"John Christopher?" Lou asked courteously. He was always polite on the phone even to telephone solicitors. He had learned from experience that you never know where your next meal ticket might come from.

"I was a detective on the Baltimore police force when you were caught. My partner arrested you," John said.

"Goodbye, John Christopher," he said matter-of-factly and started to replace the receiver in its cradle.

"Wait a minute. Don't hang up, Lou. I'm not a cop anymore. I retired."

Lou went back to suave. "What do you want?"

"I have a business proposition for you. It pays good money. Ten thousand dollars, and it's something that's right up your alley."

"Who do I have to kill?"

"No killing, Lou. Look, I can't talk about this on the phone, but I know you'll like it. It's sort of like starring in a movie." He quickly outlined the plan before Banks could ask too many questions but didn't go into great detail.

Ten thousand dollars, Lou Banks thought. If I stretch it, that's five casino trips; and (the eternal optimist) if I win . . . He let the thought hang. "Okay. I'll do it," he said as he hung up the phone.

Since women had always been his source of money, the two—money and women—were tied together in his brain. The thought of money made him horny. He stripped off his pajamas and pushed open the bathroom door.

"What time did you say you have to go to work?" he said to Frankie. She had a small towel wrapped around her and played the hair dryer over her hair while she tousled it with her free hand.

She looked at the nude man in front of her, then dropped the towel on the toilet seat and laid the dryer on it. She threw her arms around his neck, rubbed her body sensuously against his, and furiously massaged his back.

"Who the hell cares," she said, and pulled him toward the bed.

Chapter 27

*T*oday's the day, Carlo Fiore thought to himself. Friday, April 11th; a very important day in my life. I'm going to Rome to start the next phase of my career.

He had awakened at dawn and stared at his almost empty apartment. Two days ago he had watched the packers cram his belongings into cartons and felt pulled like a wish bone. I'm being yanked in two directions, he thought. I'm glad to be going to an exciting new career, and yet, I'm sorry I'm leaving . . .

"You don't have a lot of stuff," one packer interrupted his thoughts.

He's right, Carlo thought. Through this life, he mused, I have traveled light. Picking up no baggage. No wife; no kids. Never even had a long-term relationship—hell, never had a live-in. Until recently I hadn't thought much about it, and I was happy with my life. A few months ago I had no pangs about leaving the Italy, after all whom would I really have missed, and who would have really missed me? But now . . . now Judy has changed all that. I know I won't forget her, and I know I will miss her, even though she will be with me in three weeks. Enough. I must stop thinking about her.

He tried to substitute reminiscences about the good times he had in his apartment. There were many, but the highlight was the New Year's Eve party he had given two years ago. He had invited associates from the paper, relatives, and a bunch of friends. The wall-to-wall people made so much noise that at four in the morning a neighbor had called the police. When they arrived Carlo invited them to join the party and handed them drinks. "No thanks," they protested. "We're on duty. Keep it down in here so we don't have to come back and throw somebody in jail for disturbing the peace." Two minutes after he had turned down the CD player, his girlfriend of the moment had turned it back up.

The next thing he remembered clearly was waking up in the morning and finding three other naked bodies in his bed. One was his girlfriend whose arm circled his waist. There was another female (his eyes were blurred over, so he ran his hands over the body to make sure), and one male (he started to run his hands over that body, but pulled back when he felt the hairy chest). He had no idea what had happened in the bed or how the four of them had gotten there. Over breakfast, he found none of the others could remember what had happened the night before either.

After they left, he looked at the wadded-up, sticky mess in his bed. Stuffed in the pile of sheets and blankets he found a bra. How could a woman leave without her bra? he wondered. He had thrown it the back of his closet not sure whether he was saving it as a souvenir (or trophy?), or whether he was saving it in case someone claimed it later. (No one ever did.) I must have had a hell-of-a time, he decided as he crammed the sheets into his bathroom hamper.

And now I'm going to accumulate some new memories, he thought. Tonight I'm off to Rome, and Monday I start my new job. He ate a leisurely breakfast tossing the remainder of the box of Cheerios into the trash and dumping the rest of the quart of milk down the drain. After a soothing shower, he called the offices of Neuberger Roe & Price.

"She's not at her desk," the receptionist said. "May I connect you to her voice mail?" He left Judy an innocuous goodbye message ending with: "Don't forget to call me when you get to Rome." That was a disappointment, he thought. I did want to talk to her one more time before I left.

He spent the rest of the day saying goodbye to co-workers, friends, and relatives and at five o'clock, unable to postpone it any longer, he took one last look around his apartment. He touched his hand lightly to his forehead in a military salute goodbye, shouldered his garment bag and hefted his suitcase. Outside he hailed a cab and told the driver to take him to the airport. As they struggled through the rush hour traffic, a knot formed in his stomach. New job, new country, have to make new friends, he thought, no wonder you feel nervous, he told himself. You're lying, his inner voice said. You're thinking about Judy and being away from her. That's what's causing your uneasiness.

At the airport he checked into U. S. Airway's evening flight to Rome, went through x-ray inspection, and seated himself in the lounge. He hooked his fingers behind his head, shut his eyes, and tried to nap, but he wasn't tired. Suddenly someone tapped him on the shoulder. He jerked his head around and . . . Judy smiled down at him.

"I thought you might like a surprise," she said.

He stared at her open-mouthed, unable to speak.

From behind her back she pulled a bunch of flowers. *"Buon viaggio,"* she said. "Have a nice trip." She kissed him lightly on the cheek and sat down next to him.

Getting his senses back he stammered, "Thank you." And thinking of nothing else to say he said, "What are you doing here?"

"I got your voice mail, but it was too late to call you back. So I decided to see you off in person."

"I'm glad you did."

As time passed Carlo felt conflicting emotions racing through him. Eagerness to be on the plane and getting on with a new adventure clashed with his reluctance to leave the flame of love which had started to burn deep in his heart. And Judy feeling a rush of warmth snuggled as close to him as the plastic seats would allow.

In too short a time for either of them, "Flight 634 leaving for Rome is now boarding," boomed over the loudspeaker. They stood up and faced each other not quite knowing what to do next. Carlo threw caution to the winds, excitedly wrapped his arms around her, and held her close to him. Caught totally by surprise, Judy looked up into his eyes; he noticed hers were dewy, and without thinking kissed her hard on the lips. She did not resist but returned his kiss.

"I'll miss you," she whispered into his ear. Her stomach churned. This is like losing a best friend, she thought. No, he's more than a best friend. She concentrated on enjoying the feel of his body pressed against hers, and tried hard to censor thoughts of further intimacy that were starting to bubble up in her subconscious.

"I'll miss you, too," he whispered in her ear. "But we'll see each other soon."

Reluctantly he loosened his grip on her, and turned toward the cattle chute which led to the plane's cabin. He walked slowly down the ramp; and just before he rounded the last corner and lost sight of her, he stopped, turned to her and waved.

She mouthed, "See you soon," in his direction.

* * *

"Did you get my check?" the woman on the other end of the phone said to John Christopher. "I mailed it right after we spoke four days ago—last Thursday. It's a lot of money, and I'm worried about it."

Play it up big, John thought, so she thinks she's getting her money's worth. "Yes, I got it," he said. "Of course it's a lot of money because there's a lot of time and trouble involved trying to get this set up. I've made a lot of phone calls. We have to find just the right . . ."

"Cut to the chase," Kate interrupted. "Can you do this for me, or should I call someone else?" She had no idea whom she would call if he should back out.

He refused to be bullied. "I'm not sure I have every little detail worked out, but I'm almost one hundred per cent certain we have someone who can do the job for you. Let's move on to some of the nitty-gritty. For example, do you have any ideas about when we can pull this off?"

She thought for a moment. "The next to the last Thursday of every month, her office has a get-together at TGI Friday's on City Line. Do you know Philadelphia?"

"I've been there a few times. I'm familiar with Friday's."

"The party starts around four and goes on 'til who knows when. But that would be ideal since it's a public place, and there would be alcohol served."

"How can you be sure she'll be there? What if she decides to skip it?"

"There's no guarantee on that point, but she goes to most of them, and we'll just have to take our chances that she'll be there."

"And how would our operatives know what she looks like? How would they introduce themselves? And where would they get the . . ."

"Let me think this through for a while, and I'll get back to you. Those are minor problems. I'm sure we can work out the details."

"All right. But it's too late for April. The next to the last Thursday is this week, so I'll set it up for May."

"Okay, May's good. I'll be in touch."

As Kate hung up the phone she thought, if Judy won't get rid of Tony, maybe this will make Tony want to get rid of her. Either way I'm going to cause her some major heartache and grief and get my revenge.

Chapter 28

The next day Judy reported to work late. She had waited until her bank opened at nine, stopped there, and took a large envelope out of the safe deposit box she shared with Tony. During her lunch hour she hopped a cab to the Federal government office building near Independence Square. Squinting in the bright April sun, she marched up the front steps and took the elevator to the ninth floor. As the clerk dealt at length with an elderly couple, who needed every word repeated twice, Judy leaned on the counter and tapped her foot impatiently.

Finally the clerk became annoyed and turned to her. "Can I help you?" he asked sarcastically.

"I'd like to get a passport," she said, "and I need it in a hurry."

"Well, there's no way you can have it today," he said.

"No, I don't need it today. I need it by May first."

"Maybe we can have it by then. Do you have your birth certificate with you?"

"Oh, yes," she answered. She fished the document from the envelope she had taken from the safety deposit box and pushed it across the counter. "But there might be a small complication."

"One thing at a time," the clerk said. "We'll get to the complication when we get to it." He examined it carefully and ran his forefinger over the raised seal of the notary. "So you were born here in Philadelphia, and you are Gianna Orsini," the clerk said.

"Not exactly. I was born Gianna Orsini," answered Judy. "Now I'm Judy Fanelli."

He inspected the marriage license which Judy handed him. "You got married and changed your last name from Orsini to Fanelli," he said. The clerk studied it a moment more then asked, "How did Gianna get to be Judy?"

"I was christened Gianna Orsini, like it says on the birth certificate, but I never liked that name. I always called myself Judy, and when I was seventeen I had it legally changed." She handed the clerk the court document.

Once again the clerk slowly reviewed the all three documents finally saying, "Everything seems to be in order. Fill out this application, and I'll submit all your papers and forms for processing. It should take less than two weeks, and they'll mail everything back to you."

After Judy completed the form and wrote out a check, the clerk stuffed all the papers and the check in a manila folder.

As Judy settled into the cab for the ride back to work, memories flooded back. She had hated her given name almost from the very beginning because of the embarrassment and pain it had caused her. In grade school, she remembered clearly one incident where some older boys had hounded her mercilessly.

"Johneeee," they tormented her as she walked home from school. "You got a boy's name, but you're wearing a dress. Are you a boy, Johneeee?"

"My name is Giannaaaa," she wailed, "and I'm a *girrrrl*."

"You sure you're not a boy, Johneeee?" they cackled gleefully. "Let's pull off your clothes and see if you're really a girl."

They started toward her menacingly, swaggering slowly. She turned her back on them and quickly walked toward the safety of her home. They speeded up, closing the gap between them; she heard their tittering getting louder and stepped up her tempo; they walked even faster. Terror seized her as their footsteps getting closer and closer pounded in her head like sinister drums ushering in some unpleasant tribal rite. Then she panicked and started running as fast as she could, their sadistic laughter echoing in her ears. By the time she reached home she was panting and crying, scarcely able to catch her breath. With a great howl of frustration and pain she threw herself into the consoling arms of her mother.

From then on the teasing about her name grew more intense until finally, when the new school year started the next September, she asked her friends and teachers to call her Judy. And years later when her parents asked her what she wanted for her seventeenth birthday, she timidly answered—she wasn't sure how her parents would take it—that she would like her name legally changed. Her parents offered only token resistance, then agreed. She remembered appearing before a disinterested judge who, with little ceremony, slammed his gavel down, granted her request, and thundered, "Next."

Now as she got out of the cab, she had a tinge of remorse for changing her name. Wouldn't it be nice, she thought, if I could wipe the slate clean, get rid of all my troubles, and start over as Gianna Orsini again?

She leaned into the revolving door then pushed the "UP" elevator button.

Chapter 29

"Over here. I'm saving you a seat," Sara shouted to Judy from across the room. Since it was the next to the last Thursday of the month, the workforce from Neuberger Roe & Price was partying at TGI Friday's.

The partners always left the office between three and four in order to reserve tables in the far back corner for the forty or so faithful who usually showed up. They tried to isolate themselves from the raucous noise and commotion of the bar crowd in the front of the restaurant. Initially they had met on Friday thinking that the staff would be hung over on their own time, Saturday, and not on a workday. However, the restaurant was so popular that it was hard to reserve the tables they wanted on Friday, and on Fridays the noise was deafening. So they settled on Thursdays with the hope that it would be quieter and some business might get conducted. It never was.

This evening a group of five rabble rousers at the bar shouted at each other and laughed at airplane-takeoff noise levels, which made it difficult for anyone in the restaurant to hear any conversation.

Judy had attended these Thursday night get-togethers frequently in the past and was especially glad to go on nights when Tony was out of town and would be returning home late. Any excuse, she told herself, so I don't have to come home to an empty house. Despite telling everyone that she had plenty to do when Tony was gone, and she had gotten used to him being away and didn't miss his company, the truth was that she would much rather be in the company of people than sit home alone. So she enjoyed these nights with her co-workers.

Rather than scream to be heard, she waved at Sara and elbowed her way through the crowd nodding to the people she knew and quickly excusing herself from further conversation. She greeted Sara, who patted the seat next to her, and sat down.

"I noticed you took a long lunch today," Sara said. "Did you go out with your prom date again?"

Judy smiled. "No. He's in Rome. I had an errand to run over lunch."

"Personal or business?" Sara asked.

"Oh, it was business. Definitely business." She signaled the waiter to come over and ordered a glass of white wine, then folded her hands on the table and leaned forward.

"You heard I'll be out of town for a few days," she said.

"Okay. What's this all about?" Sara asked.

"You're supposed to be the queen of the rumor mill. You must be losing your grip if nobody's told you," Judy teased. "I can't believe I know something you don't know."

"I'll reorganize my KGB later. Now what's going on?" she snapped good-naturedly.

Judy told her that since she was fluent in Italian, Charles Price had asked her to go to Italy with him to attend a meeting with a potential client.

"My grapevine failed me but good. I didn't even know Charlie was going," Sara said. "So you're going with him." She smirked broadly. "Just the two of you? Now that makes really good gossip."

In her excitement about going Judy had forgotten that Price had asked her to select another lawyer to accompany them, and as she told this to Sara, a "eureka" look came over her face.

"Okay. You're dying to tell me. Who would you recommend, oh great Wizard of Oz?" Judy asked her.

"That's a no-brainer," Sara said. "He's over there." She nodded toward Paul Logan, two tables away. Sitting ramrod straight, with female daintiness—pinky extended—he sipped on straight vodka with a twist of lemon. Sara often said that, sitting or standing, he always looked like he had a broomstick shoved up his ass.

"I don't know him that well," Judy said. "Why him?"

"Two good reasons. First of all, he's a good lawyer. You'll get points with Charlie for that. Second, he's a God-fearing, born-again Christian. He's got a wife who keeps close tabs on him, and they have four children. He's not very likely to hit on you, except maybe to convert you." She leaned her chin on her hand and stared at Paul across the room. "Of course with men you never know for sure," she added. "Sometimes the milquetoasts turn out to be the tigers."

Judy thought for a moment. "I'll take a chance on him," she said.

"Now that we have that out of the way," Sara said, "we can enjoy ourselves." The waiter set a glass down in front of Judy. "Here's your wine," Sara said. "We'll celebrate your trip." She lifted her glass and clinked it against Judy's. "You wouldn't be going to Rome while you're in Italy, would you?" Sara asked slyly. "Are you planning to spend a little time with the prom king?"

"Yes. We're going to Rome, and sure I'll try to see him, but remember this is a business trip. Charlie says it's very important to the firm. The partners are really excited about this Italian connection and feel it could lead to bigger and better things from Europe. I thought I might like to be a part of that. I was even thinking about going to law school at night, get my law degree, and pass the bar."

"All this because you can speak Italian?" Sara asked. "Aren't you daydreaming a little? You think they'll let you into the chummy old boys club?"

"I don't have to be a partner. I'm looking for a challenge, and this sounds like a good one."

"Maybe they'll ask you to head up the Italian branch of Neuberger when they open it," Sara joked.

In fact Judy had been fantasizing that this might be the key to her Carlo daydream. I could be a successful lawyer in Rome, she thought, the vanguard of the Neuberger invasion into Europe. Handling legal business during the day and then coming home to Carlo at night. She pushed that idea to the back of her subconscious as she reminded herself that she was still married to Tony.

She noticed that Paul Logan was temporarily alone, excused herself, picked up her glass of wine, and went over to his table. He stood up in gentlemanly fashion as she sat down.

"Paul," she began, "we don't know each other very well, but there's an opportunity waiting for you."

He stared at her with a look Judy could not fathom. (Was that a hint of a sneer—or a leer—on his face, or surprise? she wondered.) He raised his eyebrows, and said slowly, "What kind of an opportunity would that be?"

"An opportunity to travel." He stared at her quizzically. "For the firm," she added hastily.

She explained the mission to him.

"Of course I'll do it," he said after she explained the mission. "Anything for the firm." And anything to get away from my family, he thought to himself.

Chapter 30

Saturday dawned sunny and warm. Judy lazily turned over in bed as Tony came out of the shower.

"There's something we have to talk about," she said raising up on an elbow.

Tony stared at her but said nothing. Now what, he thought.

"I'm going to Italy on business. For Neuberger."

He processed this information trying to figure out what impact this would have on his life. "Now what the hell kind of business do they have in Italy?" he said.

She explained about the firm's new client, and that she had been chosen because she spoke Italian; and she would be accompanied by Charlie Price and Paul Logan.

"Just you and two men?" he said. "I don't like it."

"Why not?"

He had spoken without thinking and wasn't sure why he didn't like it, but he knew he didn't like it. He stifled the anger he felt; she had made an important decision without asking him. If I wasn't in such deep shit with her, he thought, I'd really let her know how pissed off I am.

"When do you leave, and how long is it for?" he grumbled.

"We leave two weeks from today, and we'll probably only stay a few days," she answered.

"I suppose I can manage without you," he grouched. Now he was even more upset, realizing he would have to change his routine.

Zeroing in on what was most important to him he said, "I guess I'll eat out or eat at my sister's."

That's at the top of his list of concerns? she thought. How long 'til I can cook for him again? No "good luck" or "How wonderful that you were chosen" or "This will be a thrilling trip for you." Nothing about me; he's only concerned with his stomach. Well, that's about what I expected. She turned away from him to hide her disgust.

He dried off, he crumpled the towel and dropped it on the bathroom floor, sat down on the edge of the bed and said, "I'll go and visit Mom this morning. You can stay in bed, and you don't have to make me breakfast. My sister can make me something."

Lucia Fanelli had left the hospital and was recuperating with her daughter in South Philadelphia.

"That's fine with me," Judy said. "I've put off my spring flower planting for too long already. I'll do it today while you're gone."

She had bought the seeds as soon as the Burpee display had been set up in the supermarket, but hadn't yet found the time to plant them.

When she heard his car start, she got up from bed, dressed quickly, decided to skip breakfast, and started to the garage. The phone rang. It was her mother.

Her mother, Judy discovered, was even more excited about the trip to Rome than she was and had called almost every day since she heard. As Judy expected her mother launched into the lecture (Judy could recite it by heart having heard it many times since childhood) about the grandeur of Rome and singular honor being a Roman.

Judy interrupted her and said, "Gotta go now Ma. I hear the doorbell ringing." Then she felt guilty for cutting her mother off.

As soon as she hung up the phone, it rang again.

It was Kate. Judy told her about the coming trip to Italy.

Kate seemed unusually interested. "And you'll only be gone a week . . . or less?" she repeated.

"That's the current plan. All we have to do is have one or two meetings with the owners and maybe visit their factories and then we come home." She was ready to tell Kate of the excitement she was feeling in anticipation of seeing Carlo again when suddenly a red flag flashed in front of her eyes. She remembered the uneasiness she felt during recent conversations she had with Kate. Something intuitive warned her that it might be best to keep some things secret from Kate.

Kate interrupted her thoughts with: "And you went to Friday's for the firm's party? Did you get to brown-nose any of top brass?"

"No. Not this time. I was too busy asking Paul to go with us. He had a million questions after he said he'd go. But starting now, I'm making it my business to meet the partners at those get-togethers. This could be my chance to get ahead."

"I'm happy for you, Judy. This sounds like a real good opportunity for you . . . and all because you speak Italian. Who'd've thought?"

Judy hung up the phone and made up her mind not to answer it if it rang again and resolutely went to the garage. She took a wicker basket from the shelf and tossed the seed packets in it, then took down the trowel and the claw from the pegboard and tossed them in. Her gardening gloves (the white ones with the big pink polka dots on them) were lying on Tony's workbench; she pulled them on. As she walked briskly out to the garden, she cupped her hand to her forehead to shield her eyes from the glare of the bright sunlight. She knelt at the edge of the flowerbed, reached far into the back, and dug out the brown, withered remnants of last year's annuals. With the claw and trowel she gently tilled the soil and prepared the ground for the seeds. With a mother's love she planted larkspur in the back since it would grow tall. It would get the morning sun yet not block the sun from the shorter plants in front. Carefully she ripped open the other packets and planted the rest of the seeds.

She stood up, stretched her neck, and arched over backward to relieve the stiffness in her back and legs, then went back to the garage for the hose. As she uncoiled it, it lost its stiffness as the sun began to heat it up. She hooked it to an outside faucet and soaked the entire garden.

After she had put everything away, she stood for a moment, hands on hips, admiring what she had accomplished. Then she turned and began to walk back to the house. In an instant the brightness of the day gave way to a menacing darkening. Judy glanced up. A great black cloud had formed in the distance. As she watched, it grew larger and larger and came closer and closer gradually blotting out the sun. Suddenly the cloud appeared to come to life; she felt it stalking her ominously. Before she could move, she felt an eerie, damp, darkness surrounding her. The temperature dropped sharply; her skin goose bumped and crawled in the clammy air. Uncharacteristically, she began to sweat in spite of the cold. For a second an unnamed terror overwhelmed her; she fought it off.

Summoning all her energy she ran for the house. She yanked open the French doors in the dining room which overlooked the back yard and hurriedly pushed them shut behind her as huge explosions of thunder booming like artillery barrages began to bombard her eardrums. Panting she braced herself against a sofa. After a minute, she realized she was safe inside her house, and the fear gradually subsided.

Mesmerized she watched out the doors. There were many clouds now, and they seethed and roiled first in one direction and then another. Finally they merged into one huge, jet-black cloud in the shape of . . . (her breath stuck in her throat), a heart! The cloud attacked, hurling golf-ball-sized hail pellets which pinged and clunked as they slammed into the house. Jagged bolts of lightning zigzagged down from the sky to the ground, hissing and crackling like a thousand angry snakes. Judy staggered backward and tripped over her own feet. She fell heavily to the ground, banged her head on the floor, and passed out. In her unconscious state she continued to see the evil, black, cloud-heart. She cringed in fear as it enveloped the house, turned into a tornado funnel, and whirled the house with her in it up to the sky.

When she regained consciousness a minute later, her head was still spinning. Slowly she picked herself up from the floor, and the dizziness gradually left her. She realized she was still in her house and the house was on the ground and had not moved. Outside the thunder and lightening had stopped; the sun was shining brightly. The hail was rapidly melting. In a few minutes there was no evidence of the storm.

What did this weird attack mean? Judy wondered. She groped her way onto the couch and sank down into it. She took deep breaths of air trying to clear away the cold, clamminess she still felt.

Somewhere from deep in her inner soul, a spark of her witch's insight burst into a flame of realization. She knew what the cloud meant. The woman with the heart tattoo had planned something terrible. Something was going to happen which would turn her life upside down. In spite of the warm sun she shivered uncontrollably.

Chapter 31

$\mathcal{I}$t had been four weeks since Dominic Micaletto had been given one week to decide whether or not to go into the drug business. Because he had other things on his mind—primarily his nieces' drug dependence—he had forgotten about it; and besides he had made his decision when he had hung up the phone. After watching what happened to his nieces, there was nothing he could think of that could make him get involved in any way in the drug business. He continued to practice his "if I don't do anything maybe the problem will go away or get better on its own" philosophy, and like an ostrich, he had firmly stuck his head in the sand.

The phone rang interrupting his usual Tuesday night card game.

"It's for you," Sal said, handing him the phone.

"Who the fuck is it?" Dominic asked.

"He won't give his name, and I don't recognize the voice."

Dominic swiped the receiver from Sal and with his usual bluster, shouted a greeting into the phone.

When the voice on the other end of the line began speaking in Sicilian, he knew he was in trouble.

"This is the manufacturer in Palermo," the high-pitched voice said in a business-like tone. "My distributors in New York expected to hear from you weeks ago. Dominic," he sounded like a father rebuking a wayward son, "I can't wait any longer. I've got to have distribution in Philadelphia. Are you the man to do it?"

Stumbling purposely with his Sicilian, Sal huffed and puffed and waffled.

Angrily, the man on the other end cut him short. "I ain't got no time for your bullshit. We can't talk no more on the phone; this is too important." The voice became calmer and almost sugary. "Before I go use someone else, we should talk in person. You come to Palermo and see me. I'm sure we can work something out."

Dominic knew he was speaking to the drug lord known as Don Cesare—he wasn't sure of his last name—and was smart enough to recognize a summons when he heard one. Even though he knew exactly what the Don wanted, and he knew exactly what his reply would be, he agreed to go.

"But I got to get a passport, and . . . ," he whined.

"You get whatever you need, but you get here. You got one week. And this time it's really one week. If you're not here in one week . . . I'll have to make other arrangements."

Dominic waited for the click before he slammed the receiver into its cradle. This time it shattered into a dozen pieces. He ignored the broken phone, sunk into a chair, and buried his face in his hands. This is it, he thought. I've got to go see him. Briefly he considered taking two bodyguards with him but decided against it. If he wants to kill me, he reasoned, he's going to kill me no matter what I do or whom I bring. He went back to the card table.

"Whose deal is it?" he said.

Chapter 32

$\mathcal{I}$n the two weeks before she left for Italy, Judy heard from almost every relative she had, some of whom hadn't spoken to her since her father died. Her mother had proudly informed them that her daughter was going to Rome. Each of them asked her to deliver a message or gift to some member of the family still living in Italy.

"But it's a business trip," she told them. "These people are going to invite me to their homes, and I won't have time to see them all. I'll only promise to call them on the phone." And, she said to herself, on the day I leave Italy. Nothing will get in the way of my seeing Carlo and spending time with him, she thought.

And now it was early Saturday morning, May 3rd. Judy planned to go to the airport late in the afternoon and meet her traveling companions in time for the ten o'clock flight to Rome. As the morning light twinkled into her bedroom from the crack between the shade and the window, Judy, who had been awake most of the night with pre-trip excitement, jerked upright and poked Tony.

"Get up," she said. "I'm gong to Italy today."

Tony forced his eyes open and glanced at the clock next to the bed. "Holy shit. It's seven in the morning, and the plane doesn't leave until ten tonight. I think we'll make it."

He rolled over and pulled the sheet up over his head, but she nudged him until he woke up.

"I've got some last minute shopping to do. Besides, I'm too excited to sleep. I'm up. You're gonna be up."

Before she knew it the day had flown by and it was late afternoon. Tony, waiting in the driveway, grew impatient and honked twice. He drove to Philadelphia International Airport and pulled up at the curb baggage check-in. He leaned over and kissed her like a long-married man kisses his wife—perfunctorily—(not like that airport kiss with Carlo she thought wistfully), wished her well, and half-heartedly mouthed some banality ("I'll miss you," or some such). With her index finger she gently touched the horn hanging around his neck then kissed it. "For luck," she said.

He helped her out of the car and she elbowed him away.

"You can go home," she said as she grabbed the handle of her suitcase. "I can manage from here."

She began rolling her luggage toward the terminal.

"Call me," he said to her back.

His duties over, Tony breathed a sigh of relief, and he cautiously edged into traffic.

Inside the revolving door Paul Logan was standing his typical ramrod straight, dressed in a double-breasted, pinstriped suit. Stifling a smirk, Judy waved. Who in his right mind would wear a suit and tie for an eight-hour plane ride? she thought.

"Hi, Paul," she said greeting him with a smile.

"Hello," he said. She fully expected him to say "Mrs. Fanelli," but he didn't. "Are you aware of the seating arrangements?" he asked.

"Never thought about them," she answered. She hadn't considered them, nor were they of any consequence to her.

"Mr. Price is, of course, flying business class. He is currently in the U S Airways lounge. He gave me our tickets. As you see, we are flying coach."

"As long as I get to Rome, I don't really care where I sit," Judy said.

"You may care after being jammed into a seat with no leg room. Or you may care after the first baby starts crying. Or you may care . . ." He trailed off as he noticed her eyes glazing over. "You're obviously not paying any attention to me," he pouted.

"I'm sorry. I'm thinking about the fun I'm going to have in Rome." Hastily she added, "After our work is done, we should get some free time, and I'm making plans in my head."

"You may have fun," he muttered to himself. "I intend to do my job. Rome or Philadelphia, it doesn't matter. I was hired to work not to have fun."

They presented their tickets and passports at the check-in counter, then trudged silently down the long Terminal A corridor. Paul pointed to their gate and in the waiting area they settled into two sky-blue, plastic, body-holders. Judy closed her eyes and let her thoughts turn to the last time she was in this airport—with Carlo—while Paul stared straight ahead without speaking. He clasped his hands sedately in his lap.

Their thoughts were shattered when the loudspeaker blared, "U S Airways flight 482 to Rome is now boarding at gate A-11." When the call was made for business class passengers, Charlie Price appeared and passed them by with a wave. Shortly after, Paul and Judy boarded the plane and settled into their seats. Judy closed her eyes and remembered how frightened she had been on her first plane trip. It had been on their tenth wedding anniversary and her parents had given them a trip to California. "Hold my hand Tony," she had pleaded with him. "I'm scared to death." She squeezed his hand as hard as she could until they had been airborne for fifteen minutes. Then she was able to relax. But now there was no one's hand to hold and, she said to herself. But I've come a long way since then. I'm not afraid, and I don't need that kind of reassurance any more.

As the plane positioned itself for takeoff at the foot of the runway, the pilot called for the stewardesses to take their seats. Judy winced as the noise level escalated past droning and annoying all the way to earsplitting. Then suddenly the plane hurtled down the runway, gathered momentum, became airborne, and nose pointed heavenward, gracefully soared northeasterly.

Paul took his briefcase out from where he had stowed it under the seat, pulled a pamphlet from it, and began to read. Looking straight ahead, but straining to see out of the corner of her eye, Judy could just make out what it was about. Exactly what she expected. It was a religious tract trumpeting that sinners would surely be punished for not following the ways of the Lord.

Soon drinks were served (Paul had red wine), then supper, after which the captain turned out the lights and encouraged the passengers to get some sleep. Judy closed her eyes and tried to shut out the rising symphony of noise around her: three rows in front of her, two sets of young parents tried desperately to stifle a serenade from crying babies. Their *a cappella* soprano arias were accompanied by bursts of snoring from those fortunate enough to be able to sleep anywhere and through anything. Slamming lavatory doors provided percussion. She tried to fall asleep, but couldn't. But Paul, perhaps secure in his faith, slept like a log.

*   *   *

The heavily Italian-accented voice thundered over the public address system jolting the passengers awake. "This is your captain. We will be landing at Rome's Fiumicino airport (or Leonardo da Vinci airport, if you prefer), in about an hour. Time on the ground is now 8:15 in the morning. The temperature is a beautiful twenty-nine degrees Celsius— eighty-four degrees Fahrenheit." The announcement was repeated in Italian.

The plane landed and taxied to the terminal. Judy and Paul waited until the doors opened then Paul handed Judy down her carryon from the overhead rack and followed her out the door. She had read about the swarms of people crushing into Tokyo subways during rush hour but did not expect that this mania had been exported to Rome. It had. Crowds of people pushed and shoved around the baggage carousel straining for a glimpse of their luggage. They yanked bags off the merry-go-round often missing other travelers' toes by inches. Throngs of tourists, businesspeople, and Italians churned and darted here and there, like drops of water on a hot stove, with no apparent destination in mind. The noise level in the main terminal approached rock concert intensity; people shouted and screamed in a Tower of Babel of languages.

Judy stayed as close to Paul as she could manage; and somehow in all the confusion Charlie Price joined them. "In case we get separated," he said, "I spoke to our clients this morning from the phone on the airplane. They said they would send a car for us."

At the immigration area harried officials screeched, *"Passaporti, passaporti,"* as they fanned themselves with their clipboards to get some relief from the heat. "How long you stay?" they asked each immigrant.

Near the customs area, a short, balding, thirtyish man with a baby face frantically waved a large cardboard sign over his head. "MR. CHARLES PRICE" was handwritten on it in large, block letters.

They waved to him and made their way through the crowd.

"I'm Alessandro, your driver," he grinned broadly, and shook their hands. "Come with me. This way. Stay together, close to me," he boomed as he led them into a nearby corner. "May I see some ID?" he said. Price offered him his passport which he inspected superficially. "*Multo bene*. Very good. You are really Mr. Price. Now we go. Keep moving. No need to stop for customs. My cousin's on duty, and I told him you were coming." He heaved their luggage onto a cart and nodded to the customs agent, who smiled and waved them through. He ushered them out of the airport building.

The calm outside was in striking contrast to the turmoil inside. Judy gasped as she sucked in the hot, moist, fume-laden air. As she looked around to get her bearings, she avoiding looking at the snarled traffic around the airport entrance, and instead tilted her head up and stared. Above her was the stunning azure Mediterranean sky. She studied it for a long time. It's a magical blue, she thought. The bluest, most beautiful blue I've ever seen; and that includes Paul Newman's eyes. Alessandro's smooth voice pulled her from her reverie.

"Now, we go to the hotel," he said. He pointed toward a waiting steel-gray, Mercedes limousine, led them to it, opened the door, and helped them in. "It's not far, so I'll give you a short tour of Rome on the way there. Okay?" Charlie Price nodded as he slipped into the front seat next to Alessandro.

Both exhaustion and enchantment overwhelmed Judy. She leaned back in the seat, felt the soothing air conditioning replace the oppressive heat, and she began to relax. She shut out the trickle of conversation that rustled around her—Paul was asking how long it would take to get to the hotel—and entered a private, solitary world. The feeling of coming home overwhelmed her. Home to Rome, she thought. And to Carlo? In spite of the air conditioning she felt her body warm just thinking about him, and she smiled. She tried to force herself to stay awake and take in every tree, every house, every detail, but fatigue overcame her, she hadn't slept on the plane, her eyes slowly shut, her head drooped forward onto her chest, and she dozed.

When Alessandro droned, "On your left is the Colosseum," Judy snapped to attention. "The most *prodigioso* monument in all of Rome," he continued. He made a left turn and drove slowly around the impressive ruin. Awed, Judy gaped at the huge oval-shaped, centuries-old, amphitheater. Punched in its stone walls were four rows of huge rectangular openings topped by semi-circular arches. It looked to her like a hollow skeleton with a thousand eyes. She felt those eyes boring into her, searing her soul, branding her forever with the stamp of Rome.

The Colosseum's effect continued to haunt her even when they coasted to a stop in front of their hotel just off the Via Veneto. She floated out of the car and stood at the curb inhaling the coarse, rugged smell of Italy. Around her the locals chattered in the lilting Italian her parents spoke. Oh, this is paradise, she thought. Someday I want to live here, in this city, even if it's only for a little while. Sighing deeply, she climbed the steps and followed the three men through the door into the hotel lobby.

"I've taken care of checking you in," Alessandro said. "Today you can rest up, but if you want anything here's my pager number." He handed Price a business card. "I've been told to get you whatever you need. Tomorrow the meetings start at nine here, in the hotel conference room."

The desk clerk beckoned Alessandro, and they had a short whispered conversation. Alessandro pulled Judy aside. "Mrs. Fanelli, there is a message for you at the front desk," he said raising his eyebrows. "You have a friend in Rome?"

"It's my . . . cousin," she said nervously. "I told him I would be here, and I'm very anxious to see him."

"Ah, yes. Your . . . cousin," Alessandro said seriously.

As Judy walked away, Paul Logan cornered Alessandro. "Is the Boboli Museum open today?" he asked.

Alessandro shrugged and said, "I don't know, but I'll find out for you."

Paul said, "Can you take me there anyway after I get my bags to my rooms?"

"No problem. Here, the bellboy will take your bags up to your room. You come with me." Paul, still wearing his pinstriped suit, followed Alessandro out into the hot, Italian sunshine.

Judy stepped up to the front desk, and the clerk handed her a sealed envelope. Anxiously she ripped it open and read the note inside. "Dear Judy," it began. And then followed a plea for her to call the minute she got in. "I will be waiting by the phone with a plate of sandwiches (in case I get hungry)," it concluded. And then it was signed, "Love, Carlo."

Dear Judy, Dear Judy, Love, Carlo, Love, Carlo. She repeated the mantra over and over in her mind while her heart skipped a beat with excitement. She remembered the kiss at the airport. Was that the start of love? she wondered. Is this going to be love? Am I already in love? It feels like love. But, she thought sadly, I can't let myself fall in love. Not now, not while I'm still married to Tony.

The bellboy took her luggage, led her to the elevator, and inspected her room key. "Oh, you have a lovely room, *Signora*," he said. Exhausted she followed him up to her room. Right now I'm going to take a shower, then call Carlo, and then collapse, she planned.

The elevator whisked them up to the fifth floor. The bellboy opened the door to the room for her, and Judy wobbled in. She sprawled out on the bed and paid no attention as he tossed the bags on a luggage rack and mumbled some instructions about how to use the air conditioner. Still lying on her back she handed him two dollar bills, he dropped the key on the dresser with profuse thanks, and Judy shooed him out. She clasped her hands behind her head, crossed her ankles, and stared at the ceiling. Jet lag, the pull of Rome, lack of sleep, excitement about seeing Carlo, all jumbled together in her mind and sapped her strength. It felt very strange—this combination of exhilaration and exhaustion. She shucked her clothes, flopped back on the bed, and decided to postpone the shower for a little while. She leaned over, took the phone from the table next to the bed, and dialed Carlo's number.

"You're finally here," he gushed into the phone. "You don't know how nervous I was waiting for you. I was sure something would go wrong at the last minute, and you wouldn't come. I can't believe you're really here." Before she could say anything, he went on, "I don't know where we should go first. There's so much I want to show you. Let's start at the Spanish Steps. Take a taxi from your hotel. It's not far. I'll meet you there, and we can have lunch together."

"Slow down, Carlo, please," she said. "I've got to take a shower and rest up for a few minutes or else I'll fall asleep over lunch."

"No problem. Would four o'clock be okay?"

She agreed, "Okay. Four o'clock."

As she hung up the phone her head swam; she closed her eyes and fell into a dreamy trance. The picture of Tony in bed with the woman with the heart tattoo swam before her subconscious. Suddenly the figures became distorted and wavy like those in a Chagall painting; they writhed in a slow motion, sinuous, passionate, embrace. It took all her will to make the picture disappear.

As the couple faded, a new dream slowly materialized. A ghostly figure appeared and gradually took the form of a handsome, sensuous young man. He licked his lips, grinned, winked charmingly, and opened his arms to her. She felt a burst of lust rising. She ran to him and raised her mouth to his. Their lips touched in a sweet, gentle kiss which bit-by-bit became fiercely passionate. She pulled him close to her, molded her body into his, and surrendered herself to him. He caressed her lovingly. Embracing the ghost, she felt she was embracing Rome. He whisked his hands over her body and her clothes flew away in shreds. He lowered her gently to the ground, and in the same motion, entered her. She felt a searing jolt of electricity zigzag through her body, and she knew it was the spirit of Rome spreading inside her, burning its imprint on her soul, soldering its very essence to her. She thrashed uncontrollably in a paroxysm of combined sex and joy, then sapped of all strength, gasping for air, she lay limply, half asleep, half awake. Now she felt she had become one with Rome, joined together forever. She could never free herself. Oh, please, please God, a voice inside her begged, if there is a God, let me spend the rest of my life here in Rome.

With passion spent, release bathed over her, and she slept deeply for a few minutes. Suddenly she woke up, her eyes flew open, and she glanced at the clock. It was almost three o'clock. Omigod, she thought, I've got to hurry if I'm going to meet Carlo.

She showered in record time, dressed, and raced out the hotel's front door. "*Piazza d'Espagna*," she told a waiting taxi driver. After a short ride, he approached the top of the Spanish steps and asked, "You wanna get off here or at the bottom?"

"The top. Oh, yes, the top," she answered without hesitation. "I want to walk down, walk down the steps."

She got out of the cab, and without counting, handed the driver a fistful of money, totally unaware of what the fare was or how much she had given him as a tip. It must have been overly generous because he smiled broadly and gave her a slow military salute as he drove away.

Looking down the long flight of steps she guessed there might be as many as a hundred and fifty steps from the top to the large open square below. For a few seconds she marveled at the view around her, then took a deep breath and started walking down the steps, carefully watching the drama which unfolded below her.

At the foot of the steps was a huge open square crowded with people. A large fountain with water spouting from a dinosaur-like sculpture sat at the foot of the stairs. Sitting on the edge of the fountain, the uninhibited and foot-weary had taken their shoes and socks off, and a United Nations of feet dangled in the splashing water. Stringy-haired, unwashed, youngsters (of both sexes) with their trademark knapsacks, mixed easily with bee-hived, polyestered tourists. Roman matrons, enjoying the warm, sunny day, chatted loudly and made elaborate hand gestures for emphasis as they strolled through the piazza. Judy tilted her head as she listened to a din of voices in a variety of languages; she cocked her head and smiled. The dissonance was somehow pleasant.

She had walked halfway around the fountain when . . . there he was! Carlo. He had been pacing nervously around and around the fountain, panning the area feverishly to catch sight of her. Somehow he had missed her in the crowd coming down the steps, but now he spotted her and raced to meet her. Neither knew exactly what to do. A hug, a kiss? Carlo threw his arms around her, rested his chin on her neck, and struggled to keep his balance from the force of her embrace. She held him tightly and nestled on his shoulder.

"I'm so glad to see you," he sputtered. "I can't believe you're really here." He pulled his head back, thought he saw a flicker of invitation in her eyes, and kissed her hard as he had at the airport.

Breathing heavily Judy rested in his arms and tried to deny the warm feelings that rushed through her.

"Give me a chance to catch my breath," she gasped as a wave of fatigue enveloped her. "I've just taken a long walk down all those steps." Then, desperate to get her racing mind from thoughts of romance, she put her hands on his chest and gently pushed him back. She said, "You've got to tell me everything you've been doing. How do you like Rome? What's your job like?"

"No. No," he said. "There'll be time for that later. Now let's enjoy. Come on we'll take a walk."

The piazza and the main street leading from it, the Via Condotti, were closed to vehicular traffic. He took her hand in his and led her through the wall-to-wall people who jammed the narrow street. A short way down, on the left side, five, plain, silver letters—G U C C I—tastefully displayed above a doorway, glimmered in the sunlight. He nodded in that direction, and she smiled. Feeling suddenly faint she stumbled and grabbed his arm before she could fall.

"This isn't working out," she said. He looked at her stunned. "No, it's not your fault," she hurried to add. "It's me. I'm dead tired. I really have to go back to the hotel and lie down. As much as I'd like to be with you I've got to get some rest or I'll be dog meat at the meeting tomorrow, and they're counting on me to translate."

He turned to her with a dejected expression. "Okay," he reluctantly agreed. "I'll see you back to the hotel, but promise we'll get together when you have some free time."

"You'll definitely hear from me," she said. "Don't worry about that."

In the taxi on the way back to the Savoia Judy leaned her head on his shoulder but was unable to sleep. In spite of the heat she snuggled closer to him, and he wrapped his arms around her.

*　　*　　*

It was two days before they saw each other again. Judy hadn't been sleeping well—too excited being in Rome, strange bed, unable to see Carlo? Which one? she wondered—and awoke from another night of tossing and turning. When she looked out the window and saw a dazzling sun shining brightly, she tried to put her weariness aside, and sensing this would be a tingling, sensuously, warm day, decided to make every effort to enjoy it. Since there was no meeting scheduled this morning, she and Carlo had made plans. She ordered breakfast sent to her room, showered, dressed, and ate quickly. When she got off the elevator, she saw him waiting for her across the lobby, and kissed him on the cheek. He kissed her back lightly on the mouth.

"He's my cousin," she explained to Paul who was sitting in the lobby nearby. He had taken his nose out of the guidebook he had been reading, looked up, and stared disapprovingly at the two of them.

"Let's get out of here," she said to Carlo casting an annoying glance at Logan.

"Okay. We'll do some major league sightseeing," he said as he helped her into a taxi. "By the way how are your meetings going?"

"Dullsville. The Italians are serious business types. They came in, sit down and get right down to business. No 'Hello, how are you?' no pleasantries, no jokes, no nonsense, just business."

"And how is your translating going?"

"As far as I can tell, when they talk Italian to each other, they aren't trying to be sneaky or hide anything. It all seems to be on the up and up. And," she turned to Carlo and grinned smugly, "they are very old-world charming. They are so courteous and nice to me; one even offered to take me to lunch today. I told him 'no,' and later they offered to take all of us to lunch, but Mr. Price begged off saying we needed a break. So we got the morning off, but we have to meet with them this afternoon."

Carlo pointed out various sights as they twisted along charming, narrow streets. A fountain here, a crumbling, old building there.

"And where are we going?" Judy asked.

"It'll be a surprise. Be patient, we're almost there."

They entered a small piazza jammed with buses and teeming with tourists. As Carlo paid the taxi driver, Judy looked in awe.

"Oh, look!" she exclaimed. "It's the Trevi fountain. It takes your breath away."

Stuck on the front of an old palazzo, a huge, marble Neptune rode in a winged chariot. Below him, horses and demigods frolicked in a jumble of large rocks. Jets of water hissed and tumbled in all directions. Judy hurried to the fountain's edge and gawked at the display for a few minutes before searching through her purse for some coins.

"All I have is American coins. Will they work?" she asked.

Carlo reached into his pocket and handed her a fistful of change. "I'm not sure, but here's some Italian coins," he said, "in case it only works with Italian money."

"Okay, I'll throw them all in." She laughed and waved him away.

She stuffed all the coins into her palm, made a fist, and turned her back to the fountain. The spray tickled the back of her neck; she squeezed her eyes shut. This is more than a wish, she said to herself. This is more than a promise. This is a solemn oath. I swear I'll come back here, to Rome, some day soon.

"C'mon there's more to see," Carlo called. He stretched out his hand toward her.

"Almost done," Judy said. With a quick over-the-shoulder toss, she threw the handful of coins into the fountain. Now, she thought, it's official. It will happen. I *will* return.

Carlo took her hand and led her back to the taxi.

A few minutes later he nodded out the window to an immense, stark-white monument at the head of a huge piazza. In the forefront was a statue of a horse and rider.

"This is the center of Rome," he said waving his hand. "The Piazza Venezia. Somebody once called that monument 'The Wedding Cake' because of the way it's tiered. That's King Victor Emmanuel II on the horse; and from over there," Carlo pointed to his left and indicated a balcony, "Mussolini harangued the crowds."

The sun glinting from the monument warmed Judy through the taxi's window. She felt a glow prickling over her skin, which she understood was Rome worming its way ever more deeply inside her. She closed her eyes to bask in the moment and could not help herself; she dozed off.

"You seem very . . . thoughtful," Carlo said waking her up.

She put the back of her hand to her mouth to hide the yawn she couldn't stop. "I'm sorry. I'm just so very tired," she said. "I didn't sleep well on the plane over, and I didn't sleep well Sunday night after I left you. Monday we had meetings all day, and I was too charged up to sleep. So I haven't had a good night sleep since I left the States, and it's catching up to me."

"No problem. I can fix that. We'll stop at my place. It's not far from here." He noticed she bristled. "Don't worry, I won't try to seduce you."

It wouldn't take much, Judy thought, but she said, "Does that mean that maybe another time you will?"

"Sure. If you'd like," Carlo teased. "Anyway, when I first came here, I had trouble sleeping too, so I went to a doctor in the neighborhood. He gave me some sleeping pills that really work. I've got some left over, and you can have them." He leaned over and gave the driver his address in the Trastevere section of Rome.

"I live in the most Roman part of Rome," he said proudly. "Your mother would love it." (Judy, of course, had told him of her mother's passion for Rome.)

The ancient neighborhood was veined by narrow twisting streets full of buildings that looked like they had seen better days. Judy noticed the stone facades were crumbling badly, and some were defaced with ugly graffiti. As they stepped from the taxi, a melodious tenor voice floated down from the fifth floor of a nearby building. The operatic aria was sung with great tenderness, dripping with love. They stopped in their tracks to listen.

"Do you know what that aria is?" Judy asked quietly.

"It's from the first act of *Traviata*," Carlo whispered.

"How do you . . . ," Judy began.

Carlo held a finger to his lips to shush her. "Violetta asks Alfredo how long he has loved her," Carlo whispered. "And he says he has loved her for a whole year; since the day he met her."

"I know. I know. I understand Italian. Now you shhh," Judy said.

They stood silently, side by side, transfixed by the beauty of the music and the intensity and emotion of the singer. The tenor sang of love in a sweet, robust voice:

Di quelle'amor, quell'amor ch'è palpito,
Dell'universo, dell'universo intero,
Misterioso, misterioso altero,
Croce, croce e delizia, croce e delizia, delizia al cor.

Carlo wrapped his hand around her waist and pulled her close to him. They stood side touching side while each silently translated the words:

Ah, the love that is the heart beat
Of the whole universe,
Deeply mysterious,
Torment and rapture.

How true, how true, Judy thought. A torment and a rapture; a sorrow and a joy. That's love all right. She tried to sort out her feelings for Carlo: If I'm not already in love with him, it would be easy to fall in love with him. He is kind, interested in me, and handsome.

But she was married to Tony, she remembered, and she had more or less agreed to forgive his past infidelity after he promised not to do it again. So there was the sorrow; she must be faithful to her husband. She would make sure that nothing would come of her relation with Carlo; they could only be friends. She would struggle to keep herself from falling in love with him.

Carlo's thoughts were about the woman next to him; the woman that he had taken to a prom so long ago and now had come back into his life. The more time I spend with her, he thought, the more I'm sure she's the one I want to spend the rest of my life with. I've never been so sure of anything in my life. But she's married and doesn't seem willing to give up on Tony even though he was caught with another woman. Is there any kind of future for the two of us? he wondered.

For a few moments there was silence, then the tenor began to repeat the aria again breaking the spell for them. They said nothing to each other but exchanged looks which conveyed what they had been thinking. Carlo sighed, took her hand, and led her into one of the ancient, run down, buildings. Judy expected his apartment to be a disaster—in the same condition it was hundreds of years ago. But once inside she was pleasantly surprised. The building had been recently renovated and was amazingly modern. He noticed her look of astonishment.

"The only thing missing is an elevator," he said as he led her up a narrow staircase to the third floor.

He unlocked the door to his apartment and held it open for her. The one-bedroom apartment was tiny, but clean and modern. Judy whooshed at the beautiful furnishings: a brown-leather, sectional sofa, midnight-blue beanbag chair, and a small TV filled up the living room. Modernistic paintings, whose subjects could not readily be determined, were strung out along the wall. This must have cost him plenty, she thought.

"Wow!" she said. "Nice apartment."

"I decided to splurge," he said. "Instead of paying for a wife and children, I buy furniture and artwork."

"Like to see the bedroom?" he asked. In spite of his efforts to be nonchalant there was a tremor to his voice.

For a brief moment an idea flashed through her mind. The bedroom, she thought. I could go to bed with Carlo. His hands would caress me; his body would make love to me. How wonderful, how easy it would be. Who would know? It's not like Tony's fiasco; there wouldn't be anyone to take pictures. She startled herself with an emphatic "No!!" I can't do that, she thought. I'm still married to Tony, and I've got to try to work it out. But let that prick slip up one more time . . . She let the thought drop.

She didn't answer Carlo's invitation to see the bedroom but peeked cautiously into it. A queen-sized bed with a Ralph Lauren floral coverlet and a nondescript nightstand filled the room almost completely.

He stepped around her into the bathroom grazing his hand around her waist then brushing it across her back. Squeezing her eyes shut, she shoved the twinge that she felt into the hold-area of her mind and listened to him rummage through the medicine cabinet. When she opened her eyes, he was handing her a bubble pack with four pills in it.

"Rohypnol," she said slowly reading the label. "Never heard of it."

"The doctor said they're not available in the States, but they are the most popular sleeping pill in Europe. They worked for me, but be careful to take only one, and take it right before you go to bed. And NO alcohol. Some people who take it with alcohol get knocked out."

Judy took the pills from him and retreated to the living room where she leaned on the arm of the couch.

"Carlo, if I sit down, I'll never get up. I am really beat," she said. "Please take me home—I mean to the hotel." She smiled an embarrassed smile. "And thanks for these," she said as she stuffed the pills in her purse.

"Are you sure you won't stay?" he asked.

She didn't answer but willed herself to open the door, grasped the railing securely, and tramped down the steps.

Reluctantly he followed her.

*   *   *

That night after turning down the sheets, Judy sat on the edge of the bed. Here goes, she thought as she put a pill on her tongue and took a sip from a bottle of Evian.

Ten minutes later she had fallen asleep; she slept a deep sleep with no dreams. In the morning she had to summon all her strength to get out of bed. Even after taking a shower and eating breakfast, the drugged feeling remained, and she had trouble remembering exactly what had happened last evening.

This is a weird feeling, she thought, and I don't like it. I'm not going to take these pills again no matter how much I need sleep, she promised herself. She prepared to throw the rest of the pills in the trashcan, but a voice inside her warned, "Keep them."

She put them in her suitcase.

Chapter 33

$\mathcal{K}$ate had cleared her calendar for Thursday thinking: Judy'll only be in Italy for a few more days, I've got to make the best of a limited window of opportunity.

She woke up early in the morning and tried to drain her nervous energy. Until mid-afternoon, she scrubbed the kitchen floor, dusted the knick-knacks in her living room, and washed two large windows in the family room. At three o'clock she showered, toweled off, and sprayed perfume lightly on her neck. ("Obsession" should do it, she thought.) She leafed through her clothes until she found the extra short, black, leather miniskirt that showed off her legs and tied it around her waist. Makeup, she thought while she applied it sparingly, should make me look sexy but not whorish. As she buttoned up the white blouse which displayed a maximum of cleavage, she admired the finished product in the mirror, then smoothed her hands down her sides over her hips, and shimmied once sexily. She leered at the woman in the mirror who leered back at her.

Head high, back straight, she strutted out to the gaudy, red Pontiac Sunfire which twinkled in the late afternoon sun. As she squirmed in under the wheel and drove away, she hummed a tune and headed toward the Fanelli house. Two blocks away, she parked where she could see the front of the house but could not be readily seen, then turned on the radio, and drummed her fingers on the seat next to her in time to the hard rock music.

It was a quarter after six when she saw Tony's car pull into the driveway. As she started her engine, he got out and slung his gym bag loosely over his shoulder. He did not see the red car glide to a stop in the middle of the next block.

He's home late, she thought. I wonder who he's been out screwing? Whoever she was, I don't give a shit, because it's my turn now.

As he entered the house and closed the front door, she sprayed a short squirt of Binaca in her mouth, took a careful look at herself in the rear view mirror, patted her hair into place, then walked up to the front door and rang the doorbell.

Sounding annoyed Tony yelled through the closed door, "Who is it? I'm eating supper."

"Avon lady," she cooed. "Open up."

Trouble! echoed through Tony's head when he recognized the voice. What does she want now? he wondered as he opened the door slowly just a crack.

"Hello," she said smiling jauntily, arms akimbo, legs apart. "Hi," he replied unenthusiastically. He stood in the opening barring her way in.

"Can I come in?" she asked flippantly, cocking her head to one side.

He stared at the flawless legs and followed them up until the miniskirt got in his way. His eyes skipped up to the "V" of her blouse where he struggled to see more than was shown.

"Judy's not home," he said slowly, trying in vain to pry his eyes from her body. "She's still in Rome."

"Home, Rome. Wow, you're a poet. So she's still in Rome, so what. We don't need a chaperon, do we?" she said sweetly.

"I'm not sure I want you to come in. Bad things seem to happen when we get together."

Angrily. "I came to give you copies of some pictures I took at Nancy's wedding."

"That wedding was two months ago."

"Well, excuuuuse me. I just finished the roll of film and had it developed." She turned to leave. "I'll bring them another time when your keeper is home."

"Okay. Okay. C'mon in. I'll take a look at them."

He opened the door and stood back. As she marched past him into the house, she slid her hand across his cheek, smiled amiably, then sat down on the living room couch.

"Whaddaya have to drink?" she asked.

The alarm bells were now clanging danger so loudly in Tony's head that he was sure she could hear them, but he ignored them and answered, "There's Chianti in the kitchen."

"How Italian," she muttered. Out loud: "Would you get me a glass, please?" She kicked off her shoes, folded her legs and tucked them up under her, perfectly playing the role of the not quite demure innocent, but not quite the sex queen either.

Tony returned from the kitchen with two empty wine glasses and a straw-basketed bottle and set them on the coffee table. He eyed her warily as he filled both glasses. He handed her one, took the other for himself, and sat down on the other end of the couch—as far away from her as he could manage. He could not avoid sneaking looks at the generous display of skin the miniskirt had left exposed.

They clinked their glasses together with no toast and sized each other up as boxers do at the beginning of a fight when they circle around looking for an opening and wait for the other to make the first move. The silence clawed unmercifully at Tony; but Kate calmly took little sips from the glass of wine knowing that time was on her side.

Finally he couldn't stand the tension he felt building. "Show me the pictures," he blurted out.

"Surprise," she said in her low, sultry, sexy voice. She set her glass of wine down. "There aren't any pictures. But you knew that, didn't you?" She sidled down the couch until she was next to him and lightly brushed her braless breast against him as she threw an arm around his shoulder. "I had to see you again, Tony." She was almost whimpering. "I've got it so bad for you, and I can't get over it." She unbuttoned the top two buttons of his shirt and stuck her hand inside. The twisted silver horn hanging around his neck aroused her curiosity; she idly scratched it lightly across his chest. He struggled to ignore her but made only a half-hearted attempt to push her away.

"This is crazy. Not in my own house." His heavy breathing sucked in the perfume vapors from her neck and sent him reeling.

"Why not? It's quiet here. No one will disturb us. Judy's in Italy." Kate whispered in his ear. "It's just you and me. Okay?"

Without waiting for him to respond, she took the wine glass from his hand and put it on the table next to hers. She eased her hand down to his crotch and slowly raked the nail of her index finger up the teeth of the zipper on his fly. Prickly sensations shot through his groin. He thought about pushing her hand away and strained to summon his willpower. When she started to unbuckle his belt, his hand jerked involuntarily to his waist, found hers, and closed around it. She felt his grip was not an angry attempt to restrain her but a last feeble effort at resistance. Temporarily relaxing her efforts, she pulled her hand away but leaned in for the kill taking care to have her blouse fall away from her body.

"Look," she purred watching his eyes widen as they stared down her cleavage, "I've had this crazy hunger for you. It's driving me nuts. Honestly, I've tried everything I know to get you out of my mind. I wished, I prayed, I read self-help books, but nothing's worked. After that night in the motel, I can't think of anything but you." She began to sob. "Don't say 'no,' Tony. Please don't say 'no.' I need you so badly. Say 'yes'."

When he didn't say anything, she hiked up her skirt around her waist giving him a full view of her bikini panties, straddled onto his lap, smoothed her cheek next to his, and threw her arms around his neck. She pulled his head to her breasts, forced a tear from her eyes, and said, "You want me to beg? Okay, I'm begging. Please, Tony. Please. I've got to have you." She wriggled slowly back and forth in his lap. "I need you inside me to put out this fire that burns at me so bad."

After a few seconds of Tony's inaction she thought she had lost him when suddenly she felt his hand snaking up her leg. When his fingers started exploring inside her panties, she writhed even harder against him massaging the hard lump in his lap. Then she backed off, reached down and unzipped his fly.

Losing whatever remained of his self-control; Tony lifted her from his lap and laid her down full length on the couch. During the few days separation from Judy he had not had another woman, and now the bottled up woman-ache exploded inside him, overwhelming him like a torrent of water from a bursting dam. He ripped her blouse open; buttons popped off in all directions. He buried his face in her breasts, kissing and licking them furiously.

"Let's go upstairs," she murmured in his ear as she gently tried to get up.

"Not in my bed," he moaned.

"Anywhere," she panted. "This couch is okay. The floor's okay. The kitchen table. I don't care."

"On second thought," he said, considering that someone might look in the first floor windows, "upstairs is better."

He took her hand and almost dragged her up to the guest room. He undid the knot holding her miniskirt, tore it away, stripped the rest of her clothes off, and then his own. With raging passion he pushed her down on the bed, entered her, and rocked back and forth on top of her. She shook her head from side to side to avoid the silver horn which swung dangerously close to her eyes.

"Tony. Wait. Stop for a second," she cried. But he was in his own world, fast approaching climax, and in no mood to wait for anything. "That fucking thing's gonna poke my eye out," she growled. "Take it off." He ignored her and bounced even faster. Annoyed, she reached around his neck, unclasped it, and crumpled it tightly in her fist. A second later his breathing came faster and faster, then after a series of spasms, he lay quietly next to her completely oblivious to the missing necklace.

"That was nice," Kate said breaking the silence. "Real nice. You really scratched my itch. Oh, Tony, you're the best." She threw her arms around his neck and hugged him to her.

"I feel bad about this," he said without feeling a twinge of guilt, shame, or remorse, "because I promised Judy I wouldn't screw around anymore. We can't do this again. I only did it this time because Judy's out of town, and I got lonely."

Right, Kate thought, and I'm the tooth fairy.

In the awkward silence that followed, she smiled weakly at him, still clutching the good luck charm in her fist. Finally without another word he got up from the bed and went to the master bathroom and turned on the shower. She put on her clothes and stuffed the necklace into her purse thinking. Maybe this will come in handy someday.

She sauntered into the master bedroom and carefully scrutinized every detail. When Judy's jewelry box on top of the dresser caught her eye, she got an idea. Here's where I can make some more trouble, she realized. As she rummaged through it, a large diamond ring—it had been Judy's grandmother's wedding ring—seemed to be winking slyly at her. She listened: the water was still running in the shower, but to make sure she peeked into the bathroom. She watched: Tony's shadow dancing behind the glass shower door. She grabbed the ring, turned it over twice in her hand inspecting it carefully, then put it into her purse along with Tony's necklace.

"Anything else I can do?" she murmured softly to herself, as she began to open the dresser drawers and look at their contents. One drawer was full of Judy's lingerie neatly folded and stacked. She reached under her skirt and inched down her panties then sat on the edge of the bed and slid them the rest of the way off.

I tried this once, and it didn't do much good, she thought. Maybe this time I'll have better luck.

She picked up the panties up from the floor, wadded them into a ball, and stuffed them in the front of drawer. Maliciously, she ran her hands through the drawer rumpling its contents. When she finished, the drawer looked like a hurricane had gone through it. Noiselessly she eased the drawer shut taking care to tuck in the loose edges of clothing that stuck out.

As she left the room, she heard the shower was still running. "Now there's gonna be one real clean man," she said out loud, laughing as she made her way down the stairs.

She silently congratulated herself as she felt her revenge nearing completion. "More nails in the coffin," she thought to herself.

*   *   *

Six time zones away in Rome, it was after midnight. Thursday had changed to Friday, and Judy was fast asleep. She had only taken Carlo's sleeping pills the one time; after that, the tedium of the meetings had been her sedative and she had no trouble falling asleep.

She had not seen Carlo since she left his apartment because she had no free time. The meetings lasted all day and were incredibly dull. The Italian businessmen had warmed to the Americans, lost their serious manner, and become friendlier as time passed. Much of the conversation at the meetings now centered on discussing Rome, Italy, and trivia that had nothing to do with legal arrangements between Neuberger Roe & Price and the Italians. Sometimes Judy had to struggle to keep her eyes open, and often Paul Logan's head dipped to his chest, and he openly dozed. As far as she could tell, little had been accomplished other than that the parties had gotten to know each other quite well. Each evening Price insisted on having lengthy dinners—starting at eight and ending after ten—with Paul and her to discuss the day's events (Judy suspected they were invited so Charlie wouldn't have to eat alone.), and to hear her translation of what the businessmen discussed when they spoke Italian to each other. Judy reported that their conversations contained nothing of interest; they were not trying to hide anything, but merely used Italian because it was easier for them to communicate with each other. Price was convinced that the Italians were either on the up and up or fantastic con men, and he rejected the latter as extremely unlikely.

After Thursday's meetings, an impatient Price had informed his hosts that they would be leaving for home immediately, but the Italians had insisted that their visitors inspect their manufacturing facilities, one of which was northwest of Rome and the other due east of the city. Another wasted day, Price thought, but he agreed to go so as not to offend them.

Early Friday morning Alessandro greeted the three of them in the lobby and ushered them to the waiting limousine. As he drove them to the first plant, he chattered non-stop about the sights they were passing. An exasperated Price thought to himself, I've had enough of this shit, and at lunch he put his foot down and announced, "Tomorrow morning we are going home. I had the concierge call U S Airways, and our tickets back have been confirmed." Although his hosts begged him to stay, he insisted that pressing work was waiting on his desk, and he had been away too long already. "This," he said adamantly, "is our last day in Italy." They reluctantly acquiesced.

Downhearted, Judy listened to Price and thought about asking him for a few days vacation so she could stay in Rome and spend some more time with Carlo. How would that look to Tony? she warned herself. Me staying in Rome when he knows Carlo's here. That's all I need, him thinking I'm going to bed with another man. She rejected the idea.

Late that afternoon when she finished dressing for yet another dinner with Price and Logan—what more is there to tell him? Judy wondered—she reluctantly phoned Carlo to say she was leaving Rome the next day.

"But we've hardly seen each other at all," he said dejectedly. "Only two short . . ."

"I know," Judy interrupted. "And I'm sorry. I really am sorry, but there's just no time. I liked seeing you, and I want to see you, but tonight's another dinner with Charlie, and we leave in the morning. It's all set, and I can't change it."

"Can't you stay on another couple of days, and then go back?"

She hesitated for a fraction of a second. "Oh, I'd love to, but I can't."

"Do you know how I feel about you?" Carlo asked.

"I think I do, and I have deep feelings for you, too," Judy said wistfully. "But right now I'm a married woman, and I'm on my way home to my husband."

"Please let me see you one more time before you leave."

"I don't see how," she answered. "Carlo, I have to run now or I'll be late for dinner with my boss." Reluctantly she said goodbye and hung up the phone and breathed a deep sigh of disappointment.

After dinner as Charlie Price ground out the stub of the fat cigar he had smoked (much to the annoyance of Paul Logan who coughed politely every time he lit up), and said, "Since this is our last night in Rome, let's go for a walk and enjoy the city."

He led them outside to the Via Veneto, a street throbbing with nightlife. As they started walking, the people reminded Judy of those she had seen twenty years ago on South Street in Philadelphia when she had her one date with Charlie Price. The people who crowded the narrow sidewalk ranged from scruffy twenty-somethings with bodies pierced in every conceivable place and rainbow-colored hair, to older men in business suits (some dangling young women-not-their-daughters on their arms). Like a leaderless herd of cattle they either meandered up and down or sat nursing a drink at the outdoor cafés and restaurants which lined the street. Judy, still upset over not being able to see Carlo before she left, passed the time by studying the people, and trying to make up stories in her head of what their lives were like.

The evening was warm, and some of the men wore tee shirts. One of them, seated at a table with a woman who sported a leopard-spotted skirt with a matching top, caught her eye. He was model-handsome, and had the aquiline nose which her mother had dubbed "the perfect Roman nose." When he stood up, Judy could see he had a muscle-builder's physique. As he turned his body and exposed his muscular right arm to Judy's view, Judy gasped. There on his upper arm was a huge, blood-red, heart tattoo with a thick black border around it! As he started walking toward her, she couldn't keep her eyes off that tattoo. When he moved his arm, the tattoo seemed to come to life, dancing, winking at her, insolently taunting her. Unable to pull her eyes away, an unpleasant picture gradually took shape in the center of the tattoo, as Judy stared in disbelief. There was Tony, Tony in bed with an unknown woman, an unknown woman on whose thigh was that damn heart tattoo!

Feeling faint Judy grabbed the back of a nearby chair with both hands and tried to steady herself. The feeling worsened as a tremor similar to the one she had experienced at the office started up in her. Paul and Charlie rushed to her side and after getting no answer to: "Is something wrong?" helped her into a chair and stood over her wondering what to do. A sharp bolt of electricity shot through her; she trembled like a rag doll, then folded her hands on the table, and put her head down on them. As quickly as the spell came, in a second it was gone, and Judy started to feel better. She lifted her head and waved the men away with an I'm-okay gesture. When she stood up, something inside started to gnaw at her. It was her witch's intuition working. A submerged thought was trying to take shape, and in spite of her straining to understand it, she could not. She had walked halfway back to the hotel before it finally crystallized in her mind.

Tony had been cheating again.

Chapter 34

$\mathcal{T}$he next morning Alessandro drove them back to the airport. He dropped them off at the entrance, parked the car, and then helped them steer their luggage through the crowd to the U S Airways counter. They bid him good-bye with thanks and after an hour and a half (Price spent it drinking martinis in the VIP lounge), Paul and Judy jostled their way down the passenger walkway onto the jumbo jet. Judy was exhausted. When she had finally gone to bed last night, she had tossed and turned for hours. She could not clear her mind of thoughts of Tony. She knew her intuition was right—it had never, ever failed her—and he had certainly been to bed with that woman again. She knew it for a fact and swore to herself that she would confront him when she got home. Then she thought about how little time she had spent with Carlo and felt guilty about that. By the time she pardoned herself, realizing it was not her fault, the phone by her bed was ringing. It was her wakeup call, and she struggled to get up.

Now feeling three quarters brain-dead, she trudged down the narrow aisle with her carryon luggage, aimlessly bumping into people stowing their bags in the overhead compartments, and finally tumbling lifelessly into her seat. As she shoved the small bag under the seat in front of her, Paul Logan took off his suit jacket but left his tie on, and settled down next to her with his pamphlets.

As the plane took off, Judy sank into restless unconsciousness. In a few minutes, calmed by the monotonous hum of the engines, she fell into a deep sleep.

She dreamt of Carlo holding her tenderly in his arms.

*　　*　　*

It was late in the afternoon when the plane circled Kennedy airport waiting for clearance to land. Judy, groggy, was awakened by the end of the pilot's announcement: "We'll be landing as soon as we get clearance from the folks on the ground." In a few minutes permission was granted and the plane bumped onto the runway. In their eagerness to leave their prison of the last eight hours, passengers jumped up and clogged the aisles even before the plane was connected to the terminal's umbilical cord. Judy sat passively waiting for the aisles to clear. She tried to empty her mind of Tony and Carlo problems, but as they faded away a new thought came to disturb her. In addition to leaving Carlo, she had left Rome. I feel like I've lost a loved one, she thought sadly. She felt the pull of Rome, dragging her back. She closed her eyes and could hear a sweet, siren voice softly calling: "Don't leave me. Come back. You are mine. You belong here with me."

She grabbed her carryon and as she blindly followed Paul toward the front of the plane, she began to make plans to return to Italy. Maybe, next summer I can work something out, she thought. I'll take a leave of absence, or join an organization or work on a committee that will have a meeting there. Maybe this Italian connection will work out for the firm, and I will be a part of it. She smiled as she remembered Dorothy in the *Wizard of Oz*: Dorothy found a way back home to Kansas, she thought, and I will find a way back to Rome.

As she and Paul trudged down the long corridor, she waved him on ahead saying, "I'm exhausted, and you're walking too fast for me. Go on ahead. I'll catch up to you in baggage claim."

As he hurried away down the long airport corridor, she was startled as she caught sight of a familiar face coming toward her. He looked older now—it had been more than twenty years since she had seen him last—but she knew who it was. Even though his hairline had receded making his face look bigger, and his waist bulged with the paunchiness of too much good food and not enough exercise, she recognized the craggy, handsome man. No, there was no mistaking him; no one else walked, no sashayed, quite that way (except John Travolta in *Saturday Night Fever*). It was Dominic Micaletto, her first lover. No way she would ever forget him. Looking back it sounded sleazy—the back seat of his car. But the convertible's top was down, and twinkling rays of moonlight from a full moon had streamed down on them. As time had passed, she gradually replaced Dominic's macho arrogance and minimal attention to her needs with a much softer and much more romantic memory of that moment and of him.

As she relived that special once-in-a-lifetime, she stopped dead in her tracks and stared at him. As he passed her by, he looked her full in the face but gave no sign of recognition. Why's that dumb broad staring at me? he wondered.

Judy began to hyperventilate, and feeling woozy, reached out and braced herself against a railing. I've got to tell Kate I saw Dominic, she thought. She felt another wave of dizziness well up inside her and suddenly as she started to fall, strong arms were around her holding her up. She blinked her eyes open and saw it was Tony with a concerned look on his face.

"What are you doing here?" she asked.

"I called the airline to find out what time your plane was coming in, and I came down to meet you," he said. "Are you okay? It looked like you were going to faint."

"I had a dizzy spell. I'm all right now."

"I'm really glad you're back. I missed you," he said nuzzling her neck.

Yeah, she thought, you missed me so much you didn't even call once. And that woman; you were with that woman again.

At the baggage claim area after he yanked her luggage from the carousel, she introduced him to Paul and Charlie. Tony asked them a perfunctory "How was your trip?" then led Judy to his waiting car.

On the drive to East Falls, she asked about his mother. "She's coming along," he answered and reached over and took her hand in his.

Why is he doing this? Judy wondered.

He opened the front door for her, set her bags down in the foyer, and hugged her tightly.

"I said I missed you a lot," he whispered into her ear. "C'mon up to bed, and I'll show you how much." He circled his hand around her waist and gently nudged her in the direction of the stairs.

Judy seethed inwardly and scowled at him, but he either ignored her or did not notice. I'm so tired I could sleep for a week, she thought. But he has no consideration for me and how tired I might be. And worse, I know he's been screwing someone else while I was away. Making love is the last thing on my mind right now. But I'm caught in a bind. If I don't go to bed with him, I'll be giving him an excuse for finding another woman. So, she decided, I'll play the good wife.

She said nothing to him but plodded up the stairs. Tony pulled down the covers on the bed. Judy lay down and waited, hands clasped behind her head while he stripped down to his shorts. When he lay down next to her, and she unenthusiastically draped her arms around his neck, she realized something was missing. Dulled by fatigue it took her a few seconds to figure out what was wrong.

"Tony," she murmured.

"Mmmm," he said as he started to pull her blouse out of her slacks.

She felt thoroughly around his neck and a little way down his back, and then shuddered. "The good luck horn your mother gave you. Where is it? Your mother told you never to take it off, otherwise the good luck would go away."

Goddamn it, he thought. I never even noticed it was missing. I don't have any idea where it could be. Quickly thinking of an excuse he said, "I must have lost it at the gym. I take it off before I workout. One day I noticed when I came home, that it was gone. Somebody must have stolen it from my locker when I took a shower."

"You weren't supposed to take it off. Not for a workout. Not for anything," Judy said. "Now we're in for bad luck."

She began to sob softly—part exhaustion, part a rising fear that this was only the tip of the iceberg; things were going to get a lot worse.

"It kept getting in my way, and I was afraid the chain would break. I always left it in my gym bag and never had any trouble." He noticed her crying. "I'll get another one first thing tomorrow."

Judy didn't even try to remind him that this one was his mother's, special for the Fanelli family. Why bother, she thought. What's gone is gone. He doesn't seem to care; why should I?

Suddenly a picture flashed through Tony's mind, and he remembered: Kate took it from my neck when I was screwing her. That fuckin' asshole. I'd like to kill her. I wonder what else she did when she was here. She seems to want Judy to find out about us, even if she says she doesn't. I wonder if that's why she came over that night. I'm going to have a serious talk with that bitch.

The powerful emotions of anger and lust quickly drove all thoughts of a confrontation with Kate from his mind. He desperately needed the release that sex would provide.

He gently brushed the tears from Judy's eyes and stripped her clothes off. She felt him enter her and start to make love to her, but it was as if she was in a dream. I'm not here, she thought. But if I'm not here, where am I? She was in Rome, and it was Carlo on top of her, she imagined. It was Carlo's hands rubbing her breasts making her shiver. It was Carlo's fleshrod stabbing her causing sensations deep inside her. It was Carlo moaning with pleasure as she squeezed him and squirmed under his thrusts. She tried half-heartedly to censor these thoughts, but she was too tired and really didn't want to because they were such pleasant thoughts. They made her feel so good that she blissfully stayed with her dream climaxing an instant after Tony did.

"Take a shower with me?" Tony asked as he got up from the bed.

"Not this time," she answered. "I'm too tired. I've got to go to sleep, or I'll collapse." She had almost dozed off when suddenly she felt a chill. It was as if a window had opened in the middle of winter and a cold draft had fluttered over her. She got up to put on her bathrobe and as she turned around to lie down again, something shimmering on the top of her dresser caught her eye. She could see waves, like the heat waves rising from an asphalt road on a steamy summer day, coming from her jewelry box. She looked at it quizzically, then touched it gingerly afraid it would burn her. It was cool to the touch. She opened it, inventoried its contents one at a time, then screamed in pain.

"Omigod," she yelled. "Tony, get out of the shower right now and come here!"

Tony cinched a towel around his waist and looked at her curiously, as he walked out of the bathroom.

"What's the matter?" he asked.

"My mother's ring is missing. I always keep it in the bottom tray in my jewelry box, and it's not here."

"Look through the rest of the box."

"I did. I looked through the whole box." Frantically she pawed through the box again: "Where is it? What happened to it? Tony find it," she pleaded frantically.

"I don't know where it is. Maybe you put it somewhere else. Maybe it fell on the floor." He got down on his hands and knees and started to search under and behind the dresser.

"I never put it anywhere else."

"The maid was in to clean while you were away. Maybe . . ." He left the thought unfinished.

"We've had the same woman for five years and nothing's ever been taken. Why would she start stealing now?" She fell onto the bed, put her head to her hands, and sobbed uncontrollably. I can't fight this, she thought. I'm so tired and things are going so wrong.

Tony stood up and shrugged his shoulders.

She shooed him away. "You're no fuckin' help. Get back in the shower," she shouted at him in a final outburst of frustration.

She crawled under the covers and forced herself to relax. I'll tackle this another time, she thought. Right now I have to get some rest. She turned over once or twice, sound a comfortable position, and promptly fell asleep. Tony waited until he was sure she was sleeping then slid into bed beside her. He tossed a while before he dropped off, but she did not move. She slept soundly—the sleep of the dead, but as morning approached a nightmare came to haunt her. The man from Rome with the heart tattooed on his arm, his face contorted in a mocking grin, drifted toward her. One corner of his mouth turned up in a jeering smile and, as he bent forward, she could see a tiny silver horn dangled from a thin chain around his neck. When he lifted his hand to stroke the chain, sparks flew in all directions from a huge diamond ring perched on his finger.

"My mother's ring," Judy cried out in her sleep. "He's got my mother's ring."

She snapped awake. Bathed in a pool of sweat, she shivered; goose bumps rose all over her body. She jerked upright and gasped for air. A sharp pain shot through her chest. She felt her windpipe constrict. Minutes passed before the suffocating feeling passed. It's all connected, she thought. The heart tattoo, Tony's horn, and my mother's diamond ring. Suddenly she felt overwhelmed. Everything's piling up on me, she thought, and I can't handle it. She leaned back against the headboard and drew her legs up to her chest, then let her head fall on her knees. She slowly rocked back and forth, calming herself, soothing herself, getting control.

As the soft pink light of the rising sun slowly trickled into the room between the slats of the Venetian blinds, she got of out bed and stepped into the shower. She luxuriated as the warm water cascaded over her. Gradually she made it hotter and hotter and commanded: Wash my troubles away.

All the time she was in the shower Tony remained in bed asleep, snoring lightly. When she got out, she decided not to wake him, toweled off, and started to get dressed. As she opened the drawer with her underwear, she gasped. The drawer was a snarl of tangled lingerie. I did not leave it this way, she thought; and he can't blame the maid for this. She doesn't go into my drawers. Then she noticed the crumpled panties in the front of the drawer and gingerly unfolded them. They were obviously not hers. Bile rose to her throat making her nauseous.

Tony had that woman in this house, she thought. The dickhead bastard fucked her in my house. I wonder if they screwed in my bed? The thought revolted her and her head began to pound. Not only was the shithead unfaithful to me again, she thought, but whoever this woman was stole his horn and my ring. I know she did it. Goddamn it, she swore to herself, when he gets up he has a lot of explaining to do. And if it's the last thing I do, I'm going to find out who that fucking woman with the tattoo is. And when I do . . . She left the thought unfinished.

*　　*　　*

Monday morning Judy called Kate from work.

"I'm back," she said.

"You don't sound very happy. How was it?" Kate asked.

"I'm still tired and worn out. I looked forward to going, but it turned out to be very draining. I don't know what we accomplished other than they got to know us, and we got to know them." She took a deep breath. "Tony was at it again."

"What do you mean?"

"He had a woman in the house while I was gone, and I think she . . ."

"How do you know?" Kate interrupted.

"Little things. No big things. It's as if she left me a calling card. The good luck charm that his mother gave him is gone and so is my mother's diamond ring from my jewelry box. And I got another pair of her panties, this time stuffed in my drawer."

"Whoa! Serious stuff. What are you going to do about this?"

"I've got to pin Tony down. I wanted him to tell me who the woman is, but he raced out of the house yesterday saying he was going to the gym. Then he called me and said he was having dinner with his mother who's staying at his sister's house. By the time he got home late last night, I wasn't in any mood for a confrontation. But I'm not giving up. I'll get to the bottom of this."

Neither said anything for a few seconds.

"Kate?" Judy said.

"I'm still here," Kate said. "I was thinking about how much grief Tony's screwing around is causing you. You know you do have a choice. You could overlook what he's doing and keep on with your marriage."

"We discussed this before," Judy said. "I know that you and Greg have an open marriage, but you both agreed to that before you got married. Tony and I promised to be faithful. It's important to me that I'm the only one he sleeps with."

"Things have changed over the years. Do you ever listen to the kids talking today?"

"What kids do is all over the news," Judy said. "What you and I did in twelfth grade, they're doing in seventh grade. Teenage kids are having babies. And if it wasn't for AIDS there'd probably be a lot more screwing going on. But what's that got to do with me and Tony?"

"Okay. We know the kids today are like rabbits. Sex is a big part of their lives. You ought to face it. There's no more 'being faithful until death do us part.' Kids today think that sex is no big deal. In marriage or out of marriage they're gonna have a lot of sex."

"Number one: I'm not a teenager any more. I want to live in my own generation, not in someone else's. And, number two: After marriage and before marriage are two different things. Before marriage, screw around all you want. I did. You did, and I'm sure

Tony did, although I never asked him. But after marriage I wanted it to be different."

"Tony's only a man. He's no different than all the others. He's going to chase women, and he's gonna screw some of them."

"If that's the way he's going to behave, then I don't want to be married to him. I can't cope with that, and I won't ever get used to it. But what really pisses me off is that he promised—we both promised—to be faithful. He promised before we got married, and he promised again after I got those pictures. He broke his promise twice. And every time I think about my mother's ring I could strangle him. I'm sure whoever was in my house took it, and that really hurts."

Judy looked up and saw Charlie Price was standing outside her cubby trying to look like he wasn't eavesdropping. She ended the call quickly and turned to face him.

"Nothing important," he said hanging back in the hallway. "I wanted to compliment you again on how well you handled yourself in Rome. You made some good suggestions. You seem to have a knack for lawyering. You really ought to go law school and get your degree."

"I'll consider it very seriously," Judy said.

As he left, he said—somewhere between a question and an order, "You will be at Friday's this week. Remember it's this Thursday— this week and not next week because of Memorial Day. I'd like you to keep in touch with the top brass."

"I'll be there," she said as he walked away.

*   *   *

That evening after dinner, Judy stacked the dishes in the dishwasher and prepared to confront Tony. I'll be direct, she thought, and I'll get to the bottom of this. Confidently, she went upstairs to Tony's office.

"Tony," she said to the back of his head. "We've got to talk."

"Umm," he said without looking up.

She snapped. That does it, she thought. I tell him it's something important and he ignores me. She clenched her fists in anger and shouted, "Would you fuckin' pay attention to me?"

Startled, he turned around. "What the matter with you?" he asked.

Before she could censor it, she shouted, "Did you have a woman in this house while I was gone?"

"I told you the only one in the house was . . ."

"I know you told me, the maid. Now why would she mess up my underwear drawer and leave a pair of panties in my drawer?" she screamed.

"What?"

"You heard me. My drawer was all messed up, and I found another pair of panties that aren't mine."

"How do expect me to explain that?" Tony said angrily. What now? he thought. He had called Kate that morning to ask her about the horn and the ring.

"You were too far gone to listen to me," she had said. "So I took the horn from around your neck before it could poke my eye out. But I left it on the bed for you. What the hell would I want that thing for? And I wasn't in your bedroom, so I don't know anything about a diamond ring."

He had searched the guest room from top to bottom and had found nothing.

Judy stood glaring at him nervously clenching and opening her fists, shaking with frustration. Tears streamed down her face.

"Judy," he began, "I can't explain these things. Nothing happened in this house while you were gone. I'll call the maid and see what she knows about this. I'll fire her, and tell her not to come back again. I don't know what else I can do."

Emotionally a basket case, Judy crumpled to the floor, buried her face in her hands, and moaned.

Tony stared at her in disbelief.

"Just tell me one thing," she managed to sob.

"What's that?" he asked.

"The name of the woman . . . the woman in the pictures."

Tony hesitated before answering, "She was a secretary I met in Baltimore. You wouldn't know her."

"Her name. I want her name," Judy moaned.

"Pam Gallagher," he lied.

Exhausted, Judy crawled into their bedroom and pulled herself up onto the bed. She sobbed softly until she fell asleep.

*   *   *

Two days later John Christopher called Lou Banks to make final arrangements.

"Lou, listen to me carefully. I don't want you to screw this up."

"No chance of that." Lou sounded confident.

"It's this week. Thursday is . . ."

Lou Banks interrupted him, "I know—tomorrow. I take the train to 30th Street Station. You FedExed me the locker key; I've got it. I forget the locker number right now, but it's on the key, and I wrote it down on the train tickets. I get the stuff out of the locker and rent a car. A nice car since you're paying."

"Yeah, I'm paying. But don't go overboard on me. No Cadillac."

"I go to the motel—yes, I know how to get there—and rent a room."

"Be sure to get there early enough to allow time for something to go wrong. Maybe a traffic jam . . ."

"Nothing's gonna go wrong. I'm in control of everything."

"And don't forget your equipment. Test it before you go and make sure it works."

"Relax, would ya. Consider it all taken care of."

"You remember the story of how you know her?"

"I know the story. I saw her at the wedding," he said indignantly. "Now get off my case."

As John hung up he covered his face with his hands. Am I really doing this? he thought. After being a good, honest cop, for so many years, now I'm breaking the law. And there's a chance someone might be seriously hurt. I never thought I'd cave in for money, and here I am doing just that. Is this what it all comes down to? Money? I suppose we all have our price, and she met mine.

*   *   *

Sara popped her head in the doorway of Judy's cubicle and said, "It's Thursday and time for Friday's. Will you be there?"

"I'm still worn out from the trip, but I promised Charlie I'd go, so I'll be there. Save me a seat at your table."

"Aren't you going to hang out with the big shots and make some points?"

"Just save me a seat," Judy said.

"Okay, okay. Don't get testy."

Later as Judy opened the door to the restaurant, she was grateful she had come a little early since the noise was at a bearable level. I am definitely pre-headache, she thought. I hope I make it through this. Oh, well, I can always leave if I feel worse.

She noticed Sara sitting at a table by herself with a jacket draped over an empty chair next to her. "I've saved this for you," she said, patting the chair.

"Where's the rest of your crowd?" Judy asked as she sat down.

"They're coming," she answered. "But before they get here tell me about Italy. Did either of those lawyers hit on you? Did you find an Italian gigolo to fill those empty nights?"

"Charlie and Paul were too busy with the Italians to pay any attention to me. We had meetings all day long and post-mortems until late in the evening. The only male in my life was my cousin, Carlo, who . . ."

"Cousin? You didn't mention anything about any cousin before you left."

"I must have told you. He's a journalist working out of Rome, but he was born and lived here in Philly until recently."

"Is he good looking?"

Judy nervously looked around the room for an excuse to end the conversation. She was afraid she would slip and tell Sara that Carlo wasn't her cousin and that she had strong feelings for him. That's all I need on top of everything else, she thought, to become the focus of office gossip.

Failing to find a convenient excuse to avoid Sara's probing questions, Judy grabbed her purse and before Sara could volunteer to join her, excused herself, and rushed to the ladies' room.

On the way back to her table a tall, handsome man stood up and blocked her path. He was immaculately dressed in a nicely tailored, gray suit with a red tie which had large black polka-dots on it. An attractive woman, but one whose sad eyes showed she had seen better days, sat at his table.

"Excuse me," he said in a suave, cultured voice. "Are you Judy Fanelli?"

Astonished she asked, "How do you know me?"

"I'm . . . ummm . . . we . . . are acquaintances of Nancy Tanner. We saw you at her wedding, and Nancy pointed you out as one of her oldest friends. Please sit down and have a drink with us." With a broad sweep of his hand he gestured to the seat next to him.

"I really can't. I have friends waiting over there." She nodded in Sara's direction where a raucous group had formed around her table.

"Just for a second. I understand you've recently returned from Rome. You simply must tell us all about it. We're planning to go there in August, and it's been eight or ten years since we've been there. There must be a lot of changes."

She took a long look at the distinguished man and his companion and sat down.

"My name is Louis, Louis Carter and this is my wife, Frances." Frankie gave him a sly smile. She had never been called Frances in her life. Her real name was Felicia which she hated, but she liked the way Frances sounded—classy. From now on I'll be Frances, she thought.

"What are you drinking?" he asked.

"Merlot, please," Judy answered.

"Frances would you get our friend some wine at the bar and another Scotch for me. We don't want to keep her from her friends too long, so let's not wait for a waiter."

Frankie slid from her chair and elbowed her way to the bar. "Glass of Merlot and a J & B rocks with a twist," she said. In her fist she held the two white pills she had squeezed from the bubble pack they had taken from the locker in the train station.

When the drinks came she cautiously looked around to make sure no one was watching, then she slipped the pills into Judy's glass of wine. Daintily she took a swizzle stick from the mug at the edge of the bar, swished it around a few times in the wine, then dropped it on the counter and headed back to the table. She set the drinks down, the wine in front of Judy and the Scotch in front of Lou, and took her seat next to him. Lou had refused to allow her to order her favorite drink, Miller's Lite (So unrefined, he had tsk-tsked.), so an untouched glass of white wine marked her place.

John Christopher had sent a Fodor's Italy travel guide the week before, and Lou had studied the section on Rome thoroughly. Knowledgeably, he began discussing the sights with Judy. They had finished with the Trevi fountain and had started on the Colosseum before Judy started drinking the wine Frankie had brought. Within a few minutes her speech became slurred, and her eyes began to blink rapidly.

"Oh," she said woozily, "that drink went right to my head." She shut her eyes tight and willed herself not to faint.

"Let's get you outside for some fresh air," Lou offered. He casually glanced over to the table where Judy's friends were laughing loudly. Sara was in the center of a group of five people and was so absorbed in the banter that she had forgotten about Judy's absence.

"It looks like we're in the clear," Lou said quietly to Frankie. "Gimme a hand."

He stood up, grabbed Judy by her elbows, and gently lifted her up. Frankie picked up Judy's purse and slung it over her shoulder. Together they managed to steer Judy out of the bar and into the parking lot. The fresh air revived her momentarily, but she was still too weak to resist when they pushed her into the back seat of the rental car. Lou handed the keys to Frankie saying, "You drive." He slid into the back next to Judy, who had lapsed into semi-consciousness.

As Frankie slowly drove out of the parking lot, Lou pulled Judy's blouse out from her skirt and slipped his hands underneath it. Reaching around to her back he unclasped her bra and began to massage and fondle her loose breasts. In her twilight zone Judy imagined the hands she felt were Carlo's hands fondling her willing body giving her pleasure. She sighed and did not resist.

As they drove by Philadelphia International Airport, an airplane taking off rose sharply over the road, its belch of noise startled Judy. Momentarily she snapped fully awake but quickly faded out again. From there it was a ten-minute ride to the motel in semi-seedy Essington. Frankie opened the door while Lou dragged Judy's limp body from the car and into the room they had rented earlier. With an "Ooooff" he plopped her on the bed, stared at her for a second, then undressed her. He threw her clothes carelessly in a corner of the room and stared at the unmoving, corpse-like body.

"This is creepy," he said to Frankie. "I hope she's not dead."

Frankie squeezed her thumb on Judy's wrist and said, "She still has a pulse and a strong one. I've seen you in worse shape after one of your heavy drinking binges."

Lou took Frankie's shoulder bag and went into the bathroom. After he removed his clothes, he took a blonde wig from the purse and preening in the mirror, settled it firmly on his head. He smoothed the hair in place with the palms of his hands. Then he fished a Gene Shalit moustache from her purse, smeared it with a dab of paste, and pressed it firmly on his upper lip.

While Lou was changing his appearance, Frankie had gone to the car and brought in a small Sony video camera from the trunk. She opened the case and after she checked to be sure there was tape in the machine, looked through the viewfinder, and set the date and time.

Lou looked at himself in the mirror and admired the finished product for so long that Frankie finally said, "Are we going to do this tonight?"

He folded his glasses, put them into her bag, and took one more glance at himself in the mirror. Even my mother wouldn't recognize me now, he thought as he stepped from the bathroom.

"Roll 'em," Lou whispered as he straddled the nude body on the bed, "and don't take any close-ups of my face."

Frankie pushed the "Record" button as Lou, facing away from the camera, began to caress Judy's body.

"Oh, Carlo," Judy moaned.

Lou continued to fondle the lifeless body under him.

A few minutes later Judy cried out from her dream world, "Now, Carlo. Fuck me now, Carlo."

Lou signaled Frankie to shut the camera off, then draped Judy's arms around his neck, lay down on top of her, and, as Frankie started the camera again, he began to simulate intercourse. Slowly at first, then gradually faster and faster, he battered the unconscious form beneath him. After a few minutes Frankie shut the camera off, put it on the nightstand, and sexily started to wriggle out of her clothes.

"I got so hot watching you. We've gotta do it now," she said breathlessly as she pulled Judy's arms away from him. She pushed her to the edge of the double bed, lay down on the unused half and dragged Lou on top of her. Excitedly she raced her hands over his nude body.

"This business," he panted as he guided himself inside her, "has made me horny as hell, too."

As they bucked in their orgasmic dance, Judy lay unconscious without moving.

An hour later, Lou dressed and packed taking great care not to forget anything. He put his hand on Judy's heart—"Making sure she's still alive," he said—then took a towel from the bathroom and dampened it. He rubbed the wet spot over the cake of soap.

"What are you doing now?" Frankie asked.

He didn't answer, but methodically wiped and scrubbed every fixture, every piece of furniture, the doorknob, and even Judy's still body.

"Fingerprints," he said. "They're gone now."

*   *   *

At eleven o'clock that evening, Tony, who had been dozing on the couch, glanced at the clock on the mantel. She's not home yet, he thought. I wonder where the hell she is. He looked up Sara's phone number and apologized for calling so late.

A hint of worry crept into his voice as he asked, "Is Judy with you? She hasn't come home yet."

"Noooo," Sara said. "The last time I saw her she went to the ladies' room at Friday's. I got to talking and never saw her come back. Maybe she stopped to talk to someone else."

Tony hung up and watched the news on the TV. In fifteen minutes he was asleep again.

*   *   *

The next morning Judy fought to open her eyes. She couldn't. She tried prying her lids open with her thumb and forefinger, but when she let go they flopped shut again. Finally when some of her strength returned, she opened her eyes, and stared at the dirty-white, cobwebbed ceiling.

For a long time she was disoriented and struggled with different scenarios trying to determine where she was. Am I in Rome? she wondered. Looking around the grungy room she knew it wasn't the bright, cheerful, clean suite she had there. Am I home? she asked herself. No, this isn't my bed or my bedroom. Where am I? What day is it?

And then the headache started. There was no gradual tightening of the forehead followed by slowly rising pain. This one was the sudden, throbbing CLANG-CLANG of the blacksmith-hammering-on-the-anvil type. To ease the pain she squeezed her eyes shut. It didn't help. She felt hot, then cold. Suddenly she realized she had no clothes on. Struggling through exhaustion like she had never experience before, she swung her legs over the side of the bed, and with a great effort brought herself up to a sitting position, then noticed her clothes piled on the floor. Trying not to move too quickly, she managed to put on her bra, panties and the rest of her clothing.

She forced herself to ignore the pain in her head and the limbs-like-lead-weights fatigue she felt. How did I get here? she wondered. Then slowly she began to remember some of the events of the last twenty-four hours. She remembered going to Friday's and talking with Sara. She remembered going to the ladies' room but after that, though she concentrated as hard as she could, she couldn't remember anything. Absolutely nothing came to mind. She began to worry about what had happened to her memory.

Then she laughed softly. This is a new one, she thought. Waking up naked and alone in a motel room.

The pounding in her head lessened somewhat. Feeling stronger, she washed her face with cold water in the bathroom sink, then pulled the curtain on the window aside. She winced and let it go when the bright sun sparkled through and burned her eyes. What time is it? she thought. Twisting her wrist she read nine-thirty, Friday, May 16th, from her watch. I should be at work, she thought. Suddenly the pain in her head began again in earnest. It pounded unmercifully and a giant wave of fatigue came over her. Her arms and legs felt numb, and she crumpled back onto the bed. Fumbling around on the nightstand, she found her purse and took out her cell phone. She dialed Neuberger Roe & Price and barely able to talk to the receptionist called out sick. The small amount of energy expended for the phone call was more than her drugged body could handle, and she lapsed back into unconsciousness.

When she woke an hour later, her headache was bearable, and feeling marginally stronger, she was now determined to go home. Not wanting to risk standing, she knelt in front of the window and squinted cautiously into the bright sunlight. I'm in a motel, she realized. At first glance the parking lot appeared to be empty, but as she looked carefully, she spotted a single car a hundred yards away in front of the office. She mentally made a note of the motel name on the sign. That's not my car, she thought. I wonder how I got here, and how do I get home?

I'll call Tony, she thought, as a hoard of questions flashed through her head: Is he home? Does he know where I am? Does he care? Can he come and get me?

She flopped back on the bed and dialed her East Falls home number. After five rings and no answer, she hung up before the answering machine could kick in. She dialed his cell phone number. On the second ring she heard his voice, "Fanelli," he said.

"It's Judy."

"Where the hell are you?" he asked. He sounded frantic. "I was worried when you didn't come home at all last night."

"I'm at the Red Rooster Inn near the airport in Essington. I have no idea how I got here, but my car isn't here. Can you come and get me?"

"I'm on my way. I'll be there in half an hour."

I'm going to need every minute, she thought. I hope I can stand up by then. Twenty minutes later she forced herself back to the window. Resting her chin on her elbows on the sill she kept an eye on the entrance to the motel. When she saw Tony pull up, she opened the door to the room and waved him over. She looked around the room one more time to make sure she hadn't forgotten anything then managed to walk to his car.

"What's this all about?" Tony asked her as she slid into the passenger seat beside him.

"I honestly don't know. I can't remember much about last night other than I do remember meeting Sara at Friday's and going to the ladies' room. After that, the next thing I remember is waking up here with the mother of all headaches."

"What did you have to drink?"

"To be honest I don't remember drinking anything." She closed her eyes and concentrated. "Wait. It's coming back to me. Some of it is. Be quiet for a minute. Let me think."

Tony drove up the entrance ramp to the Schuylkill Expressway and eased his way into traffic.

"After I came out of the ladies' room, a man stopped me. He said he was a friend of Nancy Tanner's, and he recognized me from her wedding. He invited me to sit with him—he knew about me going to Rome, so I trusted him. Then the woman with him brought us drinks—me a glass of Merlot. I had one or two sips and . . ." The memory dissolved. "The next thing I remember is waking up in that awful motel this morning."

"Are you sure that's all you remember?" Tony asked suspiciously.

"What else did you have in mind?"

"I don't have anything else in mind. I only want to know if that's all you remember."

"Are you accusing me of something?"

"What would I be accusing you of?"

"Shut up with the damn questions," she said. "My head is splitting." She pointed to the City Line Avenue exit. "Get off here." He looked at her as if she was crazy. "I want to see if my car is still at Friday's."

She guided him to where she had parked the night before. Her car was still there.

"Can you drive?" he asked.

Angrily: "Whether I can or not, I'm going to. Because I'm not going to sit here and be accused of God knows what. Look, if I did something wrong last night, would I be dumb enough to tell you to pick me up at a motel? Wouldn't I have called a taxi?"

"Maybe. Unless this is your clever way of covering up what really happened."

Furiously she yanked the car door open, got out, and slammed it shut. Without looking back she drove home and dragged herself upstairs and into bed. She lay still for a long time trying to shake her pounding headache and sort out what had happened to her in the last twenty-four hours. It was no use. She couldn't remember anything that took place after she sat down with the two strangers and had a drink.

Was I drugged and abducted by aliens? she thought. That's too stupid to even consider. In spite of her headache she laughed at herself. Too much *X-Files*, she thought. I haven't felt like this since . . . She tried hard to remember when she had ever felt so completely washed out and unable to move. The only thing that even came close was waking up in Rome after taking the sleeping pills Carlo gave me, she thought. That's it! That must be it. I must have been drugged. That couple that cornered me must have slipped something into my drink.

More of last night started to return. She pictured the events in her mind, then thought: The woman—Frances, he had called her—went to the bar to get me some wine. She must have put some knockout drops in my drink. But why would she do that? What happened to me at the motel? Why did I wake up naked? Did he rape me?

Her head started to clear more. Carter. He said his name was Louis Carter, she remembered. And he said he knew Nancy.

She reached over to the bedside phone and dialed Nancy's work number.

"Louis Carter?" Nancy said. "Never heard of a Louis Carter. Never heard of a Frances Carter either. And they said they know me?"

"They said they were at the wedding, and that you pointed me out to them."

"I can't remember doing that. Maybe they're my husband's friends."

"No. They specifically said you. You were the one who showed them who I was, and that's how they recognized me at Friday's."

"What's this all about?" Nancy asked. "Why are you interested in these people?"

Judy, exasperated: "It's a long story. Thanks for trying to help. I'll talk to you soon."

Now what do I do? Judy thought. So far this is another dead end like the woman with the heart tattoo. Without even checking, I know there's no secretary named Pat Gallagher. Tony made that up to shut me up. And the cleaners didn't take my ring, and Tony didn't lose his horn at the gym. It's all lies and dead ends, and I'll bet anything Louis Carter (if that's his real name), is part of this. I've got to find out who is behind this, and why, before I go nuts. I've got to put an end to this.

Her headache returned full force, but in spite of its relentless pounding she fell asleep.

*　　*　　*

Much to Judy's relief, the weekend and Monday passed without incident. She worked long hours to clear the backlog that had built up on her desk while she was gone. After she had called out sick Friday, she had gone in and worked half a day on Saturday and taken a stack of papers home with her to finish on Sunday. Though it was always nagging at the back of her mind, she had no time to dwell on her experience at the motel.

On Tuesday Tony stopped home for lunch. As he took in the mail, he noticed a padded manila envelope addressed to him. Curious, he thought twisting it in his hand, no return address. He felt the package; there was something hard inside. He ripped open the envelope and slid out a videotape. On a Post-it stuck to the side was the message, "Watch this tape when you are alone." Tony brushed his hand through the envelope, but there was nothing else inside.

He pyramided four pieces of Italian ham on a slice of white bread, draped two slices of cheese over them and slapped another slice of bread on top. He poured himself a beer, pushed the tape into the VCR on the kitchen counter, took a bite out of the sandwich, and sat down to watch.

In the first scene the camera was focused on a prone, nude, blond man, then slowly panned down to show a woman lying underneath him. The man started to caress the naked woman's body. The woman moaned something Tony could not understand, but a minute later she cried out, "Now, Carlo. Fuck me now Carlo." At first Tony could not see the woman's face—the blond man's body hid it. But when the man suddenly jerked out of the way, Tony could clearly see it was Judy. Her eyes were shut, and she seemed totally unresponsive to the blond man's passionate caresses. Riveted to the pornography playing out before him, Tony watched in amazement, unable to believe what he was seeing. The scene faded out and a new scene faded in. Here Judy had her arms around the neck of the man and appeared to be pulling him to her. As he thrust repeatedly, Judy bounced wildly around on the bed. When the scene was over, white, diagonal, wavy lines flickered across a gray background. Stunned, Tony continued to stare at the screen. Finally he pushed the "Stop" button.

Slowly he got up from the table and paced back and forth in the small kitchen not sure what to make of the video. Carlo, he remembered, was the skinny guy Judy had made a fuss about at Nancy's wedding. She said he was her senior prom date, and then Judy mentioned he was going to Italy. Did she meet him there? Tony wondered. Was this why she wanted to go to Italy? But this is not like her at all, he thought. I can't believe she would do something like this. But if she did, he thought brightening, then I'm off the hook. If she can go and screw this guy, Carlo, then she can't complain about me, can she?

Tony smiled to himself as he went back to work. He couldn't wait until evening to confront Judy. He rushed through his last appointment in order to get home before she did and when she walked in the front door, Tony followed her into the kitchen. While she busied herself preparing dinner, he attacked.

"When you were in Italy, did you go to bed with anybody?" he sneered.

Her jam dropped in astonishment. "What the hell are you talking about? Are you crazy? I take my promise to be faithful to you seriously, and I wouldn't break it in Italy or anywhere else. And besides, we had meetings every day—all day. And at night Price made Paul and me have three hour dinners with him. It was all business. I didn't have any spare time, and even if I did, I was so exhausted I couldn't have gone out screwing even if I had wanted to." She took a deep breath.

"Yeah. You sure looked exhausted," Tony muttered.

"Say what?"

"Nothing." He paused for a moment and stared at her. "In Italy did you see . . . your prom guy?" Tony rubbed his chin. "The one you met at Nancy's wedding? Now what was his name?" Tony said sarcastically.

"You mean Carlo?" Warning flags went up in Judy's mind. Where is he going with this? she wondered. "Yes, I saw Carlo. Twice. He took me sightseeing for maybe a total of two hours. But he's only a friend, and there wasn't any sex."

"Then how do you explain THIS!?" Triumphantly, Tony brandished the tape in her face.

"I don't feel like playing games. What is THIS?"

"It's a video of you and Carlo in bed naked, and it looks like you two are having sex."

He slammed the tape into the VCR with a show of anger that he didn't really feel, and pressed the "Play" button. In shock Judy stared at him, then slowly turned toward the TV.

She breathed a sigh of relief as she saw the back of an unknown blond man. She sucked in a deep breath and prepared to scream at Tony and ask him what kind of trick he was trying to pull. But just as the words "That's not Carlo" formed in her brain, she heard the woman cry out, begging Carlo to take her. The words choked in her throat, her mouth dropped open in horror when she saw herself appear on the screen, and she struggled to catch her breath.

Before she could speak Tony said, "Well? Is that you and Carlo in bed together? Is this your way of paying me back and getting even?"

"That's not Carlo," Judy sputtered. "You met Carlo at Nancy's wedding. Does that blond, husky man look like Carlo? Carlo's thin as a rail and has thick, black hair. And Carlo doesn't have a moustache."

"All I know is that's you lying on a bed calling out for a Carlo to fuck you. That is you on the bed, isn't it? And you said you did see him in Rome."

"Stop!" Judy shrieked. She clamped her hands to the sides of her head. "Yes I saw Carlo in Rome. Why would I NOT see him in Rome?"

"Did you go to bed with him?"

"NO! NO! How many times do I have to tell you? NO!"

"Then what about the tape?"

Suddenly Judy understood. "Someone must've taken those pictures when I was drugged. That's why I was at the motel where you picked me up. They took me there to shoot this tape." He raised his eyebrows and gave her an "Oh, sure" look. "You don't believe me, do you?"

"Why did you call out for Carlo to fuck you?"

"Can't you see I was drugged? I wasn't conscious. I didn't know what I was saying or doing."

"Drugged or drunk?" Tony muttered loud enough for her to hear.

She slammed her fist on the table. "I suppose I had some fantasy, some weird dream, about Carlo, but that doesn't mean I went to bed with him. And don't tell me you're not fantasizing that I'm some big-boobed, gorgeous movie star when you're fucking me. Now once and for all I have NEVER, EVER done it with Carlo. Not in my whole life. Not even after my senior prom."

Tony stared at her in silence. Deep down he knew she was telling the truth. He could sense it in her voice, and Judy had never lied to him or anybody.

Judy knew exactly what he was thinking. Tony doesn't believe I would go to bed with another man, she thought. And yet he's putting me through this torture because in his pea-brain this is his way of getting even. I threw a fit when those pictures of him came, so he's going to bust my chops now. But he knew what he was doing when he was in bed with that whore. I was drugged.

Revulsion welled up inside her. This is really shitty of him, she thought. She felt herself starting to hate him, and wishing she was out of the marriage.

I've got to find out who's is behind this and soon, she thought. It's crushing me this one thing after another. I can't take much more of this. That cutesy heart tattoo, that's the key to this. I've got to find out who that goddamn woman is.

"Tony I need your help to find out who's behind this," Judy started.

Tony interrupted her saying derisively, "Why don't you use your witch's powers?"

She stifled a strong urge to kill him on the spot and stormed out of the kitchen.

*　　*　　*

The next day a frazzled Judy called Carlo in Rome and told him what had happened.

"Someone drugged you?" he asked incredulously. "To take pictures of you . . . What the hell for?"

"I wish I knew, but I don't. Oh, Carlo, I feel like I'm headed for a nervous breakdown," she said. "This is taking so much out of me that I can't handle it anymore. I feel all twisted and knotted up inside like an over wound spring ready to snap."

"Judy," he said seriously. "I'm worried about you, and I wish I could be there to help." And then he blurted out, "I'm in love with you. Do you know that?"

"Not now, Carlo, please. I'm too upset to deal with that right now," Judy said. But after a moment when his words sunk in, she added softly, "I wish you were here too."

"Leave Tony," he said. "Divorce him. Only a real shit would treat you this way. Come marry me and live with me in Italy. You belong here with me."

"It's a lovely offer, but I'm not quite ready to pack it in yet."

Not until I find out who belongs to that tattoo, she thought.

Chapter 35

Dominic Micaletto had made a mistake. A bad mistake. When Judy had seen him in the airport—they had actually been on the same plane—he was on his way home from Sicily.

He had called Don Cesare and tried to postpone their meeting, but the menace in the Don's voice convinced him that he had reached the end of his patience. Reluctantly Dominic had flown to Rome and then to Palermo, arriving before noon. A swarthy, short man with an ugly two-inch scar on his cheek, wearing a dirty, torn, gray sweatshirt had approached him at the airport.

"Are you Micaletto?" he asked in a flat voice devoid of any emotion.

Dominic nodded and followed him to an ancient sedan which had seen better days. The paint on the midnight-blue taxi was badly faded; its body sported an assortment of dents and scratches. The left end of the front bumper hung down almost to the road, so from the front, the car looked like it was frowning. After the first few minutes of the cabby's kamikaze-like driving, Dominic was sure he would not survive the trip. With each squeal of the brakes or swerve of the wheel, he closed his eyes to avoid witnessing what he was sure would be a fatal collision. But an hour later, the taciturn cabby swung up the driveway in front of the Don's villa and delivered his still-shaking passenger without a scratch.

The villa stood on a small knoll on the main road from Palermo to Monreale. The tall columns fronting the main entrance indicated that this might have been a grand mansion or even a palace at one time, but as he glanced around, Dominic noticed signs of genteel decay. Cracks and potholes dotted the asphalt driveway which semi circled up to the front door. And as the cabby wordlessly opened the door for him, he noticed an apron of crumbled stone around the villa's walls. He stood for a moment in front of the huge, wooden front door—surely someone had seen him drive up, or heard the screech of tires when the wild man braked to a stop—but when no one came to let him in, he looked for a doorbell. All he found was a brass doorknocker which he banged authoritatively three times. Instantly the door swung open. Dominic marveled that in spite of all the decay around him, the door opened noiselessly. A sixtyish man with neatly combed, silver hair, dressed in a brightly colored Coogi sweater, eyed him up and down before saying, "Welcome to Palermo. Did you have a good trip?"

Dominic recognized the distinctive, high-pitched voice he had heard on the phone a week earlier. "Are you Don Cesare?" Dominic asked, already knowing the answer.

"Yes. Come on in," the man replied.

Dominic followed the man into a large sitting room at the rear of the house. Although it appeared to be comfortably furnished, modern, and clean, Dominic detected a faint, musty odor. A sectional couch curved around a glass-topped coffee table in one corner of the room, but his host led him to two stuffed armchairs which faced each other near a large window. Cesare motioned him to sit down in one, then seated himself in the other.

A fawning servant appeared and the Don asked his guest, "Would you like something to drink? Paolo will bring us something to eat in a minute."

"Beer is fine," Dominic answered.

Paolo opened two folding tables and set one next to each armchair. He left the room but quickly returned with a tray full of dishes and glasses. With a flourish he set a plate of a broiled fish fillet, a plate of spaghetti, and a drink on each tray. Then carefully laid a place setting around the main dish. Throughout this performance Cesare leaned back in his chair and waited silently with his hands clasped in his lap.

Dominic burned to ask, "Why did you call me here? I know what you want to ask me, and I've already given you my answer." But instead he began to eat the fish and sip his beer.

Halfway through the meal, Don Cesare put down his fork and asked, "Do you like this?" He gestured to the food in front of them.

"Oh, yeah. It's pretty good," Dominic said taking another mouthful.

The Don watched him eat for a minute then said, "We have business to discuss."

Micaletto said nothing.

"As you know, I'm interested in moving large amounts of merchandise through Philadelphia the way I do in New York City," the Don paused to let the words sink in. "I need someone with an organization to handle the distribution. I had my representatives in New York contact you, but you never got back to them."

Dominic continued eating.

"I am prepared to make you a handsome offer," the Don continued and mentioned a percentage.

Doing some quick calculations, Dominic realized his annual income would be in the millions, but even so, he never considered accepting the offer. He loved his sister's daughters as if they were his own children, and he had suffered the torments of the damned, watching helplessly as they became addicted to drugs. They had no lives but lived only from dose to dose. My two beautiful nieces, he thought, are now two nothings. There is no way in hell I will ever get involved in this dirty business, he had promised himself.

The Don slid forward in his chair, put his hands on his knees and peered intently into Micaletto's eyes. "I can see you continue to refuse my generous offer, even though you are silent; but I want you to reconsider. You have the people and connections to make this a success, and there's a lot of money to be made. We here in Sicily," he waved his arm expansively, "are not greedy men. All of us can do very well from this business."

Don Cesare studied Dominic carefully, and sensing that his visitor was still resisting, increased his offer by fifty per cent.

Dominic stifled the urge to tell the Don exactly what he felt— that however much he offered, he would have no part of any drug operation. After all, he reasoned, he was already taking in a small fortune every week from his existing operations. What did he need more money for? The government watched his every move as it was, looking for a way to send him to jail for tax evasion. But even more important to him were his nieces, those two ghosts of human beings who haunted him wherever he went.

He said to the Don, "That's a very attractive offer. Let me think it over. I'll give you an answer in a week."

The Don's smile evaporated from his face, and he struggled to keep from showing his anger. He pushed himself back into his chair and again clasped his hands in his lap. "Very well," he said. "I am a patient man, but patience has its limits. One week. No more. If you refuse, I will have to . . . make other plans."

As if by some silent signal, Paolo appeared and piled the dirty dishes on his tray. After he returned to the kitchen, Cesare said, "You are welcome to stay here in my house as long as you want. Let Paolo know when you are ready to leave."

Without another word or gesture the Don got up and left the room. Dominic summoned Paolo and informed him he was ready to go back to the airport immediately. It was when he had landed in Philadelphia that Judy had seen him.

A week after meeting with the Don, Dominic had called Palermo and respectfully turned down the offer saying it was a business he did not care to get involved in. He wished the Don good luck in finding another "distributor."

But Don Cesare was in no mood to find anyone else, and there was no one else but Micaletto who had an organization in place that could handle the Philadelphia drug business. After he hung up, the Don made a phone call to New York and instructed his associates to effect a change in the top management of the Dominic's organization.

At the same time a horrified Judy was watching the tape, Dominic and his usual Tuesday dinner companions had just finished eating at La Luna restaurant in South Philadelphia. Back in his own element, Dominic was a different person—loud, coarse language and obscene jokes spilled from him in torrents. He was a thug—crude, arrogant, and rude.

"Call my fuckin' driver for me," he shouted at the owner as he paid the bill. "Tell 'im to come and pick us the fuck up."

He pushed the restaurant door open and stepped out into the warm night with his companions. One of his them, who had returned the day before from Mexico with five boxes of Cuban cigars, pulled one from his pocket with a flourish and handed it to Dominic. Dominic sniffed it, grinned broadly, and stuck it in his mouth. He fumbled for a lighter, flicked it, held it up to the end of the cigar, and puffed it to life. He concentrated so hard on lighting the cigar that he failed to notice the black Cadillac sedan slithering down the narrow one-way street toward him. As Dominic checked the end of his cigar to be sure it was properly lit, he glanced up. The bright lights of the oncoming car momentarily blinded him. When it had pulled alongside, the rear window slid down noiselessly, and two gun barrels poked out. Quick tap-tap-taps pricked the still night air. After each of the men was raked with a dozen bullets, the black car, in no particular hurry, pulled away leaving blood and life oozing from the mobsters.

An hour later the phone rang in Don Cesare's Palermo villa. Paolo answered it, listened for a moment, then hung up.

"It's done," he said to the Don.

Chapter 36

$\mathcal{I}$nstead of providing relief, talking with Carlo and his declaration of love made Judy all the more uptight. In addition to trying to sort out her feeling about him, she constantly obsessed about all the bad things that had happened to her since Nancy's wedding. From the spasm she had in the office to the episode in the motel, she reviewed all the events over and over again in her mind. I feel like I'm carrying a ton of lead on my shoulders, she thought. If one more thing happens to me, I'm going to collapse under the weight. A nervous breakdown might not be a bad idea, she thought. I'd be sheltered and cared for, all my needs catered to; I wouldn't have a worry in the world. No, she decided, that's not for me. I've got to tough it out; I've got to deal with all this. In a few days I'll be caught up on my work, and then I can concentrate on finding out who's behind this and put a stop to it. Maybe I'll ask for a leave of absence, take some time off, and get this monkey off my back once and for all.

As she walked along the corridor to her office, she was so engrossed in her thoughts that she didn't notice Sara fell in step behind her and followed her into her cubicle.

"Did you see this morning's papers? It's in both of them—the Inquirer and the Daily News." Sara twittered. She stood in the doorway with her hands on her hips.

Judy was in no mood to gossip. She dropped her purse in the file cabinet, slammed the drawer shut, and plopped into her chair. She began to take sheets of paper from the pile on the edge of her desk and smoothed them out in front of her. Keeping her eyes on her work she said, "No. I hardly ever read the papers anymore." Since Carlo left, she had stopped looking for his byline. "I get the news on TV. What did I miss?"

"There was a big spread right on page one. Here. Look." She unfolded the Inquirer and flattened it out on the desk and pointed. "Last night six guys were offed in front of La Luna. Shot to death from a passing car. There's a picture of them lying on the sidewalk, and . . ."

"Why do you think this would interest me?" Judy tried to push the paper out of her way.

Sara, having missed the course in sensitivity training, was certain that everyone with an Italian surname was related, and all of them were involved with the Mafia.

"They were all Italian," she said defensively.

Annoyed, Judy glared at her and bristled.

"And you think we're all related, is that it? You think one of them might have been one of my brothers . . . or an uncle? Well, if it was, I would have heard by now. We do talk to each other."

"I was only trying to . . . ."

"I'm sorry. I didn't mean to snap at you," Judy said without meaning it. "Everybody thinks all Italians are Mafia and one big happy family. I get upset when I get stereotyped."

"The paper called them alleged Mafia, I didn't." Sara sniffed, turned on her heel and left.

Without looking at it, Judy folded the newspaper, stuffed it in the wastebasket, then plunged into the pile of work on her desk. But slowly, though she tried to ignore it, something gnawed at her, her witch's sixth sense prodded her to get the newspaper and read it. Before she could get it from the wastebasket, her hands started to become clammy, and she shivered violently. She trembled so badly that she dropped the pen she was holding. She felt a pain in her palms and realized she had dug in her nails almost to the point of breaking the skin and bleeding. She squeezed her eyes shut and fought to gain control over her body but couldn't. As she shook uncontrollably, her mind raced, and a terrifying sense of impending disaster flooded through her. In a few minutes the feelings faded, but a message thundered through her mind: there was a connection between those dead men and the woman with the heart tattoo. She was sure of it.

When she stopped shaking and the tension subsided, she fished the newspaper from the wastebasket. A huge headline announced the deaths of six "reputed mobsters." The story detailed their gruesome deaths—victims of a drive-by shooting. The police spokesman said they weren't sure if this was the beginning of gang warfare or the men happened to be in the wrong place at the wrong time.

On page 12, where the story continued, there were head-and-shoulders pictures of the murdered men splashed across the width of the page. Judy gasped in astonishment as she recognized Dominic Micaletto even before she read the name underneath his picture. At first she couldn't believe what she had seen and read, but as the news gradually sunk in she felt a deep sense of sorrow. I just saw him at the airport, she thought, and now he's dead.

He played a very important part in my life, she thought. Inadvertently, she quickly replayed the scene of the night in the back seat of his car. His experienced hands had unhooked her bra then caressed her body under her clothes. His raspy voice told her what to do. "Lay down," he said. She lay flat on the seat, and he slid her jeans and panties down to her ankles then off. And then the pleasure/pain mixture of sensations. It was the one and only time with him, she thought, but I'll never forget it. Because he was my first.

The more she thought about him the more she realized she was not surprised that he ended up dead in a mob shooting. The glitzy, chromed, convertible, the fancy clothes, the wads of spending money. In high school when she and Kate asked what he did for money, he sidestepped their questions. "I work for my father doing odd jobs," was all he would say. I should have guessed he was involved in some criminal activity, Judy thought.

The grandfather clock in the hallway outside her office struck noon jarring her from her reminiscences. As the last chime's mournful sound slowly died away, a pinprick of an idea formed in her head which eventually blossomed into a realization. Her intuition told her that Dominic was the one that was going to lead her to the woman with the heart tattoo.

Chapter 37

Both Judy and Tony slept late on Saturday, woke without talking, then sat in silence across from each other over brunch. Tony, faking interest in the paper, buried his face in the sport section, while Judy struggled trying to find some plan to get her life back to normal. (Would it ever be normal again? she wondered.) When she got up to clear away the dishes, Tony grabbed the opportunity to leave the table and raced upstairs and packed his gym bag. He was angry with her. He knew she was telling the truth about being drugged when the tape was shot, but he was determined to get maximum mileage out of punishing her for getting angry with him for his indiscretions. He had decided on the silent treatment along with depriving her of his company for as much of the weekend as he thought she would put up with.

"I'm going to the gym," he said not bothering to give her a goodbye peck on the cheek. "I'll be home for supper." Without looking back he hurried out the front door.

To hell with him, Judy thought, as she started to do the laundry and prepared to follow that with some dusting. While I'm doing these mindless chores, I'm going to do something nice for myself, she decided, and found herself fantasizing about what life would have been like if she had married Carlo. Here he comes now, she daydreamed, home from work. He swept her into his arms and pressed his lips to hers. They were soft and yielding and hinted of delights to follow. And the flowers. He held a dozen pink roses behind his back and whisked them out to surprise her. Romance, love, passion; she worked it all into her dream.

Suddenly the phone rang, splintering her fantasy and wrenching her back to the present. She put down the dust cloth, took the cordless into the living room, and flopped on the couch.

Without a "hello" the voice began, "Did you see in the paper about those men who were killed?" It was Kate. She sounded weepy. "I forgot. You don't read the papers."

"I read them this time," Judy said. "Sara brought the paper to work made a point of showing me. I was going to call you about . . ."

Kate sobbed the words out: "You noticed his picture? Dominic? He was one of the ones . . ." She couldn't bring herself to add "who died."

"You sound really upset about this," Judy said sympathetically. "It was years ago that you went out with him, and if you still care this much about him, that's a hell-of-a torch you're carrying."

"It was a long time ago, but in a way I never got over him. He was the first man I ever really loved. He meant so much to me." She broke down and cried for a minute then regained her composure. "I'll have to call you back. I can't talk about this right now. No, you call me back. I've got to show a house. Call me on my cell phone in two hours. 215-543-2118. I'll be done by then." Sniffling she hung up abruptly without saying goodbye.

Judy put the phone back on its base, scribbled down Kate's phone number, then went back to her housework. She shook loose from fantasizing about Carlo and forced herself to concentrate on formulating a plan to find out who belonged to the heart tattoo. Phone number, she thought. I just wrote down a phone number— Kate's cell phone number. Phone number, phone number, ran through her head. Why didn't I think of this before? she asked herself. Tony must have phoned the woman with the heart tattoo to arrange to meet her at the motel. If he did, he wouldn't call her on our home phone, but maybe he was dumb enough to call her on his cell phone.

Judy knew Tony threw all his bills and receipts into a shoebox for the accountant to use in April when he prepared their tax return. Methodically he had stacked up these boxes of receipts going back ten years, in the closet in his study and labeled each box by year.

Let's see, Judy thought. He must have made those calls in February or March, so I need this year's box. Excitedly she ran upstairs and yanked the closet door open. The box she needed sat on top of the pile. She slid it gingerly from the shelf and set it on the desk. Panting with excitement she systematically searched through every scrap of paper putting the cell phone bills in a separate pile. On the March bill—dating from just before the pictures came—there were a number of calls to a familiar number—215-543-2118! Holy shit, that's the number Kate just gave me, Judy realized.

Stunned for a few seconds she tried to make some sense out of this discovery. Tony called Kate—his cell phone to her cell phone, she thought. Why would he do that? Was it to arrange to meet her at a motel? Was Kate the woman with the heart tattoo? Hold on, she cautioned herself, let's not jump too fast to conclusions. There's probably some good reason that I've forgotten about for him to make those calls. She racked her brain for fifteen minutes searching for a reason but couldn't think of any. The only reason he would call her from his cell phone so many times would be if he had something to hide, she thought. He would sure as hell want to hide what he was doing if he was screwing her. And Kate knew about my going to Friday's and could have set me up there.

Her heart raced; a flash of red light exploded in front of her eyes temporarily blinding her. Seething with fury, she crumpled the receipt and threw it in the closet, then angrily swept the rest of the papers off the desk onto the floor. Still raging, she slammed her fist on the desk. "It looks like it's been fucking Kate all along," she said out loud. "My supposed best fucking friend's been screwing my husband and torturing me."

With great effort she tried to calm herself and plan her next steps, but her heart continued to throb out of control. First I've got to be a hundred percent sure it's Kate, she thought. Then I'd like to know why she hates me so much. What did I ever do to her? And then I'm going to get even. I'm going to get even big time!

She glanced at the clock in the corner of the desk and saw the two hours had passed. It was time to call Kate back. She picked up the papers from the floor and smoothed the phone bill from the closet floor. She put a rubber band around the cell phone bills and put them and the rest of the receipts back in the box. Then she put the box back on the top of the pile, sat down in Tony's desk chair, and angrily dialed Kate's number.

"Yeah. It's okay to talk," Kate said. "This couple was only looking; they're not ready to buy. I'm in the car on my way home."

Afraid to speak with all the hostile feelings boiling inside her, Judy said nothing.

After a huge sigh, Kate began to sob softly. "I haven't told you everything," she said. "You know Greg and I have an open marriage. Both of us agreed that we could see anyone else we wanted after we got married. I wouldn't have married him if he hadn't agreed . . . because of Dominic." She paused, unsure how to go on, then blurted out, "I was obsessed with Dominic for a long time, and I saw him even after I married Greg. From the first time I went out with Dominic he was my lover, my friend, my life . . . my everything. Even though he married someone else, it didn't change the way I felt about him. I can't begin to tell you the stupid things I did because I wanted him so badly. I gave him sex whenever he wanted it." She tittered through her tears as she remembered, took a deep breath and rambled on. "We even did it under the boardwalk in Atlantic City. Once we went to a party and did it in the master bedroom on top of the coats lying on the bed. But he wouldn't marry me, and kept seeing other women. I was furious and decided to get even so I did the bar scene. I slept with anything that wore pants and then told him about it to make him jealous."

Judy couldn't help herself. She interrupted, "My God. You never told me any of this."

There was no stopping Kate. She continued to unburden herself. "One of the bums I picked up at a bar asked me if I wanted to star in an X-rated movie. I figured that would get Dominic's attention, so I said 'yes.' He told me I would have to audition. Can you believe how dumb I was? He took videos of me screwing five different guys before I caught on that there wasn't any movie. When I told Dominic I was going to be in a dirty movie, he couldn't have cared less."

Breathing erratically Kate began to hyperventilate. Judy heard a screech of brakes and a thud as Kate's cell phone fell to the floor. "I just missed hitting another car," she said. "I'm not myself today." She spoke calmly now. "I loved Dominic for a long, long time, and I'm not sure that I don't love him even now."

Judy was astonished. "This is unbelievable. You never told me you were so crazy about him."

"I know. I kept it a secret because it was so . . . immature, so insane. Most people grow up and grow out of bad relationships. I carried mine past the point of good sense hoping it was puppy love or a first crush. I thought it would pass, but it never did, it only got worse."

"But why did you marry Greg. Why didn't you marry Dominic if you loved him so much?"

"Dominic told me his parents wouldn't let him marry anyone who wasn't Italian, and they were really insistent about it. He cared for them so much and didn't want to hurt them, so he wouldn't marry me. He begged me to find a husband who would understand that I would be loving two men, so we could continue to see each other."

It was all a lie. Kate made up the story about Dominic's parents and Dominic begging her to find an understanding husband. She needed to believe it to soothe her damaged ego, but the truth was Dominic didn't care for her, didn't love her, and certainly didn't want to marry her. The truth was that she chased him so hard, throwing herself at him at every chance, that he looked at her as a convenient piece of meat; she was his last resort when he had no one else to satisfy his lust. Dominic loved the thrill of the chase, but when the game lay down, nuzzled at his feet, rolled over, and waited for the arrow to be shot into its heart, he wasn't interested.

"Like I said, even after I married Greg, we were still lovers." Though she had dogged Dominic as fiercely as ever after she married, his attitude toward her remained unchanged. "He finally married an Italian girl—it didn't last long—but even when he was married, he kept on seeing me."

They had only been married a few weeks when his wife found out that Dominic continued to go out with other women, including Kate. She immediately began divorce proceedings. Shortly after the divorce became final, Kate became noticeably pregnant with her first child. Dominic reacted with disgust, called her a "fat cow," and never phoned her again.

"I can't believe it," Judy said. "This is so bizarre."

"Believe it. It's true. Fortunately my marriage with Greg worked out. We have a good, functioning marriage. But," she said, "I loved

Dominic so much . . . you won't believe this, Judy, I even got a tattoo for him."

Judy's heart pounded, the veins in her neck bulged, she snapped to attention. "A tattoo?" she said cautiously.

"He said it would really turn him on if I got one. He saw a go-go dancer in a nightclub with tattoos on her boobs. He said it got him hot, so I figured I'd get one too. Can you believe me getting a tattoo? You know how much I'm into health foods and exercise—I try to do good things for my bod, and I went and got a tattoo. They prick your skin and force the colors in. It hurt like hell, and it's permanent—I've still got it. I was scared to death, but I did it for him." She broke down and cried. "See how much I loved him?"

Judy spoke slowly and lowered her voice. "I never saw a tattoo on you, even when you wear a bathing suit. Where are you hiding it, and what does it look like?" To keep Kate from getting suspicious she quickly added, "Maybe I'll get one, too."

"It would be hidden by a bathing suit. It's so small—a tiny red heart on my left thigh—but high up, almost at my waist. I've grown to like it, because it reminds me of him. Sometimes I think it's cute, even though it's not hygienic. I did it for Dominic, but . . ."

Kate rambled on, but Judy had tuned her out. Her heart jack hammered in a frenzy that frightened her (Am I having a heart attack? she wondered.). Her blood boiled violently in her veins. Her jaw clenched; her face and ears flushed red as a whirlwind of disjointed images swirled in her mind: Tony was screwing the woman with the heart tattoo. The woman slowly turned to face Judy; it was Kate. Kate was smirking and then screeched a laugh that pierced Judy's soul. Using all her will power, Judy struggled as hard as she could to stop the chaos in her brain; she desperately wanted to think clearly. There's no doubt any more, a voice shouted inside her, that Kate is the bitch with the heart tattoo. She's the one in the picture in bed with Tony, and the one who drugged you. The voice became a roar. The one who took your mother's ring and Tony's horn. She was in this house when you were in Italy, and must have fucked Tony then too.

As Kate's monologue droned on in the background, Judy thought, how could this happen with me never suspecting a thing? Of course she's not the only one in the world who has a heart tattoo, but I know she's the one in that picture. She summoned the picture from her subconscious and mentally examined every inch of it. Look, she said to herself, look at that shape. It's Kate's. Goddamn that bitch, she screamed inside herself. I'll get even with her. I'll get even with both of them.

"Judy? Are you still there?" A worried Kate's voice broke in on her thoughts.

Judy managed to sputter, "Uh. Yeah." She clamped her eyes shut as a new jumble of scenes streaked by like a videotape on fast forward. Tony and Kate writhing in bed in ecstasy, reaching a spectacular climax, gradually changed to Tony and Kate writhing in agony, dying a horrible death. She tried to think clearly, to devise a plan, but with her thoughts in confusion she was paralyzed.

"I'm almost home now," Kate said. "Thanks for letting me unload on you. I needed someone to listen. I'll talk to you soon."

Judy mumbled a "goodbye."

She waited until Kate had hung up, then slammed the phone angrily onto its base. She balled her hand into a fist and slammed it down on the desk over and over again as hard as she could. She shrieked in agony as jolts of pain surged up her arm and finally stopped. As she rubbed her aching hand, she wondered what she had ever done to Kate to make her do all those cruel things? She thought, I don't know what I'm going to do to her, but I'll get even, and I'll get to the bottom of this. Maybe she's in love with Tony and trying to take him away from me. Whatever. I'll make her tell me the truth, and then I'm going to pay her back.

Exhausted she folded her aching arms on Tony's desk, put her head in the nest they made, and passed out.

Chapter 38

Judy lifted her head a few minutes later, staggered into her bedroom, and fell down on her bed. She beat her head into her pillow over and over again in an effort to make sense out of what was happening but had no success. When she had worn herself out, she lay on her back, put her arm across her forehead, and tried to regain her self-control. It was no use. She began to shiver violently, unable to check the smoldering rage she felt for Kate and Tony. It overpowered her; it took control of her and wouldn't let go. Her mind raced wildly: thoughts, pictures, and fears created bedlam; her mental circuits overloaded, and she became disoriented. Soon she was physically and mentally exhausted and blacked out again. Fifteen minutes later she woke, oddly refreshed, her mind clear.

I've got to get my act together, she thought. A jumble of ideas gradually formed themselves into a plan. Judy ironed out the details, reviewed it one more time, then cool and composed, went down to the living room couch, folded her hands in her lap, and waited for Tony to come home.

Over dessert she asked him about his plans for the week. "Will you be home for supper every night?" she asked innocently.

"Why do you ask?"

"So tomorrow I can shop for the week. I ask you the same question every week."

"You don't ask me every week. You've never asked that I can remember."

She gritted her teeth. "Well, I'm asking you now. Will you be home every night?"

"Except Friday. Friday I have a four o'clock with a big customer. I'm going to take him out for dinner, so don't expect me home before midnight."

Good, she thought, he won't be home Friday. That's when I'll do it.

*　　*　　*

The next day Judy woke up early and dressed in her best clothes.

"Where are you going?" Tony asked.

"It's Sunday, and I'm going to church," she answered.

"How come? It's not Christmas or Easter."

She couldn't tell him the real reason.

"I just feel like it," she said.

"You don't expect me to go with you?" he said.

"No, of course not, you asshole," she muttered to herself. Out loud: "You don't have to go."

She paid no attention to the service or the priest's sermon but spent the entire time reviewing with God what Kate had done to her and what she planned to do in return.

"Of course," she said to Him, "right now I don't have proof beyond a shadow of a doubt that Kate is behind this, but I'll get it from her, from her own mouth." Then she told Him that in His eyes what she was about to do was might seem to be sinful in the extreme, but she was determined to go ahead with it. "I hope you'll see why I have to do this, and I hope you'll understand," she confided.

When she came home from church, she felt at peace with herself because intuitively she knew that God would support what she was about to do. She dialed Kate's number and with great difficulty—she really wanted to yell and scream at her—exchanged greetings.

"Is Greg still going to that engineering convention in California?" Judy asked, straining to keep her voice pleasant, struggling to keep the hatred that churned inside her from spilling out.

"Sure he is. He tries to keep current, and this is a once-a-year conference with superstars from all over the world. He wouldn't miss this for anything. He's leaving today, and he'll be gone a week. Why?"

"I was thinking. You'll be alone, and it's been a while since I've had you over for dinner. Why don't you come over for dinner some night when he's away?" She stopped talking for a second as if considering her options. "Friday's good for me. I'll go all out and home cook you something good. We can relax and have some fun. Maybe it'll take your mind off Dominic."

"Oh, Dominic," Kate said and sighed. "I do keep thinking about him." She paused. "Friday dinner sounds great. I'll put it on my calendar."

Judy waited until Tony had gone outside to prune some shrubs then went up to his study and took out the box with his receipts again. I've got to be one hundred per cent sure, she thought, that Kate is behind all my misery. Looking carefully through Tony's cell phone bills she found many suspicious phone calls. In addition to calls to Kate's cell phone, Judy noticed he had made calls to Kate's work number and to her home. One especially caught her eye: a call to Kate's cell phone on the evening of March 20th which, she remembered, was the right date for the night they spent in the motel. She shoved the papers back in the box. There was a lot of contact between Tony and Kate, she thought, and for no good reason. Something's went on between them, and I'll get the truth Friday night.

When Tony came in for supper she said, "Since you won't be home Friday, I invited Kate for supper."

Tony eyed her warily and thought, I wonder what's going on? Is she suspicious about Kate and me? Is she trying to get Kate to tell about us? "What for?" he asked.

"Nothing special," Judy answered. "Greg's going to be in California, and you won't be home, so I thought it would be nice for us to get together. After all she is my best friend."

"But you've never had her over before when he was away. Why now?"

"Because I want to," she snapped at him. "Any objections?"

"No objections. You two have fun," he said reluctantly.

Oh, I'll have fun all right, Judy thought, but Kate won't.

Chapter 39

At work on Friday Judy watched the clock, begging it to move faster. She tried to get some work done, but it was no use. Every thirty seconds she would glance up and curse the clock for moving so slowly. At three-thirty she couldn't stand it any longer and left work early. "I've got a bad headache," she lied to the receptionist on her way out. "I'll be at home if anybody needs me."

"Yeah, right," the receptionist replied.

When she got home, Judy leafed through the mail, dropped it on the hall table without bothering to read any of it, then went straight to the kitchen. She tied an apron around her waist and began preparing dinner, attending to each detail meticulously, determined that everything would go exactly as she had planned. Carefully she set the table with the two silver candlesticks her parents had given them for their fifteenth wedding anniversary. ("Silver for the fifteenth? What will you give us for our twenty-fifth?" Judy had asked. "It'll be a surprise," her mother had said.) As she seated long, white candles in the candlesticks, she decided not to use the good silverware, but she would use her good Villeroy & Boch dishes—the ones with the basket design.

The clock in the living room was chiming six when Kate rang the doorbell. Judy untied her apron and draped it over the back of a kitchen chair. She opened the front door and looked Kate over from head to toe trying to discover what Tony could find so fantastic that he would break his promises and jeopardize their marriage. She had to concede, that this was one pretty woman standing in front of her: cut-short, flaming-red hair, porcelain-skinned face, pert, tiny nose. Lightly dressed for the warm summer evening, Kate wore a loose, stark-white blouse and black short-shorts. Kate's figure gave no hint that this woman had given birth to two children. Yes, Judy was forced to admit, she was very attractive.

Kate twittered, "Hello," and handed Judy two bottles of wine. Judy studied the label.

"Orvieto. This is the wine Charlie Price ordered for supper in Rome. How did you know I like it?" she said.

"There's no conspiracy," Kate said. "Just a lucky guess on my part."

Judy mumbled a "Thank you," air-kissed Kate halfheartedly near her cheek, and led her into the house. She took the bottles into the kitchen and cut the foil neatly away from the neck of one. As she viciously twisted the corkscrew into the cork, she took secret delight in thinking: I'll make believe I'm twisting this into her heart. She peered into the dining room where Kate was seated at the table. My best friend, she thought. Not for much longer. Tonight's payback night. She stared at Kate trying to see if there was anything, tangible or intangible, that would give away the fact that she had been secretly going to bed with Tony, but she noticed nothing unusual. Judy glanced away quickly when Kate turned suddenly and caught her staring.

She poured the wine and handed Kate a glass.

"Let's have a toast," Judy said. "What should we drink to?" She eyed Kate warily.

"Good times," Kate said.

"Good friends," said Judy, hoping Kate would miss the sarcasm in her voice.

Judy avoided drinking too much of the wine by taking her glass with her when she went into the kitchen and pouring some of the wine in the sink. However, she made sure to fill Kate's glass whenever it got low. Soon they had emptied the first bottle of wine and with no fanfare, and without asking, Judy opened the second one and filled Kate's empty glass.

Kate was a happy drunk and soon began giggling at everything Judy said. "Remember the time when . . . ," Judy began, and before she could get the next word out, Kate burst into gales of laughter.

Glad I can make you laugh, bitch, Judy thought, but you won't be laughing when I'm done with you tonight.

Smoke trickled from the kitchen and Judy jumped up from the table. "The lamb chops are done," she announced. "I'd better get them before they set off the smoke alarm."

In spite of the turmoil she was feeling inside, Judy concentrated on enjoying every mouthful of food. She tried hard to focus on the conversation but with little success. I want to remember everything about tonight, she thought. Soon, soon, it won't be long now, I'll have my life back to normal. She squirmed in her chair, struggling to maintain her composure.

"Ready for dessert?" Judy said. "I bought key lime pie, and I made the whipped cream topping myself. It's real whipped cream not plastic goo from a can. Tony loves key lime pie." She stressed the word "Tony" and looked carefully for a reaction from Kate, but there was none.

"Sounds great," Kate said.

Judy slid from her chair and went to the kitchen. She unboxed the pie and dabbed it with big globs of whipped cream then sliced two pieces and carried them into the dining room, thinking, it's time to get the show on the road.

As she set the pie in front of Kate, she said sweetly, "Remember the tattoo you mentioned on the phone?"

"Oh, I remember it all right. It's with me all the time, and I can't get rid of it." She broke into a fit of laughter.

"Since it's just the two of us here, could I see it?" Judy asked.

"Suuure," Kate slurred. She stood up on wobbly legs, held onto the table with one hand, and hiked up the left leg of her shorts with the other.

Judy bent over to see it clearly. There it is, she thought, a small red heart tattooed on her hip, almost at the waistline. It was a perfect match, identical to the one in the photograph.

"Nice," Judy said her voice dripping with contempt. Now to the next step, she told herself.

She went to the kitchen for some iced tea which she knew was Kate's drink of choice. A tremor of excitement fluttered through her— it's all downhill from here, she thought. She took the whistling teapot from the stove, dropped a handful of ice into a glass, and poured it half full of tea. While the ice crunched and crackled as the hot liquid scalded it, Judy fished two pills from the pocket of her apron—the remainder of the pills Carlo had given her. Good thing I saved these, she thought. She recalled Carlo's warning about taking only one, and no alcohol, because with alcohol, he had warned, they're like knockout drops.

Should I give the bitch one or two? Judy thought. After what she's done to me, . . . two. She dropped the pills in the glass and stirred them until they dissolved. She stabbed a sprig of mint viciously into the glass (like a knife in your heart, she thought), then made herself a glass of tea.

"Special iced tea," she announced, as she brought the two glasses to the table.

"This pie is delicious," Kate said. Half her slice was already gone. "Where did you say you bought it?" She set her fork down and took a deep drink of the tea, then puckered her lips and grimaced. "The tea has a strange taste. What kind of tea is it?"

"Regular chamomile," Judy said.

She watched as Kate held the glass under her nose, sniffed, shrugged her shoulders, and drank another mouthful.

Kate felt a wave of malaise wash over her, but she credited it to the wine, ignored it, and continued to eat the dessert and sip the tea. Suddenly, she felt nauseous and light-headed.

"Oh, shit," she said. "I don't feel so good. I must've eaten too much."

Judy smiled amiably but said nothing.

Kate pushed her chair back from the table and tried to stand up. She raised herself a few inches up from her chair and then collapsed back down. She stared at Judy, her eyes pleading for help, but Judy calmly folded her hands across her chest and grinned at her like the Cheshire cat in *Alice in Wonderland*. Kate stared at her and her eyes widened as she realized that something was terribly wrong.

"I get it," said Kate doubling over. "You put something in the tea or the pie." She gripped the table with both hands and dug her fingers in as a fresh wave of nausea gripped her. "It was the tea; I knew it smelled bad. You put something in the tea."

"Good detective work, Sherlock," Judy said insolently.

"You poisoned me?" Kate's face contorted as she fought to stay conscious.

"No, it's not poison. You'll live."

"What the fuck is going on here? Why are you doing this to me? What did I ever do to you?"

"Let me count the ways," Judy said sarcastically. "Let's talk over a few little things." She glared at Kate, and her voice rose to a shriek. "Let's talk about you and Tony. You and Tony in bed together. You and Tony fucking each other's brains out. That's what this is about."

"Me . . . Tony . . . ," Kate hunched over the table and sank her head into her hands. She tried to laugh but didn't have the energy.

"My dear friend," Judy screamed. "There's evidence . . . in color. You remember the pictures you sent me? The pictures of Tony wrapped around a woman."

"I didn't send you anything, and it wasn't me in those pictures," Kate said.

"Oh, I think it *was* you. One picture showed the woman with a small heart tattooed on her left hip." Judy reached over and poked Kate on her hip so hard that she winced. "Right there where you have your tattoo, and, funny thing, it looked exactly like yours."

Unable to speak, Kate waved her arms frantically in an it-wasn't-me gesture.

"But it was you. You're the woman in that picture. Aren't you? . . . Aren't you?" Judy screeched.

Kate moaned an unintelligible reply. "Answer me, damn you! Aren't you that bitch?" Judy shouted.

Slowly Kate tried again to stand up. Judy sprang from her chair, put both hands on her shoulders and pushed her back down, saying, "You sit here until I'm done with you." Kate fell onto the chair with such force that it teetered backward on two legs then fell over. As she hit the floor she moaned in pain then fell unconscious.

Furious, Judy straddled Kate, sat down on her stomach, and smacked her across the face with all her strength.

"Wake up, goddamn you," she roared in her ear. "I'm not done with you yet."

Kate's eyes blinked rapidly then jerked open. She twisted and squirmed in a vain effort to get out from under Judy's smothering weight, then flailed her arms weakly and tried to push her off. Judy grabbed her wrist and clamped them so tightly that Kate winced with pain. Kate opened her mouth as if to speak, but no words came out.

"You were that woman, weren't you?" Judy shouted in her ear, not a shred of pity in her voice.

"Help . . . me, pleeeease," Kate pleaded, gasping for air. "You're so heavy, it hurts. I can't breathe."

Judy leaned down, her face just inches away from Kate's. Kate cringed.

"After I get some answers, I'll get off." She lifted some of her weight up a little to allow Kate to catch her breath. "It *was* you in that picture, wasn't it?" She spit the words out. "It *was* you in that motel. It *was* you with the cutesy tattoo. It *was* you fucking Tony. Wasn't it?"

Kate realized there was no point in denying it; she sucked in a deep breath, and said angrily, "So what if it was? You did the same thing to me. I was only getting even."

Judy's mouth fell open. This was something she didn't expect.

"What the hell are you talking about? I never slept with Greg, and why would you care if I did? You keep telling me you have an open marriage."

Kate drew on what little strength she had left and snarled, "I'm not talking about Greg, you asshole. I'm talking about Dominic. You tried to steal him from me." Kate continued to struggle to breathe. Somehow she summoned a burst of energy, pushed Judy off her, and pulled herself up to a sitting position. She leaned against a table leg for support and coldly looked Judy in the eye.

"And don't you try and tell me you didn't," she said. Judy started to speak but Kate held up her hand. "Remember the night of the prom?" Judy nodded perplexed. "After the prom. You . . . my . . . best . . . friend."

Judy closed her eyes and the memories flooded back.

Chapter 40

$\mathcal{A}$ month before her senior prom, Judy didn't have a date. She wanted to go to the prom but hadn't been dating much, and one by one the boys she knew had asked other girls. During their senior year, Kate, on the other hand, refused to go out with anyone except Dominic. Even though he bragged to anyone who would listen that picked his dates at random from a harem full of girls, about once a month he would deign to take Kate out. Kate was his fallback; he knew she would drop everything and cancel any plans she might have to go out with him. He dated her just enough to keep her on the hook so he wouldn't have to risk her saying "no."

And then there was sex. Dominic discovered early on that Kate was so crazy about him, she would do anything he asked. So when he felt his voracious sexual appetite needed instant, no questions asked, satisfying, he would call Kate and she would oblige. Once they even did it in the downstairs hall closet in Kate's house with her father upstairs reading a book in the bedroom.

Kate badgered him endlessly to go steady. He would snort derisively and tell her that he wasn't ready to limit himself to only one girl.

"I'm a young guy," he would say, "and I'm gonna play the field. I'm not gonna be tied down to any one woman, and if you don't fuckin' like it, you can go find someone else."

Blinded by love, Kate lived with his promiscuity but didn't like it. She was pleasantly surprised when, with a minimum of nagging on her part, he agreed to take her to the prom. The truth was that he wasn't about to ask anyone—it was beneath his dignity—and she was the first girl to ask him. Also he didn't much care what girl he went with—to him it was only another date and nothing special.

Kate and Judy spent many hours tossing on Judy's bed struggling to come up with the ideal prom date for Judy.

"I've gotten to meet a lot of Dominic's friends, and let me tell you, they are really scary," Kate chirped. She was lying on her stomach, knees bent, legs waggling in the air.

"Scary? Meaning what?" Judy asked.

"Spooky. Weird. Just scary. I wouldn't let you go out with any of them." She flipped over on her back and clasped her hands behind her head. "But Dominic has this cousin, Carlo Fiore, who's really nice. He hasn't been kicked out of parochial school like Dominic was." She laughed. "So how bad can he be?"

Judy sighed and said unenthusiastically, "Okay. I guess I'm desperate. But I'll only do it if we double date."

*   *   *

On prom night Carlo knocked on Judy's door promptly at eight and escorted her to a gleaming, white, Ford convertible (top up). Judy sized up Carlo as they walked toward the car: he was thin, soft-spoken, and a winner in his black tuxedo; but she gasped as if she had been punched in the stomach when she saw Dominic. As he slowly disengaged himself from a clothes-mussing embrace with Kate, Judy devoured him with her eyes. His shiny, raven-black hair was plastered tightly to the sides of his head; his swarthy face was perfectly tanned; every muscular bulge was accentuated by precisely tailored clothes. As she stepped closer, the powerful odor from his sweet-smelling cologne made her head swim. For a fleeting second she closed her eyes and fantasized that he was *her* date, and Mr. Perfect would be caressing her. Uh oh, she thought, Kate's my best friend. I'd better snap back to reality.

Halfway through the prom, Dominic grabbed Carlo by the arm and pulled him outside. When they returned Judy asked, "What were you guys up to?" When Carlo opened his mouth, his breath reeked of alcohol, so she wasn't surprised when he answered, "We went for something to drink. Dominic's got a bottle of Scotch in the car."

His words were so badly slurred she barely understood him. And when she pulled him out onto the dance floor, his head flopped onto her shoulder, and she had to prop him up and lead for the rest of the evening. Dominic, on the other hand, showed no signs of being drunk. At the end of the evening, he appeared to be as sober, calm, and in control, as he had been at the beginning.

When the prom ended and the band starting packing up their instruments, Kate and Judy went to the ladies' room and changed into casual clothes. They had agreed to meet two other couples at the New Jersey shore where they had rented a beachfront house for the night. As they neared the car, they saw Carlo slumped over the steering wheel, his arms circled around his head.

"Get in the back," Judy yelled at him. "You're plastered and in no shape to drive." He gave no sign that he heard and didn't move. She bent over to shake him awake.

"Don't worry," Dominic said. He leaned forward from the back seat and put his hand gently on her arm. Funny, little, shooting tingles ran up to her shoulder. "Carlo's all right. He's just resting. A little more fresh air, and he'll be as good as new." He pushed the front seat down, and held his hand out to Kate. She took it eagerly and giggling, stumbled purposely into his lap.

"Hey c'mon, I don't think we should let Carlo drive," Judy protested to Dominic. "It's a long way, and if he conks out, we'll all be dead."

"Don't worry, I trust him. If I see he can't make it, I'll take over. Sit down next to Carlo, and let's get going." He gestured for her to get in and patted the back of the front seat.

She couldn't bring herself to argue with the grinning, handsome demigod, who had settled Kate on the seat next to him and began playfully biting her neck. Angrily, Judy slammed the door shut. Carlo, like a puppet whose handler had jerked his strings, sprang to life and tried to shake the cobwebs out of his head.

"Let's go, cuz," Dominic commanded.

Without a word, Carlo, ostensibly conscious, started the car and began to drive. Judy soon realized why Dominic had been so insistent that Carlo drive. While Carlo silently concentrated on his driving, Judy could hear soft, animals-in-heat grunts coming from the back seat. She softened, smiled, closed her eyes, leaned back, and let her body relax. Visions of Dominic taking her in his arms, caressing her, and making passionate love to her played in her mind. I wish this could be my night for some romance too, she hoped.

Carlo focused trance-like on his driving, but soon the moans from the back seat attracted his attention, and he tried to adjust the rear view mirror so he could see what was going on.

"Watch the road and don't get us killed," Judy snapped at him.

In spite of her worries that Carlo would wrap them around a tree, they reached the shore without accident or incident around midnight. Shortly after the car with their classmates arrived. While they were sitting around the living room talking, Carlo's eyes closed, his head bobbed then fell to his chest, and he dozed off. A second later he jerked awake.

"That drive down knocked me out," he said. "You'll have to excuse me, while I go lie down." He groped his way upstairs.

"That leaves me to take care of both of you girls," Dominic said as he smiled broadly at Kate and Judy. Kate winced as if someone had punched her.

She growled into his ear, "I'd prefer you concentrate on me. I'll be enough for you to handle."

"Hey, Kate. You know I was just kidding," he said. He mumbled something to her, they both smiled smugly at each other, then disappeared upstairs.

An hour later, Dominic, in a change of clothes, strutted down the steps—alone—and brazenly reached out and took Judy's hand.

"C'mere, I wanna talk to you," he said as he pulled her into the pantry and shut the door.

She trembled with anticipation, not really knowing what to expect.

"I've been watching you for a long time," he oozed, holding both her hands and staring directly into her eyes, "and there's no use foolin' around. I think you're a really beautiful girl, and I'm crazy for you, and . . . well, let's go for a ride and get to know each other better."

He flashed his best seductive smile at her.

Judy's mouth dropped open, her legs wobbled, and she grabbed onto a pantry shelf to keep from falling. She hadn't counted on him being interested in her or being so direct. Think, she implored her brain. Come up with something to say.

Finally: "Kate's my best friend. I can't go riding around with her boy friend," she said faintly. And lacking enthusiasm: "I don't think we should get to know each other better."

"Kate and me ain't going steady or nothing," he said. "She knows I go out with other girls, and she doesn't care. Besides, I told her I might go out with you tonight, and she said it was all right with her."

To Judy that didn't sound like the intensely jealous Kate, who called her crying every time Dominic went out with another girl. But, Judy thought, maybe something happened upstairs to change her mind. Dominic sure is handsome, and I wouldn't mind going out with him, but I wish I knew if he was lying or not.

Inside Judy the battle of heart versus head began. Her head told her getting romantically involved with him wasn't a good idea. She wasn't concerned about losing her virginity; she put no great value on keeping it. It was the fact that it would be Kate's boyfriend performing the operation made her uncomfortable. This could be a dangerous undertaking; she might lose her best friend. But worse, she knew Kate was vindictive—there were many girls at school Kate no longer spoke to because they had gone out with Dominic.

In her heart, however, the thrill of romance was a powerful force. Ever since Kate had described to her in great detail the sensual pleasures that Dominic provided, Judy had been eager to experience some for herself. She had been fantasizing about an erotic adventure with Dominic since the she had first seen him in the convertible, and here was the opportunity to turn her dreams into reality.

Fight's over; heart wins, she decided. Tonight's the night for excitement, love, and adventure. Logic and reason are for another time.

He put his hands on her shoulders, stared deeply into her eyes, and said, "Let's get in the car. Anytime you say you wanna come back here, I'll bring you back. Whaddaya got to lose?" He noticed her ashen face. "Besides, you look like you need some fresh air."

Judy put her brain on autopilot, ignored the lump forming in her throat, and followed him numbly out the back door.

Dominic drove to a deserted spot with a magnificent view of the ocean. The sky was clear, and the full moon sent silvery rays flickering over the water and dancing playfully on the sand. Ocean waves lapped lightly on the beach. Judy was lulled into a dreamy fantasy world. Softly, slowly, he spoke the passionate words he knew she wanted to hear, and masterfully he let the tension build. When she closed her eyes and turned her face toward his, he drew her to him and kissed her hungrily. Without a word of protest or an ounce of resistance, she melted into his arms.

With no help from a semi-conscious Judy, Dominic rocked her from side to side as he struggled to pull off her jeans and panties. Sweating profusely, he laid her flat on the seat, guided himself into her, and began to bounce up and down. After a few minutes, he spasmed violently. At the same time Judy, experiencing erotic feelings she had never felt before, threw her head from side to side and panted with growing passion. Shortly after he climaxed, she answered with her own, shuddering head-to-toe orgasm. Gradually as her writhing subsided, she locked her arms tightly around his neck, pulled him to her, and kissed him forcefully. He struggled to sit up, but she didn't want to give up the comfortable feeling of his male warmness inside her and squeezed him tight and would not let go. He finally untwisted her arms from around his neck and pulled himself free.

They rode back in silence: Dominic mentally carving another notch in his conquests' belt, while Judy began having second thoughts as reality began to replace the receding afterglow. Would Dominic tell Kate? she wondered. Would Kate care if she found out? From deep inside, her intuition sputtered to life then screamed that she had made a terrible mistake.

Chapter 41

*J*udy lurched back to the present as a groggy Kate pulled at her leg to get her attention.

Kate said, "I watched you and Dominic from the window that night, and I saw you two get into his car. You were gone a long time. Where did you go? What did you do? I know you weren't talking. No, Dominic didn't like to talk. He liked to fuck. That's what he did to you, didn't he? He took you out and fucked you. And you wanted him to." Her voice became a shriek: "Didn't you?"

Judy, dazed, stared in disbelief at Kate. "That was twenty-five years ago, for chrissakes. I can't believe you've held that grudge against me for all these years. Besides, he told me he asked you if he could go out with me, and you said it was all right."

"Hah! You're a liar. He never *asked* anybody for anything. Use your head, dummy, would I have said 'yes'? I was crazy for him. I wanted to marry him. Why would I agree to him screwing another woman? Don't you remember how upset I used to get when he went out with other women? I wanted him for me," she hissed the words, "and you knew it." She paused to catch her breath. "I told you I loved him," she panted. "I told you everything about Dominic and me; and even though you knew how I felt, you had to try to steal him from me, didn't you? I've *always* hated you for that. But you couldn't get him, could you? You must have been a worthless shit of a screw, because he didn't even call you again after that one time, did he? He could have any girl he wanted, and you weren't even on his list."

Exhausted from venting these long pent-up emotions, Kate keeled over flat on the floor.

Judy leaned over grabbed her shoulders and shook her. When she failed to revive, Judy slapped her again across the face. A crimson bruise blossomed on her cheek. She wagged her head from side to side, and her eyes blinked open.

"You planted the panties in Tony's laundry, and you mailed me his address book?" Judy asked.

Kate nodded her head. One corner of her mouth turned up in a hideous grin and she barely managed to say, "Yeah."

"You were in this house when I was in Italy and took Tony's horn and my mother's ring?"

"I fucked him in the guest room, and afterwards while he was in the shower . . ." Kate wheezed. "They're in my purse. I don't want them. I only took them to prove to you that I could fuck Tony any time I wanted to. Take them back."

The blood pounded in Judy's head; a knot began to form in her stomach.

Kate said, "I wanted to hurt you the way you hurt me. You got Dominic to fuck you, and you hurt me really bad." She started crying. "So I fucked Tony . . . twice, and now we're even." She struggled for breath then gasped, "Take the jewelry out of my purse, I don't want it."

In a daze Judy went to the hall table and yanked Kate's purse open. When she shook the contents out, a wadded-up Kleenex fell to the floor. She picked it up, unwrapped it carefully, took her mother's ring out, slid it on her finger, and angrily slapped the horn onto the dining room table unsure what to do with it.

She sat back down on Kate's stomach, grabbed a clump of her hair with each hand, and pulled her head up until their faces were almost touching.

"And you set me up for the video? You had me drugged?"

Kate grimaced in pain and weakly tried to slap Judy's hands from her hair. "I did it," she whispered. She huffed for a minute like a woman in labor, trying to catch her breath. "I had to get even with you. The pictures of me with Tony weren't working. Fuckin' Tony managed to talk his way out of everything I tried. And you're such an asshole you believed him. After his father died, you took pity on him. But I had to get even; I had to give you as much heartache as you gave me. It took me a long time, but we're even now." Kate tried to laugh but only a hoarse cackle came out. "I got what I wanted," she said. Suddenly she grimaced and grew angry. "I've told you everything. Now let the fuck go of me," she demanded, swatting weakly at Judy's hands. "My head hurts."

Judy shoved Kate's head free not caring that it thudded on the floor. She sat down at the kitchen table as powerful emotions swirled through her, the last of which was relief. My nightmare's over, she thought. I've got the truth, but where do I go from here? For sure I'm through with goddamn Tony. His promises were worth shit. In my house . . . he . . . She briefly pictured Tony and Kate in bed together in the guest room and shuddered. This house is contaminated, she thought, and I won't stay in it another minute.

After a quick glance at Kate who remained motionless on the floor, she ran upstairs to her bedroom and threw a small suitcase on the bed. She packed clothing, cosmetics, and other essentials then snapped it shut. In her purse she checked for her wallet and checkbook and noticed her passport was still there. She looked at it and smiled; she knew what her next step would be.

On her way out she stared at Kate, who was still lying on the dining room floor, until she saw her chest rise. She's still alive, she thought. She squelched the urge to kick the unconscious body and yanked the front door open and made a special effort to slam it loudly behind her.

This is the end of Mrs. Judy Fanelli, she thought.

Chapter 42

Two days later, early in the morning, Carlo Fiore folded his shopping list, and stuffed it in his pocket. As he closed the apartment door behind him, he heard the phone ring. He briefly considered turning around and answering it, but he didn't. Let the machine pick it up, he thought.

Outside on the sidewalk, he stopped for a moment to let the hot, humid air drape over him like a cloak. He shivered as he felt the special Mediterranean warmth and sunshine that hung over Rome this day. Down the street he heard the tenor bursting into the aria from *La Traviata* that he and Judy had heard. Pavarotti would be singing the Alfredo role at the baths of Caracalla in October, and Carlo had promised himself that he would go. Even though he had heard the aria many times, he stood patiently and listened, because it reminded him of her. It will be our song, he thought as the love he felt for her rose inside him.

Goosebumps prickled at him as the tenor's words enveloped him: Love, a torment and a delight. Mostly a torment now, Carlo thought wistfully. The singer finished, and Carlo went sadly on his way.

Two hours later he returned to his apartment with his arms full of groceries, fumbled for the key, and let himself in. Momentarily he had forgotten about the phone call, but the answering machine's blinking red light caught his eye. He set the groceries down in the kitchen and pushed the "play" button.

"I'm back in Rome," the familiar voice began. "If you're still interested in . . . If you want to . . . talk, call me at the Savoia Hotel. Oh, yes, and ask for Gianna Orsini."

Eagerly Carlo grabbed the phone and began to dial the hotel's number.